It's Not You, It's Me

HELEN DUNNE

First published in Great Britain in 2007 by Orion Books,
an imprint of The Orion Publishing Group Ltd
Orion House, 5 Upper Saint Martin's Lane
London, WC2H 9EA

1 3 5 7 9 10 8 6 4 2

A CIP catalogue record for this book is
available from the British Library.

ISBN-13: 978 0 7528 6063 3
ISBN-10: 0 7528 6063 1

Typeset by Deltatype Ltd, Birkenhead, Merseyside

Printed in Great Britain by Clays Ltd, St Ives plc

The Orion Publishing Group's policy is to use papers that are
natural, renewable and recyclable products and made from wood
grown in sustainable forests. The logging and manufacturing
processes are expected to conform to the environmental
regulations of the country of origin.

www.orionbooks.co.uk

To my mother Lily
For her unfailing support and generosity
With love

I am aware that this book has tested the patience of many people. Heartfelt thanks are due to my editors Sara O'Keeffe and Jane Wood for their support in difficult times and unerring good advice. I would like to wish Jane all the very best in her new chapter, and look forward to a long and rewarding relationship with Sara. Thanks are also due to Will Geddes at ICP Group for his advice on corporate investigations, and to my unpaid readers Adrienne, Rosie, Sarah, Emma and especially Christina! Ms Mills, you have missed your vocation.

I suppose it was my fault. Looking back, I should have acted differently. But, in my defence, it was an extremely provocative situation. It would have taken somebody with the heart of Mother Teresa and the acting ability of Nicole Kidman to keep a straight face. When your boyfriend of four weeks and three days turns up for your latest date in a peacock blue satin shirt that makes him look like a refugee from *Mamma Mia*, what is a girl to say? Okay, so I now know – with the benefit of an hour's hindsight – that yelling 'Has *Cirque de Soleil* called you yet? They need the Big Top back for tonight's performance' across a crowded bar was not it.

Nat just froze in his tracks, waiting for the cacophony of sniggers to die down, before he carried on wending his way through the maze of chrome bar tables to where I was sitting. In spite of everything, including his rather cross expression, he was looking good. The offensive shirt had an open neck, and the black hairs that sprinkle his chest poked through a criss-cross of satin strings. He was wearing the tortoiseshell glasses that I always thought perfectly framed his green eyes, and his black hair, with its slight dappling of grey, was set with a dash of gel. The girls on the neighbouring table certainly appreciated the view. I heard a slight intake of breath from a rather busty blonde, but she could just have been asthmatic.

He pulled out the chair beside me, and sat down. No kiss, no hug, not even a cursory peck on the cheek. Just weeks ago the first minutes of our meetings should have come with a

Parental Guidance rating as we devoured each other. Greedily. Passionately. But today he just leaned across as if I wasn't really there, grabbed the wine bottle out of the ice bucket beside me and poured himself a large glass of pinot grigio. There was no chivalrous offer to refill my half-empty glass, I noted. His puff sleeve, decorated with faux diamond cufflinks, flapped in the slight breeze, fanned by the door that kept opening to admit customers. Look, it was a gift. I would defy anyone to resist such temptation, particularly if they're irked at poor manners. And I am only human, after all, so I tugged on it.

'No, seriously ...' I pulled the puff, stretching it out like thin pastry; 'there's enough material in here to make party dresses for the entire Girl Guides' movement.'

Nat sighed. He took off his glasses and rubbed his eyes with his free hand, as if in distress.

'Stop it, Holly,' he finally said, jerking his arm away. 'This is a Roberto Cavalli shirt. It recently proved a huge hit on the Milan catwalk. David Beckham bought it in three different colours.'

I should have recognised the warning signs: the irritability, the irrational snappiness, the petulant stance. I know that now. But I was distracted, you see, because I, Holly Parker, who is 32 but looks about 27 (in the right light), had actually enjoyed the best working day since I started as a corporate investigator, which is not to be confused with a private eye. I do not rifle through underwear drawers, unless it's a new boyfriend and I still have the pre-emptive right to dump him on the discovery of cartoon characters on his underwear or old-fashioned white Y-fronts. I do not take dodgy photographs of people in compromising positions, unless it is specifically requested by a long-standing boyfriend and on the strict understanding that they are not developed at the local chemist. And I do not dress in dirty raincoats. Well, okay, there was that one time, but it wasn't work-related, and it definitely aided the recovery of one hospitalised boyfriend. He certainly perked up on realising that, in my haste to make visiting hours, I had completely forgotten to dress under the coat. I think he made it to the disabled

2

toilets in less than two minutes, which was miraculous as he was suffering from a very bad ingrowing toenail.

No, I am not a private eye. Instead, I check out the backgrounds of people applying for the country's top jobs. I make certain that they really did pass the exams they claim, discover whether that permanent sniffle truly is the result of a persistent sinus problem, and basically rattle around their closets for any skeletons. And today I won a major contract with a new client. Ilyax Insurance is the country's largest insurance company. It probably covers more houses than Dulux paint, and I have just been employed to check out its potential new finance director. I've got to make sure he's absolutely perfect and squeaky clean. It is hard to explain how exciting this contract will be for me. It is like Justin Timberlake turning up for a date without any clothes on, dangling the keys to a five star hotel suite from his nether regions. Multiplied five-fold.

So, you see, I was rather preoccupied. I wanted to get through the opening greetings and onto the celebratory champagne. I was so desperate to toast my great success with Nat that my antenna wasn't fixed onto the warning signs, which was silly really because, after my recent string of disastrous love affairs, I should have been highly tuned. Instead I carried on mocking, like a child picking at a scab until the wound reopens and starts to bleed once again. I clung on to the sleeve while he pulled his arm away, emphasising the vast expanse of material with a not-so-subtle 'wow' before I released it. I then stroked the fabric very carefully and puffed it gently back into shape. One final pat to say good-bye.

'I think you mean David Brent,' I teased, filling my glass from the dwindling bottle of wine. 'Beckham's got impeccable fashion sense.' I corrected myself: 'Apart from that one occasion he wore a skirt that wasn't even a kilt, but I suppose we're all allowed a couple of mistakes.' I stared pointedly at the shirt, ignoring Nat's incredulous look. My boyfriend, the fashion student who prides himself on his style, was in shock at my treachery.

And that was the moment. Looking back, that was the

exact point when I nailed the lid on the coffin of our short relationship. One smart quip too many, and bang. The lid was down, never to be lifted. Because that was when Nat started the speech. The one I'd heard so many times before. The one that men all around the world recite when they dump their girlfriends. I swear that somewhere out there is a 'How To' book that men share. A book that offers them advice on how to let a woman down gently. How to dump her so that she won't seek revenge with a rabbit and a saucepan of boiling water. And the final chapter is 'How to leave something on the table so that she still thinks you're a good guy.' Because there's always a small part of the speech that holds out that little bit of hope. A hint of maybe. The false promise that then prompts thousands of usually sensible women around the world to spend days on the phone to their friends analysing the 'what if?' The 'he said it wasn't me ... he said the timing was wrong ... do you think if I called him in six months ... do you think he really meant it?' conversations. I swear dumped women across the world prop up the global telecom system. They should get a special rebate. I know I'd vote for a political party who suggested it.

Then there are those men who improvise, offering a few extra seeds of comfort. Like my old boyfriend Rob. He told me that if you truly loved somebody then you should be prepared to set them free. Now I'm not quite sure that the Prison Service would agree, but somehow it all made sense when he said it. And I spent weeks afterwards in a state of blissful ignorance, believing that Rob had ended our short relationship for my own good, because he believed that he was not good enough for me, that somehow I was worth more. And his selflessness made me want him more. I spent days yearning for him, thinking of ways that I could persuade him that I really wasn't out of his league. And then I learned about a lap dancer named Krystal Tits with whom he had been two-timing me. Apparently once you've touched silicone, it ruins you for the real thing. Especially if they're a modest 34B.

Then there was Jasper, who fancied himself as an actor and

4

managed to bring tears to his eyes as he ended our relationship. I learned later that he had smeared a lick of Vicks under his eyes to make them water. Apparently, it's an old stage trick. If he'd only asked, I could have found a much easier (and for me, more satisfying) way to achieve the same objective.

But Nat isn't like them. He didn't indulge in any stunts or digressions. He is a gentleman, and he stuck rigidly to the script.

'I thought I could do this,' he sighed, placing his half empty glass on the chrome bar table and staring at it. 'But this just isn't working.'

'Come on, it's not that bad an outfit,' I said breezily, examining it again. 'Perhaps if you didn't wear it with the black trousers,' I suggested helpfully. 'Maybe faded, torn jeans instead?' See? I really hadn't noticed that hammer hit the wood.

'I really don't think you should be giving me fashion advice,' he muttered under his breath, before adding loudly, 'Look, Holly, you're a lovely girl. Really lovely. Truly.' My stomach lurched as realisation dawned. Unsolicited flattering from a boyfriend is never good. 'You're,' he hesitated, clicking his fingers as if searching for the correct adjective, before adding: 'funny. And kind. And you've got that great career thing going on, but ...' Nat swiftly drained the contents of his glass, and I just knew what was coming next. 'I'm just not the right person for you. I'm at that stage in my life where I don't know what I want to do.'

'I thought you liked your degree?' I said sharply. 'You told me that your creative juices were flowing like Niagara Falls.'

'They are,' he sighed. 'That's not what I meant.' He paused before taking a deep breath, bracing himself. 'I just don't think that I'm ready for a, well, a relationship. With anybody. Not just you. I need time to discover myself. Who knows?' He shrugged, smiling at me and his eyes filled with cheap concern. 'Perhaps if we had met six months from now, I might have had all this stuff sorted out in my head.' Ah yes, I thought bitterly, the keeping his options open phase, just in case he gets lonely in the future and decides a night of passion might fill the gap. 'But right now, I'm just not in the right frame of mind. I'm not at that place yet.' He grabbed my hand across the table. 'Believe me when I say right now that this has nothing to do with you. Honestly. It's me. All me.' He thumped his chest with his spare hand, as if emphasising his 'pain', and stared intently at me, searching for a reaction.

What do you want from me, I thought. For me to break down, beg you to stay, and give you another chance? Or to absolve you of all blame, and tell you that I understand? To send you away guilt-free.

'Look, I know this has all come as a shock to you,' he continued.

'But I'd really like us to stay friends. Really. I think you are a wonderful woman.' Patronising git, I thought. 'Truly amazing. Any man would be proud to call you his girlfriend, but I'm ...' he searched for the words. A tosser, I thought. A snivelling wretch who had none of these qualms last night in bed. A bastard who spends more time in the bathroom than any female I know. Strangely, he didn't opt for any of my preferred choices. Instead, he continued with that old faithful: '... not ready for this right now,' he said solicitously. 'Look, I know this has come out of the blue to you, so if you have anything to say, please tell me.'

I slowly stood up, pulling my hand free from his clasp. 'Cowboy boots went out with *Dallas*,' I finally replied.

His face recoiled in shock, as if I had just slapped him hard, which theoretically I suppose I had. Nat considers himself an expert on footwear. It is his passion. He is considering specialising in shoe design when he leaves college. It was a low blow. Literally. He sighed, took a deep breath and retorted bitchily – like a true fashionista – 'And your bum does looks big in that.' He pointed to my tartan pencil skirt.

I was momentarily speechless. The wind was taken out of me. But I determined to get the last word: 'Please don't get me started on size.'

And I turned on my scuffed kitten heel, and left.

CHAPTER ONE

'Personally, I don't know how you avoided mentioning the cowboy boots for so long.' My best friend Louise looks horrified. We are sitting cross-legged on her massive chocolate brown suede sofa in the massive sitting room of her four-storey house on one of those beautiful Georgian garden squares in Islington, and I have finished recounting the events of just over an hour ago. It was the only place to come after my ordeal. My own flat, five minutes down the road in Canonbury, seemed too empty and cold. Louise had quickly assembled the essentials for an emotional evening, after I rang her from a cab to say I was on the way. A box of tissues and packet of plain chocolate Hobnobs now lie open on the coffee table in front of us, resting beside a half empty bottle of Chablis. Condensation drips off the bottle, making a small puddle on the table's glass top. Louise's fastidious husband, Sam, will not be pleased. He has even banned red wine from the house in case it spills on the mock Persian rugs that cover the wooden floorboards, although sometimes Louise and I secretly break the rules, sharing a bottle (or two) in their designer kitchen where the black granite floor tiles don't show the stains. I clutch two crumpled tissues in my hand, but my tears, which have now run dry, were more of humiliation than sorrow.

'I mean, if the boots ever had anything going for them, that was lost as soon as George Dubya wore them in public,' said Louise, refilling my glass. 'It'd be like wearing your parents' clothes.'

'I suppose Dubya's allowed,' I muse, carefully holding my glass steady. 'He's from Texas. They all wear them there. They're almost like a national costume.'

'It doesn't mean he has to inflict them on the world fashion scene,' retorts Louise. 'After all, you don't see, say, the Dutch prime minister wearing clogs and one of those frilly triangular hats every time he's out in public.'

'And who is the Dutch prime minister?' I ask, totally confident that my friend's knowledge of European politics is as limited as mine about the off-side rule.

'Well, I don't know,' Louise reluctantly admits. 'But I'm sure it'd have been front page news if he made a public appearance in national costume. And what if the French president started strutting about in a navy blue and white striped tee shirt and beret with a string of onions around his neck? It just doesn't happen. They have manners, and style, but those bloody Americans.' She tuts. 'They think they don't have to worry about the sensibilities of the rest of the world.'

'Sam having problems with the boys in New York?' I hazard a guess, glad to have something to distract me from the evening's events. Louise's husband is a dealmaker in the City, working for the London office of Bush Merriman, an American investment bank. He joined last year from UK rival Browns Black, selling his soul and social life for a salary that sounds like a phone number. It has bought my friend a lifestyle that even Madonna would be impressed with: expensive holidays in exotic five star resorts, a weekend estate in Gloucester, his and hers matching sports cars. And, last year, Sam's bulging bank balance allowed Louise to indulge her dream of giving up her job as a tax lawyer to establish a party planning company.

'No more than usual,' she says. 'I just think they work him too hard, although he got home early enough tonight.'

'He's here?' I try to keep the alarm out of my voice, surreptitiously checking that my shoes have no mud on the soles. Thank God I took them off before curling up on the sofa. A lecture from Sam would be just too much tonight.

'He's in the kitchen, making himself useful. I'll call him in later. But look, how are you feeling? Nat is such a bastard. I really thought he was a nice bloke. It just goes to show ...' She sighs. 'And to think we invited him to Gordon Ramsay. Those tables are like gold dust.'

'I know,' I shrug my shoulders, shaking my head in despair. 'Why couldn't Nat just be honest about everything? Look, we both knew we didn't want anything serious, it was just a bit of fun, but no. He had to make all those usual "not ready" bullshit excuses. To make out that somehow I'd changed the rules; that I was looking for more than he was able to give. And then when I retaliate – out of hurt, mind you – he snaps that my bum looks big in this,' I tug my skirt. 'Typical man, attacking because he knows he's in the bloody wrong.'

'Oh God, you're so right Holly.' She reaches across and hugs me.

'Yes, but *does* my bum look big in this?' I shake myself out of Louise's grip and stand up with my back towards her, breathing in deeply so that my tummy is flat and keeping as upright as I can to make my bottom look extra pert. Nat's biting comment has opened up a Pandora's box of insecurities.

'Not at all,' she says emphatically. 'You look like one of those fifties starlets in that skirt, who wiggle along on four inch heels. It's like something Marilyn Monroe would wear, but without the polo shirt.'

'Marilyn Monroe,' I explode. 'But everybody knows her bum was big.'

'Well, I didn't,' Louise soothes. 'Your bum is perfect. Anyway, Nat was just lashing out. We all say things we don't mean in the heat of the moment.' She beckons me back to the sofa. 'You're just feeling insecure. It's only natural after this evening. Men are such pigs,' she sighs. 'I'm so grateful that I've got Sam, and no longer have to subject myself to the humiliation of the dating scene.'

'Well, some of us have no choice,' I mutter, feeling slightly irritated. I know married people can't help it, but do they always have to seem so smug?

'I'm sorry, I'm being insensitive,' smiles Louise. 'In some ways I was lucky. Sam and I got together before answer machines, mobile phones or 1471 took over, so you could always kid yourself that the bloke had rung while you were out. But I do remember how stomach turning it was just waiting for a call. Jumping up every time the phone rang. Now, there's no excuse. Today's single woman can be contacted twenty-four-seven. It must be terrible waiting for a guy to call you, all the time knowing that there's no real reason for them not to manage it.'

'And this is meant to help me how?' I ask sarcastically.

'I'm trying to tell you that I can remember what it's like,' she smiles kindly.

But you don't, I think sadly, because once you find The One, all the pain of the search disappears. Just like mothers who no longer recall the agony of a forty-eight-hour labour the moment the child arrives. You can't truly appreciate how the disappointment of a love affair ending can overwhelm your whole being. The constant nagging ache that ruins your appetite and depletes your energy. The shock. The horror. The grief that turns sensible high-flying women into nervous wrecks. But, even as I recall these emotions, I know that tonight will not affect me like that because, honestly, I had never classed Nat as 'The One' or even 'The One in Waiting'. He was fun to be with, interesting, urbane, good in bed – a temporary fling rather than the love of my life, and yet, even in that carefree capacity, by abruptly ending our relationship, he has somehow made me feel that *I* am not good enough. Not just for him. Tears of hurt pride sting my eyes. 'Stop that, Sam will go mad if salt water stains the sofa,' orders Louise. 'I think you need this.' She carefully fills my glass, replaces the bottle back into the centre of its puddle, and passes over the biscuits. I grab one and dunk it into my wine.

'Look, I know it was never really going anywhere. We both knew that. Hey, I've got pairs of tights that have lasted longer than our relationship, but I did quite like Nat. He was fun to be with. We had a laugh, and – before you say it – I *know* I've chosen the old Flings-for-Me lifestyle.' I take a deep breath, my voice starts to break and I blink back the tears that again threaten to fall. 'But do you know how many men have dumped me over the past two years?'

'Seven,' she replies without hesitation.

'You're including Pete?' I'm puzzled. 'I dumped him.'

'You didn't have a choice. He was gay.'

'You liked him.'

'What's not to like? Your best friend's new boyfriend,' she pointedly curls her index fingers to indicate quotation marks while saying the b-word, 'comes round to dinner, and insists on washing up while everybody else is drunkenly playing Twister, because he can't abide to see a cluttered sink.'

'I thought it was nice of him,' I say defensively.

'Hey, I thought it was fantastic. That man is welcome at my house anytime he wants. And I still rely on his tip to keep my cushions plump.' She points at the perfectly plumped up velvet cushions that are scattered over two chocolate brown leather armchairs nestling beside an open fireplace.

'It sounds like you always knew he was gay.'

'Well, I've never known a straight man who popped around unexpectedly with some colour swatches that he thought would be "just perfect" for my en suite bathroom.' She laughs at the memory.

'He wasn't that obvious,' I say defiantly. 'I'm not that stupid.'

'I'm not saying that you are,' she replies evenly. 'Pete wasn't one hundred per cent sure about his sexuality when he asked you out, and don't forget that the two of you dated for less than a week.'

'Great, I'm so awful that men become gay in my presence …' I glug back a hefty sip of wine.

'That's so not true, and you know it,' retorts Louise. 'Pete paid you a tremendous compliment. He was on an emotional roller coaster, uncertain of everything about himself, and when he met you, he bonded in a way that he didn't think possible. He thought you two really had a chance. Sadly it

11

didn't work because, ultimately, genes will out ...'

'Not that Pete's jeans ever did for me,' I admit. Louise raises her eyebrows inquisitively. And I shake my head, before admitting, 'But he seems really happy with Angus now.' Hey, I mightn't be able to find suitable men for me, but I can find them for each other. Angus is a colleague who invited me and my new boyfriend to a Shirley Bassey concert. His treat! Apparently his former boyfriend had bought the tickets before running off with the motorcycle courier, who, it seemed, had been delivering a lot more than a package from Amazon. It was our third date and I wasn't really keen to go, but Pete was so excited at the prospect of seeing the Welsh diva that I gave in. Well, I'd have had to be in Australia not to feel the frisson between them. Our box at the Albert Hall crackled with so much electricity that I'm surprised it didn't affect the microphones. And suddenly everything was clear. To both of us. I excused myself during the interval, and a week later Pete moved into Angus's minimalist apartment in Hoxton. Obviously it was really awkward at the beginning, particularly at office get-togethers, but now, a year later, it doesn't really bother me. In fact, they seem to have morphed so much into each other that sometimes I have trouble telling them apart.

'I know these relationships have not been serious, but what am I doing wrong, Louise? Why can't I hold onto a man? Six,' I hold up my fingers to emphasise the point, 'have dumped me after less than three months together. That's been my record in recent years. It's atrocious. I've had longer relationships with some of the items in my fridge ...'

Louise tops up my glass. 'Any man should be glad to be with you long term, and if he isn't then he's an idiot,' she says. 'I'm serious. You're just picking the wrong guys at the moment. You need to change your requirements.'

'So I can't have tall, dark and handsome any more? I thought you were meant to be making me feel better.'

'Of course, you can. But I'm just not sure it's enough. The guys you choose just don't really seem to make you happy. Sure, they look great and you have some fun initially but there's ...' she pauses, trying to avoid upsetting me. 'There's no real connection between you. It's been that way since ...'

I hold up my hand to stop her. There are some parts of one's life where even best friends mustn't trespass. Episodes that you lock away, until, occasionally, when you feel able, you unwrap and re-explore them. But then you discover, all these years later, that the pain is still there, so you bury them again. I swallow hard, push the memories back into their box and throw away the key once again. I don't want to talk about Jake right now. Louise nods, understanding. She pauses – a quiet moment of companionship – and then she carries on, a softer tone to her voice.

'The problem is, even if they are flings, you have really nothing in common with these guys ...'

'How can you say that? Nat was a fashion student. I like fashion.' I sweep my arm along my body, indicating my tartan suit, complete with mock sporran, and thick red tights. It's my take on Vivienne Westwood.

'I rest my case,' she mutters, before leaning forward to shake the wine bottle, checking out the contents. 'Sam,' she yells towards the kitchen. 'Be a darling, and bring us in another bottle of Chablis.' Yikes. Sam Alert. I lean forward, quickly place both our glasses on their sterling silver coasters and use the (non-puff) cuff of my shirt to soak up the spillages.

'Don't be silly, Holly,' insists Louise. 'Sam doesn't worry about things like that anymore. He's really mellowed. Last night I burned a non-stick pan he bought in the January sales and he didn't say a word. Honestly, we went to bed in silence.' There's a quick rap on the door, and Sam appears with alcohol reinforcements and an empty glass. He's wearing an apron that declares Domestic God. 'Christmas gift from his mother,' Louise whispers. 'Wearing it to keep her happy.' I don't like to point out that Sam's mum is not actually here.

'Hope I'm not disturbing a girlie chat,' says Sam, grabbing another coaster for the bottle and surreptitiously using his apron to wipe a small puddle that I missed. Damn. 'Don't you need plates for the Hobnobs? And napkins?'

'Sit down, Sam,' we order simultaneously.

'You're not disturbing anything,' I say bravely. 'I'm just describing to Louise how I got dumped again tonight.'

'Was it Alan?' Sam asks. He fills his glass before settling himself on the floor in front of Louise. She leans forward, kisses the top of his head, wraps her arms around his shoulders and gives him a sharp pinch. 'Jasper?' Another pinch.

'Actually, it was Nat,' I reply. 'You met him at that Chinese takeaway party I held two weeks ago, and on New Year's Eve. And you took us both to Gordon Ramsay.'

'Was he the guy wearing tartan trousers?'

I nod. 'The other two were last year, remember? Jasper came away with us for that week in Cornwall, and ended it the day after we returned.' Before we had finally split all the bills. 'But, hey, I really don't want to talk about Nat,' I lie.

'Student, wasn't he?' I nod again. 'Never can quite understand a grown man going to college. Needlework, wasn't it?'

'Fashion,' I correct. Sam raises his eyes to heaven. Despite his whopping annual salary, he still fumes over the taxes he pays and the 'scroungers' that benefit from his hard work. 'Honestly, though, I don't want to talk about him.'

'Quite right too!' Louise says firmly. 'He's just not worth our time.' She reaches forward and refills my empty glass but, just as she holds the bottle over her own glass, Sam places a firm hand on her arm and shakes his head. Louise slowly nods, replaces the bottle on its coaster and sits back. There's an air of tension in the room. For a moment I don't understand what is going on. Don't tell me that my best friend is ...

'Don't worry,' says Louise, reading my mind. 'I'm not pregnant.'

'Not yet,' mutters Sam.

'Sorry?' I ask.

'We wanted to tell you,' she continues, holding her hand up to hush Sam, 'before it's too late.'

'Tell me what?'

'We're trying for a baby.' They both look at me, their faces beaming with excitement. They have been together for over ten years, since we all met at university, and I always knew that this day would eventually come. I just wish it wasn't now. It's yet another reminder of my own solo status. Louise's life is about to change irrevocably. Our last-minute nights out or weekends at the spa will be confined to history. How can I compete with nappy rash or colic? It's bad enough when Sam has a cold. And a teething baby will mean a harassed friend, too busy to chat with her old buddy. I know I sound selfish, but why do other people's lives seem to progress at a faster pace than mine?

'But you're not pregnant?' I quiz.

'Not yet,' answers Louise.

'Er—' I'm a bit puzzled. 'Then wouldn't it be better to wait and tell me when you are?'

'Holly, this is such a momentous decision for us that we want all our friends and family to share it,' explains Sam pompously. 'We're going to start trying for a baby.'

'Well, technically we started already,' smiles Louise. 'Last week.' She and Sam exchange glances at each other. Secret memories. Dreamy smiles. An intimate moment. Married bliss.

'Whoa! I really don't need the details.' I put my hand up to stop further information spilling forth. I don't care what those girls in *Sex and the City* do, but I don't need to know about my best friend's bedroom antics. 'Look, I'm really pleased for you both, truly, but don't you think telling everybody that you're trying for a baby will just place an extra strain on the situation?'

'Not at all,' beams Louise. 'Look, Holly, you're my best friend. How could I do this without telling you that I'm planning to be a mummy?'

'I'm sorry about the timing,' says Sam, twisting around on the floor to gently stroke a slither of Louise's washboard flat stomach peeking out from under her cashmere sweater. 'We'd hoped to tell you before this, but somehow it never seemed appropriate.' And it is now, when I've just spilled my guts about another chapter in my lousy love life?

'Oh, don't worry about me and my stupid romantic mishaps,' I wave my hand in the air in an act of dismissal. 'That's great news. I'm truly pleased for you.' I lean over and hug my friend. 'You'll make a wonderful mother.' She beams with pleasure.

'And you will too,' Louise reiterates. 'Some day soon. I just know it.' But you don't really, I reflect. There are no guarantees in life. Nobody has a divine right to a successful relationship and a healthy family. It's just that some people get lucky. Sometimes they meet their partner without even looking, while others spent their lifetime unsuccessfully searching.

'We'll see,' I say, in a noncommittal tone, 'although I think I lack a rather vital ingredient for that at the moment.'

'There's always sperm banks,' says Sam.

'Sam!' Louise exclaims in a sharp tone. 'Don't say such a thing.'

'What?' He looks completely bemused. 'I don't know what the big problem is. Holly's made no secret of the fact that since ...' Another sharp pinch and he stops short. 'Okay, look, I don't understand you women. Holly is always boasting that she's happy to play the field, that she isn't in it for the long run, but then, when she finds the guy isn't either, shock, horror, she gets upset.'

I can feel my face reddening. It sounds silly when Sam puts it like that. He's right, though. I haven't really wanted a serious relationship since Jake. Or have I? Am I fooling myself? When Louise announced her plans, didn't I just feel a twinge of jealousy? Don't I sometimes secretly read those quizzes in women's magazines in an effort to discover what sort of man I'm compatible with? I shrug. It's the wine talking. I'm tired, that's all. I'm happy with my status quo. Truly. Honestly. I'd hardly lie to myself about that.

'Holly is bound to meet somebody soon,' Sam says. I smile gratefully. 'She always does.' The smile freezes. 'But personally, I wonder why she bothers with half these guys.'

'Sam,' Louise hisses.

'What? Can't I have an opinion?' Not when it seems to

16

attack me, I ponder sourly. 'I think it's all rather ironic really. Here's Holly who spends her working life picking right 'uns for companies, and yet when it comes to her love life, for the past two years she seems to have picked an assortment of boyfriends that she has about as much in common with as I have with Pamela Anderson. I don't know why she doesn't just use some of her professional skills to pick people who are more suitable.'

'God, you're so right, Sam,' Louise again kisses the top of his head. 'I'd never thought of doing that. Had you, Holly?'

What does Sam think I am? An idiot? Of course, I've pondered the irony. I can discover any candidate's foibles and discard those unsuitable for a post, but I constantly fail to find anybody suitable to meet my requirements.

'It's not quite the same thing,' I point out. 'Anyway, the companies are looking for somebody on a long term basis. I keep telling you that I'm not interested in anything serious.'

'Hmm,' mutters Sam. 'So you keep telling us, but then you always turn up in tears when it ends badly. Look,' he ignores a gentle kick from Louise, 'I'm not saying that you're not welcome – our door and wine cellar are always open to you – but I really think you should start thinking carefully about what you truly want. Relationships are a bit like a merger. One company taking over another.'

'You didn't take me over,' Louise taps his shoulder playfully. 'Although you may have taken me ...'

'Er, yes, let's not go into that at this moment,' he says edgily. 'But seriously. The basics are the same. If company A is bigger than company B ...'

'I wasn't bigger than anybody,' I interrupt indignantly.

'And company B is not really interested in company A, then company A can go hostile. Force B into a merger. Display all its assets and appeal to B's owners, who ultimately are the shareholders.'

'You've lost me,' I say, 'I should flash my tits at a prospective boyfriend and ask his parents to make him go out with me?

Or maybe I should flash at his father?' I look at Louise, who shrugs in a 'haven't got a clue either' kind of way.

'Well, obviously that analogy doesn't quite work here,' admits Sam.

'I can see why you earn those huge bonuses now,' I mutter.

'But,' Sam continues, 'if it were a merger of equals, or almost equals, and one party was still reluctant to engage in discussions, then the other one has to sweeten its offer. It has to make itself more attractive to the opposition.'

'What are you saying?' Louise asks quietly.

'I'm saying that Holly has been involved in hostile take-overs for the past two years,' he looks at our blank faces. 'She's been dating guys who she was, metaphorically speaking,' he holds up his hand to halt any dissent, 'bigger than. There was too much of a gulf between them for it to ever work. But the problem is complicated somewhat because we are looking at it from the wrong direction.'

'Oh? That's why it's complicated?' I interrupt. 'And there was me thinking it was because you were talking gobbledegook.'

'Look, if you girls don't want a male opinion ...' Sam shrugs, and starts to stand up.

'No!' we shriek.

Louise pushes him back down to the floor. 'Stay. We do want to hear your views. Honest.'

He smiles smugly, and continues: 'Holly has been involved in mergers with companies that, in reality, work in different industries from her own. She has little in common with them, and therefore any union is doomed.'

'Exactly what I was saying,' shrieks Louise, triumphantly.

'I know, but I understood it when you said it,' I mutter.

'Holly only pursues mergers that she subconsciously knows will ultimately fail. Now, I don't want to sound like Doctor Freud and confuse matters ...'

'Oh, why worry about that now ...' I mutter.

'... but it sounds like there are issues here that only you can sort out. But my opinion, as an investment banker who is an expert at putting together two companies, is that if you want a successful merger then you have to do two things.'

'Which are?' Louise and I ask in unison. Damn. I really am interested.

'Holly needs to find a target that is more her equal.' Louise nods in agreement. 'And she needs to package herself into the most attractive business proposition that there is for that target.'

'Eh?'

'She needs to pick the right man, and then turn herself into the perfect girlfriend.'

CHAPTER TWO

Call me old fashioned, but I've never been a great one for hanging around when my friends decide to analyse my character. It just seems so rude. Why couldn't they just talk about me behind my back, like normal people? That's what I'd do. And anyway, I think that Sam was enjoying the discussion too much. There's always been a little friction between us, since university days when we were first introduced. He was a Goth, kitted out from top to bottom in black. Even his fingernails and lips were painted black, while his eyes were outlined so thickly that Ozzy Osbourne would have shuddered. It's all a far cry from the buttoned-up investment banker he is today who thinks rebellion is an exclusive resort in the Far East. But one characteristic remains, his thick curly hair as orange as a satsuma. Well, after all the trouble that he had gone to dying everything else black, I couldn't help but express surprise at the contrast. He looked like an erupting volcano. And obviously my comment went down as well as Simon Cowell at a primary school carol concert.

Sam avoided me until one night he hooked up with Louise, who I shared a flat with, and suddenly we found that we were stuck with each other. It worked better as a foursome when Jake was around, but since he's been off the scene there's been an uneasy truce between us. I know deep down we're rather fond of each other, but sometimes his pomposity drives me up the wall, while my scattiness and constant romantic woes have the same vertical effect on him. Still, I know that he makes my best friend very happy and that's good enough for me. Most of the time.

And anyway, he was speaking a lot of twaddle. The perfect girlfriend. Pah. And then likening my love life to some big deal, where it's possible to tick all the boxes and judge that this relationship is going to work but this one isn't. And what is the 'perfect girlfriend' after all? A doormat, perhaps; somebody who doesn't complain about driving her drunken boyfriend home; a woman who acts like *Sex and the City*'s Samantha Jones in the bedroom and Nigella Lawson in the kitchen? It's intangible, surely, I mutter angrily to myself, as I unlock the front door of my house. It's not like an Olympic event, when the judges analyse a performance and then brandish cards saying 10. What happens if you're just a nine? Does that mean you're destined for the shelf? A failure?

I am just shutting the front door of the converted Victorian house where I live, when Miss Binchy opens the door across the small, carpeted hallway, and looks out. I check my watch. Ten o'clock. My aged neighbour lives in the flat below mine and never seems to go to bed. Today Miss Binchy is wearing a pleated tweed skirt and a short sleeve blouse. I glimpse the corner of the frilly handkerchief she keeps tucked under the cuff of her sleeve. I would never ask, but I'd guess she's in her mid-seventies.

'Holly dear, is that you? You're home then?' She smiles at me.

'Yes, Miss Binchy,' I reply. 'I hope I didn't disturb you.'

'Not at all, dear. I was just about to put the kettle on when I heard the door open, and I wondered if you'd like a cup of tea.'

'Well, I really shouldn't,' I hesitate. 'It's getting late.'

'Late? Listen to you. You young things have no stamina. A little bit of supper would do you good and give you some energy. There's barely a pick on you, dear.' She shivers. 'Come on, it's freezing out here. I've got two gas rings heating up the kitchen. A cup of tea and a few crumpets will soon warm you up. Or perhaps you'd prefer a hot toddy?'

21

'No, tea will be fine.' I surrender myself to the inevitable and enter Miss Binchy's flat. It's been like this since I moved in upstairs six months ago. I can barely pass my neighbour's door without her popping out and inviting me in. Now and then I make an excuse, but other times I haven't the heart. She's obviously lonely. I occasionally catch the postman sneaking the mail silently through the letterbox when he really hasn't the time to stop for buttered toast and hot chocolate. And as I walk through her doorway and across her tiny hall into the Fifties-style kitchen containing one of those old stand-alone cookers with the grill at eye-level, a worrying thought pops into my head. I may not want a relationship now, but what if I end up alone? Will I turn into a little old lady who badgers people into a quick cup of tea to stave off the loneliness?

'Now, my dear. Sit yourself down over there.' Miss Binchy points at a pine stool with a floral cushion anchored to the seat, that stands in front of a small ledge. 'A nice cup of tea then.' She pads across the linoleum floor in her fluffy slippers, opening cupboards to retrieve the tea things. Her kitchen, though old and shabby, is sparkling clean. I feel a pang of guilt at the load of dirty crockery that waits for me upstairs, and Miss Binchy's gleaming stainless steel sink, as empty as my little black book, reproaches me. 'Now where did I leave the teapot?' Miss Binchy glances around the kitchen, holding her wrinkled hand to her mouth as she ponders the problem. 'It must be here somewhere.' My neighbour can sometimes be a bit forgetful. She is constantly knocking on my door asking if I have seen her cat Marmalade. The perils of old age, I suppose.

'Shall I get the milk out of the fridge?' I offer.

'That would be kind, dear,' she replies distractedly. 'Now where on earth is it?'

I bend to open the fridge, and there, on the second shelf down, is the teapot, still wrapped in its crocheted cosy. I look over at Miss Binchy, who is busy opening cupboard doors. I don't want to embarrass her – last week she was mortified when I found her butter dish under the grill pan which, luckily, was turned off – so I silently lift it out and place it on the ledge.

'It's here, Miss Binchy,' I say. 'I think I must have been sitting in front of it.'

'Ach, not to worry,' she smiles as I pass the teapot over. 'Now how was work today? Did you get a lot of e-letters?'

'Email,' I correct her.

'That's what I said. On that spider thing.' I look at Miss Binchy blankly, as she heats the pot, before tossing in four teaspoons of loose-leaf tea. Tea bags, she once told me, never taste right. 'You know. The web. My nephew Seamus says it's changed his life. Made his job so much easier.'

'What does Seamus do?' She's mentioned her nephew before. He sounds like a surrogate son, always popping around to sort out something or other for her.

'Ah, I don't know, dear, something in an office. Did you not see him when I was away over the New Year? I went to stay with my sister Sheila and her husband Adam in Kent. Did I tell you? Lovely place they've got, and Adam's so good. He thinks nothing of driving along those motorways. I don't know how he copes. Cars move so fast these days, but he always seems to pass somebody who knows him. People are always tooting at the car. Ah, Seamus is a pet. He promised to come and feed Marmalade.' Hand on heart, I don't think I've seen the cat in the six months I've lived here. Perhaps we work different shifts. 'I told him to keep an eye out for you too. Make sure that you were alright. I worry about you, dear.'

'There's really no need.' Fantastic. Not only can I not get a man for myself, but now my neighbour is insisting her nephew watches out for me. I'm turning into a charity case. I'm glad I didn't bump into him. It would have been embarrassing.

'There's every need with a young woman by herself in a big house.' She sighs. 'Sure, I just don't understand young men these days. They've no sense of gallantry. In my day, a young man walked a lady to her door after an evening out. But what am I telling you this for? You've that nice young man I saw leaving your flat a couple of weeks ago. Early in the morning it was. I thought to myself, he must have missed the last Tube seeing her home.' She glances quickly across at me. I nod guiltily, feeling like a teenager who has just been caught snogging her first boyfriend outside the school disco. 'I liked his yellow trousers. Very smart, dear. Is he a model?'

'No, just a poseur. We're no longer together. Actually it ended earlier tonight. I've just been to see my friend Louise for a medicinal drink. To tell her all about it.' Tears of frustration once again sting my eyes.

'Ach, well, now you can tell me all about it. Is the young man mad?' And, as she pulls another wooden stool to sit opposite me, I no longer think Miss Binchy is.

CHAPTER THREE

I travel to work the next morning feeling able to cope with the world. Miss Binchy may not be the full pint of milk, but she sure made me feel refreshed. There's nothing like another woman insisting that there is nothing wrong with you. Even if she wears glasses that could be melted down to rebuild Crystal Palace, thinks rollers are a girl's best friend and wonders why young women today shun girdles. Hey, with my bum, I may have to start wearing them soon.

Shortly after I moved into my flat, Miss Binchy told me a little about her life, growing up in Dublin, the eldest of four sisters. Her eyes got all misty as she told me about the man that she had once loved, who she secretly hoped might ask her to marry him. But he never did. It was one of a string of promises that were sadly broken. They courted for four years before she realised he never would, and she moved to London to restore her broken heart. And I remember thinking how sad it was that this kindly lady, who had so much love to give, had never found someone decent to share it with. Not that she was sad. On the contrary, Miss Binchy told me that she had had a very happy life and even if the Good Lord had not blessed her with children, he had blessed her with fantastic sisters and wonderful nephews. 'There's always somebody worse off than you,' she said. 'You should remember that. Sometimes your troubles may seem overwhelming, but they always pass. Trust me. Time heals.'

And so I told her about Jake, the boyfriend I met after university. Sam introduced us; they were on the same graduate trainee scheme in the City. I recalled how I used to dream of walking down the aisle with him. How I'd while away evenings, while he was working late, sketching my ideal wedding dress, sorting out pretend seating plans and planning the five-course menu we'd enjoy at our reception. How I couldn't imagine a day without him in my life, and how he ruthlessly abandoned me when his career took off, surpassing Sam's. He didn't even call to let me know that our four-year relationship was over, to tell me that he had fallen out of love with me. I found out when I saw him hand in hand with a blonde, strolling down New Bond Street, smiling and carefree.

It was history repeating itself. My father ran out on my mother when I was six years old. The previous year he had been promoted to managing director at work. She was so proud of his success and fell for that age-old story about working late in the office. It was such a cliché. She discovered months later that he had actually been working *out* in the office – with his secretary. Miss Jones had taken more than a letter. She had taken my dad's heart and broken my mother's. He was my mum's first and last love, and the experience has left her bitter about men. She tried to ease my distress about Jake with the comforting phrase, 'I told you so'.

Sometimes I see Jake quoted in the newspapers. Once I saw him in the pages of *Hello*, champagne glass in one hand, the other solicitously resting on the blonde's shoulders. Up close, she has a wild mane of hair and horse-like features that even her mother would find hard to be kind about. It turned out she was The Honourable somebody or other. That made me laugh. What was honourable about stealing the love of someone else's life? Then last year I read that he had left Browns Black, the investment bank, to join a hedge fund which, according to Sam, would earn him millions of pounds. Money had changed Jake, though. It had turned him into somebody I no longer recognised. And, quite frankly, how much money does one person need? I'd have been happy curled up on the sofa in my little flat eating cold baked beans (I'm not much of a cook), if Jake was sitting beside me. But he wasn't. His first taste of the high life created an insatiable greed. He needed the six bedroom stucco fronted house in Holland Park, immaculately furnished by some leading interior designer, the yacht, moored off the coast of Monte Carlo, a whole range of boys' toys and Savile Row suits. But he no longer needed me.

That was six years ago. Miss Binchy may promise that time does heal but I'm not so sure. There are some days, even now, when the grief feels as acute as if I had only just lost Jake. Maybe it's because he was my first love. Sure, I'd had other boyfriends before, and I even told one or two that I loved them, but that was a different type of love. It was more fraternal. Jake was the real thing. Cupid scored a bull's eye, but when he pulled out the arrow he ripped my heart apart and I vowed that nobody would ever hurt me like that again.

Louise set me up with lots of Sam's friends, promising that another relationship would help me get over Jake. You know the sort of thing. But everything they did seemed to remind me of him. When they drew up outside my flat in the latest sports car, hood down, obviously trying to impress me, I remembered the time that Jake had taken delivery of his first company car – a convertible BMW – and how excited he had been. I recalled how we had driven straight to Brighton, top down on a bitterly cold day, to road test it. When they sent massive bouquets of exotic flowers from celebrity florists, I just got upset. Jake had taken to sending those just weeks before I discovered about his other woman. It had been so easy for him to assuage his conscience by getting his secretary to order them. There was no effort in these gestures. The guys were pseudo Jakes, and not even a patch on the real thing. When their numbers came up on my mobile phone, my heart didn't stop with anticipation. Inevitably, the relationships were doomed to failure. I dumped each of them before they could act, until Louise finally said she was not introducing me to anyone else and would leave me to my own devices.

So I chose people who were the complete opposite of Jake. Somehow I thought they would be more real, more honest. And then the tables turned. I changed from dumper to dumpee. Great! It was a massive shock to the ego and I began training myself not to care, not to expect too much from my relationships, to treat them as temporary flings. I had met the man of my dreams and if I couldn't have him, despite all his failings, then I didn't really want anyone else. Or at least, that's what I believed. But the only thing is, if I'm being completely honest with myself, I *do* now care. A fling seemed exciting and wild when I was 28, or even 30, but at 32? The truth is that I can't face getting hurt again.

The tube pulls into Knightsbridge station, my destination. Well, I can't spend any more time fretting about my self-inflicted lousy love life. I've got to be focused for my meeting with Carl Lawson, boss of Ilyax Insurance, this afternoon. He managed to keep his job last year when a major fraud was uncovered in the insurance company's Indian call centre in Mumbai, but the finance director was not so lucky. It turned out that two of his right-hand men, sent to India to oversee the operation, adopted some rather Third World accounting practices, redirecting company funds into their personal offshore bank accounts. The finance director was completely unaware of their antics, but that was no defence, as he soon learned. With the trappings of his position, came the buck. And it stopped with him.

It was a major public relations disaster for the insurance company. The headlines were damning, particularly after it emerged that he had been paid nearly one million pounds to soften the blow of losing his job. And then some investigative reporter discovered that he had not actually got a first class degree in economics, as he claimed on his CV, but a third class in anthropology. The newspapers were filled with stories of irate policyholders, furious that Ilyax had refused to pay out on their claims for leaking pipes and burnt out cars, but was willing to reward someone who had failed in his duties and lied about his qualifications. So it's totally understandable that Carl Lawson is determined his new finance director is scandal free.

Investigations-R-Us is located just a few streets away from Harrods. Its shiny black door carries a discreet brass plate that only says IRU. As the founder Boris says proudly, you'd only find IRU if you knew what you were looking for. In fact, most people scurry past, thinking it's an offshoot of the Inland Revenue, without any knowledge of the ex-SAS men and paratroopers who work here, plotting the rescue of some kidnapped banker in Colombia, or the security gadgets that would amaze even James Bond.

There are twenty full time staff working here, operating in four-person teams. In my group there's Donna, aged 26, who has a figure like J-Lo and a voice like Barbara Windsor. Today she is wearing a black pencil skirt with a wide patent leather belt that pinches in her already narrow waist. A red Lycra top clings desperately to her 34D bosom. She is perched on the corner of Angus's desk, chatting to him about Jude Law. Her skirt is split almost to the waist, and her legs are casually crossed to reveal just a hint of orange-peel-free thigh. She doesn't have a clue about the problems of other women. When I bemoaned my cellulite, she thought I was talking about a new type of slimline mobile phone. Men love her, and she likes them back. A steady relationship for Donna means the man stays for breakfast. She never gets dumped. The concept is as alien to her as paying for her own drinks in a nightclub. She is only interested in champagne cocktails and one-night stands.

Donna joined Investigations-R-Us about three years ago, just a few months after Angus, and is really the team's trainee. Today Angus is wearing a grey cashmere V-necked sweater that shows off his fantastic muscular frame – God, it's such a waste. The fourth member of our team, James, joined about nine months ago from our Irish sister company, and is nomi- nally the leader, although it's quite democratic. We all muck in together. He is hunched over his desk, studying a pile of documents. His glasses perch atop his shaven head in a futile attempt to disguise his receding hairline. I once saw a picture of him with a full head of hair. I didn't like it. As usual, his tie hangs at half-mast and his collar button is loose. James is something of an enigma to me. He's friendly and takes part in the team banter (of which I am usually at the receiving end) but I don't really know him that well. I love his distinctive Irish lilt though, even when it makes it difficult to work out whether he's teasing me or not.

'So?' Donna looks up expectantly as I pull my chair out. 'How did it go last night? Spill the beans. We're dying to know. Aren't we, Angus?' He nods, a sheepish look on his face. Sometimes, after a few drinks, Angus admits he still feels guilty about Pete, even though I tell him to put it behind him.

'It was alright,' I shrug my shoulders. 'Nice place. You should go there.'

'And?' Donna looks slightly disappointed.

'And what?' I feign ignorance.

'When are you seeing him again?'

There it is. The killer question. It hangs in the air like a noose round my neck. 'I don't know,' I finally reply. 'We didn't really discuss that.'

'Nat dumped you?' Trust bloody sixth-sense Donna.

'What makes you say that? I could've dumped him.' Donna and Angus raise their eyebrows, challenging my comment. Even James appears interested when he looks up. 'Okay,' I hold my hands up in defeat. 'I was dumped.' I don't need to add 'again'. They know.

'Yes.' Donna punches the air in delight. 'Angus you owe me twenty quid.'

'You bet on me getting dumped?' I ask, incredulous. I survey my colleagues as they simultaneously defend themselves.

'Actually I bet that you wouldn't be,' corrects Angus, waving his finger at me. 'I thought this one would last.' He pauses. 'Well, at least for a few more weeks.' He throws up his hands in a 'what can I do?' gesture.

'Don't look at me,' shrugs James. 'I know nothing about this. Your love life is a complete mystery to me.' And me, I add silently.

'Hey, I needed the money,' Donna responds defiantly. 'There's a new top in Zara that I simply can't live without. I was a bit short.'

'So you bet on my misery?' I shriek at her. 'Couldn't you just have borrowed the money? Or bought a lottery ticket like normal people?'

'Ah, but this was more fun,' she smiles, 'and besides, the chances of your relationship lasting was about as remote as me winning the lottery. Look, don't act all indignant with me. I know you weren't really that serious about the guy.'

'Why do you say that?' I say indignantly.

'When was the last time you went for a bikini wax?' she retorts. My two male colleagues and I blush furiously. 'Anyway, he was so wrong for you. He was so boring, always talking about appliqués and hemlines.'

'I liked him,' Angus cuts in. 'He had fantastic dress sense, darling, very flamboyant.' He delves into his wallet, fishes out a twenty-pound note and hands it to Donna.

'You think so? I thought he looked like Laurence Llewelyn-Bowen in drag, and that's saying something,' insists Donna, grabbing the proffered note. 'He's a male peacock. Who wants to go out with a man like that?'

'I do,' I reply.

'Me too,' mutters Angus.

'Oh, come on Angus,' snaps Donna. 'You can't lust after all Holly's men.' Angus blushes. 'And Holly,' she turns to me, 'Nat was just another fling for you. Did you honestly see yourself settling down with him? Buying a place together? Maybe having a child?' No, I silently concede, but that's not the point. 'Anyway, how could you enjoy dating a man with better manicures than you?' Subconsciously I scrunch my hands into fists – hiding the badly polished nails. Correction: chipped nails. 'You're so much better than him.' I look over at James, secretly imploring him to save me but he just smiles.

The man seems to enjoy seeing his colleague in distress. I won't forget that.

'Look, can we all get on with our work?' I plead. I really don't need this psychoanalysis today and I turn on my computer. 'I've got a very important meeting this afternoon that I really do need to prepare for.' A pink Post-it note stuck on the handset of my phone says: 'Carl Lawson. 3pm. Ilyax offices. London Wall.' My stomach turns when I spot it. I'm already nervous at the challenge.

'I'm worried about you, Holly,' Donna taps my shoulder. 'Don't you want a real boyfriend? Is that what it is? You want to remain an old maid?' She looks at me in puzzlement.

'Of course I don't want to remain an old maid.' I burst out. 'Anyway how can I be an old maid? I'm 32 – that's not even halfway to my bus pass.'

'But the little hand's gone way past six on your body clock,' retorts Donna. 'We need to analyse this problem, and we need to work fast.' I redden, put my hand up to signal enough but she just ignores it. 'You spend your life analysing other people, and you won't even spend a few minutes on something as crucial as your own happiness.' I suppose she has a point, I think grudgingly. 'I know I'm right. Gather round, boys. We're going to sort out Holly's disastrous love life.' Angus pulls his chair closer with alacrity, and James swiftly follows. Donna retrieves a wire-bound notebook from a drawer and seductively slithers back to her chair. She looks sexy without even trying. 'Right, I've taken the liberty ...'

'You can say that again,' I interrupt.

'... of analysing your exes,' she barely flinches, 'although I'm aware that past performance cannot necessarily be viewed as a guide to future success. I've studied Nat, Jason, Jasper, Alan, Sean and Rob.' She turns to Angus. 'I disregarded Pete. I view him as a momentary blip.'

'Oh, believe me, sweeties, there's nothing momentary about his blip,' mutters Angus.

'The six,' Donna checks her notes, 'share common traits.

They're all tall, dark, reasonably good-looking and of a similar age to you. And they all dumped you. One by text message?'

I nod. It was Alan, a plumber I met when he came to instal my washing machine. We went out for about six weeks, before the text arrived. It said: 'Cnt do ths @ mo. Nt rt time 4 me. Nt u. Me. Soz.' It took me two days to decipher, and realise the relationship had ended.

'So?' I finally ask. 'What does it mean, Freud?'

'That you go for the same type,' she shrugs. 'And that's where you are going wrong. You need to break the mould.'

'I disagree,' interrupts James. Thank you, I think. Now exercise your authority and tell Donna to go back to work. 'There's probably nothing wrong with any of these men.' What does he mean 'probably'? Does he think I date psychos? 'But they sound like they were all losers. 'This conversation has a ring of familiarity.

'They were not losers,' I say indignantly. Angus mutters archly about Pete most certainly not being a loser.

'Oh, come on Holly,' James persists with remarkable forcefulness for a man who hardly knows me. 'According to Donna, over the past two years you've dated an art student, a plumber, an electrician, an actor working as a barman ...'

'There's nothing wrong with that,' I defend my old boyfriend Jasper. 'He could still be discovered. It takes years for some actors to get a break. George Clooney worked with killer tomatoes before he got that part in ER.'

'Okay, you were dating an actor working as a barman while he waited for the call from Hollywood,' concedes James, 'and then there was the guy who used to deliver sandwiches to the office.'

'I liked Sean,' interrupts Angus. 'When he was seeing Holly, I used to get the hummus and alfalfa sprouts on rye bread at a special discount.'

'Nobody else ever wanted them,' I say. 'You were the only customer.' Sean had been fun. I used to look forward to his morning visits, to my tomato, avocado and mozzarella with basil drizzle on granary, and to our flirtatious chats. I enjoyed the buzz of knowing that somebody liked me. I didn't reciprocate at first, but that's the funny thing about relationships. Sometimes you end up falling for the guy whom you'd never usually give a second glance just because you discover he likes you – perhaps it's because you initially enjoy the flattery – and then that somehow transforms into something more significant. My heart leapt the day I unwrapped my sandwich to find a poem asking me out.

> *To Holly,*
> *Don't make me melancholy,*
> *Come on a date,*
> *Just don't be late.*

Okay, so he was no Poet Laureate, but it seemed so romantic, just like the movies. And then he turned up for our first date. Prince Charming doesn't usually arrive on his bicycle, walk into a pub encased in Lycra – revealing a figure better than your own – to discover he has left his wallet in his jeans. At home. Yet even that didn't dampen my initial enthusiasm. But there's only so much conversation one can have about sandwich fillings. We parted over Brie and bacon baguettes that had been left over from the day before. The bread had gone stale very quickly, and so had our relationship.

'You forgot the mechanic,' exclaims Donna.

'You guys are just snobs,' I interrupt angrily. 'There was nothing wrong with any of those people. And there's nothing wrong with me. They all said so. Each of them said that it was nothing to do with me. They all said that it was their issue. Their fault.' The trio burst out laughing.

'See, I'm right,' says James, while the others nod in agreement. 'The classic kiss-off. I realise that we don't know each other very well, so I may be speaking out of turn here.'

'Really?' I interrupt. 'You think?'

'But guys always say that,' he continues, ignoring me, 'otherwise you women want a big long post-mortem on what went wrong. It goes on and on and on ...'

'We do not.' I defend my sex. Donna looks confused. This is alien territory to the woman who never gets dumped.

'You do. It's too hard for a woman to accept that a guy just doesn't fancy them anymore. That he's dumping them because, I don't know, suddenly he's irritated by their habit of singing in the shower, or he thinks their bum really does look too big in their jeans and is fed up saying otherwise.' My face flushes at this point but James carries on regardless. 'Or because he's just met someone else. There's a mountain of reasons that men dump women, none of them very complicated, but the simple truth is you don't want to hear any of them. You want a big in-depth discussion on what went wrong with the relationship, and to analyse it all. It's like you all want to be the host on Trisha.'

'We do not,' I repeat again.

'Alright, so if one of your former boyfriends said he was dumping you because he thought you talked too much or you, I don't know,' he throws his hand into the air, 'were obsessed with soap operas, wouldn't you want to discuss it further?'

'No, I'd accept his decision and move on,' I lie.

'I just don't believe you, and nor do any of them,' he continues. 'You'd want to know exactly how much talking was too much, or you'd try to educate him on the finer points of *Coronation Street*, and then promise to change to make him happy. It's embarrassing for men and humiliating for women. It's far better to tell you that it's not you. It's a cop-out. A get-out-of-a-long-intense-discussion-with-crying-girlfriend card.' He looks at my stunned face, before continuing in a softer tone: 'But personally, my honest opinion is that it really wasn't you in the case of all these guys.'

'Yes, but they dumped her,' points out my tactful colleague and former friend Donna.

'Yeah, but not because Holly did anything wrong,' reiterates James, turning towards her. 'Any guy would be lucky to date her.' I feel my face burning, and an involuntary tingle through my body. 'I don't know why but Holly is picking guys who, frankly, aren't good enough for her, and I think they realise that. I know you won't believe this, but we men are sensitive souls. I think these guys probably guessed that there was no real future in the relationship, and their egos couldn't bear that. They expected Holly to find somebody else more suitable for her and dump them. Better to act first and save face.'

'That's ridiculous,' I exclaim. 'I wasn't about to dump Nat.'

'Actually I think James is onto something here,' says Donna, nodding her head knowingly. 'And it would have ended sooner or later. If it hadn't happened last night, I'd have given it another week at most.'

'I *am* right. What's a girl like you doing with a plumber?' James holds his hand up before I can protest. 'Don't get me wrong. I'm not a snob. Far from it. There's nothing wrong with plumbers – but when the attraction of his muscles and discussing his U bend runs out, what's left? He doesn't understand your world, and you really don't understand or care about his.' I don't say anything. There's a lot of sense in what James is saying – but I'm blowed if I'm going to tell him. Not when he's simultaneously embarrassing and flattering me in front of my colleagues.

'I can just imagine you trying to mask your boredom as he tells you about his washing machine adventures by making those little quips of yours. Just the sort of ego boost a man needs. But I bet he still fancied you when he dumped you. You should ask one of your exes to tell you the truth about why your relationship failed. I'm sure I'm right.' He winks at me, and I find myself blushing again.

'Look, you guys,' I continue. 'This is all very amusing. Really. And you've all had a great laugh at my expense. But now, do you think we could leave it, and maybe, and hey I know this sounds radical, get on with some work?'

'We're doing this for your own good,' insists Donna.

'Public humiliation is not for my own good.'

'If you feel like that then you shouldn't have worn that suit today,' mutters Donna, just loud enough for me to hear.

'There's nothing wrong with this suit,' I snap, looking at my Prince of Wales check outfit, with its wide shoulders and nipped-in waist. 'It's vintage.'

'What you mean is, you found it in the back of your wardrobe, realised it still fitted and prayed that it had come back into fashion. Well, I hate to break it to you, but it hasn't. It's still out of date.'

'Girls, girls,' James holds his hand up to silence us. 'This isn't sorting out Holly's problem with men.'

'I don't have a problem with men,' I protest.

'Yes, you do,' my three colleagues insist.

'Look,' says James. 'You seem like the sort of girl to remain on good terms with all your old boyfriends. Why not meet up with one of them for a coffee or something, and ask a few probing questions? What about the delivery guy, Sean?'

'So I then casually ask whether he felt inadequate when we went out?' I laugh sarcastically at their great plan.

'Holly, you spend your life researching people and what makes them tick. Are there any skeletons in their closets, any foibles? And you use that information to judge whether they are right for the position they have applied for. All I'm saying is why not use your professional talents on yourself? You want to be one part of a successful relationship.' James smiles sympathetically.

'Exactly,' interrupts Donna. 'You want to be the woman that men can't dump.'

James goes on. 'I think you need to discover what makes a successful relationship, and find out where you're going wrong. You're a professional investigator, so – investigate. What do you think?'

He smiles. Donna jots her final squiggle, and looks expectantly at me. Angus indicates his mobile phone, silently mouthing that he'll call Pete to seek his advice if I just say the word. I pause, pretending that I'm considering the matter.

'I think you're all mad, and extremely rude. I'm not some character in a soap opera that you can analyse and take apart.

I'm a real person with a busy schedule.' I gather together some papers that are scattered on my desk, and place them into an already bulging file. 'Who is now going down to Starbucks to enjoy a skinny latte in peace, and prepare for her extremely important meeting this afternoon.' I grab my coat and leave without another word.

Chapter Four

They say you need a period of mourning to get over a relationship. I usually agree. It took me five days to get over Jasper, four for Alan and three days apiece for Jason, Sean and Rob. I'm not even mentioning Pete. That was shock rather than grief – although I was bitter we hadn't got around to colour coding my wardrobe as planned. As for Nat, well it's been less than twenty-four hours and I think I'm over him. In fact, I really want to be under someone else – I think it's what is called the recovery position – because I've fallen in lust. It's hit me like a thunderbolt. My hands are clammy. My mouth is dry. I'm talking like a parrot with a throat infection. And it's all because Carl Lawson is sexy.

It was the last thing I expected to happen to me today. I swore off men when I finally managed to prise myself away from my colleagues and their unsolicited, humiliating advice. Work, I decided, would be my salvation. And luckily that seems to be the case. In the form of a man who, quite frankly, would not normally attract my attention. It's weird. He's a bit older. He's not exactly good looking, but he's got something – that X factor – and it's currently playing havoc with parts of my body that clients should not reach.

Obviously I had done my research on Ilyax Insurance, and had read all the articles about its boss, Carl Lawson. They informed me that he was 45, separated from his wife (a former catwalk model), and has three sons, ranging in age from seven to twelve. I found a tabloid list of the City's most eligible single men, where he was placed at number eight between a 60-year-old property tycoon and a 21-year-old internet millionaire. I learned he had a degree from Cambridge University, started his career as a management consultant and took home enough money last year to buy my tiny flat several times over and still have change. But what I didn't expect from my extensive research was the impact Carl Lawson has had on me. It's a total bolt from the blue. Ever since Jake, I have never once been attracted to a successful man. Hell! I disconnected the relevant hormones.

I didn't truly notice Carl at first. We had the usual small talk about the weather (rain again), traffic (slow again) and a new office development across the road from his office (modern again), but I was so determined to make my presentation without a glitch, to demonstrate why Ilyax Insurance had been right to select Investigations-R-Us, that I didn't really pay attention to the person sitting opposite me. I was worried about flip charts and graphics, so I wasn't aware of his azure blue eyes that seemed to burn right into me. And now I can't stop staring into them. They're mesmerising – possibly the sexiest eyes I have ever encountered – and they truly twinkle. Every incisive comment is met with a flicker of appreciation. It's so understated, almost imperceptible, and yet so blatantly sexual. My stomach is already turning in anticipation of the handshake I'll receive when this meeting ends.

I started with the PowerPoint presentation of past investigations designed to demonstrate Investigations-R-Us's phenomenal success in uncovering skeletons in unlikely closets. I told Carl how my colleague James once uncovered an irregularity in the bank account of a leading candidate – I called him Mr X – for a top City job. He couldn't work out why Mr X made a significant payment every month to another bank account. It wasn't any of the myriad of bank accounts belonging to Mr X that James already knew of. So my determined colleague delved a little further and, lo and behold, discovered the account belonged to a Portuguese waiter named Juan. Well, that posed a few other mysteries. First, how could a Portuguese waiter earn such phenomenal tips to afford a top floor flat on a rather nice garden square in South Kensington? And, second, what was his connection to Mr X? A bout of twenty-four-hour surveillance soon solved those posers. Juan turned out to be Mr X's lover. Such a revelation would have shocked his wife – Mrs X and their four children A, B, C and D – who thought their husband and father was out playing football. He even left home in his football kit and boots, before changing into civvies in a lay-by down the road. Mind you, I always thought Mrs X was just a little bit dim. She must have thought her husband was the cleanest football player ever – he never got a drop of mud on his boots or shorts.

Obviously Mr X didn't get the job. He probably has no idea why he was rejected, and the company would never disclose the reason – after all, Mr X could sue for breach of human rights. The job was given to somebody less qualified but whose life was entirely blameless. I could tell Carl was impressed. He kept probing to discover the identity of Mr X, but I was resolute. And in doing so I emphasised the company's ability to keep information confidential. My lips were sealed but, as Carl kept teasing me to get the juicy titbits, I increasingly wished they were slightly open and pressed against his. It was the way he looked intensely at me. My stomach started fluttering.

'Okay, let's cut to the chase,' Carl finally said, laying two buff folders on the boardroom table. 'I've listened to your advertisement, all very impressive, and this,' he pats the folders firmly, 'is what I want. Here are the details of two candidates for the finance director's job. Obviously, after all the bad press we had last time, Ilyax Insurance just cannot get this wrong. I want you to look into every aspect of their lives, especially their exam results. If their granny served two months for shoplifting in the fifties, I still want to know because,' he pauses for effect, 'I guarantee that journalists will dig like crazy for dirt on our new finance director. Have you anything to say?' And then he smiled at me expectantly, and I noticed his long eyelashes. It's like being on a magical mystery tour. Every moment I am with him I notice something else.

I shake my head. Carl opens the first folder, and removes a sheaf of papers, topped by a black and white photograph. I don't look at it. I am studying him.

'Hmm,' I mutter dreamily, 'greying hair, six foot four, thirteen stone, nice dress sense ... absolutely perfect.'

'You can tell all that from this photo?' Carl stares at me in surprise.

'Er, yeah. It's, um ... I've, um ... Trained eye,' I stutter, looking down to the folder in front of me. 'I've a trained eye.'

'But he's sitting down?' He looks confused.

'I went on a special course,' I bluff.

'Sounds interesting,' Carl smiles at me. Eyes all a-twinkle. He knows, I think. He knows why I am distracted. 'Well, this is our preferred candidate, and I'd like you to concentrate your initial efforts on him and if you turn up anything bad I want to know immediately.' I nod, trying to appear businesslike and efficient. 'His name's Clive Partridge and he currently works at one of the smaller insurance companies. Egyptia. I've enclosed a batch of press cuttings on him, and you'll find that there've been no negative articles about him ...'

'That doesn't mean anything,' I interrupt in my best professional voice – the one that doesn't sound like a smitten kitten on heat. 'The press had no reason to study him before.'

'I suppose that's true,' Carl nods. 'He could have more skeletons than the Natural History Museum.'

'Hey,' I soothe. 'If there's anything in his closet, Investigations-R-Us will find it.'

'Oh, I'm sure you will,' Carl says quietly. 'And in that event, we have a reserve candidate just in case.' He opens the second buff folder, and pushes a black and white photograph across the table towards me.

'It's a woman,' I remark in surprise.

'Really? You *are* good,' he winks. 'Can you tell me anything else about her from the photo? Something you learned on that course, perhaps. Her height? Weight?' He knows I was bluffing before, I'm sure of it. I study the picture, and realisation slowly dawns. It's a candidate from a previous search. Now if

I can only remember all her details. My mental Rolodex starts rotating ... Bingo. Located target. I casually pick up the photograph and rub my chin, as I appear to study it. Aim. Fire.

'I would say this candidate is aged about 45, height about five-five. She's a size twelve, but has quite an athletic physique, so my guess is that she works out regularly – probably favours rowing – you can tell from the shoulders,' I smile at Carl who looks at me in surprise. 'Her facial features indicate that she is of' – I shrug, as if this is all really rather difficult (and definitely worth the whopping bill Ilyax will certainly charge) – 'Celtic origins. If this picture were in colour, I would hazard a guess that she's a redhead. And you see those little worry lines around her eyes?' I point at non-existent wrinkles. I'd say she is a mother. Three, maybe four, children?'

He stares at me in utter amazement.

'Wow, that's really something. And you can tell all that from just one photograph?' I nod slowly, trying to settle my nerves. 'What happens if it's a passport photo?'

'How do you think Customs Officers know who to strip search?' I wink cheekily. 'They have an eye for detail.'

'Is this woman ideal for us?' Who knows? But I'm certainly ideal for you.

'Never judge a book by its cover,' I quip. 'But I should point out that Investigations-R-Us can't tell you who Ilyax Insurance should employ. All we can do is provide an in-depth background on each candidate. If there's any skeleton in a closet, I promise that I'll find it. If you opt for the Complete Body Check Programme, I'll trawl through Clive Partridge's finances, pore through his telephone bills, examine his tax returns, totally check out his curriculum vitae and discover whether he has a criminal record.'

'You can find out if they've been in jail?'

'We can,' I say, 'or even if they've just been in trouble with the law. It's getting more difficult though. The Data Protection Act makes it harder to find out personal details about people. It's not so easy to access information. We used to have a network of friendly policemen who, for a small fee (Carl smiles

knowingly) would check out people on their central computer for us. It's almost impossible to find one keen to do that
now with all these blasted restrictions. Now if a policeman
in Central London, say, is caught looking up the details of a
person in Edinburgh, alarm bells ring across the country. He
has to have a very good reason why he was prying or he could
go to jail. All this bloody nanny-state rubbish, and protection
of personal freedoms is destroying legitimate businesses like
Investigations-R-Us.'

'You obviously feel strongly about this,' Carl says. 'But
you're certain that you can get that information?'

'As certain as night follows day,' I smile. 'We have our
methods.'

'I'm sure you do, Miss Parker.' Carl smiles at me. 'And I
think it's going to be fun finding out all about them over the
coming weeks.' He stands up, signalling the meeting is over,
and steps nearer to shake my hand. I surreptitiously rub it on
my skirt before taking his, and then give it a firm grip, savour-
ing its softness. 'Great fun.' He squeezes my hand and twinkles
his eyes. 'I don't want you to start any surveillance operations
for now, but perhaps you could report in every few days to
update me on progress and ...' he pauses '... your methods!' I
blush. 'And we'll set a meeting up for,' he hesitates, 'ten days'
time? Friday? At these offices, same time. I'll get my secretary
to email confirming details.'

'Certainly,' I reply. 'We should have all the background
checks done by then. And if then you decide on the Complete
Body Check Programme, which I strongly recommend, I'll
organise the surveillance teams to be in place the following
day. I look forward to seeing you next week.'

'And I you, Miss Parker,' he says, escorting me towards the
lift. 'I you.'

He stands in the hallway watching me until the lift doors
close, and I experience a frisson of excitement at the feeling
that today, somehow, my life has irrevocably changed.

CHAPTER FIVE

I see Pete as soon as I enter the coffee shop. He is agitatedly picking out the raisins from the Danish pastry in front of him, while throwing anxious looks at the doorway. He smiles nervously on spotting me, dropping a raisin into his steaming cup of coffee in his panic. I signal that I'm fetching a drink from the counter and will be over shortly, and he noticeably breathes a sigh of relief. Poor Pete. He sounded very suspicious on the phone when I rang last night to request a meeting, and then quietly suggested it might be best if we kept it from Angus for the moment. Oh God. I just can't bear the inevitable 'I told you so's' when my colleagues learn I've taken their advice and contacted an ex. I can't bear the thought of their preening.

But I am prepared to go through all of that for the sake of Carl Lawson. It is three days since we met, and I can't get him out of my mind. He's not my usual type but that, according to James's unwelcome advice, might be just what I need. He's a high-flying businessman who probably doesn't know how to make a panini, unblock a toilet or change a tyre on an articulated lorry. If I can manoeuvre an evening drink to keep him abreast of my findings, then I want to make damned sure that I don't blow my chances. And Pete is probably the only person I trust to give me helpful tips on dating etiquette.

I surreptitiously examine Pete while waiting for my espresso. I can understand the initial attraction I felt. He has the sort of looks that don't turn heads, but somehow make an impression. My mother would describe Pete as clean cut. He's the type of man that most mothers dream of for their daughters. Everything about him is spotless, from his shiny black lace-up shoes to his perfectly buffed nails. But it is only now, in hindsight, that I notice the warning signs. While I'm at the counter, Pete is checking his image in a small compact mirror that he keeps in the leather attaché case that's never far from his side. It also holds a small make up wallet, which he shared with me once when I couldn't find my foundation. I was just so grateful at the time that I didn't even think it was weird.

'Hi,' I say, slowly approaching the table. I rest my coffee down and lean across to kiss him chastely on the cheek. 'How are you?'

'Fine,' he says curtly. The cerise silk handkerchief that sprouts from the breast pocket of his pinstriped suit is merely for decorative purposes. He thinks it gives him an edge over his colleagues at the Savile Row store where he works.

I flop down on the seat opposite him, tucking my feet out of sight, and toss my purple scarf and pink woolly gloves into a pile on the floor. I then bundle my coat into a ball and sling it on top.

'I hope you didn't mind me contacting you.'

'Mind? Why would I mind, darling?' His voice is getting shrill and he glances, horrified, at the way I've discarded my outer garments.

'Well, it's a slightly awkward situation.'

'Not in the least.' He almost yelps the words. 'Nothing could be less awkward.' He scrunches up a Wet One and throws it into the ashtray.

'As I said on the phone, I wanted to talk about us.'

Pete cringes at the 'us' word and sighs deeply. Great, I think. I really am that unbearable.

'Holly. Sweetheart,' he finally says, grabbing my hand solicitously and starting to speak slowly. 'Listen to me. There.' He pauses. 'Is.' Pause. 'No.' Pause. 'Us.' He shakes his head sadly. Pete strokes my hand. 'You're wonderful, absolutely wonderful, but I'm with Angus now. I thought you understood that.'

'I do,' I say quickly. 'I think you make a lovely couple.'

'We do. You do?' He suddenly looks puzzled.

'Absolutely,' I nod. 'You've got lots in common.'

'You think so?' Pete sounds pleased.

'Yeah,' I continue. 'You share similar interests.' Like men. 'You're both interested in the arts, able to whip up a cordon bleu meal from the contents of an empty fridge, and you each put down the loo seat after paying a visit.'

'My mother was adamant on that last point,' Pete waves his finger firmly. 'She said it would impress the ladies.'

'And it does,' I agree, 'although sadly it's wasted.'

'So, you're not here to ask me to try again with you?' Pete is puzzled. His forehead creases into a frown, and he combs a hand through his hair. It sticks up on end. He really shouldn't wear so much Brylcreem, but I understand his frustration at his stubborn cow's lick.

'Good God, no.' I exclaim indignantly. Relief is instantly etched on Pete's face. Bloody cheek. Perhaps he wasn't the best 'ex' to start this particular project with. 'Although I must admit that when I get home to find a block of mouldy cheddar cheese, two eggs, three bottles of wine and a can of Diet Coke in the fridge I really do miss you.'

'But I started a basic store cupboard for you for those sorts of emergencies, darling,' Pete looks irritated. 'Do you not keep it up to date?'

'Sort of, but what am I meant to do with dried porcini mushrooms and truffle oil? And what the hell are vanilla pods?'

'You could have used the arborio rice and rustled up a lovely mushroom and truffle risotto, and if you only kept a packet of Parma ham in your fridge, as I specifically recommended, then a carbonara would have been within reach.' Pete sighs. 'Did I teach you nothing?'

'You taught me loads,' I smile amiably. 'Without you I'd never have known that a dash of vinegar improves the quality of meringues, or that you can buy special detergents to keep your whites bright.'

Pete beams with pleasure. I don't mention that I've never

in my life made a meringue or managed to keep my whites brighter. Any woman who claims she doesn't have a drawer containing off-white undies is lying.

'See, I told you that not everything can be learned from the pages of *Hello* and *Marie Claire*. Do you still de-scale your kettle?'

'As often as I brush my teeth.'

'You're mocking,' he frowns.

'Only a little. You're a remarkable man, and I was lucky to count you as my special friend' – I balk at the word boyfriend – 'for a short time, and now, I hope, as my friend.' He nods. 'That's why I feel able to ask you something rather delicate.'

'Well, now I know you don't want us to try again, you can ask me anything you want.' Pete visibly relaxes. 'I'm all ears, sweetie.' He sits back, crosses his arms and throws one hand under his chin.

'This is slightly embarrassing and I'm only asking because I want to learn from my mistakes, and not repeat them ...'

'Well, I wouldn't wear that suit again,' he interrupts, closing his eyes in horror as he shakes his head.

'What's wrong with this suit?' It's the one Donna mocked, but I can't see anything wrong with it. I think it's a nice outfit. Prince of Wales check is never out of fashion, as far as I know, and skirts that come just below the knee are always flattering. I'm sure I read that somewhere.

'Absolutely nothing, if we still lived in the eighties ...'

'... and that wasn't what I wanted to ask you about,' I continue indignantly.

'Sorry, I just thought we were talking about not repeating mistakes. That suit is a big 'no-no'. I mean, come on. And *you* have the audacity to criticise others on their dress sense!'

'I don't,' I lie, crossing my fingers as I recall my comment on Nat's shirt.

'You do,' he continues. 'I mean, this must be the first time that you haven't pulled my handkerchief out of my pocket, hoping to find a string of other coloured ones. Darling, take my word for it. The best place for that suit is in the bin. Your whole outfit is wrong. You look like you've just got out of bed, and thrown on the nearest thing even if you found it on the floor.' I blush. He's not that far from the truth. I tossed this suit on my bedroom chair three evenings ago, but my aim wasn't that good and I woke to find the jacket crumpled in a ball on the carpet. Still, the blouse was fresh out of the wardrobe. 'And your blouse has toothpaste on it.'

'What.' I glance down, and see a blob of Colgate. I scratch desperately at it, leaving a white mark. It looks like a pigeon has shat on me. Pete shakes his head in horror. 'Oh God. This is awful.'

My erstwhile friend produces a pack of wipes from his attaché case. 'Try this. They work wonders. Now what did you want to ask me?'

I take a deep breath, as I dab frantically at the spearmint-flavoured stain.

'Pete, be honest, why did you stop going out with me?'

There is a stunned silence. 'Holly,' he finally says. 'I'm gay.'

I throw my hands up in exasperation. 'Duh. I know. But that's not what I'm talking about. Look, I've been dumped by – er – a number of men in a short period of time. Now I know they were never going to be the loves of my life, and that they were really only flings, but I really want to know why. What is wrong with me?' I sigh. 'I know they all say it's nothing to do with me, but it must be.'

Pete looks carefully at me. 'You really want my honest opinion on what you're doing wrong,' he asks suspiciously. 'Apart from choosing losers?'

'Hand on heart. I do.' I make a mock Girl Guide salute.

Pete takes a deep breath. 'Well, you know that my skin is as thick as the next man ...'

'I thought you used cream to stop that,' I interrupt.

'That's exactly what I was going to say.'

'You were going to tell me about your cream?' I'm confused. 'That's all very well, but I have my own skincare routine and it isn't really what I want to talk about today. I want to know what's wrong with me?'

'*That's* what's wrong with you.' His voice is gentle.

'My skin?' I put my hands to my face. 'No one's ever mentioned that before. Okay, so I get the occasional spot. Who doesn't? But they only flare up on my chin ... and the little one I have now will disappear if I just ignore it. They always do. Eventually.'

'Holly, calm down.' Pete sounds frustrated. 'Your skin is fine, although I think a little concealer for the bags under your eyes might be wise. Look, you've asked me to be honest, so please don't take this the wrong way, but you're sometimes too quick to make little jokes at other people's expense. You don't always think through the consequences.'

'I disagree. I never say anything without mentally checking that it's funny. I have an imaginary audience in my brain.'

'Sadly, I think they probably don't share the same sense of humour as your ex-boyfriends.' Pete takes my hands again – with an anguished glance at an unsightly hangnail – and looks into my eyes. 'Look sweetheart, men are sensitive folk. We don't like to be mocked. And, let's face it, some of the chaps you've dated have hardly been the brightest sparks. They can't cope with an intelligent feisty woman. Their egos can't take it.'

'You only met Jasper,' I say indignantly, recalling the awful evening when Angus and Pete had invited us for dinner at their flat. I was sure that Jasper would have lots in common with them, being an actor and all that. Sadly he must be the only homophobic one to tread the boards. He kept cracking the most inappropriate jokes, and as for his comments when Angus put on his prized Barry Manilow album ... I was so mortified that I kept making sharp asides to put him back in his place. But I only did it to make Angus and Pete feel at ease. Didn't I? I feel a little uneasy myself. Am I really too quick to quip? Didn't Nat say something similar?

'I rest my case.' Pete smiles kindly. 'You could do so much better for yourself. Frankly, darling, he was such a bore. He lacked imagination and pizzazz. I only hope he was good in bed, or you really did waste a few weeks out of your life.'

'Pete, that's unfair.'

'I thought you wanted the truth.' He lifts up my right hand, and examines it with a horrified expression on his face. 'Darling, who does your nails?'

'I do.'

'I don't mean bite them. Who manicures them?'

I look at him in confusion.

'I do.'

'Sweetheart, that's nothing to boast about. Holly, you're attracting losers because, how can I put this delicately?' He ponders. 'You look like a loser.'

'I thought you were trying to put it delicately,' I retort indignantly.

'Sometimes the truth hurts,' he shrugs. 'You're a walking disaster. You need a good old seeing to.'

'I know.' I giggle. 'That's what I'm trying to sort out.'

'If you're not going to take this seriously ...' He starts to stand up.

'I am,' I protest. 'Sit down.'

'Well, we need to sort you out,' he flicks through the diary that he's just fished out of his attaché case. 'Can't do this weekend,' he mutters. 'Dinner with Oscar and Philomena.' He runs his perfectly buffed nail down a week planner, before stabbing a vacant slot. 'Saturday week, darling, what are you doing?'

'Day or night?'

'Day.'

'Nothing. Appointment with my bed.'

'Right, you're coming with me. We are going to turn you into one sex bomb. I'm booking a restyle,' he gives a disdainful look at the ponytail that I threw my hair into this morning. 'Highlights, pedicure and manicure, and then we're going shopping.' I start to protest about funds, but he silences me: 'Did you say you wanted to change your men, and change your life?' I didn't. But when you put it like that – Yes.

CHAPTER SIX

Clive Partridge's CV tells me that he's 44, married with three children – two boys and a girl – enjoys skiing, opera and classic literature, has a clean driving licence and speaks conversational French. I make a note to get a French-speaker to call him for some spurious reason to see if he can cope. Apparently he was born in Uxbridge in Middlesex, went to the local primary and secondary schools and graduated with a first class honours degree in English from Cambridge. Clive moved swiftly after gaining his accountancy qualifications, and has had eight jobs in his twenty-year career – each one more significant than the last. I jot down the names of the companies. I'll need to verify that he did actually work at each of them, and that he left of his own accord without any hint of a scandal.

Boris Beresford, the founder of Investigations-R-Us, used to work at Check 'Em Out Now, but that company went bust five years ago as a result of a high-profile scandal when it failed to properly check the background of a candidate for a major job. His appointment was front-page news, particularly when a tabloid journalist found five former female assistants who claimed that he'd been unable to keep his hands off their bottoms. 'Boss's bum fumble' was the inevitable headline, accompanied by a series of black and white images from a closed circuit camera, located just outside his old office door. Well, it spelt the end of the man's career – and that of Check 'Em Out Now.

But Boris escaped with his reputation untarnished and set

up Investigations-R-Us, employing some of his old colleagues (the good ones), and has been working solidly ever since. Boris is an old army intelligence man, and Investigations-R-Us has a team of former SAS men and paratroopers, available at a moment's notice to go on surveillance or even, occasionally, to jet into far flung locations for emergency operations. There are some dangerous places where the locals have discovered it's quite lucrative to kidnap employees of European firms based in their countries. These fantastically fit guys pride themselves on their one hundred per cent success rate in rescue situations.

They're also available for undercover work. If a major company suspects an employee is stealing secrets and selling them to a rival, for example, then one of these former military men will pretend to be a new recruit to try to work out what is going on and which employees are trustworthy. Boris had to get special white scientist coats made for one case – they couldn't even get their wrists through the armholes on the normal ones.

But the only dealings that I have with these gorgeous specimens of mankind are when they help out on surveillance. My friends think it's like the movies, where one man in a car miraculously manages to follow the suspect across Manhattan, down every side street, through every tunnel and the wrong way along every one-way street, without ever being spotted. As if. Firstly, you need at least two nondescript cars, with two people in each – one to drive, the other to spot – and a motorcyclist, for each surveillance operation. The cars will follow from a discreet distance, swapping positions every so often, rigorously obeying the Highway Code to prevent either being noticed, or picked up by the police. If the suspect suddenly zooms off then the motorcyclist is there to follow. Then you need three teams each working eight-hour shifts. It's extremely labour intensive (and costly) so Boris brings the Golden Boys in. Many an hour I've sat in a car with one of them, waiting for a candidate to leave his house or office. But while the boys may be beautiful and as fit as Stradivarius's fiddle, conversation is definitely not their strong point. The longest I ever managed was a two-grunt response from one of them when I mentioned the weather.

Clive Partridge, if his career resumé is to be believed, has led a pretty blameless life. I decide to start with the easy bit, checking out his bank account details, and dial a number from my Rolodex. The phone is answered after a few rings.

'Basham Bank. Penny speaking. How can I help?'

'Hi, it's Holly.'

There is silence at the other end of the phone, before finally Penny says, 'I'm afraid that we're no longer allowed to take personal calls on this number. Let me give you my mobile.'

I call the mobile. It answers on the third ring.

'Sorry about that Holly, they've started taping my bloody phone line. Makes life a bit difficult.' Penny is walking as she talks. I suspect she is going somewhere that our conversation won't be overheard. 'So you want me to look up somebody's details for you?'

'That's right.' I tell her Clive's branch and account number. 'I want his statements for the last, say, five years. And information on any other accounts he may have. I don't know any other account numbers so you may have to do a bit of digging. Is that possible?'

'Should be. I'll probably have it all ready by tomorrow. Meet at the usual place?' She is talking about a Starbucks down the road from her office. 'About two? And you'll bring the usual fee, of course.' She means £300 in cash. I agree to her terms, jot the meeting in my diary and hang up. The next hour is spent ringing my contacts at telephone, mobile phone and credit card companies. Most people seem to think that corporate investigators just hack into a company's main computer system to get information on people. Well, hell, that's illegal. And Investigations-R-Us can't be seen to be doing anything illegal. It's far simpler to have a contact on the inside willing, for a price, to check out all the information you require. I arrange to meet each of my contacts tomorrow at their usual drop off points, noting that I'll be criss-crossing London all afternoon.

Getting information about Clive's career history is a little tougher, and much more time consuming. I call over Donna, who, despite the bitter weather outside, is today modelling a halter-neck top and a skirt that Miss Binchy would dismiss as a handkerchief.

'Donna, you know your friend Gavin?' She nods. Gavin is a male stripper who Donna met on a hen night. I've never actually met him, but Donna claims he's a cross between Mr Universe, Jamie Oliver and Jeremy Clarkson. I take that to mean he's muscular, cheeky and rather loud. 'Could you see if he is available in the next day or two. I need him to do some flirting. Usual rates.' Donna goes off to ring and check.

There aren't many ways to check out somebody's career history. I could just ring the personnel departments and ask a few pertinent questions, but that is fraught with difficulties. For a start, it causes suspicion and it is hard to explain why you need the information. It is also not foolproof. Companies are often reluctant to admit that somebody has left under a cloud, large or small. It reflects badly on them, and they would often just rather not admit that they'd employed a wrong 'un. But if I can get hold of a few internal phone directories then I can casually ring some numbers and pretend to be looking for an old friend who works there ... Well, it's amazing the sort of information that can be uncovered like that. You'd be shocked how people want to gossip and chat about old colleagues, but it's extremely difficult to get those directories, so I use my secret weapon. Gavin. Clad in black leather gear that accentuates his muscles and curves, he pretends to be a messenger dropping off a package, who just can't help chatting up a pretty receptionist. Then, while they search for a pen to jot down their number for the call that sadly never comes, he steals the directories that generally lie on the counter in front of them. Of course, the scheme is not foolproof – and Gavin has occasionally had to actually deliver his package – but it's not too bad. And he doesn't seem to mind that added perk of the job.

Donna returns triumphant.

'Gavin is available tomorrow,' she announces. 'He asked if you have any special requests.'

'Not really. I just want his leather to be as clingy as possible, if his muscles are anything like you say, and for him to use all his charms. I really need those internal phone lists. This is a huge contract for me. Actually I'm probably going to need some help from you as well. I'll keep you informed.'

'No worries, and I'll pass on the request.' Donna dawdles by my desk, lifting up the photo of Clive Partridge. 'He's quite cute, if you like older men.'

'He's 44,' I point out patiently.

'Exactly. He could be my father.'

'I wouldn't wish that on anyone. Not even your own father.'

'You're so funny,' Donna says in a dismissive tone. 'I was just thinking. You've never met Gavin and he is a real gentleman, in a thrusting type of way.' The mind boggles. 'I was wondering about setting the two of you up on a blind date ... he's always asking to meet you.'

'What!' I almost fall off my chair. 'Absolutely not.'

'He could analyse your dating technique, and give us a few pointers on how you can improve.'

'Us?'

'Well, there's no point in you doing it by yourself.'

'You mean that you'd come on the date? Oh, for goodness sake ...'

'Of course, we wouldn't actually come out with you. What do you take us for?' We? Us? Donna really takes the biscuit. 'Me and Angus, and we'd have to include Pete. It wouldn't be fair to leave him out. He'd have so much fun. I figure it could be like one of those makeover programmes. You know, where the relationship expert, that's me—'

I cut her off with a snort of derision. 'Absolutely no way.'

'Did I hear my name being taken in vain?' Angus is mincing

back towards his desk, with a pile of telephone bills under his arm. 'What's the story?' He peers through his wire-rimmed spectacles, which contain only plain glass but which he reckons give him an air of authority.

'Holly is going on a date with Gavin,' she lowers her voice, but it's too late. I can see James looking over from his cluttered desk, struggling to hear our conversation. 'You know my exotic dancer friend? And we're going to watch her and give her pointers on what she's doing wrong.'

'I am not.' I protest. The co-conspirators ignore me.

'I think that sounds an absolutely fabulous idea,' gushes Angus.

'Look, you two, I refuse to continue with this conversation. It's absolutely pointless. You've lost your mind.' I look down to carry on with my work, but not before I catch James's amused glance.

CHAPTER SEVEN

I have almost finished collecting all the information from my inside moles. I am just waiting for the final drop. I feel like one of those characters in the old spy movies, who casually sit down on a park bench beside a suspicious looking character reading a copy of that day's *Telegraph*, and mutter something ridiculous like 'The white bear has landed'. They never thought it looked odd that they chose to sit on the only bench that was already occupied. Or that anybody walking past would wonder what on earth he or she was talking about. How many white bears land in Regents Park?

Although I know everybody dropping off information for me, and even though we meet at venues several blocks away from their offices, they all insist on acting like a Cold War spy. Penny even wears a black beret and a taupe trench coat. Not one is happy to walk into a coffee shop and greet me like an old friend. Instead they each want to be known by pseudonyms and call me by different names. And nobody wants to pass me a plain folder containing the required information. No. Apparently that would be too obvious. So today I've collected a brown paper envelope, a plastic carrier bag from Marks & Spencer, three computer discs hidden in an empty cereal box, the latest Harry Potter novel (with pages cut out to fit the information I want, just like in the spy movies) and a birthday card. I think they like the intrigue.

I'm sitting at a wooden table close to the door of a coffee shop on Baker Street awaiting the drop from Matt, who works at one of the major mobile phone companies. I got to know him through his girlfriend Ashley, who used to temp at Investigations-R-Us and brought Matt along to a staff night out. He jumped at the chance when he heard there were free drinks, because Matt is tight, with a capital T – as I've learned to my cost over the years.

In fact, the only reason Matt is helping me out now is that he needs the cash to pay for his wedding. Or at least that's what he claims. But I know from Donna, who keeps in touch with both him and Ashley, that Matt's actually booked an all-inclusive holiday with a wedding thrown in for free. And being the tight git that he is, Matt even ditched the brochure listing all the extras on offer that make a wedding so personal and special. Nothing fancy, just the traditional flowers, musicians and even champagne. But his plan backfired when Ashley found the brochure in the bin, read it, and booked the lot.

I'm engrossed in the *Evening Standard* crossword when I hear 'Christina. Is that you? How was the conference?' I carry on reading. A throat clears, before an insistent 'Christina. How was the conference?' is repeated. Not great, judging by Christina's lack of response. 'Ahem, Christina,' another cough, 'the conference. How was it?' Slowly it dawns on me. Tonight Matthew, I'm Christina.

I look up, and smile at Matt who is holding a Tupperware box in his hands. His sweatshirt carries the name of the mobile phone company that he works at in big green letters across his chest. Even the sports bag that is swung casually across his shoulder advertises its slogan. A passer-by would probably guess he worked there, even without the tell-tale security tag that swings around his neck. James Bond? No. Cheap? Yes.

'Matt,' I smile.

He frowns. 'Anthony,' he hisses. I raise my eyebrows. 'It's Anthony. I don't want anybody to know who I am.' I casually nod towards the tag. He blushes deep red as he spots his error, and quickly flicks it over his head.

'Sorry, Anthony,' I finally say. 'My mistake. I always get you muddled up with your better-looking brother.' He scowls. 'It's nice to see you. Would you like a coffee?' I gesture towards the chair opposite me, as I reach for my purse.

'No, Christina. I really haven't time, but I was desperate to know how the conference went.' He fidgets with the box, and jiggles from side to side. A couple on a neighbouring table look over. They're probably trying to work out whether I have just been to the most exciting conference ever or am being pestered by the world's most boring nerd. Matt is positively dancing with excitement. His face is flushed. It's the thought of all the money he's about to receive. 'Did you learn about any new developments in Tupperware?'

'Eh?'

'The Tupperware conference,' he prompts.

'Oh yes, sorry.' I make a mental note never to use Matt again. 'The world of Tupperware is enjoying a major revolution.'

'So,' Matt thrusts his box into my hands, 'the days of the old style lunchboxes like these are numbered.'

I look down at the see-through box. There is no additional camouflage. No sandwiches or apples to hide the big bold words that shine through the plastic lid and announce to the world (and every body else in the coffee shop) its contents: 'Bill for mobile no: 07710 123456. Mr Clive Partridge.'

'Couldn't you at least have put a snack in the box to make it less obvious?' I hiss.

'I didn't think I could claim expenses,' Matt hisses back, before adopting his normal voice. 'So, this box is on its way out?' He thrusts it towards me.

'Indeed, Anthony.' I grab the box. 'I think I should take this and dispose of it for you, because, believe me, you're soon going to be so embarrassed to be seen in public with this box.'

'You can't have the box,' he hisses. 'What will I carry my sandwiches in tomorrow?'

'I don't want it,' I whisper. 'But how the bloody hell am I going to get its contents if I don't at least open the bloody thing?' I discreetly remove the thick pile of bills below the table, as I blabber on about the new developments in vacuum-style seals that I claim will soon make the lid of his box appear archaic.

'The bills date back six months,' he whispers. 'I can get more but it'll take a bit more time.' And money, I suspect.

'This should be enough to be getting on with,' I whisper back. 'If I need any more I'll let you know. You said you wanted fifty-pound notes?' He nods. I raise my voice: 'I've taken the liberty of bringing along some literature on the next Tupperware conference.' I pass over a thin envelope. 'You should hurry. Places are limited, so it's on a first come, first served basis. The latest developments will truly blow your mind.'

'Thanks Caroline,' Matt grabs the envelope and starts to stand.

'Christina,' I hiss.

'Huh?' He looks confused.

'You told me my name was Christina.'

'I mean Christina.' He shakes his head and blushes. 'I can't think who on earth I meant when I said Caroline. Sorry Christina.' Ah yes. When a special agent gets himself into a hole, what does he do? Dig deeper.

'I think she's the woman you slept with last week,' I smile helpfully. Before I can say anything more, Matt has rushed out the door. The neighbouring couple watch him run away as I pack the bills away into my briefcase.

I turn back to my crossword, but am getting nowhere. My mind is racing with my investigation. I am not sure how long has passed when something familiar catches my eye outside. It is a memory that fleetingly mocks my brain before dissolving, but it leaves me unnerved. I look again. There must be something there. I scan the pavements, checking out the people walking past, and the parked cars. I can't quite grab it, but I know there's something out there. I check again. And then I see it. A bright red bicycle with two empty wicker baskets. Sean's bicycle. But something's different. It takes me a moment to work it out. There's a bright red pennant flying from the back of his seat: Sean's Sandwich Express. I search for the man himself, and within minutes spot him walking out of a deli carrying a baguette. His Lycra top carries his new logo, while his tight cycling shorts carry their own little message. God. Cycling does things to a man.

I grab my briefcase and bag, and rush outside.

'Sean,' I cry from the other side of the road. He stops, looking around at the sound of his name. I wave, and Sean frowns as he spots me. I check for traffic, and dash across the road. 'Hi there. How are you?' I say feebly. 'Can't believe I've run into you. Do you come here often?' I wince at the corny opening line.

'Hello Holly,' Sean replies evenly. 'No, not often.' He indicates the baguette in his hand. 'But I'm thinking of starting a new round, and am checking out the competition.' He waves it around, and a few pieces of meat fall to the pavement. He studies them carefully. 'Well, I'm not that impressed. There's obviously not enough mayonnaise in this one, and that meat looks processed. Absolutely disgusting.'

'Enough said.' I hold up my hands in mock horror. I nod towards his chest. 'I see you've started out on your own. Congratulations.'

'Thank you,' he nods. 'I know you thought I'd no ambition, Holly, so I expect this comes as a major surprise to you.'

'I never said you lacked ambition,' I say, startled at the accusation.

'No, but you thought it,' he sighs. 'I could tell you weren't interested when I discussed my plans for new fillings. You mocked at shitake mushrooms, avocado and Parma ham, but it's one of my best sellers now.'

'I didn't mock,' I protest. 'I merely said it wouldn't be my cup of tea.'

'I think your exact words were "you couldn't get a weirder mix if you tried," but it's just as well that my customers in Marylebone High Street don't agree with you. And I can't produce hummus, spring onion and bell peppers on granary quick enough. They're flying out of the basket ...'

'Did you take my advice?' I interrupt.

'I was just going to say that I had. I throw in a free piece of chewing gum, as you suggested.'

I smile at the acknowledgement. 'Perhaps I should claim royalties,' I joke. 'So when did you set out on your own?'

'Two months ago. I had a little setback just before when everybody went crazy for Atkins, then suddenly it seemed people couldn't get enough of carbs. They were crying out for the bread they'd starved their bodies of. I was inundated with orders, and I knew I had to strike out by myself. And honestly Holly, it's the best move I ever made. My girlfriend Laura even works in the business. She gets up at five to help with the buttering.'

'You've got a girlfriend?' I reel slightly at the news. 'That's, er, wonderful.'

'Laura's a real gem,' he smiles dreamily, nodding his head. 'She was working in a greasy spoon, totally miserable, stinking of chip fat and feeling her arteries harden, when I walked in and changed her life.'

'Was it love at first sight?'

He looks closely at me, a strange expression on his face, before slowly shaking his head. 'Oh no,' he shrugs. 'I was actually sworn off women at that time. But it was one of those Saturday mornings when only a fry up will do, and I barely noticed her when I placed my order. But then when she served me my toast, that's when I sat up.'

'Was it delicious?'

'No, it was like chewing cardboard. Processed rubbish. Well, I had to complain, after I'd finished peeling it off my palate, being an aficionado of bakery products. I suggested using ciabatta, but Laura thought I was talking about a character from *The Sopranos*.' He laughs. 'Who'd have thought we'd have got together? I was all for dismissing her as an airhead, but then I saw her whisk up a batch of egg mayonnaise. I think that's when I was first smitten.' He smiles at the memory. 'It's all in the wrist action, you know. And Laura's got very strong wrists.'

'I'm pleased for you,' I reply, and I really mean it. Sean is a truly nice person, if a little obsessed with sandwiches. 'And congratulations on your new business. Your sandwiches were always the best I ever tasted.'

Sean blushes. 'So, how about you, Holly. Seeing anybody?'

'Nah,' I shake my head. 'Actually I've just come out of a relationship. He dumped me.'

'Was he mad?' Sean exclaims.

'Hey, pot calling. You dumped me too, remember?'

Sean sighs. 'Holly, when will you ever learn? I didn't want it to end between us. You're a wonderful woman. In fact I can tell you now – my counsellor says it's best to be open about these things – I know we weren't together long, but I really thought you and I had a future. I'd even planned the fillings for the finger buffet at our engagement party.' I feel confused. Why had I no idea of this? 'I dreamed of you giving up work, and us running a little sandwich shop in Bath as an old married couple. Possibly with a "ye olde" theme – you know, in a wench outfit, obviously with some sort of Wonderbra to get the cleavage, and me in breeches. But I knew you didn't share my vision. Bread wasn't in your blood. And it wasn't that long before you'd change the subject the minute I started to talk about sandwiches.' He pauses. 'It hurt me. I realised we had nothing in common. We were two slices of bread without a filling. You never really wanted more, and I did. Our relationship needed more substance.'

He sighs and looks at me with big, doleful eyes. 'What I'm trying to say, Holly, is that if you'd only been more supportive, learned about my hopes and dreams,' Sean reaches out and gently touches my cheek, before motioning to his pennant. 'All this could have been yours. And there's a little part of me that will always wish it had been.' Then he leans over, softly kisses the cheek just where his hand had rested, before quickly turning, mounting his bicycle and riding off.

CHAPTER EIGHT

I am about to put my gloves on when there's a desperate tapping at my front door. I pull it open to find Miss Binchy, looking like a refugee from a Miss Marple movie dressed in a beige twin set, tweed skirt and sensible shoes. She looks at my footwear in horror. 'You really shouldn't wear those pointy boots, Holly. You'll end up like me – a martyr to bunions. If the Good Lord wanted us to force our feet into tiny shoes, the pictures of the Virgin Mary wouldn't show Her in sensible sandals,' she says, before adding: 'Are you going out?' I wonder if it's the coat and scarf that gave it away. I nod.

'Oh well, I'll leave you to it,' she waves her hand dismissively. 'Seamus is coming over later. Honestly, I don't know what I'd do without him. Did you meet him when I was away? He came to feed Marmalade.' I shake my head. She's obviously forgotten that we've already had this conversation. 'He's a wonderful boy. Do you know that he once ran a marathon for charity?'

'Really?'

'Aye. To raise money for prostitutes with cancer.'

'Prostitutes with cancer?' I'm confused. What a saint this Seamus must be, and then the penny drops. 'Do you mean prostate cancer?'

'Aye,' she nods. 'That's what I said. Who else thinks of those poor fallen women? Our Lord took pity on Mary Magdalene, and now my nephew takes pity on her successors.' I haven't the heart to correct her. Miss Binchy lives in another world and it's definitely out of this one. 'Anyway, I better leave you to it. Going anywhere nice?'

'Just work,' I reply. 'Have quite a busy day on, actually.' I am planning to ring a selection of numbers from the internal directories that Gavin took five days to charm from a host of receptionists across the City. I'll pretend that I'm looking for my old chum Clive Partridge and then feign surprise when they tell me he's moved jobs. It might turn up nothing, or it might just reveal something outstanding.

'Well, I was wondering, my dear, now I know you have a hectic social life, but my nephew is coming to supper tomorrow evening. Nothing fancy, just boiled bacon, cabbage and mashed potatoes, plain simple food that the Good Lord would have eaten himself. And I'd love for you to join us.'

'Well, I don't know ...' I hesitate.

'Ach, listen to me. I know, you've probably got a date tomorrow with some lucky fellow. Ah well, it was just an idea.' She turns to go back downstairs, and I remember the contents of my fridge – a choice of microwave spaghetti bolognese or shepherds pie, a cardboard canister of grated Parmesan cheese and three tired looking tomatoes, sagging on a dried out vine. They seem about as appealing as a Marmite milkshake. Miss Binchy takes two stairs down before she hesitates, and turns back: 'It's just, and I know he wouldn't say it, but my nephew Colm can get rather tired of my company.'

'Colm? I thought your nephew was Seamus?'

'Yes that's right, dear. Colm is Seamus's brother, but Seamus can't come. He's busy with work tomorrow.' She smiles. 'Colm doesn't live very near, and he can only get to see me every six months or so and I really love his visits. He's a wonderful fellow, and I know he'd just adore you. He always loves to meet beautiful young women.' I throw a self-deprecating hand gesture to waft away her compliments. 'He doesn't get to spend much time with them in his line of work.'

'Why?' I joke. 'Is he an oil-rig worker?'

'Ach,' Miss Binchy bursts out laughing. 'Listen to you. So clever. Anyway, it doesn't matter. You're obviously busy.'

An evening with a potential oil-rig worker who has been starved of female company for months? Even I can tell that the odds sound good. Somehow suffering boiled bacon and cabbage is a small price to pay. It might even give me a chance to put into practice the points I've learned from Pete and Sean, and if it can help with my meeting with Carl Lawson in two days' time then count me in. I can't actually get him out of my mind. We have spoken three times since I started my research, and yesterday I could have sworn that he was actually flirting with me. It wasn't anything said, but his tone. But then last night he appeared on the Money Programme talking about last year's scandal at Ilyax and I realised that flirting is second nature to him. I could sense the female presenter reacting to his charms and I was jealous. He cracked a few jokes, calmly answered her probing questions and once, when he lightly touched her arm to convey his sincerity, I actually wanted to smack her thrilled face. Face it, I tell myself sternly. Carl Lawson is a pipe dream. My neighbour's nephew is reality.

'I'd be delighted, Miss Binchy,' I smile.

'You won't go cancelling things on my account now, will you?'

'No, honest. I'm already looking forward to it.' And I am, I realise. An evening with a sex-starved oil-rig worker, I'd be mad not to be excited. I'll practise my flirting techniques, and perhaps, later, indulge in some practical demonstrations.

'That's great.' She beams with excitement.

'Now, what can I bring?'

'Ach no. Just yourself ...'

'Miss Binchy, I cannot turn up in your flat for dinner without bringing something. It would be extremely rude,' I say firmly.

She thinks about my question for a moment and then nods. 'Well, if you're sure.' I nod. 'I don't drink myself but I know that Colm has a wee tipple every day.'

'Great. I'll bring some wine then.'

'Lovely, my dear.'

'Okay then. What time would you like me to arrive tomorrow? About seven?' She nods. 'Right, I'll see you then. Now, don't think me really rude, but I really have got to get to work now or I'll be late.'

Four hours later and I'm studying the internal phone directories that Gavin obtained. Each contains at least five hundred names, but I'm trying to dramatically narrow that down. I want to find people who may have worked with Clive Partridge. I cross through anybody who doesn't work in the finance departments where he was employed, which leaves about fifty people on each list. I try to narrow it down even further. Mostly it's guesswork but, after another few hours, I think I've got a small core of people in each company who may have worked with or closely to Clive at some point. I'm just about to make the first call, when Donna strolls over. She arrived late today after a drama with an acrylic nail that required emergency treatment with the manicurist at Harvey Nicks. Today Donna is wearing an off-the-shoulder top that owes more to gravity than Lycra, tight pedal pushers and three-inch high strapless sandals. And it's only January. I dread her summer wardrobe.

'What're you doing?' She peeks over my shoulder.

'Ringing some people from those directories Gavin got me.'

'That reminds me,' she says. 'I'm meeting Gavin tomorrow for a quick drink. Do you fancy coming along? I told you he's dying to meet you.'

'Sorry,' I reply, keeping my eyes glued to the directories. 'I've already got something on.'

'Something on?' She repeats. 'What on earth could be more important than meeting a single sexy man?' James looks across at us, casually flicking through a pile of letters that the office assistant has just dropped into his in-tray.

'Meeting a single sexy man starved of female company,' I mutter, refusing to look up.

'A single sexy man deprived of female company?' Donna exclaims.

She perches on the corner of my desk, calling over to Angus, 'Did you hear that? Holly's got a date.'

'I heard,' he shrieks, racing over from his desk, his hands flapping in the air in excitement. James looks amused, but starts opening his post.

'So, spill the beans. We want all the details, don't we Donna?' She nods. 'When? Where? How?'

'How what?' James asks. Not working that hard then.

'How good? How long? How was it? Take your pick,' smiles Angus. 'It's an open-ended sort of question. You straight guys know nothing.'

'Look guys, I do not have a date,' I finally say.

'But you're meeting a guy tomorrow?' Donna and Angus look confused. And disappointed.

'Yes, but it's not a date. My neighbour has invited me to dinner to meet her nephew.'

'Her nephew?' James repeats, smiling.

'Yes.' Does my private life have to be everybody's business?

'Does he have all his own teeth? Body parts? Mental faculties?' Donna asks.

'I didn't check,' I reply. 'I don't know about you, but I thought it would have appeared rude.'

'She knows nothing,' mutters Angus.

'Look, you've been invited to dinner to meet a single man. You're entitled to ask questions,' explains Donna. 'What will you do if you turn up and there's some old geezer sitting there who looks like he's an extra from *Planet of the Apes*?'

'I'd make polite conversation and have a good time ...'

'And you wonder why you're single.' Donna raises her eyes to heaven.

'Whoa. Just a cotton picking minute here,' Angus suddenly interrupts, holding his hand up to stop Donna. 'We seem to be forgetting that Holly thinks he's sex-starved.'

'My God. You're right.' Donna touches her forehead. 'How could I not have remembered that little gem? So Holly, what makes you think your blind date will be horny?'

'I didn't say that.' I recoil in horror.

'If he's sex-starved, darling, he'll definitely be horny,' says Angus.

'Come on,' urges Donna.

'I was only joking,' I protest.

'Not falling for that one. Spill. We'll sit here all day nagging until you do, won't we Angus?' He nods, flicking an imaginary piece of dust off his clinging cashmere sweater.

'Look, it's nothing,' I shrug.

'We'll be the judges of that. Come on,' says Donna.

'Well, Miss Binchy happened to say that her nephew doesn't get to see many women in his line of work.'

'What is he? A jailbird?' asks Donna. James is listening intently, smiling at me.

'No,' I protest, slightly worried at the suggestion. I hadn't thought of that. 'Don't be silly. Miss Binchy would have mentioned that. I kind of imagined he might be something like a, well, an oil-rig worker.'

'Way to go,' exclaims Donna, punching the air. 'Then he probably won't even make it to dessert.'

'Holly will be dessert,' laughs Angus. I blush.

'But Miss Binchy didn't actually say that he was an oil-rig worker,' reiterates James. What a spoilsport, I think.

'Of course not,' snaps Donna. 'She doesn't want to scare Holly off. Look girl, you better be prepared. Wear something sexy ...'

'If he's been on an oil-rig, he won't care if Holly turns up in a shroud,' Angus points out.

'Thank God for that,' laughs Donna. They both dissolve into fits of giggles.

'He might do something else for a living,' persists James, ignoring their outbursts. 'He might be, I don't know, a soldier or ...'

'Even better. A man in uniform,' interrupts Donna. 'But let's hope that he's not wearing it tomorrow night. I swear the last time I was with an officer, it took almost five minutes for him to undo all the buttons on his jacket, and those boots are a nightmare to get off. Honestly, I'd almost lost the mood by the time he was ready. If it hadn't been for his friend keeping me amused, I honestly would have got up and left. One was an officer, but the other was a gentleman.' She winks.

'What was his friend doing in the room?' I ask confused.
'Oh, I don't even want to know. Anyway, playtime is over. There's been enough laughing at my expense. Get on with your work. I'm too busy to cope with this frivolity.' Donna and Angus move away from my desk, comparing notes on men in uniform. I look over at James, and shrug. He smiles back in his inscrutable fashion. Sometimes I get the feeling that I don't really know my new colleague at all. He doesn't give much away. He turns back to his work. And I return to mine.

The first number that I've highlighted on my list belongs to Mrs Maisie Simpson. She is personal assistant to the senior auditor at a company that Clive Partridge resigned from six years ago. Partridge was also senior auditor when he left, and I'm betting that Mrs Simpson once acted as his personal assistant. I dial the number. It is answered after three rings.

'Hugh Wood's office. Can I help you?' Maisie Simpson sounds efficient. I can just imagine her – a short rotund woman, with her grey hair pulled tightly into a bun, pince-nez resting at the end of her nose, with a crisp white cotton shirt ... Or maybe I've just watched too many movies.

'Oh, I think I may have mis-dialled,' I fib.
'This is Mr Hugh Wood's office,' she repeats.
'I could have sworn this was Clive Partridge's number.'
'Oh, there's a name from the past,' she simpers. 'I'm afraid you're about, ooh, six, maybe seven, years too late. Mr Partridge has left this company. Mr Wood replaced him. Could he help you?'
'Clive's left?' I feign surprise. 'Oh no. That's typical of my luck.' I sigh. 'Never mind. He's an old university friend, I'm just over from Australia on a short holiday and wanted to catch him for a beer. Or two.'
'Ooh, you know him so well. Never just one beer, eh?' I make a note on the pad in front of me that Clive likes a drink.

'Now don't help me. I'm sure he must have spoken about you. He used to share everything with me. Do you know I organised all his family holidays?' Another note. 'And I never once forgot to prompt him about all their birthdays. As you would know, being a friend of his, he does have a mind like a sieve. That man needs somebody to take firm control of his diary and I find remembering dates as easy as multiplication tables. Not that Clive could do those either. You'd think, being an accountant and clever like that, he could do six times seven without hesitation but he needed a calculator. Imagine.' I jot a further note. 'Not that it held him back. He was what those magazines call, ooh what's the word? A networker,' she seems pleased with herself.

'Yes, I remember him pointing out an article and saying 'that's me, Maisie. I'm a networker. It's the only way to get on.' He was always off to some networking event, like a golf weekend or cocktail party. And look at him now. He's the finance director at a big insurance company. Egyptia. The one that's got a sheikh and a talking camel in its adverts. You can try him there. I tell you, your friend's going places,' she pauses, dropping her voice to a conspiratorial whisper.

'Actually he was desperate to take me with him. Well, it's hard to find hardworking executive personal assistants these days. The younger girls, they just spend their time surfing the web and flirting via this text-messaging lark. I don't even think they can do shorthand. And discretion? They don't know what it means, and they definitely couldn't spell it. I mean, some of these girls would just tell strangers confidential information. People could just ring up out of the blue, and those girls'd tell all. Me, I never breathe a word. Confidentiality is my middle name.

'I'd never tell a living soul anything, you don't count dear obviously as you're Mr Partridge's university friend. I certainly wouldn't tell 'em that Mr Wood sometimes plays squash instead of attending departmental head meetings. Not that he needs to go to them, really. I've got my friend Minnie, we started out in the typing pool together, and she takes the minutes of the meeting. It's very handy, I always learn every-thing that was said and I just fill Mr Wood in. Ooh, listen to me. I've gone off onto one of those tangent things. Where was I? What was I saying?'

'That Clive wanted to take you with him?'

'Ah yes. He pleaded with me. But then, after days of soul searching, he told me he just couldn't do it. He said it'd be unfair to deprive the team here of my unique skills. That's what he said. Unique. Very proud I was. And I do owe the company something. After all it plucked me from the typing pool and transformed me into the executive personal assist-ant that I am today. Mr Partridge said that Mr Wood deserved me. Those were his exact words. I was touched, I can tell you. The sacrifices that Mr Partridge made ...' I am quickly jotting everything down. 'Anyway, dear, why did you think he was still here? Don't you use email?'

'I'd one of the hand-held computers with all my phone numbers and addresses, but I lost it,' I lie. 'Luckily I found one of Clive's old cards and, seeing as I'm in town, thought I would try his number.'

'Mr Partridge was just as bad with technology. I've got it.' She suddenly shouts. 'You're not the friend that set up the fast food franchise in Melbourne are you? Finger Frigging G'day? The one Mr Partridge invested £20,000 in?'

'Er, yes. That's me,' I say, noting down the franchise name to check out later.

'You must be so pleased the way things turned out. Made a fortune, didn't you, when you sold out? And Mr Partridge, well he bought a lovely villa in Marbella. Saw the pictures. Gorgeous. Had one of those kidney shaped pools. Really classy. Anyway dear, it's been lovely chatting, and you've got a lovely voice, you know. No accent.'

'Thank you. Well actually I better shoot off now, call Clive at Egyptia. Thanks so much for your help.'

'My help? But I haven't done anything dear. Anyway, you call up Mr Partridge, and give him my best. Tell him Maisie's still looking forward to that dinner he promised, but she knows he's a very busy man. Cheerio then.' She hangs up.

I jot down the new insights into Clive Partridge that I have just gleaned from my conversation with Maisie Simpson, although none of them could possibly be viewed as worrying.

Drinks more than one beer. Hold the front page.
Can't remember family birthdays. Join the club.
Bad at mental arithmetic. That's why calculators were invented.
Kind to staff. Nice quality.
Diplomatic to gossipy old wind-bags. The man is a saint.
Invested in a fast food joint. Okay, need to check that out.
Holiday home in Marbella. Interesting. Examine further.

Still, it all adds up to a fuller picture of who Clive Partridge really is, and at least I know that he didn't leave that job under a cloud. I toss away the rest of that particular company's internal directory – I've learned as much as I need from Mrs Maisie Simpson – pull another one from the pile, and start looking through the names for one more 'soul of discretion' to spill the beans on Clive Partridge.

CHAPTER NINE

I am standing outside Miss Binchy's door, eagerly waiting for her to let me in at the sex-starved oil-rig worker. I've done my homework. I can talk about semi-submersibles, platform rigs and flotels (a sort of floating hotel for rig workers), but I'm going to steer clear of jack-ups. That's just asking for trouble. I can hear Miss Binchy chatting away as she pads down her short, narrow hallway.

I hadn't known what to wear tonight, and searched through my wardrobe in desperation. I wanted something that wasn't overtly sexy, yet I needed an outfit that sent out the right vibes. A 'come on in, the water's lovely for a dip' sort of message. So I've opted for a pair of black satin trousers and a fitted burgundy velvet blouse that I bought years ago in Marks & Spencer. Okay, so it's not the height of fashion but today everybody's into vintage. I've left the top three buttons open, and my breasts are being pushed together and outwards in an M&S balcony bra to accentuate my cleavage. Strappy sandals and long dangly earrings finish my ensemble. I don't care what Donna and Pete might think, I know I've got style. And I'm wearing a brand new scarlet coloured lip-gloss that the adverts claim will transform any mouth into a sexy pout.

'Just coming,' I hear Miss Binchy cry. 'With you now.' She opens the door wide, welcoming me with open arms and a beaming grin, and ... Oh no! I recoil in horror. My jaw drops in disbelief. I try to say something but nothing will come out, so I shove my gifts across to my neighbour, playing for time because my septuagenarian neighbour, who dithers between a pink hairnet and a powder blue one, is … I can't actually accept it. I close my eyes tightly, shake my head firmly and open. Shit. It makes no difference. My neighbour is wearing exactly the same blouse in exactly the same colour as I am. The only difference is that she has buttoned it up to the throat, and accessorised with a frilly white apron and black Crimplene trousers. And there is nothing I can do about it. So I stand motionless praying for the floor to swallow me up. 'Would you credit it, Holly?' she cries out in surprise and pleasure. 'I just can't believe this. Colm,' she calls over her slightly rounded shoulder, 'Holly is wearing the same blouse as me. And there's me,' she pats her ample bosom in delight, 'I only picked it up this morning in the fifty pee box at Help the Aged.' Hey, it's one thing to ignore my prayer; it's quite another to rub it in. 'Is that where you got yours?' she asks, ushering me through the door and down the hallway towards her 'parlour'.

'Er, no,' I reply grumpily. 'It was in my wardrobe.'

'Look at me, the height of fashion,' she cries, throwing open the doorway and rushing to her nephew. 'Have you seen what Holly's wearing, Colm? Are you proud of your fashionable auld auntie now?'

Colm untangles himself from a deep sunken chair and stands to greet me. First impressions are favourable. He is tall. Very tall, with broad shoulders and a body that, despite a thick woollen polo neck, I can tell is in good shape. Colm is neither particularly handsome, nor disappointing. He has one of those faces that are attractive without being threatening. His sandy red hair is pushed back from his face, and a sprinkling of freckles cover his nose. I extend my hand to shake his, careful to stand straight so that my chest is well displayed and my stomach is pulled in.

'I'm always proud of you,' Colm says, putting one arm around her thickened waist and giving her a friendly squeeze. 'And Holly, I've heard so much about you. It's such a pleasure to finally meet you. And I must say, you have excellent dress sense.' He winks at his aunt, who giggles in appreciation. 'You could be twins.'

Great, I think, he has just likened me to an old age pensioner. It may have only started but could tonight get any more embarrassing?

'Get away with you.' His aunt waves her hand dismissively at him, but I can tell she's delighted. 'And look,' she waves the bottle in the air, 'she's brought white wine. Your favourite, eh?' I had dashed into the local off-licence and picked up a chilled bottle of hock and a box of After Eights (in for a penny, in for a cliché). My two companions smile appreciatively.

'It's very good to meet you,' I finally respond to Colm.

'What a lucky man I am. Dinner tonight with two beautiful ladies dressed in lovely outfits,' he continues, gallantly. Miss Binchy disappears to the kitchen to 'see to the potatoes', Colm nods towards an empty armchair and I sit down. The centre of the seat cushion is squashed from regular use, and my bottom makes contact with the wooden base. It is as uncomfortable as a futon, and almost as unfashionable. The chair is covered in dusky chintz adorned with huge bunches of vibrant pink peonies caught up into arrangements by twists of ivy. Crocheted flower mats cover the arms, hiding the slight fraying of the material, while a similar mat is draped over the chair back, masking the dark stain that has developed over years of use. A small teak table with a crimson faux leather top covered in glass, taken from a nest standing in the corner of the room, is by my knee. A small glass of sherry and a wooden bowl of Wotsits rest there.

I had never been inside this room before, and I glance around quickly. The walls are hung with a pale floral paper, vertical stripes of lily of the valley interspersed with swirling ivy, and are covered with mock oil landscapes in faux gilt frames and china plates painted with pictures of cats at play. A Siamese cat with a ball of wool. A tabby frolicking in the snow. A kitten waving a paw at a passing butterfly. Over the original fireplace, with its iron grate and tiled surrounds, hangs an oval mirror, the glass dulled from age around the edges. There are photographs everywhere. Babies in christening gowns. Young boys with toothy grins and slicked back fringes posing, with ties slightly awry, for their school photographs. I spot a photograph of three young red-headed boys, who I assume are the nephews Miss Binchy talks so fondly of. One of them must be Colm, I think. He catches me looking.

'The downside of a proud auntie,' he explains. 'Embarrassing photos. I tried to take them all down before you arrived but Auntie Maureen wouldn't let me. She thinks the one of me without any front teeth is charming.'

'I'll have a proper look at it and the others later,' I laugh, as he excuses himself to open the wine. On an occasional table, beside my chair, there are three black and white wedding photographs. I think the brides must be Miss Binchy's sisters because, even all these years on, it is easy to recognise her as the chief bridesmaid in each picture. But there is no attendant man to balance out the numbers. I wonder what happened to her young man and if he attended the weddings. Perhaps that was yet another broken promise, I think sadly. She is smiling in each of them, but in one, maybe I'm imagining it, I sense Miss Binchy is not as content. She probably never imagined she would always be the bridesmaid. An involuntary shiver runs down my spine. Is this my future? I shake my head and gulp down my sherry.

The room is dark despite the pale wallpaper. Heavy full length pink dralon curtains hang at the window, while the dark purple carpet seems to dominate the room. I am startled by the contrast to my own living room upstairs. My windows have no nets or blinds, but are framed with light calico curtains while the carpet has long since been replaced by stripped floorboards. With the pale cream walls, it makes my room looks at least twice as big as this. Where Miss Binchy has chosen dark wood, I have selected maple while my sofas are covered in the palest leather.

But if my room is minimalist, this is definitely maximist. There are ornaments everywhere. I have just counted ten china cats when Miss Binchy enters, carrying a small plate of cocktail sausages and cheese and pineapple cubes on sticks.

'Have a chipolata, my dear. You must be absolutely starving,' she says, placing the plate on a small paper doily on my side table by the waiting sherry. 'Dinner won't be long now.'

'Can I do anything to help, Miss Binchy?' I ask as she places the other plate on a table beside Colm's chair. The smell of roasting bacon is wafting through her flat. Today the weather has been freezing, with a slight drizzle of snow this evening, and this is exactly the comfort food that the doctor ordered.

'Not at all,' she replies. 'You sit there looking pretty. Colm, entertain our lovely guest.'

'My aunt says you're a successful career woman,' says Colm. 'What company do you work for?'

'Investigations-R-Us,' I smile politely.

Colm ponders for a moment, before adding, 'That sounds familiar.' That's a good sign, I think. There is absolutely no way that Colm could have heard of Investigations-R-Us – it prides itself on its secrecy and is never in the news – he's trying to impress by appearing interested. 'Have you ever heard of it, Auntie Maureen?' he asks his aunt who has just re-entered the room.

'Oh, sure what would a silly sausage like me know about posh companies,' she says, waving her hand dismissively. 'I just know it's a good one if it employs my lovely young neighbour.' She smiles at me, and I blush again. Miss Binchy is definitely trying to set the two of us up, and I can't say I really mind. 'Anyway, dinner is ready. Would you like to come through to the dining room? And' – she looks around the room – 'have you seen Marmalade? She must be around somewhere.' Miss Binchy is making a swishing sound, rubbing her fingers together, as she bends down looking under the chairs for her errant cat. 'She'll be dying to see you, Colm.'

A strange look shoots across Colm's face, but he swiftly recovers.

'And me her, Auntie Maureen,' he says with little enthusiasm. I sense this man is not a cat lover.

'Ah well, no doubt she'll arrive when she smells the food,'

Miss Binchy straightens up. 'I've done all your old favourites, Colm.' She shoos us through into her dining room, which is decorated in a similar style to her living room. A large mahogany sideboard matches a round table and four chairs, and is covered with ornaments and souvenirs of past holidays. I spot a straw donkey in a sombrero, at least three flamenco dancers and a little wooden Russian doll, the type that has identical smaller ones inside.

'Colm, your aunt tells me that you don't get down to London much,' I say, as Miss Binchy places bowls of tomato soup in front of us.

'It's only Heinz,' she mouths, 'Colm's favourite.' She sits down heavily on her chair.

'Great,' I smile. 'Aren't you having any?' I point at her empty bowl.

'Oh no, dear,' Miss Binchy beams. 'Tomatoes repeat something awful on me. I'm a martyr to those salad vegetables. You young people carry on. Sure it's a delight to have company in the house. It can get awfully quiet at night.'

Colm leans over and gives her hand an affectionate squeeze, then we simultaneously dip our spoons into the soup. And sup. Whoa! We look at each other in horror. The tomato soup is cold, as if Miss Binchy has spooned it straight from the can into our bowls. We gracefully swallow a couple of mouthfuls, then Colm gets up from his seat.

'Actually Auntie Maureen, it's so cold out there and I'm still frozen through, that I think I'll just put my bowl back into the microwave for two seconds to make it piping hot.' His aunt starts to protest that she'll do it for him, but Colm insists: 'Nonsense, you've done quite enough. You rest there. Holly, would you like me to zap your soup for two seconds?' He winks, and takes my bowl. Miss Binchy appears blissfully unaware of her error, chatting amiably to me about how Colm has always been so good around the kitchen. She is definitely setting us up, I feel.

Within minutes he returns to the table, and resets the soup in front of me. I notice how he lays an affectionate kiss on his aunt's head as he passes her on the way back to his seat. Poor Miss Binchy. She does seem to be getting forgetful. Only last week she asked me to help find her reading glasses, when they were hanging on a chain around her neck all the time. I want to tell Colm this and to ask about the mysterious Marmalade, but I don't want it to appear that I'm interfering in family matters, so instead I quiz him once again about his infrequent trips to London.

'The problem is that I only get so many days leave a year, and I've got to see my family back home in Ireland. They'd love to visit me on the odd weekend, but it just isn't possible, and it's difficult to use the phone when I'm at work. It's kind of frowned upon.'

'Hmm,' I say, trying not to slurp. 'I suppose mobiles don't work out there.'

'It's not that they don't work, it's more that they're not allowed. They sort of interfere with things,' Colm replies.

'Like signals and that?' I persevere.

'Something like that,' he replies, while liberally buttering a slice of white bread, tearing it into small chunks and dropping them into his bowl. 'So Holly, what do you actually do at, er, Investigations-R-Us?' I'm not falling for that line. Too many ex-boyfriends have commented on my lack of interest in their careers, so I shrug off Colm's question and continue probing him on his.

'Your job sounds really exciting.'

Colm looks at me in surprise and laughs. 'I don't think I've ever heard it called that before. Interesting, yes. Rewarding, yes. But exciting? No,' he shakes his head. 'That's not a word I'd ever use.'

'Oh, come on now Colm,' Miss Binchy rises to clear the bowls away. 'There have been some high points. What about when you met the Pope?'

'Pope Benedict? The new one? Did he come to visit you? To bless you all?' I'm confused. Surely it would have been in the newspapers if the Pope had visited a North Sea oil-rig.

'Oh no, he's far too busy for that,' Colm says, as Miss Binchy brings in serving dishes filled with cabbage and mashed potatoes with mounds of melting butter on top. She leaves, and returns with two plates over-laden with bacon.

'Now serve yourselves, dears, before it gets cold. And I don't want to see anything left on your plates.' For the next few moments all three of us pile our plates high, then Colm fills our crystal glasses with wine.

'You were saying about the Pope?' I prompt.

'Oh, yes,' replies Colm, returning to his seat. He squirts a generous dollop of tomato ketchup onto his plate. He piles his fork high and eats greedily as though he hasn't been fed in months. I suppose the food on the rigs is lousy. It'll be like school dinners, pre-Jamie Oliver, made with stores of dried and frozen food. I can't imagine there's the opportunity for the rig's chef to catch a little tugboat to the nearest supermarket and stock up on fresh fruit and vegetables. How do they prevent scurvy, I wonder. The old Holly would probably ask, but the new-turning-herself-into-a-perfect girlfriend will just stick to polite conversation. 'He invited a delegation from my unit to the Vatican.'

'Really?' I wonder why oil-rig workers warrant a special meeting with the Pope. 'Did you do a big sponsored swim across the North Sea or something?' I ask. 'Raise thousands of pounds?'

'Aren't you a card, Holly dear? I told you she was a sweetie,' Miss Binchy ladles more mash onto my plate, ignoring my protestations. 'You'll waste away. Men like women with a bit of flesh on them, don't they Colm?'

'Er, yeah.' He blushes, barely meeting my eyes. Uh oh. Do I detect a hint of interest from my sex-starved companion? I flick my hair back coquettishly, before lightly resting my hand gently on his arm.

'I think your aunt wants me to end up like the Michelin man.'

'I don't think there's any chance of that,' he stammers before moving his arm ever so slightly, knocking my hand off in the process. I'm momentarily confused at this gesture, but then figure he probably wouldn't want to embarrass his aunt. I wink knowingly at Colm, and am flattered by the red glow that immediately inflames his face. Somehow my blouse doesn't matter any more.

'So tell me a bit more about your work. Is it all men in your unit? Or has the industry been worried by all these sexual discrimination claims that you read about in the paper, and decided to admit women?'

'No, it's still all men,' replies Colm, looking at me rather oddly. 'I really can't see that changing in my lifetime. The Pope even said as much when we visited him.'

'The Pope has views on women?' I'm shocked. 'I wouldn't have thought it's his business. If a woman decides that's how she wants to spend her life, then I don't think he has any right to stand in her way. Okay, so I know he'd probably worry about potential sexual tension building when men and women are cooped up together, but frankly it's so unrealistic of him to expect people to remain celibate, waiting for their wedding night ...' Colm looks at me strangely, and I spot Miss Binchy blessing herself from the corner of my eye. Shit, I think, you're so tactless, Holly. There's poor Miss Binchy who never had a wedding night ... and I feel a surge of warmth towards Colm who is so obviously sensitive to her discomfort. I swiftly change the subject. 'So, do you ever get bored? Stranded for weeks and months on end?'

'Not really. There's a hectic schedule and everybody has individual duties. My day is planned from the moment I wake, so I haven't got time to get fed up. Plus, I'm doing something that I truly love. It really is a vocation.'

I'm slightly surprised. I mean, I love my job but I doubt I'd call it a vocation, and extracting barrels of oil is hardly life enhancing. Still, I am intrigued by his career. I persist with my questioning. Donna would be proud.

'What happens to those men with families?'

'Our families adapt,' replies Colm. 'Mine did. Some parents believe there is no more fulfilling role for their sons. I know mine feel like that. Others pray, from the moment their sons are born, for them to follow this career path.'

'Is it because of the pay?' I never knew working on a rig was such a hot career. 'Do you get special danger money for working in such difficult conditions? How do you cope with thunderstorms? They must rock the place a bit.' I lean over and fill Colm's empty glass, careful to give him a brief glimpse of my voluptuous cleavage.

Miss Binchy and Colm burst out laughing. This wasn't exactly the reaction I had expected.

'Ach, isn't she a card,' Miss Binchy giggles. 'Imagine. Danger money. I think you've been watching too many horror movies.'

Colm laughs. 'The biggest danger I face is dealing with aggressive drunk beggars.'

'I suppose drink is a problem where you are,' I say. 'People with nothing else to do.'

'I don't know about nothing else to do, but the new twenty-four-hour licensing rules haven't helped. It just encourages people to drink from dusk to dawn.'

'Oh, I thought you'd have had different licensing rules where you work.'

'No, same as everywhere,' he smiles, finishing his meal.

'What about shift workers?'

'Eh?'

'Well, some of them must go on benders once they've finished a difficult shift.'

'That's certainly true,' Colm smiles at me. 'Once we had eight drunks arriving together at the door looking for rooms for the night. We had to double up to give them a bed each.'

'Did they row across for a bed?'

It's Colm's turn to look confused.

'Row? Why would they need to do that?'

'To reach you.'

'What? As in "Michael, row the boat ashore, Hallelujah?"' He laughs.

'Er, no.' I'm puzzled, and add hesitantly, 'As in you being in the middle of the sea ...'

'... the sea?' He shakes his head. 'Well, Brighton is by the sea, but I'd hardly say it...'

'Brighton?' I interrupt. My geography isn't great, but I know that's not by the North Sea. I'm sure Brighton is known for antiques, Fat Boy Slim and a nudist beach, but oil? The only slicks in Brighton are the baby oil ones on the pebbled beach.

'Yes, that's where I'm based.' Colm looks at me intently.

'There's an oil-rig in Brighton?'

'Not that I know of,' he replies. 'Why?'

'I thought...' I hesitate. What the hell have you done, Holly? 'I thought you worked on the rigs?' I feel my face reddening.

'Me?' Colm and his aunt exchange bemused glances. 'Whatever gave you that idea?'

'Well ...' How can I explain my reasoning? That a man who doesn't get out much and doesn't see many women in his line of work must be an oil-rig worker? It made sense at the time. 'I just, er ...' I pause.

'An oil-rig, eh? That's a good one. What would the abbot say?' Miss Binchy laughs out loud. 'Goodness, you are a card Holly. Didn't I tell you that she was priceless, Colm?'

'Abbot?' I repeat slowly. 'As in ... monk ... abbot?'

'That's right.' Colm holds his hand out to shake mine. 'Father Colm. I don't think we've been properly introduced.'

CHAPTER TEN

Louise's mouth is open wide in amazement, like the lost fish Nemo. I shrug as she shakes her head once again. It is five minutes since I told her of the little misunderstanding, and all that my best friend has done is laugh. She has cried with laughter. Shaken with laughter. Spluttered with laughter. The diners on the neighbouring tables keep looking over. They must think I am the funniest person in the world. Now Louise giggles, shrugs her shoulders incredulously, takes a deep breath, and finally speaks.

'So, let me get this straight,' her words are slow and considered, 'you were gearing up to hit on a priest. And you actually stroked his arm?' I nod in shame. 'That's absolutely priceless. You're like a character from Father Ted. Wait till I tell Sam.' She dissolves into a fit of giggles. 'Perhaps I should call him now?' She lifts her mobile off the table.

'Leave it,' I order in a tone like a police officer in an American movie. 'Put your hands flat on the table. That's right. Okay.' I lean across and confiscate her mobile. 'It wasn't like that. Obviously I didn't know he was a priest. He wasn't wearing a dog collar.'

'But he looked like an oil-rig worker?' She thrusts her hands out to make a point. 'Was he carrying a pipe?'

'I wish I hadn't told you now,' I sigh. 'You're as bad as James ...'

'You told him? Are you nuts?'

I nod in disbelief at my own stupidity. I was desperate,

wracked with guilt and shame, convinced I was set for an eternity of hellfire and damnation, so I confessed my transgression to the only Catholic in the office, hoping for assurances. So much for the sanctity of the bloody confessional. James kept it to himself for about as long as it took me to eat five comforting chocolate Hob Nobs. And in two minutes he had shared my humiliation with Donna and Angus. The past three hours have been unbearable.

'He told Donna and Angus.' I admit.

'No.' Louise slams her palm over her mouth in horror. 'What did they say?' The look on her face suggests she has already guessed.

'Oh you know,' I say nonchalantly. 'Plenty more priests in the Holy See. Every font has a silver lining. Any others to join the pew? What are my thoughts on Cardinal sin?'

'They took the piss?'

I shrug.

'I'm sorry.' At least Louise has the grace to look sympathetic.

'Oh, it doesn't matter,' I sigh, as the waiter serves our lunch. I offer a taste of my deep-fried Camembert to Louise but she shuns it, muttering about the parasites in soft cheeses. 'I haven't told you the worst bit.'

'It gets worse?' Louise is incredulous. 'What can be worse than trying to jump a priest?"

'I didn't try to jump him,' I correct. 'I merely thought about it. Oh God,' I sink my head into my hands, 'I'm going to hell. Anyway, this is the worst bit – Miss Binchy was wearing the same blouse as me.'

'No! Your neighbour who normally wears curlers and wrinkled stockings? That's appalling.' My style-conscious friend is horrified by my revelation. 'Which blouse?' She sounds panicked.

'Does it matter?'

'Well, I'm just checking that I don't have one too.' I look at my friend, elegant in a mink coloured cashmere top with chocolate brown trousers and suede boots. A shearling coat is draped casually over the back of her wooden chair. Her make-up is barely perceptible, apart from the dark brown kohl that frames her olive-green eyes. Louise is every inch the wife of an investment banker. And, if there were any doubt, the massive princess-cut three-carat diamond that sparkles on the third finger of her left hand confirms it. There is no way she owns an eight-year-old Marks & Spencer velvet blouse. She probably doesn't even own an eight-week-old one.

'You don't. And nor do I any more. I tossed it in a building skip on my way to the station this morning.'

'Isn't that an overreaction?' She picks happily at her chicken stir-fry. Already I've noticed subtle differences with Louise. She was only available for lunch, when I called in a last minute panic, because she's abandoned her step class. Too much exercise, apparently, is a bad thing as it may inhibit ovulation. And it took almost five minutes for her to choose her stir-fry – the broccoli ingredient swung it in the end because, according to her 'How to Get Pregnant Without Even Trying' book, broccoli is full of beneficial folic acid. But I digress ...

I answer Louise. 'Miss Binchy bought it in a discount bin in a charity shop. What does that say about my style?'

'Lots of celebrities scour charity shops,' soothes my friend. 'The ones in Notting Hill and Kensington are stuffed with designer gear. All the top stylists check them out.'

'This wasn't designer gear.' I pause, wondering if I'm just about to open some huge Pandora's box. 'Look, I took your advice, and spoke to a couple of old boyfriends ...'

'Who?' she asks eagerly.

'That doesn't matter, but all of them mentioned my lack of sartorial style.' I look down at my lace-up brogues. 'Louise, be honest, what's wrong with this outfit?' My best friend carefully scans my ensemble. She sighs and takes a large gulp from my glass of white wine.

'There's nothing wrong with elements of your outfit,' she finally says in a diplomatic tone.

'But?' I suddenly wish I hadn't started this.

'The trousers you're wearing are gorgeous ...'

'Thank you.'

'... but they don't match your top.'

'Oh?' I look down at my outfit.

'Personally I think herringbone trousers, and by the way I'm not making a judgment on whether they're this season or last, require a plain top. Not a floral one.'

'But there's grey in the trousers and look,' I push my sleeve towards her, 'the flowers are grey. I'm coordinated.'

'You sound like Sam, when he tries to put a blue striped shirt with a patterned blue tie,' she laughs patiently. 'Not that I could tell you what he's been wearing recently. He's working on some major deal eighteen hours a day and it's playing havoc with our baby trying.' Does everything have to come back to babies, I think sadly. 'Holly, your outfit just doesn't go. Take my word for it.' I silently digest my friend's comments. Finally, she lays down her knife and fork, and says, 'I'm sorry, but you insisted. You're my very best friend and as far as I'm concerned you can wear a hessian sack every day if you want, but admit it; you're not really interested in clothes. Shopping is a chore to you. I've watched you walk into a boutique, pick the first pair of trousers that you see, buy them without trying them on and walk out. You've got your credit card out before I've reached the first rail.'

'So I look a mess?'

'I didn't say that,' Louise replies kindly. 'You've got other interests in life. Who cares about clothes?'

'My old boyfriends did ...'

'So what?' Louise pushes her half-empty plate away. 'Their opinions no longer matter.'

'But what if I wanted to impress somebody? If I worried about their opinion?'

'Who?' Louise looks confused. 'The priest?'

'No.' I flap my hands to quieten her. 'This is a huge secret. You can't tell Sam or anybody, but I think I may like my new client ...'

'Your new client,' she repeats slowly.

'Shhhhhh.' I quickly scan the neighbouring tables. 'I don't want anybody to hear. This is awkward.'

'You're telling me.' She wags her finger. 'Mixing business and pleasure never works.'

'I know. Anyway, it's unrequited lust on my part. He'd probably walk past me in this restaurant and not notice, but I'm off to see him in,' I check my watch, 'in an hour to give an update on the investigation, wearing what can only be described as rags.'

'I didn't say that,' Louise retorts.

I sigh. I never worried about what I wore when I was dating my 'flings', but today I'm really nervous about my appearance for meeting Carl Lawson. I have butterflies in my stomach.

'You can impress him at your next meeting,' Louise soothes.

'There might not be a next time,' I admit. 'I've done a very thorough job. Unless he requires surveillance for the candidate, my work there is done.' I feel deflated. I've suffered the humiliation of hearing what two former boyfriends think of me in an attempt to learn from my mistakes and transform myself into a perfect girlfriend, and I've blown it at the first hurdle.

'There's always time.' Louise is getting excited. 'We've got forty minutes to buy you a plain white shirt, new shoes and do your make-up. I'd say that's definitely achievable. Now settle this bill, and let's get going.'

Chapter Eleven

Carl Lawson is seated at a mahogany boardroom table, in a room on the twenty-second floor of Ilyax Insurance's head-quarters. Every wall is made of glass, offering a birds-eye view of the City. I can see the dome of St Paul's cathedral, the mottled grey concrete of the Barbican Centre, the pale granite walls of the Bank of England, the cigar-shaped glass-walled building predictably dubbed the Erotic Gherkin, and a forest of cranes signalling the continuous building work that goes on within the Square Mile. He waits for a liveried butler to serve coffee from a sterling silver pot into bone china cups, with saucers so translucent that I worry about just resting the spoon on mine. I am feeling nervous and unsteady. Louise has given me a completely new look. She found me a chocolate brown fitted shirt – opened three buttons – stiletto boots and daubed me generously in make-up. But despite worrying that I mustn't smile or I'll crack it, the look is very subtle. And my lips look extremely kissable, even though I do say so myself.

'So, Holly, do you want to kick off and tell me what you've discovered about Clive Partridge? Candidate A.' Carl Lawson beams at me. He is in his shirtsleeves, having thrown his navy-blue jacket over the back of his chair. Silver bulldogs fill his double cuffs. 'Have you completed all the searches?'

'Indeed I have.' I take a buff folder containing my findings from my briefcase and rest it on the table. The front cover carries no subject name. 'And you'll be pleased to know that I can't find any skeletons that might concern you. There are no unseemly habits, no mistresses, and no spending patterns that might alert the Inland Revenue. Clive Partridge is, to all intents and purposes, a model citizen.'

'Really?' Carl's eyes flicker to my cleavage. 'That's great news.'

'Before I hand over this information, I need your personal assurance that it will remain confidential.' I say firmly. 'These investigations do breach certain privacy laws, and Clive Partridge could sue both you and Investigations-R-Us if he ever discovered we'd accessed his personal bank accounts, for example.'

A fleeting look of impatience crosses Carl's face, but he soon recovers and smiles broadly.

'It's for his own good,' he says. 'This is a major job, but I understand your concerns.'

'Nevertheless, I need assurances before I pass over any information.' I spent an hour yesterday searching for an Internet café to print out these findings to ensure the printers within Investigations-R-Us's offices contain no record. The paper is flimsy, cheap and untraceable. Not one page contains my company's name or that of the candidate. If this document ever gets left on a train or in the pub, then it will probably get tossed into a dustbin because it looks dull and boring. Hell, it *is* dull and boring. Clive Partridge is hardly the world's most exciting executive.

'You have my assurance,' Carl Lawson says. I slide the folder towards him.

'If you'd like to turn to Specimen A in the folder' – Carl opens the cardboard file and shuffles through its contents – 'You'll see Clive Partridge is referred to throughout as Mr Pear-tree, so if the file falls into the wrong hands, his anonymity remains protected.' Carl opens a five-page document on the table in front of him. 'This is a detailed schedule of his tax returns over the past five years,' I explain. 'Every number filed has been checked and double-checked. Clive Partridge is so honest he even includes the abominably low interest he receives on his high street bank account. He also makes substantial annual donations to several charities, reflecting his kind nature that several acquaintances have referred to.' Carl nods appreciatively. 'I know it's hearsay, but I believe comments like those highlighted in Specimen B' (Carl draws out the relevant part), 'provide a fuller picture of an individual.' He skims the three pages. 'I constantly heard the phrases, "family man", "kind hearted", "well-balanced", "animal lover", and "respectful of staff",' I tell him.

'We're not looking for Mother Teresa,' Carl mutters. I blush. James had warned me that Specimen B might prove over the top when we ran through my presentation yesterday morning, but I felt it key to establishing Clive Partridge's personality. I give my rehearsed response.

'I'm aware of that,' I say diffidently. 'But I got his former colleagues and acquaintances to open up by pretending to be an old friend of his. Imagine if I'd have been a tabloid journalist waving a blank cheque? Isn't it comforting to know the only insights they can buy are as trivial and mind-numbing as these?'

'You've got a point,' says Carl. 'Any negatives?'

'He has trouble with his multiplication tables.'

'Hell. He's going to be a finance director ...'

'What's eight times seven?'

'Eh?' He looks flustered. 'Fifty, er, sixty two, no, um ...'

'Eight times seven is fifty-six. Surely you must know that,' I sigh. 'You're the boss of a major accountancy firm.' Phew, lucky I checked my maths on a calculator this morning.

'Touché,' he blushes. 'More coffee?' I nod. It gives me a moment to study Carl Lawson. Dear God, I silently pray, I know I probably offended you in my near wanton displays of lust with Father Colm – rest assured, he was totally blameless and didn't encourage my attentions – but please don't let that stand in my way today. This man is crying out for Holly Heaven. Amen

'Specimen C,' I continue, 'reflects his personal expenditure. I've balanced out his monthly earnings, offset his monthly outgoings, and discovered Mr Pear-tree is a model of financial rectitude. His only indulgences are a monthly trip to his local book shop, where he favours crime novels, and a personal investment in an Australian franchise specialising in battered chicken wings.'

'He may have to sell that,' mutters Carl.

'He already has,' I reply. 'Last month, but not before it paid for a very attractive holiday home in Marbella.' Carl Lawson raises his eyebrows. 'There is absolutely no hint of impropriety. His investment is detailed in the franchisee's accounts.'

'Why did he get involved?'

'An old university friend.' I check my notes. 'Actually I think she was a former girlfriend. Not that that matters. Shows he's a healthy red-blooded male.' Carl laughs as he continues to read Specimen C. His Adam's apple wobbles, and I feel all giddy. He flicks through the file again. 'There don't seem to be any bank statements or utility bills.'

'We wouldn't disclose those,' I reply. 'This may sound strange after I've spent the last few days probing through them, but it wouldn't be right to pass them over to you. If there was anything out of the ordinary, I would have mentioned it in my report.'

'So there's nothing to suggest that Clive Partridge is anything other than an ideal candidate?'

'My professional opinion, on the basis of the information I have here, is that Mr Pear-tree is ideal. But I've only partially completed my investigation. I'd need to conduct a surveillance operation on the candidate to provide a definitive opinion. I could start tomorrow. Saturdays are always interesting. People do strange things at weekends ...'

'That won't be necessary,' Carl closes the files.

'I'm sorry?'

'I think I've all I need. Clive Partridge seems ideal.'

'But ...' I protest. He puts up his hand to stop me.

'Honestly,' his eyes flick again to my chest. 'I think we've pried enough into his personal life. Let him have some secrets,' he laughs.

'Yes, but I thought the point was there were to be no secrets ... .'

'Holly, honestly. Set your mind at rest. The work you've completed is brilliant. I'm delighted.' I flush with pride. 'Actually, I'm so pleased that,' Carl appears to hesitate, 'I want you to take on another investigation.'

'Another one?' So I'll see you again. Thank you God, it is true you are a merciful man. Sorry once again for the mix-up with the priest. Amen.

'Well, two actually,' he beams again. Carl's teeth should star in a toothpaste advertisement. They're absolutely perfect, white, straight and gleaming.

'Two?'

'Yes, Ilyax Insurance has a major dilemma. Our Human Resources boss is leaving soon and we have two internal candidates. It would send a fantastic message to our staff if we could promote one, and even better, they're both women.'

'And you want me to check them out? I wouldn't have thought the position was serious enough to warrant the cost of an investigation.'

'Holly,' Carl ignores my question, 'something's been bothering me since you walked in today. You look different.' My heart misses a beat. 'Have you done something to your hair?' I shake my head, unable to speak. 'Hmm, I can't put my finger on it but it certainly suits you. Anyway,' he smiles at me, 'where were we?'

'Two female internal candidates for Human Resources.'

'Ah yes.' He reaches into his briefcase. 'I've their personal details here. And photographs.' He shuffles two black and white photographs onto the table in front of me. Bloody hell. They're stunning. Both these women could be models. 'Now I obviously know both these candidates so I think Investigations-R-Us can bypass the preliminary investigations. I'm just interested in surveillance operations on them both.'

'That's not standard procedure,' I begin, thrown by the scale of the project. 'Surveillance is usually done after other lines of inquiry are exhausted ...'

95

'Holly,' Carl suddenly interrupts. 'I know this isn't exactly professional, but I'm just looking at my watch. It's five o'clock on Friday evening. Would you like to continue this meeting over a drink?'

CHAPTER TWELVE

Slowly, and with difficulty, I open an eye. I repeat the painful process with the second one. My head is pounding, making it hard to focus, but eventually I make out the pale calamine pink Farrow & Ball colour that Louise and I spent a weekend painting onto my bedroom ceiling. I turn my head slightly to the right – ouch – to check the light fitting. Yes, I think with relief, this is my bedroom. The only question is: how did I get here? I can remember leaving Ilyax Insurance with Carl Lawson, walking down Bow Lane, bustling with early evening shoppers, to the Wine Vault. I can recall perching on a wooden stool at the bar while he flamboyantly ordered a bottle of vintage champagne. A second bottle being popped open. Life stories being exchanged. Lots of giggling. Some tentative touching of fingers. Frissons of delight. An extra couple of glasses 'for the road'. Tottering down the cobbled lane in unfamiliar, and painful, stiletto heels, until eventually I wrenched them off and walked barefoot, to hail a cab. I can see the amused cab driver watching me thrust my aching feet onto Carl Lawson's lap as he asked where we were headed. And Carl's husky whisper into the ear attached to the lobe he was nuzzling. Bed.

Bed!

Shit.

I'm in bed!

Shit.

If I am in my bed, then where is Carl?

Without moving my body, I slowly edge my right hand across the Egyptian cotton sheet that covers the mattress. Waiter, there's a man in my bed! I look across in a panic at the person lying there. Carl Lawson is smiling at me.

'Good morning,' he finally says. 'Well, that certainly wasn't in my Microsoft Office diary yesterday.'

'Nor mine,' I admit, feeling shy and embarrassed.

'So you didn't intend to seduce me with that thrusting cleavage yesterday?' He winks suggestively, as I casually try to pull the quilt up to chin level to cover my nakedness.

'No,' I mutter.

'Hey, I'm not complaining.' He slowly edges the quilt down my upper body. My cleavage is more alluvial flood plain than Himalayan peaks now I'm lying on my back, but Carl doesn't seem to mind. 'I think it's trying to seduce me again,' he whispers hoarsely, moving towards me.

Twenty minutes later, and I'm watching a freshly showered Carl Lawson dress in the clothes that somehow, in the heat of last night's passion, he managed to fold neatly and place onto the chair in the corner of my bedroom. In contrast, the clothes I wore yesterday are strewn across the floor, making friends with the garments already there.

'Cleaner's day off?' he laughs, nodding at the debris.

I blush. This is not exactly the image that I had hoped to convey.

'Nah. Tracey Emin's latest artwork,' I smile. 'It's a work in progress. I wasn't expecting visitors or I'd have told her to finish it.'

'And I wasn't expecting to visit.' Carl sits at the side of the bed looking down at me. His shirt, yet to be buttoned up, reveals his muscular chest. 'I wouldn't like you to think, Holly, that I make a habit of doing this.' He lightly touches my cheek and shakes his head. 'But it just felt so right. This feels *so* right. You feel it too, don't you?' He softly drags a finger across my cheek to my lips, and tenderly pushes them open. 'I can't believe this is happening to me. To us.' My lips gently kiss his finger. 'You're definitely not how I imagined before I first met you.'

'What did you imagine?'

'I don't know,' he shrugs, 'somebody uptight and professional, who kept her mind focused on the job, not the sultry, curvy woman who arrived at my office. You've been on my mind since we first met. I even looked forward to your progress calls.' He takes my hand. 'I don't want you to think I'm a ladies' man. I'm not, Holly. Hell, I was married for fifteen years and never once strayed. Not once. I don't do things like this. I'm not some teenager looking for a quick leg-over. This really meant something to me.'

'Yeah, I know. The earth moved ...' I reply flippantly, before biting my lip. That's exactly what Pete warned me about. Accept a compliment, Holly. Enjoy it.

'I don't know about earth, but the bed certainly did.' He rubs his back. 'You might need to get a new mattress before we do that again.' I can't speak. This can't be true. Carl Lawson, who I've lusted after for ten days, is talking about a repeat performance. My dream man may actually become a reality. 'I don't know about you, Holly,' he continues, 'but I don't do flings. I'm not interested. I really want to see you again, but I'll understand if you just want this to be a one-off. I won't pressurise you, but I can't say that I won't be disappointed and it won't affect our professional relationship. I like you, Holly.'

My heart slips a beat. Carl Lawson wants me? He doesn't want a fling? He is offering a serious relationship?

'It'll be difficult. You're my client. I could lose my job.' A torrent of reasons not to take the situation further spill from my mouth without warning or thought. Carl frowns.

'It will be difficult,' he agrees, 'but not impossible. For the time being, if you decide you want to take things further, then we'll keep it quiet When the contract expires, we can shout it from the rooftops.' He smiles at me. 'If you like?'

I like, I think, but I keep that feeling to myself for the moment. Instead I smile enigmatically.

'I'll call,' he says. 'As soon as I get home, and every other time today that I think of you.' He giggles. 'Holly, I don't think I'll be off the phone.'

'You could just stay,' I say quietly.

'I could, but I have to get back to take my sons to football. They're expecting me. Not that I'll be able to concentrate on their games. Holly, I think you are one very special lady.' He kisses my forehead. 'And this might just be the start of something sensational.'

Chapter Thirteen

Nothing can deflate my good humour. I am on Cloud Nine. Thirty minutes ago Carl Lawson left my now tousled and sweaty bed, and he wants a relationship. Not a fling. Not five dates, eight bonks and countless snogs over two weeks, but a proper boyfriend-girlfriend relationship when a couple eats at restaurants with clean linen and silver tableware. Louise doesn't sound quite as excited as I'd expected when I ring her, minutes after Carl slammed the door behind him, and mutters on about 'hardly knowing him' and 'it all seems rather quick'.

I can't help feeling a little put out at her attitude. Louise is, after all, the woman who, on meeting Sam at the uni bar, attached herself like a Dyson cleaner to his mouth within minutes, and then hours later disappeared on a marathon bedroom session. The only person to see them over the next two days was the pizza delivery man.

'Aren't you the person who always said I'd know when I met the right one?' I point out. 'Well, don't ask me why, but I think it's him. Everything just felt so normal. Apart from the initial shock of seeing him here this morning, there weren't any awkward pauses. It felt so right. You old married people, you forget how it used to be...'

'I'm sorry,' says Louise. 'I'm just a bit irritated. Sam was meant to have today off, but he's been called into work. I'm going to make him pay, though. I'm buying the latest Mulberry handbag.'

'Not that he'll mind,' I soothe. Sam is many things, but he wouldn't care if Louise bought the latest collection from Joseph, just as long as she colour co-ordinated the items on wooden hangers. 'Hey, why don't you come along with me today? I'm going shopping.'

'You! Going shopping twice in two days? What is the world coming to?'

I admit to Louise that Pete has 'offered' to take me out for the day to sort out my style. 'And after the impression that my new clothes made yesterday on Carl, I'm actually quite keen,' I confess. 'We're starting at Toni & Guy's. You could come on later.'

'Not likely! If Pete is going for the complete package, I'm there from the start. Don't you watch those makeover programmes on telly? Gay men are *so* in these days.'

'Great! Come along then. The more the merrier. Nothing can upset me at the moment, I'm walking on air.'

'He's that fantastic?' she asks.

'And more besides,' I sigh. 'See you in an hour.'

One hour later and what the hell was I thinking? The more the merrier? Pete, who by the time I arrive has ingratiated himself with Louise with tips on the perfect bedroom ambience for conception, has invited spectators. Angus and Donna shout out 'surprise' when I walk through the glass doors.

My four 'stylists' are sitting in the reception area, sipping takeaway hot drinks from large paper mugs and browsing through magazines in search of the 'perfect' hairstyle for me. Louise is drinking peppermint tea, which she tells Donna is good for morning sickness. And the woman isn't yet pregnant. My colleague is pointing out a fringe that she claims will narrow my nose. Louise nods enthusiastically. Suddenly I feel like Pinocchio and the air I have been walking on since getting out of bed this morning evaporates, bringing me back to earth. They follow my stylist Henri and I to his workstation, gathering around while he disdainfully lifts one lifeless tress after another, dropping its predecessor with a distinct tut. After all this humiliation, Carl Lawson had better call.

Henri is dressed from head-to-toe in black, a flick of vibrant red through his hair his only concession to colour. A leather tool belt hangs around his narrow waist, filled with brushes, scissors and a host of other stainless steel items that wouldn't look out of place in a gynaecologist's consulting rooms. Henri has that uncanny hairdresser's knack of making clients feel unfashionable. My skinny-rib polo neck and faded jeans combo appears tired, while every member of my entourage appears to have stepped from the pages of *Vogue*. Louise is wearing a bandanna – 'don't want the hairdresser to see my roots,' she whispers – a cheesecloth smock-style top and jeans. She has effortlessly transformed herself from wife of investment banker to rock chick. Or, more accurately, rock chic.

'Your hair,' Henri finally sighs. 'It eez so,' Henri swirls both his hands in the air, 'dull.' He shakes his head in disgust at the word. 'Eez just not good. Who cut zis hair before?'

'I had a go,' I admit shamefacedly, before blurting out in explanation at the horrified gasps, 'I didn't have time to go to the hairdresser. I was on a job.'

'Was it down ze mine?' Henri asks. Donna giggles. I glare at her reflection in the gigantic mirror facing me. 'You must use conditioner. I need to cut at leezt six centimetres to get rid of ze split endz.'

'How long is six centimetres?' I ask. Pete and Angus simultaneously demonstrate with their thumbs and forefingers.

'Rupert,' they both exclaim, before bursting into giggles.

'I was thinking that Holly needs a wispy fringe,' interrupts Louise, bringing the gang back to order. Henri considers the matter, and nods.

'Eez good idea.' He pulls strands of hair around my face. 'I wizzzp around ze cheekbones, too. Give definition.'

Pete remembers he's in charge, and steps forward. 'Henri, what colour do you think for Holly?'

'Somezing warm and light. I need to get rid of zis grey.' Henri shakes the hair on the crown of my head. 'Zis mouse is sooo last year. I look at coppery tones.'

'Copper?' say Angus and Pete. They stare at my hair, turn to each other and nod decisively. 'Absolutely.'

'Can I say something?' I put my hand in the air, like a small child in an infants' class trying to grab his teacher's attention. 'It is my hair.'

'Madam,' Henri looks over my shoulder into the mirror, studying my face. 'Zat is not something to boast about. Please leave this to the experts.' He turns on his heel to fetch strips of silver paper, pots of ammonia-smelling creams and a variety of brushes, before transforming my head into a festive hedgehog. He sits me under an electronic contraption that I swear would beam me up if I only asked it to, and disappears for twenty minutes.

'We're not sure what your look should be,' concedes Pete.

'I think Boho chic,' says Angus, his chin resting in his cupped right hand. 'I can see you in gypsy skirts and bangles.'

'But I'm thinking dominatrix; I see you in leather and killer heels,' Pete gives my shoulder an affectionate shove. 'Show off those legs.'

'We could go for Boho-trix,' persists Angus. 'Peasant tops and leather bottoms.'

'Holly'd be out of date before she even left the changing room,' says Pete. 'She just couldn't pull off that look.' They glance at each other, before pursing their lips and staring at my reflection. 'But I'm not seeing her as Boho. It's too unstructured for her. This girl has so little dress sense,' he shakes his head in frustration, 'she needs discipline in her wardrobe.'

'But I don't see her as a dominatrix,' huffs Angus. 'She hasn't the attitude or the oomph to work it. She's not like Donna,' he smiles at my colleague, who is sitting at one of the mirrors checking her hair for split ends. She pouts at him.

'You're so right,' sighs Pete. 'Holly is too demure. She's not a slut.' Louise stifles a snort. I glare at her.

'She has the air of a naïf,' says Angus. They continue studying me. 'Are you ...' He suddenly looks at Pete.

'... thinking what I'm thinking?' says Pete excitedly. 'I think I am.' They high-five each other. 'I'm thinking ...'

'Audrey Hepburn!' they exclaim together.

'She's just perfect,' says Pete. 'Oh, this is going to be so much fun. Quick, back to the fashion mags. Come on Donna, we haven't a *moment* to waste.'

They disappear off to the reception. Louise and I watch them leave.

'Guess what I bought yesterday after I left you to go to your meeting,' she asks excitedly.

'A Maserati?' I say flippantly. 'Just a little runabout for town.'

'If you're going to be childish I might as well leave.'

'Don't be silly,' I quickly soothe. 'What did you buy?'

'One of those temperature thingummies so I can find out when I'm at my most fertile. All I've got to do is make sure that Sam is with me at that exact moment. It's going to be such fun.' Louise giggles.

'But what happens if he's out when you're most fertile?'

'I've bought him a special pay-as-you-go mobile and if that ever rings he knows that it's all systems go. Literally.'

'And if he's at work?'

'What's more important?' she sniffs, turning away to read her Mother and Baby magazine. It all depends on whether a multi-million pound bonus is riding on it, I think. I look at her sadly. My best friend's life is moving on, and a small selfish part of me fears that, in a short time, I'll no longer play such a major role in it. It's strange. We used to do everything together – joining the University Archery Club (we left after one lesson; nobody told us about the bruises), joining the Real Ale Club (we didn't drink ale, but it was held in the pub and we were told lots of boys were members), starting work, getting a flat, sitting around the breakfast table at the weekend with our boyfriends. Sunday lunches by the river as a foursome. And then Jake left me for old horse-face, Louise got married, and all her subsequent firsts happened with Sam. Mine became solo events. It could have been so different. We might have been giggling about trying for babies at the same time, arguing about natural birth or having an epidural (as if

105

there is any choice!) and comparing our bumps. Funny the cards that life deals us. Or rather me.

'Now ...' Henri checks beneath one of the foil strips, clicks his fingers at a passing junior, dressed from head to toe in black. 'Alfred, I wish you to wash my client's hair. Use the shampoo for one,' he makes a fist, holding up the thumb, 'dry ends, two,' another finger is unwound, 'greasy scalp, three,' another finger, 'dandruff,' another finger, which also casually flicks a few of my errant flakes from his black top, 'and last' – the final, and most insulting, finger of all – 'greying hair.'

But I forgive him when, almost an hour later, Henri holds the vanity mirror behind my head to reveal the back view of my new hairstyle. My hair has more bounce, more life and the cluster of highlights and lowlights on my crown give my face a halo-like reflection. And, though I never thought I had a hooter the size of Eurotunnel, Louise is right, the wispy fringe makes my nose seem narrower, while the feathery ends that frame my face make it appear more delicate. I look again. This image cannot be me. Can it?

'Our duckling,' says Angus with pride, clapping his hands in excitement, 'is turning into a ...'

'Swan!' exclaim Angus and Pete simultaneously.

'You look fantastic,' gushes Louise. 'Absolutely gorgeous.'

'You clean up really well, sweetie,' gasps Pete. 'But this is just the beginning. Donna, what's next?' He claps his hands. 'Jump to it. We're on an extremely tight schedule.'

My ever-efficient colleague springs open her Palm Pilot, and starts dictating. 'Paraffin manicure and pedicure in twenty minutes. Venue: beauty salon downstairs. Waxing – eyebrows, legs, bikini and any other rogue hairs surplus to requirements (her eyes inadvertently scan my top lip), in ninety minutes. Same venue.' She stops and addresses my entourage. 'I suggest we then meet for lunch, before we hit the shops to choose Holly's new wardrobe.'

'Will I have any say in the matter?' I ask.

Pete gives my outfit a quick up-and-down look as Angus stares at me in amazement for suggesting such a thing. 'You can't be trusted,' Pete finally says. 'Angus and I will go recce the shops and select some outfits to save time. Right Holly, what's the budget?'

'You mean I have to pay for this humiliating experience?'

'Darling, we,' Pete throws his arm around Angus, 'are donating our time for free.'

'What do you mean?' mutters Donna. 'I wouldn't miss this for the world. I'd pay to come along today.'

I ignore her. 'How much do you think I'll need?' I ask Pete.

'How much do you spend on clothes every month?'

'I don't know,' I shrug. 'Forty pounds? Fifty? Give or take.'

There is a resounding roar of laughter from the group. Even Louise joins in.

'I think we might need to use the reserves from the months you didn't spend anything on clothes,' replies Pete.

'That would be every month over the past year,' says Donna. 'Somebody told Holly about vintage, and it's become her excuse to wear all her old clothes.' My cheeks burn with embarrassment.

'So we've got a maximum of £600?' Pete asks.

'Eh?' I reply. 'I don't know about that. I might need to check with my bank manager.'

'Nonsense,' he says firmly. 'Use your plastic. What on earth do you think God created it for? Anyway, it's hardly Harvey Nicks' scale funds. We'll have to make do at Top Shop, Oasis and Zara. Right Donna, you're in charge of the next stage of Holly's day. Remember not to let her loose on nail colours. Nothing says style and elegance more than a French manicure, and on the waxing front, try to persuade her to have a Brazilian ...'

'I can choose where the waxers come from?' I ask. 'Which nationality is best?'

They shriek with laughter.

'As I said, Donna. A firm hand.' And with that final instruction, Pete and Angus flounce out of the salon to source my new wardrobe.

CHAPTER FOURTEEN

Eight hundred and twenty-two pounds and thirty-seven pence later, I return home with my purchases. I feel giddy with excitement. Pete and Angus selected six outfits that they claim provide the foundation of a wardrobe. Or, as they called it, 'a capsule wardrobe'. It sounds like a closet found on the Starship Enterprise, but apparently it will transform the way I put together an outfit. Each top selected can be worn with any of the skirts or trousers. And the two jackets can be worn with everything.

I have twelve carrier bags, including a fancy turquoise blue cardboard one with bright pink ribbons for handles, that the shop assistant filled with pale pink tissue paper before carefully placing my purchase, already folded into more tissue paper, on top and sealing the bag with a tulip-shaped sticker. I've never in my life owned anything before that deserved tissue paper – and coloured paper at that.

Today was a complete revelation. In one boutique, there were special silk scarves hanging in the changing rooms, which apparently you're meant to put over your head to stop your make-up staining the clothes, and a special area for tired husbands and boyfriends to sit, drink coffee and watch sports – not that Angus and Pete went there. They were on a mission.

'We've come here,' Pete said, waving his hands at the antique clothes rails filled with designer labels, 'to find you a dress for special occasions.'

'An LBD,' giggled Angus.

'Isn't that a bacon sandwich?' I ask.

'A little black dress,' he sighed. 'Something stylish. Something that says elegance.'

'I'm thinking *Breakfast at Tiffany's*,' added Pete. 'Holly Golightly meets Bree from *Desperate Housewives*. Accessories? Hmm, pearls. Don't you agree, Angus?'

Angus stood, one hand on his hip, with one finger tapping his lips, and considered. 'Pearls are always classic but, do you know Pete, I think sparkles – diamanté could do it.'

'Oh, perleaase.' Pete threw his hand across his face in a dismissive action. 'They can be so gaudy. Too Duran Duran.'

'I'm not talking Christmas baubles,' argued Angus. 'Bling can be tasteful.'

'We'll see,' Pete finally replied. 'Perhaps long satin gloves.' He shivered with pleasure. 'Just imagine how seductive that would be if Holly ever had a date.' A snort from Donna. 'She could peel them off on arrival. Right, let's get searching.'

And that's how I ended up with the slinky shift dress now folded in tissue paper. I couldn't believe it was me when I emerged from the changing room and looked at my reflection in the full-length mirror. My two male stylists were in raptures when I revealed myself. They kept 'oohing' and 'aahing', before Pete turned to Angus and said in a mock upper-class accent, 'By George, I think she's got it.' Even Donna was sufficiently impressed not to mention the manky knickers she glimpsed while I was changing. And now, as I'm turning the key in my doorway, I feel a frisson of excitement as I imagine Carl's reaction on our first date (he will call, won't he?) when I casually slip off my coat to reveal this sexy outfit. I know this is probably tempting fate, but I've already decided on stockings. Just in case.

'Holly, is that you?' Miss Binchy peers out of her open door and smiles as I enter the hallway. I freeze. I haven't seen my neighbour since the evening I met Colm. I was going to drop in a 'thank you' note, but somehow I hadn't. She's wearing one of those old floral aprons favoured by actresses starring in

Second World War movies, and there's a dash of flour on her chin. 'Look at you,' she exclaims. 'You've had your hair done. It looks absolutely lovely. And the colour ... you've such a shine there.'

'Thank you,' I beam, immediately forgetting my embarrassment.

'Ach, not at all, sure it's grand to see you looking so pretty. Not that you weren't lovely already. Give me a twirl.' I happily oblige. 'It's truly gorgeous. And I see you've been shopping.'

'Guilty as charged.' I hold up my bags in a 'you caught me out' sort of gesture. 'I decided my wardrobe could do with a bit of brightening up,' I smile. 'To go with the new hairstyle.'

'Ach, you young things. I remember being fashion conscious too. Well, now, I've just finished my weekly bake. It's not for me, dear, but Seamus does like a piece of my Victoria sponge when he calls over, and I like to feed him up. Between you and me, I think he looks a bit thin. He needs a woman to look after him. So, come on in and show me everything you bought, and have a nice cup of tea.'

Actually I'm secretly thrilled to have somebody to show my purchases to; I was a bit disappointed that I had no plans for this evening – feeling a bit like Cinderella without any ball to go to. Still, I tell myself, I soon will have. I settle into one of Miss Binchy's well worn armchairs, while she disappears into the kitchen to fetch the tea. The National Lottery is playing on the television, and a bag with knitting needles and grey wool is resting by her chair.

Miss Binchy returns with tea and a plate of fairy cakes sprinkled with multi-coloured hundreds and thousands. 'So, what did you buy?' she asks, looking at my shopping.

The magic words. I immediately start opening bags, holding up their contents and explaining how the outfits will fit together. Miss Binchy claps with delight at each one.

'Did you win the lottery?' she laughs. 'You must have spent a fortune.'

And then I gently lift out my pièce de résistance; the little black dress. I hold it against me, and Miss Binchy 'oohs' and 'aahs' in admiration, before going very quiet.

'Do you know, dear, I've got something that would be perfect with that,' she says quietly. 'I'll be back in a moment.'

She pads out of the room in her fluffy slippers. I hear doors opening and slamming, and then Miss Binchy returns with a calico suit carrier over her arm. She opens it, and pulls out a beautiful red satin coat with tiny embroidered green and purple flowers.

'Miss Binchy, it's so beautiful,' I exclaim, as she holds it against herself.

'It's hand embroidered, you know. But I never wore it,' she sighs.

'Why?' I ask gently.

'I thought he was about to propose,' she says quietly. 'I was giddy with excitement when I saw this jacket and a matching dress; I just adored it. I'd never seen anything so beautiful in all my life, so I bought it, for my going away outfit.' She sighs. 'I know I was foolish. I should have waited, not tempted fate, but all I could think of was his face filled with pride and love when I wore it, as *his* wife, to leave for our honeymoon. But he never asked.' Tears glisten in her eyes at the memories of yesteryear, which are more vivid to her now than those of yesterday. 'I wore the dress to work, it was too expensive to waste, but I never used the coat. Somehow it seemed too extravagant for the office.' She sniffs, pulling out her handkerchief from her sleeve. 'Listen to me sounding foolish. What a silly thing I am.' She dabs her eyes.

'No, you're not.' I place a comforting hand on her arm. 'You were in love.'

'Ay, well,' she shrugs, 'life moves on.' Miss Binchy holds the jacket towards me. 'I'd like you to have this now.'

'Miss Binchy, I couldn't,' I protest. 'It's too beautiful. It means too much to you.'

'It would mean more if you had it,' she says firmly. 'It deserves to be seen. Go on, dear. Wear it, and remember that things don't always turn out the way you expect.'

Chapter Fifteen

It is eight o'clock on Monday morning and I've been at my desk for almost an hour. A giant sheet of graph paper is spread out in front of me, beside a huge desk diary that shows the availability of Investigations-R-Us spooks for undercover work. I want to start watching the two contenders for head of human resources at Ilyax Insurance on Thursday morning, so that I have excuses to ring Carl regularly and update him on the situation. He rang my mobile last night, as I was practising sliding my long satin gloves seductively up and down my arms, and suggested dinner on Friday. I was more than a little disappointed that we couldn't meet earlier, but I realise he's a busy man and that this situation has caught us both by surprise. His evenings are probably planned months in advance. As for me? Well, obviously I'd cancel any evening at a moment's notice, although I did play the usual game of 'let me check my diary', as I flicked through the TV guide.

But I have to put Carl out of my mind this morning, which isn't easy – I keep getting those bursts of 'I can't believe I'm so happy' feelings – because I have to sort out two simultaneous surveillance operations, which is about as easy as getting British Rail trains to run on time. The two women live in completely different locations – North Finchley and Highbury – and I'll need about forty people for the operation. Three teams, comprising two cars and one motorcyclist, will be assigned to each subject on eight-hour shifts to provide round-the-clock surveillance, plus weekend and sickness cover. I spend the next hour working out different permutations for each team, and am completely engrossed when a cup of coffee is placed in front of me.

'Thought you could do with this,' I look up. James is dressed casually in navy jeans, a thin grey woollen sweater over a white tee-shirt, and Timberland boots.

'Cheers,' I say, lifting the plastic lid off the cup and blowing gently at the steaming liquid. 'Are you going out on a job?'

'Just back. I was out on the early shift this morning, but I was pinged.' Poor James. Pinging is every undercover agent's nightmare. It means the target either spotted James or made contact with him. 'I followed him into a greasy spoon café, where he was obviously meeting somebody, but I'd hardly sat down at a table when he walked over and asked to borrow my bowl of sugar. I just walked out,' he sighs. 'Minus the cooked breakfast that I'd just ordered. I hope my replacement enjoyed it.'

'Well, I'm pleased that you're free,' I say. 'I might need you later on this week. I'm putting together a huge surveillance operation, and it's all hands on deck. Maybe we could team up together? I'd appreciate some guidance, this is my first big operation after all.' James nods amiably. 'God, I'm stiff,' I say, standing up from my desk and stretching my limbs.

'Nice outfit,' remarks James, slowly looking me up and down. 'Is it new?' I'm wearing the first combination from my capsule wardrobe. Smart black trousers teamed with a pale pink satin shirt and long black cardigan. Casual yet elegant was how Pete described the outfit when he selected it on Saturday. 'And, I'm meant to be observant, but I've only just noticed the new hairdo. It's nice. Suits you.' He nods in approval as my cheeks burn with embarrassment. 'Anyway,' James looks down at the graph paper, 'what sort of a job is this? Two candidates? I thought you were checking out that potential finance director at Ilyax Insurance? Didn't you have a meeting with the boss on Friday? How did you get on?'

I didn't get on, I think, I got under. I feel my cheeks burn even brighter. My heart starts fluttering. Stop it, I tell myself. Calm down.

'Fine,' I eventually say, trying to sound nonchalant. 'He was very pleased with my findings.'

'So, you're now organising a surveillance operation just to be sure?'

'Not exactly,' I hesitate. 'Carl Lawson didn't think it was necessary.'

'Not necessary?' echoes James. 'That's strange. Most companies insist on surveillance to verify all the information from the background checks.'

'What can I say?' I reply breezily. 'I'm very thorough.'

'I'm not doubting that for a moment, but you've got to admit it's unusual.' I shrug nonchalantly. 'So, what's this job then? I didn't think we had any other new operations on the go.'

'Ilyax has another surveillance job they want done.'

'Which is?' James looks interested.

'They've got a vacancy for the head of human resources, and apparently two internal candidates are ideal for the post, so we've been hired to check them out.'

'Head of human resources?' James appears confused.

'Yes, personnel and all that.'

'I know what it is,' he replies. 'I've just never heard of any company putting so much time and money into picking one. Does this boss at Ilyax ... what's his name again?'

'Carl. Carl Lawson,' I say, trying to sound casual.

'Does this Carl Lawson know how much this will cost?'

'Obviously. I've explained it all to him.'

James shakes his head. Carl's request may be unusual, but the man is running a major company and he must know what he's doing. And, as long as he pays Investigations-R-Us's bills, then James shouldn't really worry. I know he's been doing this line of work much longer than me and I value his advice, but right now I just want him to butt out.

'I'm sure you have, but it's just not standard practice. So does Carl Lawson want you to do background checks on the candidates too?'

'No,' I admit. 'He doesn't think that's necessary. They're already employees so he's familiar with them.'

'That's unusual,' James shakes his head in bemusement. 'Who is this?' He lifts a photograph from the file open on my desk.

'Tracy Bruce,' I smile. 'And this,' I pass him a second photo, 'is Alice Kelly. These are the people I have to watch.'

'Bloody hell, either of these could be on the cover of *Vogue*.' James looks impressed. 'Well, you can definitely count me in for surveillance on this one,' he taps Tracy Bruce's photo, 'she's gorgeous.'

'Just your type, eh?' I tease.

James looks at the blonde beauty and shakes his head.

'Nah, if I'm honest she's a bit too perfect for me, but, hey, I've got no problems getting paid overtime to stare at her. But why do both simultaneously?' He lifts up the CVs of the women, and starts reading. 'Wouldn't it be better to do the preferred candidate first, and then see how that pans out?'

'My impression is that the company can't make their mind up,' I soothe.

'Still strange,' he mutters. 'Tracy Bruce sounds fun though. Her hobbies are flamenco and *pole* dancing.' He raises an eyebrow suggestively.

'It's the latest rage for keeping fit. Sadie Frost has a pole in her bedroom apparently.'

'You serious? How come I never meet girls like that? So when does the surveillance kick off?'

'I'm hoping for Thursday.'

'Okay, count me in, but do me a favour. Ring the client and give him an approximate estimate of the cost. I don't want him ringing to complain when the bill arrives. This is going to make some dent in his budget.'

Four hours later and I'm finished. I have planned the operation for the next two weeks. I've booked the cars and bikes from the motor pool and called all the agents. I've got the perfect excuse to call Carl now. It's silly, I know, we're 'going out' but it's early days, and I'm still not quite sure when it's okay to ring. But this is business, not pleasure. I ring his mobile.

'Hello.' He's terse..

'Carl, it's Holly.'

'Holly, hi.' His voice immediately softens. 'I was just thinking of you.'

'You were?' I feel an excited buzz.

'Yes,' he replies. 'I was just wondering what you were doing, if you were having a nice day, what you had for lunch, if you have had lunch. I just can't get you out of my mind.'

'Really,' I say softly.

'Really,' he replies firmly. 'So what have you been up to? Anything I should be jealous about?'

I giggle. 'Not that I can think of,' I reply, 'although I did lust at a picture of George Clooney in the newspaper on the tube.'

'Clooney's a has-been.'

'Really?' I laugh.

'Yeah, anyway those Hollywood types are so shallow and fickle. You're far better off with a staid businessman. You know where you are with them. Exactly where you are.'

'Is that so?'

'It is,' he says softly. 'So it's just as well that you've just met one who is very keen and interested, particularly in your day-to-day activities. Like today.'

'I've been sorting out the surveillance.'

'Great,' Carl sounds excited at the news. 'When can you start?'

'I'm aiming for Thursday, but it's going to cost ...' I quote a horrendous figure at him and wait for the uproar.

'No problem, babe, just carry on, I know you're not going to rip the company off,' he says. 'Look, got to jump, the other line's going. I'll call.' He hangs up.

CHAPTER SIXTEEN

It is six o'clock in the morning and I am sitting in a car with James outside Tracy Bruce's Victorian house in Highbury. Our back-up car is parked about two hundred metres down the road, and a surveillance officer on a motorbike is even further away. Angus, Donna and their back-up team are currently parked outside Alice Kelly's house in North Finchley. It is raining. Hail ricochets off our windscreen, but the wipers remain turned off. We can't risk the Neighbourhood Watch brigade spotting two strangers sitting in a car for hours on end. I am just passing James a mug of hot coffee from the flask I made at some ungodly hour when a light goes on in Tracy Bruce's upstairs room.

'Flamingo is awake,' I whisper into my walkie-talkie, alerting my team. 'Be prepared.' Slowly the terraced house comes to life. The landing lights up, then the stairs, and soon there's a dim glow through the green glass panels of Tracy Bruce's front door. 'Flamingo is downstairs,' I inform my team, logging the movement on my day planner. 'Probably the kitchen.'

Within an hour the street where Tracy lives has become a blaze of lights and activity. Her next-door neighbour leaves to walk a charcoal-grey Great Dane that could give any horse a run in the Grand National. Both look unhappy at the pounding rain. Other front doors open and their inhabitants face the inclement weather with their dogs; the postman, wearing waterproofs, pushes his red trolley along and drops several items through Tracy's letter box. I note all the activities and their timings. My mobile buzzes, disturbing the silence. I'm thrilled to see it's a text from Carl wishing me good morning. He's got into the habit of sending one every morning, and a good night text in the evening. It's comforting to know that I'm the first thing he thinks about in the morning and the last thing at night.

James glances over, and finally says:

'Do you come here often?'

I laugh. 'Is that your winning chat-up line?'

'That, and "do you believe in love at first sight, or shall I walk past again?"'

'Works every time, huh?'

'Makes me irresistible to women, and sometimes even men,' he smiles at me. 'So, what's the worst pickup line you've ever heard?'

'Hey, according to Donna, my whole life has been one bad pickup, but I think the worst line was when I met that plumber, Alan, and he told me that if I was going to regret anything in the morning, then we should stay in bed until the afternoon.'

'And did you?' he laughs.

'Yes, and yes! But don't tell Donna.'

'Hey, she's young and insecure. I think she's used to being the prettiest girl in the room, and isn't able to cope when she's not,' says James. I almost choke on my coffee. 'She's just trying to make herself feel better but, in her own way, I think she really likes you. Honestly, she and Angus are always talking about how nice it would be to see you settled.'

'Yeah, on the other side of the world,' I joke, trying to lighten the atmosphere. I'm feeling slightly uncomfortable at this conversation. 'The only reason Donna wants me settled is to be certain there's one less woman competing for the men out there,' I laugh. 'And I haven't a clue why she sees me as a threat.'

'I do,' says James quietly.

'Anyway, perhaps she won't have to worry about me soon,' I reply quickly, without thinking.

'Really?' James looks interested. Shit! I couldn't help myself. It was a knee-jerk reaction, but I am so excited about my date with Carl Lawson that I want the world to know about it. I know I can't say anything, especially to James. He would be appalled at the breach of company rules. Luckily I'm saved from answering when the front door opens. 'Is Flamingo married?' asks James.

'Not according to her CV.'

A man is leaving her house. Tracy Bruce is standing in her dressing gown on the front step, kissing him good-bye. I wipe my window, clearing some of the mist, to get a better look and take a few photos. Twenty minutes later the door opens and Tracy emerges. She is dressed in a bright red tracksuit with a rucksack on her back.

'Is she serious?' I look at the pounding rain in horror. 'Please don't tell me that she's going for a jog, and that I have to follow her.'

'I won't tell you but you know,' grins James.

'But I'm not dressed for it,' I protest. 'I haven't got any trainers.'

Tracy is stretching out in her pathway.

'You haven't got much time,' says James, as he obligingly leans across me and opens the door. 'Just make the most of it.'

'Can't we just track her in the car?' I try to pull the door back, but James is stronger.

'We'll stand out like a sore thumb. We'll start holding up traffic. Take your walkie-talkie to keep me informed, and I'll see you back here in ...' He looks over at Tracy, who is jogging on the spot. 'How long do you think a woman like that runs for? Five miles? Come to think of it, judging from her backpack, I'd say she's running to work.'

'Bastard!'

'I prefer loveable rogue, now go,' he nudges me out of the car. 'Flamingo is on the move.'

I reluctantly get out of the car. Luckily I am wearing waterproofs but my Timberland boots are not meant for running.

I glance back at James, but he just pulls the door shut. It is at times like this that I wish, once again, that I had gone on one of Boris's fitness refresher courses.

Just over an hour later and Tracy Bruce is showing her security pass at the turnstile entrance to Ilyax Insurance's magnificent art deco hallway. I watch her from outside as she enters a lift. I am freezing. My legs are aching, a stitch pounds at my side, my hair is dripping and my jeans are soaked through. I am the human equivalent of a drowned cat and about to collapse in an exhausted heap on the kerb when a car pulls up beside me, and James shouts across.

'How much for a quick one, love?'

'I am going to organise a slow and painful death for you,' I snap.

'Don't be like that,' he flicks open the door. 'Sarcasm is such an unattractive feature in young women, don't you think?' I note that he has thoughtfully covered the passenger seat with a plastic bag, to prevent any damp marks. 'So how's your day been?'

'Don't push your luck,' I mutter, grabbing the flask of coffee in my glove compartment and pushing the heating on full blast.

'Oh, me? I'm having a great time, thanks for asking, although traffic was murder getting here. Still, at least I had Terry Wogan's dulcet tones to keep me company. It stops the old road rage.' He looks at me and smiles. 'You look awful.'

'Thanks,' I reply sarcastically.

'That new hairstyle is definitely not waterproof.'

'I'm warning you.' My feet and legs are starting to painfully thaw.

'Well, we can't sit here chatting all day,' he continues. 'We're on a double yellow line in the middle of the most security-conscious mile in the country. It's a no go. And you'll catch your death of cold sitting in those wet things. I'm going to call in one of the agents from the back-up team to sit in that coffee bar over there and keep an eye on things.' He motions to a Starbucks on the opposite side of the street. 'This is the only entrance, so they'll see her if she leaves. And I'll swap with the back-up vehicle, take this vehicle back to base, exchange it for a black cab and come back.' A black cab can sit outside a building in the City all day long. The traffic wardens will leave it alone, and a security guard will just think it's waiting for some banker caught up in an important meeting.

'Look.' James indicates a figure approaching Ilyax Insurance. 'Isn't that Alice Kelly? I recognise her from the photograph.' A tall blonde woman in a trench mac stands in the doorway, pulls down her umbrella and shakes off the excess water before she enters the lobby. 'And she wins the prize for thoughtful employee of the year,' he laughs. 'Look, there's Angus following her on foot.' He passes by our car and, like a true professional, gives no hint of recognition. 'You're not the only one to suffer.'

'If you carry on like this I definitely won't be.'

'And there was I, Sir Galahad, about to offer you a lift home. Or even a shot of hot toddy.' He holds up a silver hip flask. I grab at it. 'Manners, Holly! Say *please*.'

'Please,' I say sarcastically. He hands over the flask. The liquid burns through my body. 'Take me home, Chivers,' I giggle.

'I thought you'd never ask.'

CHAPTER SEVENTEEN

Today James and I are in front of Alice Kelly's house, while Angus and Donna replace us in front of Tracy Bruce's house. I am studying the notes from the other shifts. Nothing very exciting appeared to happen in Tracy Bruce's life yesterday after I signed off. She left work at six, stopped at the local Corney & Barrow wine bar where she met an unidentified female friend and had two large glasses of pinot grigio. It would have been cheaper to get the bottle, I reflect. Tracy then caught the bus home where, judging by the lights from the front room, the agents assumed she spent the evening in front of the telly. Alice Kelly had a similarly dull day. It reached a pinnacle with a lunchtime kickboxing session, which unfortunately Donna wasn't prepared for. Last night I sent a memo to all agents on this job that, in future, at least one person on each shift must be wearing sports gear. It just won't be me.

Alice Kelly lives in a modern development of townhouses in North Finchley, just moments away from the bustling High Road where the old stalwarts of urban high streets vie for space against the new titans – the coffee shops. The baristas at Caffe Nero obviously rise earlier than Alice, because, while James and I drink steaming espressos, her house is still in darkness. It is seven-thirty and if she doesn't get up soon, she'll be cutting it fine to get to work on time. That's the trouble with surveillance, you want to go in and sort out the subject's life. The temptation to offer her a lift to the station when she dashes out the front door will be intense.

Actually, it would be ideal if we could offer Alice Kelly a lift to Ilyax Insurance, because at least then I wouldn't have to dash after her and hope that I manage to catch the same train. I've already been to the station and bought my ticket. So, after checking that Alice Kelly is not a regular jogger, I dressed as a City worker – complete with briefcase, high heels and a copy of the *Financial Times*.

The development where Alice Kelly lives is only half completed. Several houses at the far end of her road are still empty shells, lacking windows and doors. A concrete mixer stands in a muddy yard, a portable loo occupies the street corner. Building sites are useful camouflage. Cars and trucks constantly arrive, and nobody blinks an eye. It means James can keep the engine running, and we can sit in the car with the heating at full blast and Johnny Vaughan prattling on Capital Radio.

'I never thought I'd be able to say that I woke up with Holly Parker two days running,' James finally says, draining his espresso.

'I think that's technically incorrect,' I point out. 'We actually woke up separately.'

'Believe me, I'm not awake until I've had my first shot of caffeine, so I stand by my assessment. Good morning.'

'Good morning,' I reply, 'and you're lucky then. Most men don't usually get this far so early on.'

'It must be my magnetic personality,' he grins, tossing his empty espresso cup onto the back seat.

'Stylish,' I glance at the litter gathering there. 'You can take the man out of the zoo, but ...'

'Uh oh,' interrupts James. 'The lights are turning on; it's all systems go.' I alert the other members of the team that 'Swan' is up and about. 'I don't get what this client wants,' he adds, as Alice pulls back her bedroom curtains. 'We do surveillance for big ticket jobs, to make sure there's no skeleton that the candidate could get blackmailed over, not for a personnel boss. I bet all these women will do for the next few weeks is get up, go to work, possibly jogging.' He gives me a smile. 'They might pop to the gym at lunchtime, and stop off once or twice to meet a friend on their way home. Okay, so maybe this weekend they'll let their hair down, go clubbing or drink too much, but that's hardly a crime. As far as I can see, both these candidates lead pretty boring mundane lives, although we now know, and let's hold the front page here, that Alice Kelly oversleeps. But if they've been working for Ilyax for years then their colleagues would know most of their foibles and secrets. I think this exercise is a huge waste of money.'

'Look,' I admonish, indignant on behalf of Carl. 'It's not for us to question the client's logic. There is obviously some compelling reason that has made Ilyax Insurance opt for this surveillance and, anyway, I'm surprised at you. Aren't you always saying that first impressions can be deceptive? These women might appear nice and ordinary during the working week, but who's to say that they haven't got some horrendous secret. One of them might be having an affair.'

'That's not a crime.'

'But it might be embarrassing for Ilyax if it emerged that its new personnel boss was having it off with somebody inappropriate.'

'Embarrassing, possibly, but it's hardly going to knock the share price, is it? And the share price is generally the only thing that these big companies worry about. A senior director having an affair is barely going to register on the Richter scale. They happen all the time,' reasons James.

'Have you never heard that the customer is always right?'

'Apart from when he's wrong,' he counters.

'I'm sure he knows what he's doing!'

'But what is he trying to find out about these women?'

'He's trying to assess whether they are suitable for the job.'

'Then he should study their CVs, interview them and not waste company money on a futile task like this.'

'I will not have you challenging the client,' I snap. 'You wanted in on this surveillance, but if you now find it questionable then perhaps it is better that you step down.'

'Oh for God's sake,' retorts James. 'I'm only expressing a view. And don't tell me that yesterday, when you had to jog in the pouring rain, a little part of you didn't question why? I know I would.'

'The only question I asked myself was why my lousy colleague wouldn't act like a gentleman and insist on taking my place,' I bark.

'That "lousy" colleague was just following *our* pre-designated plan that *you* should follow the candidate.'

I bite back a reply. James is right. We had decided on our roles yesterday and I was just unlucky. And, if I'm truthful, he does have a point about the surveillance. These women don't seem important enough to warrant such attention. I was going to ask Carl about it yesterday but we didn't get the chance to chat. Besides my 'wake up' and 'good night' texts, I got three others but no phone calls. One text explained he was in meetings all day and unable to chat, but I was really disappointed.

'Uh oh! Swan is moving,' James nudges my knee. 'Come on. Shift out of the car. And, before you complain again, we did agree that you would also follow Swan.' Alice is pulling on her coat, as she emerges from the house.

'I know, I'm sorry.'

'Fine. Now let's get a move on.'

'She's obviously just going straight to the station. Couldn't you drop me there?' I plead.

'What, and miss Swan popping into the newsagents to buy some illicit cigarettes and chewing gum? I don't think so.' He grins. 'Hurry. She's walking quite fast. Almost jogging pace, I'd say.' I open the car door and stick out my tongue at my colleague. 'That's a very sexy look to go with your new hairstyle. Now move.'

'Remind me again, why you can't do the legwork?'

'How would I cope if she popped into the ladies on the way? I'm an innocent fellow.' I get out of the car. See you outside Ilyax Insurance,' James says. 'I'll have a coffee waiting!'

CHAPTER EIGHTEEN

I am sitting on a purple velvet chaise longue in the bar of Pierre's, a restaurant tucked behind Islington's bustling high street, waiting for Carl to arrive. He finally rang at five to say that he had booked a table here, only ten minutes from my flat, which he assumed would be convenient for me. Convenient for both of us, I thought wryly. My stomach is filled with fluttering butterflies. Carl is ten minutes late. I was disappointed that he wasn't waiting for me when I arrived. It meant that the waiter, Marc, was the only one to benefit from the seductive peeling off of the long satin gloves. But I could tell he was impressed. My glass of champagne came with a complimentary bowl of nuts.

The waiter tried to take my coat, the one Miss Binchy gave me, but I demurred. (I want *some* peeling to go on, or is it off, in front of Carl.) It's funny but this outfit makes me feel so graceful. My back is perfectly straight, and my legs are tucked neatly to one side. It's just how Bree sits in *Desperate Housewives*. Audrey Hepburn would be so proud. As would Pete and Angus.

It's been a bit of a mad day. Alice Kelly's train journey took forever. The tube got stuck in a tunnel for twenty minutes, forcing me to read my two-day-old copy of the *Financial Times*, where I spotted a small article about Ilyax Insurance, claiming that the search for a new finance director is no closer to ending. Journalists, I think smugly, what do they know? I followed Alice on foot to Ilyax, where I caught up with James.

I then popped across to Starbucks, while James stayed with his car until Investigations-R-Us's 'black cab' arrived.

Unfortunately a black cab in Knightsbridge can be a rare sight, so when it swept out of Investigations-R-Us's garage doors, five Japanese tourists jumped in demanding to be taken to 'Hallads'. It took almost thirty minutes for the harassed driver, Will, an ex-SAS officer, to persuade them that the world-famous store was literally five minutes' walk away. He finally arrived, in one piece, two hours after he set off. I can't risk such delays again, so from next week I have decided that the 'black cab' will be parked outside Ilyax Insurance from nine every morning. It's just as well it's not a real one. I don't think the client could afford the waiting time.

Alice Kelly had a busy lunchtime. She must have popped into every food store down Bow Lane, picking up six organic lamb shanks, fresh vegetables and a selection of farmhouse cheeses, so I guess she's holding a dinner party this weekend. She then stopped off at The Thin Line for a glass of wine and a sandwich. I sat at the next table pretending to read the *Daily Telegraph*, but I couldn't really concentrate. I was too excited at the prospect of seeing Carl. I just wanted my shift to end, which it finally did just after two, so that I could dash to the hairdresser and start the preparations. I decided on a chignon for tonight; it just feels appropriate for the outfit. Miss Binchy certainly thought so when I popped in on my way out to show her how the coat looked. There were tears glistening in her eyes as she muttered that I looked just as she had once imagined how she herself would. I gave her a 'wish me luck' hug and promised to fill her in on all – well, nearly all – the details.

But that wasn't my only preparation for this evening. Last night I thought carefully about how to behave on this date. I made a list of pointers, which I jotted down on Post-it notes that are now stuck on the inside flap of my new clutch bag.

Tips for a perfect date
Compliment him

Be attentive

Do not make any wisecracks

Do not criticise

Ask about his work (but be careful not to turn this into a business dinner)

Avoid garlic, chilli, pepper sauce, spinach (can get caught in teeth), and smelly cheeses

Avoid excessive alcohol

The last point came from Louise. Personally, I always think dates go just that little better when both parties have consumed a bit too much alcohol. It somehow relieves the initial tension. But she is adamant that, while men find a tipsy woman amusing, they don't want to spend the rest of their lives with her. Indeed, she says that Sam insists that a drunken woman is a big turn-off. I listen to her advice with a wry smile. It's amusing how Louise and Sam re-invented themselves and their history once they became a perfect married couple. They obviously can't remember the students who guzzled Babycham and Snake Bite, whose favourite games involved drinking, and who spent the day after their second date tending each other's hangovers.

Still, her comments have made me a little wary. I am sipping my champagne *very* slowly at the bar when Carl walks in. He takes a moment to spot me, which gives me a chance to look him over carefully. Hmm, he's definitely got something. Today he's wearing a charcoal grey suit, pink shirt and tie. The outfit isn't exceptional – it's a typical choice of any successful businessman, expensive and well cut – but it's the way he wears it. The clothes hang well on his lean yet somehow muscular frame. He moves effortlessly, almost gliding towards me, and as he gets closer, the smile on his face widens. Sitting on my bar stool, we are exactly the same height.

'Holly.' He throws his arms around me in a huge embrace. 'Have I been looking forward to this evening?'

'Have you?' I ask quietly.

'What do you think?' His eyes twinkle at me. 'I can't tell

you how many meetings I've sat in this week where I've just ended up daydreaming about you.' He laughs. 'Hey, we could have sold the company three times over and I wouldn't even have noticed.' A pause. 'Wouldn't even have cared,' he adds in a softer voice.

I can hardly breathe. This is heady stuff. None of my boy-friends in recent years has said anything quite so romantic.

'Can I show you to your table?' Our waiter Marc hovers by our side. Carl nods and helps me down from my stool. His hand gives my arm a comforting squeeze, and then he softly glides his hand, sending shivers down my spine, along my arm until he takes hold of my hand and we follow Marc down the few steps into the restaurant. (I pray that I don't trip up in my new stiletto sandals.) Carl watches appreciatively as Marc takes my coat and pulls the upholstered carver chair out for me.

'You look sensational,' he shakes his head in wonder. 'Absolutely stunning. Am I one lucky fellow.'

'Thank you,' I nod in gratitude. My long diamanté earrings jingle with the movement. Angus was right. Bling feels so right tonight. Carl reaches across to gently stroke my face.

'Beautiful,' he mutters. 'Absolutely beautiful. Do you have vintage Krug?' he asks Marc, who has been shuffling uncomfortably at this overt display of affection. 'We'd like a well-chilled bottle.' Marc disappears to fetch our order. 'We're celebrating,' Carl tells me.

'Celebrating? What are we celebrating?'

'This,' he motions towards the table. 'Our first date. Our first kiss. Our first ...' I blush but he doesn't finish the sentence. 'Meeting each other. There's so much to celebrate.'

Marc returns, pops open the bottle and fills our crystal flutes.

'To us, Holly,' Carl says softly.

'To us,' I repeat.

We clink glasses as I pray that I never wake up from this dream.

'Hmm, that's good, although I prefer the '76 myself,' Carl

says, placing his glass down on the table, and covering my hand with his. His thumb gently caresses me.

'So, tell me, I've been wondering about this, how did a nice girl like you get into this line of work? It's not usually what the career officers recommend.'

'True,' I nod. 'I knew someone at university on an Army scholarship who used to do a bit of undercover work to make extra money. He helped out a friend who owned a corporate investigations business, and I thought it sounded really cool. I'd always been fascinated by the world of spies. Who doesn't dream of being a Bond girl?'

'Me.'

'Sorry?'

'I wanted to be 007.'

'Ah, right,' I laugh. 'Well, maybe after Daniel Craig! Anyway, this friend needed someone to pose as his wife for one under-cover job and I begged for the chance. We spent a weekend in a five star hotel observing the target, and I got the bug.'

'What about the friend?'

'We lost touch. Last I heard he'd been posted overseas.'

'I suppose, in your line of work, you could find out what that friend was doing now if you wanted.'

'If I wanted, probably,' I concede, sipping my champagne. 'But I'm not really that bothered.'

'But I thought you could find out about absolutely anybody. Hey,' he laughs. 'I *hope* you haven't been investigating me.'

'Why? Are there some nasty skeletons lurking in your closet?' I'm joking, but for a split second I swear Carl Lawson looks uneasy, then the moment passes and I'm not so sure. He holds his hands up in mock surrender just as Marc arrives to take our order. Mindful of my 'tips for successful dates' list, I opt for smoked salmon to start, followed by broad bean risotto. They seem to be the least troublesome dishes on the menu. But I pass on the rocket salad. Stuffing green leaves into my mouth will not be a pretty sight.

'What you see is what you get.' Carl throws his hands open.

Believe me, I think, I want to get it.

'This is going to sound totally contradictory, considering tonight and all that, but I don't really like to mix business with pleasure,' I say. 'It's fraught with enough difficulties checking people out for professional purposes. Just imagine if I started checking out all my friends for fun. I'd never be able to look anybody in the eye again without thinking about his or her credit card debts or secret fetishes or scandals. It'd be a nightmare. Nope, I prefer to find out about my friends the old-fashioned way, by talking to them and allowing them to keep their little secrets.'

'What do you want to know about me?' He smiles. 'I'll even share my secrets. I could tell you all about my clandestine love affair with the sexiest business associate ever to walk into my office.'

'How did it turn out?' I tease.

'I'll let you know, but I'm betting on a happy ending.'

'I'm a sucker for those.'

'Well, I wouldn't like to disappoint.'

'You're not,' I say quietly.

'So I suppose you've read all the newspaper profiles about me?'

'A few,' I lie.

'The ones that drone on about how I married my childhood sweetheart, had three children and am now separated. Blah, blah, blah.' I blush, as that *was* the part I was most interested in. 'We grew apart,' he continues. 'We started off together with similar interests, but our lives took different paths.' He places his hands side by side on the table, keeps them locked as he moves them across the table and then suddenly separates them. 'Just like that.' He sighs sadly. 'I never thought I would become another statistic.' I rest my hand on his arm. 'It's hard sometimes.'

The moment is broken when Marc lays the starters before us. Carl has opted for foie gras with apricot relish.

'Are you still friends?' I ask.

'We try for the sake of the children, it's not their fault that mummy and daddy are no longer in love. But basically she lives her life, which includes dating, and I live mine which until now did not include dating.' He smiles at me.

'But no divorce?' I'm probing, but try not to sound too nosy or desperate – rather, genuinely interested and concerned. Which I am, obviously, but selfishly I also want to hear that his wife is out of his life and I am not some rebound fling.

'Well, the papers have been served, but we're just sorting out the financial settlement. It is never as easy as people think.' Carl seems reluctant to discuss the matter further, so I drop it. There will be another time, I'm sure. 'And what about you? This is going to sound like a cliché,' he beams, 'but why hasn't some young man snapped you up?'

'Life's eternal mystery.'

'It is to me,' he says softly. 'So what have you got planned for the weekend?'

This is a tricky question. If I sound really busy then he might take it as a reason not to see me, but if I have nothing planned I might exude an air of desperation as in, 'I've kept the weekend free, changed the sheets, waxed my legs and collected a pile of takeaway menus so we don't even have to leave the flat'.

'I'm meant to be seeing my mum for Sunday lunch,' I finally admit. It's our regular get together, when I tell her about my romantic adventures and she lectures me on how men just can't be trusted. Such fun times we share.

'What about your father?'

'Not around,' I say firmly.

'Oh?' He raises his eyebrows quizzically.

'He left when I was six, and I haven't seen him since. Fathers didn't go to court then or dress up as Batman and scale Buckingham Palace for the right to see their children. Mum kept refusing him access and, after a while, he just gave up. I don't know where he is. He could be sitting in this restaurant now for all I know.' I scan the faces of the other diners. 'Mum did the bitter cheated wife thing, cutting his face out of the family pictures and dumping the rest. I don't blame her, but

I can't remember what he looked like. I don't even know if I take after him. Sometimes I wonder if I've walked past him on the street.' Not that I really care, I think. The man has given up all parental rights. I'm not sure if I could even be polite if we ever met.

'I'm sorry.' Carl links his little finger through mine. 'It must be very hard for you. I'm lucky that my parents had a long and happy marriage. I can't imagine how you must have felt. That's why I worry about my children and how they are coping with the break up of my marriage.'

'We're more resilient than you think,' I say quietly. 'And besides, at least you are still in their lives. You haven't abandoned them.'

'I couldn't,' he says in horror.

'I know. And I couldn't be in a relationship with anybody who could.' I smile at him. This man, I think, loves his children desperately and is prepared to do anything for them. I hope they appreciate how lucky they are.

'Are you okay?' he asks tenderly. Carl seems to sense my sadness.

'I'm fine,' I say. 'It's such a long time ago. What you never had and all that ... what about you? What have you got planned for the weekend?'

It's the killer question.

'I've got my children staying.'

I feel a momentary pang of disappointment, but catch myself. His children need him at this difficult time, they need to know that daddy still loves them. All I need to know is whether it is possible that daddy could love me too. It is not a question that will be answered overnight.

'That'll be nice for them.'

'Yeah, sorry love,' Carl pulls a disappointed face. 'I didn't like to say sooner and ruin the evening, but my driver is arriving in an hour or so to take me back to Kent so that I'm there when the children wake up.'

'To the family home?' I'm surprised and a little uneasy, but it's too soon in our relationship to ask difficult questions.

'My wife, Gloria, moves out to her parents' house when I stay.' He senses my confusion. 'It's just better for the boys if they have some stability. Hey babe, we've still got an hour,' his eyes twinkle, 'maybe two if I delay my driver, and it'd be such a shame to waste them. What would you think if I suggested skipping the main course and getting the bill?'

'My appetite has suddenly disappeared,' I say seductively, as I lean across to kiss Carl on the lips.

'Well, mine is just starting to waken,' he replies, as he leans forward to respond.

CHAPTER NINETEEN

Staying well groomed, I now realise, is an ongoing process. Lipstick has to be re-applied every few hours, especially if you wear liner. Hair cannot just be brushed once in the morning. It needs to be brushed, gently lacquered and then spruced up at least twice during the day. Even perfume needs to be sprayed a couple of times over the working day. I quite enjoy the admiring stares my new look is getting, but I can't help feeling a bit irritated with cosmetics manufacturers. If I bought gloss paint that on the pot claimed to be long lasting and it chipped within a week I'd be mighty peeved, but apparently that is quite acceptable for nail polish. So, I'm currently sitting on a chrome stool with my hands resting flat under a hot plate waiting for a new coat of polish to dry. My mobile phone has vibrated several times alerting me to text messages, but I'm trapped. The manicurist comes over as the mobile shakes for the sixth time.

'Someone's popular,' she says, gently touching my scarlet talons. Pete may think French manicures are stylish, but I think red varnish is much sexier. I smile. Since I saw him (and boy, did I see him!) on Friday night, Carl Lawson has become a text-pest. Not that I'm complaining. It makes me feel warm inside knowing that, even though he is spending the weekend with his children, Carl is still thinking of me. Yesterday he rang or texted me eight times. 'I think you're done,' she smiles. 'Shall I help you put your jacket on? And remember, be extremely gentle for the next hour or so. No rough games.'

Chance would be a fine thing, I think.

I gently press the mobile's buttons, careful to avoid touching my nail polish.

9.50
From: Carl (moby)
Am tkg kids to local farm to c the animals. May b out of range for a while. X

10.20
From: Carl (moby)
Range ok here. Kids running after sheep. Thinking of u. X

10.35
From: Carl (moby)
Btw, did I tell u how much I enjoyed Friday? X

Several times, I think, but I'm not complaining.

10.40
From: Carl (moby)
It is beautiful here. I wish u could b here. XX

Me too, I think.

10.42
From: Carl (moby)
Am I sounding smitten? XXX

Yes, I think. It's a lovely sound.

10.50
From: Carl (moby)
Am trying not to appear 2 keen, but it's hard. I can't get u out of my mind. I miss u and hope u feel the same way. XXX

I do, I think. I definitely do. Excitedly I dial the number. My heart is pounding. I'm acting like a schoolgirl with a crush, but it feels lovely. I feel truly alive for the first time since Jake. I don't want to jinx the situation by even thinking it, but I really am falling for this guy. I'm not quite sure of the etiquette of calling. It is early days, after all, but I figure six text messages (and I haven't counted today's 'Good morning. X') give me the right. Blast. It's gone straight through to answerphone. I feel an irrational stab of extreme disappointment, and swallow hard to stop any tears welling up. I leave a breezy non-desperate sounding message and then, with heavy heart, go off to visit my mother for lunch.

Our Sunday lunches are a long-established ritual. Sometimes, when I lived with Louise, she would come along, but eventually she tired of the constant 'men are useless' rant from my mother. My father was the love of her life. She could never understand how women could get divorced and yet still believe in love. When Jennifer Aniston split with Brad Pitt, she was quoted saying she still believed there was somebody else walking around who could be the father of her children. My mother would never accept it wouldn't be Brad. She wouldn't be able to move on.

But my mother is a mass of contradictions. She will love my father until her dying day, while professing to hate him. She claims to no longer believe in love, but she truly thinks that there is one person in the world for each of us. But *only* one. One chance. No more. When Jake left me, when I sobbed on her shoulder that the man of my dreams had betrayed me, she said that was what men did. They had no integrity, she insisted. They just couldn't be trusted. And successful men were the worst. They thought rules only applied to other people, to the little people. She told me that I was now on the proverbial shelf. I had missed my one opportunity. And I thought she was right, because at that moment I could never imagine loving or wanting anybody as much as Jake. Until now.

My mother is a passionate woman. As this emotion is no longer directed towards men, it erupts in many forms. It has currently manifested itself in her love of line dancing and all things Western, which probably explains my severe reaction to Nat's outfit and his cowboy boots. I couldn't even tell Louise, but my mother and I were probably the only family in England to eat Tex-Mex turkey and Mississippi mud pie on Christmas Day. Not that Mum is much of a cook. They were straight from the freezer. She hung up her oven gloves when my father left, claiming it was a redundant skill. She had filled my father with cordon bleu meals, but it hadn't kept his heart faithful. Apart from my birth and graduation, the best day of Mum's life was when the microwave arrived. She and I can now zap for England.

So, while I would have liked to meet my mother at a charming country pub with thatched roof, we are actually meeting at 'Sally's Steak House – Yeehah!', a huge mock farmhouse with bales of hay piled up against the entrance, in Ruislip on the outskirts of west London, just a few miles from where I grew up. There's a life-size model of a cowboy standing at the doorway, a lasso in his hands framing the menu. The interior of the restaurant looks like the set of a Hollywood Western. Tractor parts and farm equipment hang from the ceiling, while sawdust and straw covers the wooden floorboards.

I'm shown to the table by 'Wayne' – 'it's actually Hans but the management said that wasn't in keeping with the image' – complete in Stetson and suede chaps. 'Your saloon girl for the evening is Calamity Jane, but don't worry. She won't drop anything in your lap,' he says, pushing open a pair of saloon doors to reveal a small alcove. Plastic bullhorns decorate the backs of carver chairs and a big oil lamp sits on the middle of the table, which is covered with a multi-coloured rug, like those thrown over the shoulders of swarthy Mexican cowboys in Clint Eastwood films.

My mother is already waiting for me. She is dressed in a white frilly shirt, with a bootlace tie fastened at the neck with a small silver stag's head, and a turquoise waistcoat trimmed with curved lines of red sequins. A sparkly red Stetson is hanging on her bullhorn.

'Holly,' she cries. 'It's so lovely to see you. I've ordered a pitcher of margaritas. Isn't this place wonderful.'

'This isn't quite what I imagined, Mum,' I say tactfully. 'It's not often you hear Dolly Parton singing while you eat.'

'I know, it's great, isn't it?'

Calamity Jane arrives to take our order. A twenty-pound note is sticking out of her cleavage. Mum orders barbecued spare ribs, and giggles as Calamity Jane ties a big plastic bib around her neck.

'Isn't this fun?' she giggles. I nod indulgently as Calamity places plates of complimentary nachos in front of us, with a dramatic 'yee hah!' We pass the time with pleasantries while 'Sitting Bull', resplendent in a massive feather headdress and ragged suedette trousers, serves our drinks, with a 'How!' and an alarming American Indian war cry.

'You look different, Hol. Have you done something to your hair?'

'I've gone for a restyle,' I say, shaking my head gently to emphasise how now my hair just bounces back into place.

'It's nice.' She chews on a bone. 'But there's something else.'

'I'm wearing make-up,' I giggle. 'Louise taught me how to put it on so that it blends in together, and people don't really know you're wearing it.'

'What's the point of that?' snaps my mother. I flush with embarrassment. My mother still applies make-up the way she did when my father left. Blue eye shadow spread along the lid, pencilled-in eyebrows, bright pink lipstick and a liberal application of Max Factor powder. She looks like the Bride of Estée Lauder or a news reporter for Channel WXKRJ in some Midwest American state.

'I don't know really,' I reply. 'It's just the fashion these days.'

'I haven't seen that outfit before,' she adds suspiciously.

'Right back at you.'

'Oh, this auld thing,' she says in her best Daisy-from-the-Dukes-of-Hazzard accent. 'I bought it for the Middlesex Line

Dancing Championships last week. My cha-cha-cha was unbeatable.'

'How did you do?' I ask.

'Second place.'

'That's great, Mum!' We clink tumblers, and watch as some of the salt on the rims flutters on to the table. 'Another trophy for the sideboard. You'll be running out of space soon. Maybe you should move the darts trophies into the cupboard?'

I am wearing a baby blue woollen sweater and jeans, with strings of mock pearls twisted around my neck. Last week Pete taught me how to 'make the most of my accessories'. He also ripped these old jeans at the knee to give me 'street cred'. 'I went shopping with Louise and Pete,' I say airily.

'You? Shopping?' Mum stares intently at me. 'You've met someone,' she accuses. A look of disapproval flashes across her features. 'I can see it in your face. You've got a glow ... don't tell me you're falling in love. Oh Holly, I hope you know what you've got yourself into,' she adds in a quieter voice.

'I ...' This is so strange. Most mothers would be delighted at such news. 'Look, it's early days, Mum. It's too soon to talk about love. But I definitely like him. Who knows what will happen?'

'I do.'

'No, you don't.' I'm angry that my mother's bitterness at my father prevents her from celebrating my news. What kind of a woman wants her only child to be permanently miserable, I think to myself. 'I'm happy. And I think this man, Carl, he could be the one.'

'Pah!'

'Mum, don't be like this,' I bite back. 'I want you to be pleased for me. I'm getting too old for the fling lifestyle; I want to settle down. Hell, Mum, Louise and Sam are trying to have a baby.' I shrug. 'Maybe I want one too. I want to take this chance, Mum. It might all go wrong, but I'll never know if I don't. Hey, who said "it's better to have loved and lost than never to have loved at all?"'

'A liar,' she retorts.

'Mum, I'm happy. I really like him, and he likes me.'

'Where did you meet?' she finally asks.

'Through work.'

'He's a colleague?'

'No,' I say carefully. 'It's difficult. He's my client.'

'So, he's some rich businessman?' My mother's voice sounds venomous.

'Yes.'

'Why does he want to go out with *you*?' She stabs her forefinger in my direction.

'Mum!' I say firmly. 'For once in your life, stop being a bitter, twisted woman and listen to yourself. Why wouldn't he want to go out with me? What's wrong with me? I'm a nice person and I'm getting just a bit fed up with everybody criticising me. Telling me my failings. Well, do you know what, Mum? You're not perfect. You've got many faults.'

'Don't you talk to me like that, young lady. I'm your mother,' she snaps back.

'That's right. My mother! You are meant to support me in everything I do, and yes I know that sometimes things may not go the way I want them to, but that's life, Mum. Life means taking chances.'

'Life means being miserable,' she screams.

I look at my mother, really look at her, and I see a sad middle-aged woman. She may have been dealt a duff hand years ago, but she has chosen to let that control her life ever since.

'I am not going to turn into you,' I say in a softer tone. 'I am not going to give up on life.'

'You're just like your father,' she says bitterly. I look at her in surprise. It is the first time she has ever likened me to him. 'He was stubborn, always on the look out for opportunities. He thought everyone was entitled to happiness. Pah!'

'People aren't born unhappy,' I say softly. 'It's not genetic. Mum, what Dad did to you was awful. Truly awful, but it's time to move on. I am not saying forget – just move on.'

My mother sighs. 'It's hard. Every time I look at you, I see

141

him. In your smile. In your eyes. You're my beautiful daughter, and you're my constant reminder.'

'I didn't know,' I reply. 'I'm sorry.'

'Don't be. You're my greatest achievement, I'm so proud of you, but I also think you're incredibly naïve.' She sees my puzzled face. 'Look at yourself. You've changed, wearing fancy new clothes and a glamorous hairstyle to win this man, and I bet he doesn't change one iota of his life for you.' She places her hands over mine. 'Men are different animals from us. They always have motives for their actions. I sincerely hope his are true because I really do want you to be happy.'

CHAPTER TWENTY

I am standing beside a white board, marker pen in hand, holding a meeting with the surveillance team members who aren't actually out on the job. Those working are linked in via satellite phone, although I have told them that their priority remains the subjects, Flamingo and Swan. It is Tuesday. We have almost finished a complete week of surveillance on the two subjects, and I want to recap everything we have found out about them to date. Tomorrow I am scheduled to meet Carl at four to discuss the findings, but I won't be able to go on for a drink with him as I'm then booked to team up with James on surveillance later that evening.

I haven't seen Carl since Friday night, although we've spoken on the phone several times. Much of the time we communicate by text which is not exactly ideal. Obviously, it makes me feel special knowing that he's in some super-important meeting (and he seems to attend a lot of them) and is surreptitiously texting me, with his mobile under the table like a naughty schoolboy. But texts never really tell you anything. It is hard to sense the tone of a message, or its mood. He has apologised many times by text for not calling more, but says it is difficult at work to get an uninterrupted moment to himself, what with endless meetings and a major business to run. I understand, truly I do, but it does get a bit frustrating.

So, I'm really looking forward to seeing him, but I also want him to be pleased with our work to date. I want him to be proud of his new girlfriend, and her professionalism.

About thirty of us are crammed into one of the meeting rooms at Investigations-R-Us. It is mostly used for planning overseas operations. Metallic bookcases line two walls. They are filled with reference books on obscure places in Eastern Europe and South America that I can barely pronounce, let alone recognise. I once tried to borrow a dictionary to help me when I holidayed in Portugal, but there wasn't one. If I had opted for Libya, Saudi Arabia, Tunisia, Afghanistan or some other popular war-torn hotspot then I'd have been in luck.

One wall is covered with maps; some are dog-eared and faded, but a large-scale map of Bogotá, the capital of Colombia, looks fresh. Coloured pins are dotted across it, and lime green arrow-shaped Post-it notes are centred on a main square. Flight numbers, hotel addresses and a series of phone numbers are jotted on the wall beneath. I vaguely remember my boss Boris talking about an overseas operation last week – I think a UK engineer had been kidnapped while on a business trip – but in this business it is best to forget almost everything you hear in the office. Somebody's life may depend on it.

I have drawn a big vertical black line to divide my white board in half, and have pasted blown-up mug shots of Tracy Bruce and Alice Kelly on either side. Underneath I have listed their personal details and as detailed a timetable of their lives over the past six days as we have been able to compile from our surveillance. There is also a selection of the photos taken over the past six days. It looks like a missing persons board from an American crime show.

'So, has anybody got any additional comments to make about Flamingo and Swan?' I ask the assembled crowd. 'Bert.' I smile at a middle-aged agent who was in charge of the week-end surveillance teams. 'I've read your reports, but I wonder if anything stuck in your mind?'

'Right you are, Holly,' Bert gets to his feet and nods at his colleagues in the room. He looks like an aging fifties matinee idol, while his lenses have the telltale line of bi-focal glasses. Today he is wearing a brushed cotton brown and green checked shirt, chocolate brown slacks and sensible, slightly scuffed leather brogues. A beige anorak hangs on the back of his chair. That's the trouble with this job. You can't ever just glance at somebody: you're trained to notice every single detail, which might just come in handy later on. Bert's third button on his shirt is unfastened. A wisp of grey hair pokes through the gap. 'Well, I was detailed to watch Flamingo, aka Tracy Bruce, for the daytime session, but was also acting head of both teams. Now you may have seen in the report that both targets received bouquets on Saturday morning, at roughly the same time.'

'Yes, I noticed that,' I reply with interest. 'Did we get the florists' names?'

'Poppy's Posies,' says Bert, checking a spiral bound note-book.

'It was the same florist for both?' I'm surprised.

'Yes,' Bert nods. 'I thought it was strange too, so I rang Poppy's Posies and posed, no pun intended there, Holly' – he wags his finger in delight at his unplanned humour – 'as the sender. I was checking that "my flowers" had arrived at Flamingo's house. The florist was very friendly and told me that both my bouquets had been delivered.'

'Both?' I am even more surprised. 'So the same person sent flowers to both of them.' How strange. The only connection between these two women is their place of employment. It must have been a colleague. But why would a colleague pursue two women? My mind races with the possibilities. I feel unnerved by this discovery.

'Yes,' nods Bert. 'It seems so. I tried the old trick of wanting to check that there had been no problems with my credit card, but the florist got a bit suspicious. I think the sender paid cash.'

'Which means he must have visited the florist,' pipes up James.

'That's my guess,' agrees Bert.

'And we've no idea who it was?' I ask.

'None at all.' My elderly colleague shakes his head in frus-tration.

'There's something else,' Mark, a former paratrooper stands up. I notice Donna checking out his tight jeans and clinging black lambs' wool jumper that reveals the distinct contours of his six-pack, and empty wedding finger. 'Alice Kelly, I mean Swan, refused to take delivery.'

'Maybe she's allergic to flowers,' suggests Angus.

'Maybe,' Mark says. 'But she had five friends round for dinner that night.' I was right about her trip to Bow Lane, I think. She was buying the ingredients for a dinner party. 'One arrived carrying a huge bouquet, and she didn't reject those.'

'Perhaps she didn't want to appear rude, and threw them out after the guest had gone?' James pipes up.

'Nah,' shrugs Mark. 'I did a recce of the bins after Swan went to bed, and the flowers weren't there.'

'I don't like the sound of this.' I jot the information on the board. 'It has to be a colleague sending these flowers. We haven't found any other external connection, have we? They aren't cousins or anything?' There is widespread shaking of heads. 'But why would she turn away flowers?'

'Doesn't like the sender?' suggests James.

'But Flamingo accepted them. If he or she were that awful, surely she would have declined as well.'

'Maybe she didn't realise who they were from,' he says. 'It could be her first bouquet. Perhaps Swan has received some before?'

'Maybe we should do a check on Poppy's Posies next Saturday, casually canvas the assistants. Something doesn't smell right here.'

'Let's hope it's not the flowers,' Bert jokes lamely.

'Keep me informed,' I order. 'Right, anything else?'

'I've found out who the man is that left Flamingo's house on Wednesday morning. He also spent Friday and Saturday night,' says James.

'Who is he?'

'Peter Porter. He works at Ilyax Insurance as an actuary. He's 36, joined the company in 2001 and lives in a modern

146

apartment block in Wimbledon. It seems like they've been dating for a few weeks, no more.'

'Well done, James.' I jot that detail on Tracy Bruce's side of the white board, under the heading: Boyfriend? 'Right, anything else?' Apart from a few coughs, the room is silent. 'Okay, that's it, folks. Same place next week. I'm on the evening shift this week, so page me if anything unusual comes up during the day.' A handful of team members nod at me. Then the room is filled with the sound of chairs scraping across the wooden floor and my teams depart, leaving an assortment of empty paper cups and water bottles in their wake. And a lustful Donna exchanging phone numbers with the walking Action Man, Mark.

CHAPTER TWENTY-ONE

As I shut the big red front door on my house, I realise that I haven't seen Miss Binchy for a few days. Obviously I filled her in on what a success her coat had proved to be on my date with Carl on Friday night, which really seemed to please her, but since then she has been remarkably elusive. It occurs to me that I actually miss the old girl, miss her friendly face popping around her door to coerce me into her flat for a nice cup of tea. The alternative is often only a night by myself in front of the TV, which reminds me. There's been a major advertising campaign playing during the *Coronation Street* break, telling people to keep an eye on elderly neighbours during this cold snap. I make a mental note to check on her later. I wish I could bump into her nephew Seamus to tell him of my concerns, but our paths never seem to collide.

Miss Binchy's absentmindedness does seem to be getting worse. She was out cleaning her front windows on Sunday morning in just her short sleeves. She had barely noticed the smattering of snow on the ground until I mentioned it, but she did accept my invitation to a warming cup of cocoa. It was nice to be the host for a change.

I am wrapped up warm in my torn jeans, polo neck and an old sheepskin jacket that Pete said is so *Starsky & Hutch* that it might just be cool. A gym bag is slung across my shoulder, just in case, and I am carrying another holdall filled with Thermos flasks of coffee, sandwiches and a portable DVD player. James is waiting outside in the car.

'Have you been here long?' I settle in the passenger seat.

'Not really,' he replies, 'I had some business in the neighbourhood.' I look at him curiously, but he doesn't elaborate.

We drive to Ilyax Insurance's headquarters to relieve the earlier shift. It is now quite dark which makes surveillance difficult. It is a problem with winter work. Bulky coats, long scarves, pashminas and woolly hats can make it hard to distinguish a target. We are watching for Flamingo, aka Tracy Bruce. Donna and Angus are parked behind us in an anonymous-looking blue Ford Mondeo waiting for Swan, Alice Kelly. Both targets usually leave work at about six-thirty.

'I thought the meeting earlier was useful,' says James.

'Thanks,' I smile. 'How did you spend your afternoon?'

'I went for a run around the park.'

'In this weather? You must be mad.'

'I'm in training for a charity run I promised to do,' he explains. 'What about you?'

I can't tell James that I spent a large chunk of the afternoon on the phone to our client, Carl Lawson. An important meeting was cancelled, which left him with unexpected time on his hands, and he seemed quite happy to gossip to me, which certainly beat doing my laundry. Just then my phone buzzes to signal a text message.

5.30pm
From: Carl (moby)
Hv just looked out of window on 8th floor & saw 2 cars parked at front of building. I guess u r in one of them. Hope so. Like 2 thnk u r close 2 me. XXX. PS Miss u.

Without thinking I look out of my car window, count eight floors and wonder which window Carl Lawson is standing by at this very moment looking out at the world. I feel a buzz of excitement knowing that there's this small, almost illicit, connection currently between us.

'Someone's popular,' observes James. 'That must be the

eighth text you've received today.' I glance across at him nervously, but he's still staring at the entrance.

'Uh oh,' he says. 'Flamingo is moving. She's leaving early.' I alert the team, and jump out of the car carrying my gym bag to move in behind Tracy Bruce. I wonder briefly if Carl has noticed me. Just then the Ford Mondeo's door springs open and Donna jumps out, clutching her sports bag. Alice Kelly is also emerging from Ilyax's entrance. She calls out to Flamingo, runs up and they link arms. Donna and I look at each other in surprise (although part of my reaction is at the ear muffs that Donna is wearing). It seems our targets are going somewhere together. Until now our surveillance hadn't revealed that they even knew each other. I feel a tingle of excitement at the discovery.

'Where are we going?' hisses Donna.

'Shh,' I warn. 'Please, don't talk to me. We mustn't do anything to jeopardise this operation.' I nod at their backpacks. 'But I think they're off to the gym together.'

'Great,' mutters Donna through gritted teeth. My colleague prefers to get her aerobic exercise in a quite different forum.

The two targets are walking at quite a pace, but traffic is gathering behind James and Angus as they tail us. I signal them to drive on. We will alert them on reaching our destination. Flamingo and Swan walk past Bank Station towards Moorgate, passing a mixture of elegant buildings that have stood on their sites for centuries and modern glass developments that house the world's leading financial institutions. The duo keep walking north towards Old Street roundabout. They continue on for about five minutes, before turning towards a pub down a small side street.

'That's not a gym.' Donna sounds relieved, before spotting the blackboard outside the entrance to the cellar bar of the Horse and Hounds. 'They're doing pole dancing lessons. I'm going to get paid to do this? Sometimes I love my job!'

Pole dancing! I alert James to our location, and we follow the targets down a wrought iron spiral staircase into a dark room containing a handful of women. Most are dressed in tight shorts, bandeau tops and high heels. A few have feather boas strung around their necks. I note that Tracy and Alice are nowhere to be seen and assume they're changing in the Ladies'. A couple of full-length mirrors have been wheeled into the room, and three poles are fixed from ceiling to floor. Kylie is 'Spinning Around' on the stereo.

A peroxide blonde adorned with three feather boas is dressed in matching leopard-print bra and knickers. She marches over in six-inch patent leather ankle boots. The muscle definition in her arms and thighs is worthy of Kelly Holmes. 'Hi, I'm Feather. I'll be your instructress tonight. Are you first timers?'

'God, no,' shrieks Donna. 'I can't remember the last time I was a first timer in anything.'

Feather smiles. 'If you'd like to get changed, we're starting in ten minutes. Unfortunately tracksuit bottoms and tights are not allowed. It's bare legs only or you just won't be able to grip the pole. High heels are optional but they do give you that extra strut, I always think.' She shakes her booty. 'Now, what names would you like to be called?'

'Sorry ...' I'm distracted. Tracy and Alice have re-entered the room and are chatting to each other. They're both wearing Lycra cycling shorts and tiny, cropped tops. Neither has an inch of flab on their stomachs.

'While there's no stripping at this session, we find it helps clients to relax and get into their part if they adopt a nom de plume,' gushes Feather. 'Hi Gemini, hi Aurora.' She waves at our targets. God, this is confusing. Now they've got two extra names each. 'Are you ready for the upside-down scissor kick tonight?' They nod.

'I'm Passion, and she's Honour,' Donna announces. 'I'll just go change.' She disappears off to the loos.

'I'm afraid I might have to sit this one out,' I tell Feather. 'I haven't brought the right kit.'

'Oh Honour,' Feather swishes a purple boa in my face startling me, 'you're very naughty. Well' – she sighs – 'It can't be helped. Watch and learn. I can tell Passion's going to be a natural. She's got the sort of body that contortionists pray for.'

My smile is frozen on my face. Feather is the most predatory woman I have ever met. God, Carl, I think to myself, I'm lobbing danger money onto the overtime bill. If I was working for anybody else, I would be out of here quicker than Feather can say Scissor Sisters.

Donna, aka Passion, emerges from the loo in gold lamé shorts, a skimpy halter-neck and strappy sandals. It is the perfect outfit for clubbing. My colleague doesn't go anywhere without such an option. I call her over and discreetly warn her not to talk to either target. We have already been pinged, because they have seen us, but we just can't leave (unfortunately) without making the situation worse. We still need to remain as anonymous as possible, although, after tonight, we won't be able to do any more legwork on this operation in case they spot us again. From tomorrow, Donna and I will swap places with Angus and James and take over the driving. Let them try pole dancing!

'Girls, girls, girls.' Feather claps her hands and the group gathers around. 'Let's start with some warm-up exercises.'

For the next half hour the class is put through an aerobic regime worthy of an army boot camp. There are lunges, press-ups, star jumps and squats. Even Donna abandons her heels halfway through.

'Give yourselves a round of applause,' Feather finally shouts, and gather round the poles. I'm going to show you a few gentle moves. This is the Walk Around.' Donna Summer's 'Love To Love You Baby' is booming through the speakers as Feather hooks her arm around the pole and, on tiptoes, walks slowly and sexily around it. Everybody giggles as they follow her lead. It is a simple move to gain their confidence. Then Feather places the pole between her legs and, staying on tiptoes, drops backwards towards the floor. A raft of laughter greets each girl's effort to copy her.. I note that Tracy can arch her back perfectly, and her hair sweeps the floor as she stretches backwards.

The music changes to Britney Spears' 'Toxic', then Feather jumps onto the pole, grips it between her legs and holds on with both hands. She lets one hand go, leans back, straightens her left leg and spins around the pole like a whirlwind. Feather urges 'Bambi', a red-haired lady in matching shorts and top, to try. Unfortunately, Bambi doesn't live up to her graceful name. She grabs the pole above her head, kicks her legs in the air ... and slides straight to the floor. 'Texas' 'Atlanta' and 'Georgia' suffer similar fates. Alice Kelly and Tracy Bruce simultaneously step forward, grab adjacent poles and do perfect pirouettes. They high-five each other when they land. They are obviously good friends, I note. Maybe I have got it wrong. Perhaps a mutual friend sent them flowers, not a colleague. But then again, why would Flamingo refuse them if a friend sent them? It's a puzzle.

'Now Passion, don't be shy,' says Feather, pushing Donna forward, but my colleague needs little encouragement. She steps forward, jumps onto the pole, leans back and does a perfect pirouette. 'Fantastic,' calls Feather. 'You're an absolute natural.' Then Donna jumps onto the pole, gripping it with both hands and kicks her legs up above her head. The force of the movement turns her body completely upside down and, in that position, she spins perfectly six times around the pole. Her legs stay rigid, circling the pole, like a pair of scissor heads. Feather claps her hands in delight. 'Fantastic technique,' she cries out, as Donna grips the pole between her legs, throws her arms out, spins again before cartwheeling into standing position.

I'm furious. I told her to blend in and not attract too much attention, but Donna can't help herself. Her behaviour is totally unprofessional. The other participants, including our surveillance targets Alice and Tracy, burst into applause. Feather twirls a cerise pink boa in the air in appreciation.

'Passion,' she cries, 'you're ready for the master class. Have you ever tried it with two poles?'

'Yes,' replies Donna blithely. 'But I didn't realise it at the time. I thought one of them was Hungarian.'

CHAPTER TWENTY-TWO

I am still angry when I meet Donna the day after her pole dancing antics. Last night Tracy (Flamingo) and Alice (Swan) made a beeline for Donna immediately after her Olga Korbut routine to ask for tips on the backflip. She was pinged more times than a ping-pong ball. Donna is now totally compromised and cannot be used on any more surveillance operations involving these targets. She even left the pub, chatting away to them like old friends, and, without thinking, walked up to the Ford Mondeo and offered them both lifts home which, luckily, they declined. To cap it all, I got home to discover that I'd missed three calls from Carl – two 'where are you, I miss you' messages on my mobile, and one on my answerphone. His voice sounded a bit sharp, but I expect he was just disappointed that I was out. I was certainly disappointed that I was. I did call back but his mobile was switched off. I guessed he'd already gone to bed.

'What were you thinking?' I demand. Angus, James, Donna and I are sitting in an Italian café just down the road from our office. We have ordered paninis and cappuccinos all round. 'I told you to blend into the background. I didn't expect you to audition for Spearmint Rhino.'

'You were that good?' asks James, his voice filled with obvious admiration.

Donna gives him a 'what do you think?' lift of her eyebrows.

'But where did you learn?' he continues.

'I've been in a lot of four poster-beds,' she sighs.

'Sweetheart, what did you wear?' Angus taps her forearm.

'You know that outfit I wore clubbing at G.A.Y. with you and Pete? When I danced in that cage hanging from the ceiling?'

'Sensational,' he exclaims, slapping his mouth with surprise. 'And you, Holly, what did you wear?'

'Me?' I snort. 'Am I the only one here who thinks that Donna overstepped the mark?' Stupid question, I think. I've got a straight guy imagining nipple tassels and whips, and a gay guy thinking of feather boas and sequinned mules. They've got the same stupid dreamy expression on their faces.

'Why didn't you have a go, Holly?' James finally asks. 'I'd have really liked to see that.' He winks at me.

'Look, I was trying not to stand out, not to engage with the targets, to behave like a professional.'

'Holly's right,' Donna says quietly, surprising us all. 'I was out of order. I just,' she shrugs, 'got carried away. It was just the music, the lights, the ... you know ...'

'Action,' claps Angus.

'Yeah. I guess I'm programmed to perform. I understand that I can't go on these operations again.'

'I can't take the chance that they will recognise you,' I reply. 'You did end up chatting to them for quite some time.'

'What did they talk about?' asks James. 'Even if we can't use you for surveillance, we can at least exploit all the gossip.'

'Nothing much,' replies Donna. 'They asked if I'd ever like to go for a drink. Swan gave me her card and said to call.' Now, I think, now she's acting professional and using the code names. 'Actually, I think Swan might be gay,' she adds.

'What makes you say that?' James is intrigued. Men, I think, they're all the same.

'Dunno, just a feeling I have. Can't quite put my finger on it. Tracy is going away soon for a week's winter sun with her boyfriend ' She turns to James. 'He's that guy you mentioned at yesterday's debriefing session.'

'Anything else?' I ask.

'No,' she thinks for a minute. 'Oh, there's some guy at work that they both think is pretty creepy. They wouldn't say who he was, but apparently lots of women feel the same.'

'Do you think he's the same guy who sent them flowers?' I quiz.

'I really don't know,' replies Donna, 'but it's an interesting theory.'

'It is, isn't it? I wonder who this creep is. They offered no clues?'

'Nothing that I can remember, but I *was* on an adrenalin high,' giggles Donna.

'Perhaps it is something we should look into,' suggests James.

'Perhaps, but it's not really relevant to our work. It is just a footnote as it is,' I reply.

James shrugs. 'Well, it's got my interest piqued,' he says. 'Don't rule it out. It might be important.'

'Let's just stick to the plot, shall we?' I snap, irritated that he's challenging my authority. 'I'm getting another cappuccino before my meeting with Ilyax Insurance.'

Carl Lawson's eyes twinkle as his secretary, Jackie, shows me into his office two hours later. I can sense the way he looks me up and down, taking in the stiletto boots (which have become my favourite shoes since Louise helped me choose them), fishnet tights, black pencil skirt and powder blue sweater. Again, I have accessorised with strings of cheap pearls. Almost imperceptibly, Carl nods in appreciation. He is looking good too, in a crisp white shirt and charcoal grey tie. As soon as Jackie closes his office door behind me, Carl leaps out of his ergonomic black leather chair and rushes across to hug me. I glance at the glass walls in panic, but notice that the slats on the blinds have been closed. Nobody can see in.

'God, I've missed you,' his voice sounds husky, 'I called last night. Where were you?'

I explain about the pole dancing, which he listens to with an expression similar to the one James had over lunch when he heard about the evening. Pah! Men, I think, they really are just oversized boys with tufts of hair. His eyes light up at the part regarding Donna.

'Some day I'd like to meet her,' he sighs.

'Not if I have anything to do with it,' I reply.

'You're not jealous, are you?'

'No, just protective of my goods!'

'That's good to hear,' he teases.

I remove two buff folders from my briefcase as we take our seats at a large oak table. They contain details of the surveillance operations on both Flamingo and Swan, and a selection of photographs taken over the course of the past week. He flicks through the snaps, pointing at the picture of Flamingo's boyfriend leaving her house.

'Who's this?'

I report James's findings about Tracy's lover. Carl nods, reading through the folders' contents, as I explain how the targets' daily lifestyle patterns are pretty normal and mundane and that, so far, there is nothing to suggest either would be unsuitable for the job. 'So, there was nothing out of the ordinary?' he mutters.

'No.' I mention Swan's dinner party as the height of the week's excitement for her. 'Oh, there was something. Both targets received flowers on Saturday from the same person. We're going to check out the florist this weekend, see if the guy returns to place another order.' Carl nods, barely paying attention. 'And Donna said something strange.'

'Oh?' He looks up from reading the folders.

'Well, we have no evidence so it shouldn't be relied upon, but Donna thinks Swan is gay.'

'Swan? As in Alice Kelly?' I nod. 'That could be a problem.'

'Look, there's no evidence. I probably wouldn't even mention it if we weren't ...' I hesitate at the word, but Carl fills in the blank.

'Dating?' I smile. 'It's such a pity that you're going back to work after this meeting,' he adds.

'I'm the lead officer on the operation,' I say. 'It would look unprofessional and suspicious if I missed a shift.'

'I agree,' he nods solemnly. 'But I have cleared the decks.' With a sweep of his hand, he knocks the contents of the folders onto the floor. 'And it would be a shame to waste the opportunity.'

Twenty minutes later and we're tidying ourselves up. I'm simultaneously appalled and thrilled at my behaviour. Even when I dated Jake, and he used to show me around the trading floors and meeting rooms of Browns Black after a night at the wine bar, I always refused a liaison. I was so scared of getting caught by either the security guards or one of his colleagues. But now, with Carl, it's almost like I don't care. I feel reckless, relaxed and confident. He is so cool and unfazed by anything. Throughout I could hear the chatter of his staff, working just beyond the glass walls, and it merely heightened the experience and pleasure. Somehow it felt more intimate and private. Us against the rest of the world. I feel so safe with Carl. He is so kind and tender, an unselfish lover. I trust him to protect me from all evil. This must be what love is, I think. And maybe that wasn't what I had with Jake.

Carl Lawson is marvellous. He returns to business mode instantly as if a switch has been flicked in his body. He quickly gathers up the papers and photos, places them tidily into their folders and buzzes Jackie to bring in tea. I glance around the office. There are three silver-framed photographs of his children on a low oak cabinet, but none of his former wife. Several newspaper cuttings about Ilyax Insurance, including a front page from *The Economist*, hang in frames on the walls.

'By the way, Holly,' Carl says casually, as he sips his Earl Grey. 'I'm sorry to do this to you, but I'll be out of reach over the next few days. I'm going on a bonding session with senior management in the Highlands somewhere. I expect it'll be paint-balling, white-water rafting and role-playing, all that sort of rubbish, but I've got to show willing. I am the boss.' He places his hand over mine, adding softly: 'But I know who I'd rather be spending the time with.'

CHAPTER TWENTY-THREE

I arrive with Louise at Angus and Pete's fifth-floor apartment in trendy Hoxton just after one for Sunday lunch. They have also invited James and Donna – I think they're trying to matchmake. Poor James. Their building is on the site of a former art deco cinema that was knocked down to build the six-floor utilitarian block they now call home. Two walls are made almost completely of plate glass and steel girders, while the others are built from a silvery-grey stone. None of the residents bother with curtains or blinds though. Not only are they untrendy but they are totally redundant. The windows have been coated with something that allows the inhabitants to see out, yet prevents anybody having a nose in. The view from one side of the building is of half-derelict tower blocks and bleak wasteland. From the other it is possible to see the City skyline. Angus and Pete have a balcony which is fitted with the ubiquitous aluminium planters and bay trees. I press the buzzer.

'Apartment 5a. Can I help you?' asks a voice I don't recognise.

'They must have invited some other people,' I say to Louise, before announcing us into the speaker. The door is buzzed open, and we walk through the empty reception area to the lifts. My friend's surprise is visible as soon as we emerge from the lift. A man, resplendent in butler's uniform, with a tailcoat and black tie, is waiting at their door. He takes our coats, and invites us to go through to the drawing room where our hosts are waiting. Scissor Sisters is playing in the background.

'You've got a bloody butler!' exclaims Louise, as she hugs the boys excitedly. 'I'm so jealous.' They are wearing matching embroidered Nehru jackets and slim-line cropped trousers. James stands up to greet us. He is sitting with Donna, and somebody I don't know, on the massive white leather L-shaped sofa that dominates the living part of the vast open space, sipping champagne. 'That is so cool.'

'He's not exactly a butler,' admits Pete, nodding admiringly at my latest outfit from the capsule wardrobe. 'He's more of a male *au pair* and general dogsbody.' He and Angus giggle. 'He's Juan from Valencia. We met him in Ibiza over Christmas. He's here to study. He was looking for somewhere to stay, and we were looking for somebody to buy the loo paper and bleach.'

'He lives here?'

They giggle and nod simultaneously. 'In the spare room,' they reply.

'And he's a marvel with a dab of Jif and a J-cloth,' says Pete. 'Honestly, even I've picked up a few tips from him.'

'Naughty,' says Angus, playfully shoving him.

'But I thought you liked cleaning,' I say.

'No time for it now,' says Pete firmly. 'Because,' he and Angus air-tap a mock drum roll, 'we're getting a ...'

'... puppy,' they shriek.

'He's arriving next week,' says Pete. 'It's a black Labrador and we're calling him Gabbana.'

'Our hero,' they simultaneously exclaim.

'So what's with Juan's uniform?' I ask.

'Hired it, darling. We were at a *Gosford Park* party last night,' replies Pete, 'and I went as an under-butler.'

'How appropriate,' mutters Donna.

'And I went as Dame Maggie Smith's character, Constance, Countess of Trentham,' giggles Angus, 'from the bed scene, the one where she turns up her nose at the marmalade. Maggie is fab. I just love her. There's not one Harry Potter film that she doesn't steal.'

Juan appears with flutes of champagne on a silver platter.

'Darling,' says Pete, gallantly turning to Louise. 'Would you prefer something soft?'

My friend shakes her head, and grabs a flute. 'This is absolutely perfect,' she says. 'I'm having a well-deserved day off from worrying about pregnancies and folic acid. Anyway I've been a banking widow for the past few weeks, so there's absolutely no fear that I might be even a tiny bit pregnant.'

'Sam's working on a major deal,' I explain to the others. 'He's been very busy.' They nod knowledgeably as if they understand what investment bankers do.

'And besides,' Louise adds, 'my temperature thingummy says I'm not even fertile at the moment, so there's no worries.'

'Way to go, Louise,' Donna giggles. 'By the way girls, let me introduce Gavin.' The man stands up, revealing a six foot five stature, and moves across to shake hands. Gavin's shoulders are reminiscent of an American football player's – with all the padding. This man has muscles on his muscles. I can see how he is able to distract bubbly young receptionists, and even some older ones. Pete and Angus can barely keep their tongues from hanging out as they stare at his physique. Only James remains unmoved. He just watches us, his expression inscrutable.

'The exotic dancer?' I splutter. Louise takes a huge gulp of champagne. 'Is this a set-up?' I hiss at Donna. She smiles innocently.

'Actually that, along with my undercover work for you, is just a sideline,' says Gavin. 'I'm really an astrophysicist.'

'Really?' Louise and I morph into Angus and Pete and ask questions as one.

'Really,' he nods. 'But there just isn't much demand for somebody who wants to study pulsating neutron stars.'

'I thought those celeb mags sold pretty well,' mutters James. I glance over at my colleague. It's unusual for him to be snide, particularly to somebody he doesn't know. He shrugs in an 'I'm sorry' sort of way.

'But I have to pay for my PhD studies somehow,' continues

161

Gavin, 'and I admit there are some highly attractive fringe benefits from my other careers!'

'And some mingers, I bet,' Louise pipes up. 'You'd be my husband's hero. Sam hates anyone who scrounges off the state. Honestly, you'd think he'd never been a student. I remember when he used to march for better grants.' But Sam, I reflect, has wiped those years from his memory. His old Goth image would sit badly with his American bosses.

'Gavin's here to meet you, Holly,' Donna smiles at me. 'Mohammed wouldn't come to the mountain, so we brought the mountain to Mohammed.'

'And what a mountain he is,' mutters Louise in my ear.

A bell tinkles in the distance. 'Ah, Juan is now ready to serve.' Pete leads us across the room to a long trestle table with two benches on either side. White cards with italic writing indicate our places. Donna and I are on either side of Gavin. Louise is placed opposite me beside James. Angus and Pete are at either end of the table. 'Juan is not *au fait* with the traditional Sunday roast.' Pete drops his voice. 'Between you and me, we tried him on Yorkshire puddings yesterday but they were as flat as Tara Palmer Tomkinson, so we relented and let him make his local speciality, paella.'

'I thought *you* liked cooking,' I remark pointedly.

'I do, darling, but how can I manage with a puppy? I'll have his organic feeds to make, walks to organise, animal recognition classes ...'

'What?'

'He's going to be an urban dog.' Pete looks at me as if I'm simple. 'I don't want him to be scared by a cow or a sheep, but when will he ever see them in Hoxton? He'll have to have lessons, perhaps a week's course in the country.'

'Sangria, anyone?' Angus minces across with a cut glass jug and the next ten minutes are a whirl of plate and glass passing. When everybody is served, Juan does a little bow and retires from the room. Pete raises his glass: 'Let's have a toast ...'

'Darling,' interrupts Angus, 'we want to make it special. Forget all that good friends crap. It goes without saying. Has

162

anybody here got something they want to celebrate?' I glance anxiously at Angus to make sure that this isn't some elaborate ruse to make me confess to my new relationship. But he's scanning the table hopefully and hasn't looked at me. Relax, I tell myself, they don't know. Suddenly Louise pipes up.

'I've got something to celebrate.'

'I thought you weren't pregnant,' Donna says tactlessly, pointedly glancing at the near empty sangria tumbler in front of my friend.

'I'm not,' Louise shakes her head. 'No, it's the next best thing.' She claps her hands in excitement. 'I've just been hired to organise a huge engagement party for one of Sam's old colleagues, Trixie something or other. She's a trader or saleswoman or something. Anyway, that doesn't matter. It's the biggest contract since I launched my party planning business.' Everybody raises their glasses in salute as Louise leans across to refill hers. 'I'm a last-minute replacement, though. Poor girl only found out yesterday that the venue she'd set her heart on was double-booked. She's distraught – the event's on Friday ...' She drains her sangria. 'I've got five days to find a new venue, entertainment, waiters, caterers and notify all two hundred guests. Can you see why I need a drink?'

We clink glasses with Louise in sympathy and excitement. For the next hour we suggest alternative venues, where we've previously enjoyed a good party, and different sorts of entertainers. Not surprisingly, perhaps, Gavin has more ideas than most. Louise scribbles down everybody's suggestions, when Pete suddenly shrieks: 'Hold the front page!' The table goes silent. 'Why not have it here?'

'Here?' Louise looks around the room. Angus looks startled.

'We don't know this Trixie woman, dear,' he says. 'She could be psychotic for all we know, and think of the mess.'

'Not *here*,' says Pete, gesturing to the wooden floor, 'but upstairs in the penthouse.' He points to the ceiling. 'It's huge, it has just the most fantastic views of the City, and it's been empty for months. The landlord would probably welcome some money for an evening showing.'

'Darling, I think you've got it,' exclaims Angus. 'If the land-lord hears it'll be filled with rich City types, he'll be gagging. He couldn't pay for that sort of advertising. Maybe we can get *Harpers & Queen* to cover it. Is this woman, Trixie, well known? Does she have any celeb friends?'

'I know nothing about the woman,' Louise says, 'although Sam said something about her stepfather being in ice cream.'

'Who cares about the paparazzi! Think about it, Louise. It could be amazing. You just need to decorate the room,' insists Pete. 'Plus, it's surrounded by balconies.'

Louise is in party planning mode. Her mental Rolodex is checking through all the possibilities. 'I'd need to instal a bar, possibly two, but the caterers can take care of that. A couple of tasteful ice sculptures, massive arrangements of flowers, maybe a disco. I need to hire at least a dozen patio heaters, some stocked up planters ... maybe a hot tub?' she pauses. 'I think this could be spectacular.'

'Ooh, and fireworks,' pipes up Pete. 'Mask those awful tower blocks. I don't know which prat on the council placed a pres-ervation order on them.'

'I've got a giant Jenga in my cellar,' offers James.

'I bet you say that to all the girls,' Donna cries. James turns crimson.

'I've got an even better idea,' says Angus. 'Let's all work on the evening as ... .'

'Waiters,' he and Pete cry. 'I was thinking exactly the same thing,' says Pete. 'I just love wearing a tux, and as for seeing Angus in a tux, well, hold me steady! My knees are buckling at the thought.'

'It'll be such fun,' continues Angus, ignoring his frisky part-ner. 'It'll solve part of one of your many problems and our surveillance operation should finish this Tuesday?' He raises a quizzical eyebrow towards me. I nod. Investigations-R-Us will by then have completed two full weeks of surveillance and, on current trends, Flamingo and Swan display nothing to concern Ilyax about appointing either of them. 'It'll be the ultimate undercover work,' giggles Angus. 'And it'll be comforting for

Louise to have some friendly faces in the crowd. *And* Pete and I can christen the hot tub as soon as it's installed.'

Gavin turns to me, while the others are chatting excitedly about the event, and quietly says, 'I've been wanting to meet you for a long time.'

'Really?' I'm surprised. Gavin has the most startling green eyes. They're so deep and penetrating, and intelligent. Despite his image, Gavin feels like the sort of man you would trust with your life.

'Yes, Donna is always talking about you. Between you and me, and she'd deny it if questioned, I think she secretly admires you.'

'Me?' I look over at Donna, gorgeous in a turquoise silk halter-neck top and chandelier-style earrings which emphasise her long, elegant neck. She has the unknowing arrogance of somebody in their twenties for whom wrinkles and grey hairs are inconceivable.

'Yeah. You're your own woman. You're comfortable in your skin and all that. Donna has yet to get to that point. I love her to bits, but she's very young. She's like my baby sister. The real her is very vulnerable, I'd do anything for her, but what she shows the world is just show.' As he glances across at Donna, I catch a fleeting glimpse of something. My God! I suddenly think. This man is in love with Donna, and she hasn't a clue.

'And I suppose what you see with me is what you get?' I prompt.

'I'd hope so,' he smiles. 'You seem honest, down to earth. A woman with her head screwed on.'

'You're not what I expected,' I reply quickly. I did not go through my day of humiliation at the hairdressers, beauticians and boutiques to be described as 'down to earth' by a good looking man.

'Thought I'd turn up in baby oil and a loin cloth, huh?'

'Something like that,' I giggle. 'A little leopard skin, perhaps? I never imagined you to be so ...'

'Educated?' I cringe at my small-mindedness. It wasn't exactly the word I'd use, but then I'm not actually sure what

165

word I planned. 'I'm not the stereotype,' concedes Gavin, 'but in a few years' time, I'll give it up, find a chair at some university and become a lecturer. I know, hard to imagine me in flannel shirts and cords.'

'And a tweed jacket with elbow patches. Don't forget that. No self-respecting professor would be seen dead without one.'

'I'll probably have to have them specially made,' he flexes his biceps. 'So, tell me about you.'

I lose track of time as we chat about our backgrounds, our fears, hopes and dreams. I glance across at Donna, who is chatting to a rather distracted looking James. He looks so moody today, I think. Not at all like the good-humoured person I know. Maybe he's had some bad news, he's barely spoken to me. As for Donna, she looks as vibrant as ever and, as I learn about Gavin's love of opera and his captaincy of the local pub quiz team, I realise that his will be an unfulfilled love. Donna needs excitement, she's too young to settle down. I sigh inwardly. Timing, I think. The ultimate curse of relationships.

Louise leans across me. I sense my friend with the massive party to organise will have a rather nasty hangover tomorrow. 'Holly, Sam's just called. He's leaving the City now, and is on his way to collect me. Do you want a lift?'

'I'm sorry,' I say to Gavin. 'I'll have to go, because I don't think Louise'll find the car without me.'

'It's been really lovely to meet you, Holly,' Gavin says, rising to his feet. 'I'm sorry that I've monopolised you.' His eyes inadvertently dart across at Donna. That's what this is about, I think to myself. He wants to see if she has noticed our lengthy conversation and whether he's sparked some jealous feelings in her.

I haul my drunken friend around the table to say our goodbyes.

'You've been very quiet,' I say to James. 'Are you okay?'

'I'm surprised you even noticed,' he snaps. 'You seemed very busy with macho man.'

'Are you jealous, James?' I ask in surprise. Shock registers in his eyes. 'Do you think your muscles don't measure up?' The look of shock changes to a look I do not recognise. Men, I think, their egos are just so fragile. 'Book yourself in for some bodybuilding classes if you're so insecure.'

And then we leave.

CHAPTER TWENTY-FOUR

I light several scented candles and settle myself on my sofa with a large glass of merlot. Sam rang ten minutes ago to say he'd put Louise straight to bed when they got home, and that she was now snoring loudly and dribbling like Niagara Falls onto their new cashmere throw from The White Company. I felt a tinge of guilt at his tenderness as I saw his look of loving amusement when she tried six times to fasten her seatbelt. True love, I think, means putting up with each other's failings.

Sam looked tired. Sometimes I envy Louise her lifestyle – able to book a five-star holiday without first seducing the bank manager and the kudos to dine at celebrity restaurants without sitting at the table next to the ladies' loos, but she definitely pays a price. So, undoubtedly, does Sam. As his career has progressed, so has his unreliability. It is no longer possible to count on Sam turning up for a social function. If he has an important deal on or a meeting with a big client, they come first.

Once, a few years ago, he was thrilled to act as best man for a colleague, but the groom was unable to stay for the reception – a client was in the middle of a crisis and he had to rush back to the office to discuss tactics. Sam had less than an hour to organise a video satellite link-up to relay the groom's speech from the office to the reception. Unfortunately, he had less success consoling the bride. She filed for divorce two months later (on her return from a solo honeymoon cruise) on the basis of unreasonable behaviour.

The theme tune to another murder mystery set in Victorian times blares from my TV, breaking into my musings. Great, just what the doctor ordered, a night of slobbing in front of inane programmes on the box. I watch as, during the opening credits, an unknown man's hand stabs a chimney sweep returning from his rounds but, just as the sweep's dirty brush falls into a puddle, my door buzzer sounds. It can't be Miss Binchy. She'd just walk up the stairs and rap on my internal door. I shout through the intercom.

'Holly?' It's Carl. 'I thought I'd surprise you.'

I quickly shove the Sunday newspapers into a tidy pile and throw a few dirty clothes from the bedroom floor into a laundry basket. I check my reflection in the mirror over the fireplace, and dash to the door.

Carl Lawson is leaning against the wall, wearing an amused look, when I finally open the door. He is carrying a massive arrangement of red parrot tulips and has a suit bag swung over his shoulder.

'I hope you weren't tidying up on my account,' he smiles. 'By the way, why is there a set of saucepans in the hallway?' He pants at a selection of cookware by Miss Binchy's door.

'It's probably my neighbour. She's a bit absentminded. Just back from Amsterdam, I see.' I nod towards the tulips, as we climb the stairs to my flat.

He walks into my apartment, places the flowers gently onto my coffee table and tosses his carrier onto the floor. Then he moves forward and hugs me tight. I can hardly breathe.

'I have spent the past few days desperate to do this,' he whispers into my ear. 'To hold you in my arms, to breathe you in, smell your perfume. God, I've missed you.' He disentangles himself and, still holding my shoulders, steps back, and looks me up and down. 'Let me look at you. I know it's early days and we haven't spent that much time together, but I just can't stop thinking about you.'

'I've missed you too,' I say quietly.

'It was hell not being able to contact you. Absolute hell.' He closes his eyes and shakes his head at the nightmare memory of it all.

'Did you have a good time?'

'What do you think?'

'I think you did,' I tease.

'Then you'd be wrong,' he says softly. 'I was in a hotel with fifty senior managers all trying to bond, and I've never felt so alone in my life.'

'No women?'

'Not that I noticed.'

'Seriously?'

'Holly, I don't think you know what you do to me.'

'I've got a feeling I do ... at this exact moment,' I giggle, glancing down.

'I'm serious. You've got to me like no other woman ever has.'

'I bet you say that to all the girls.'

'I'm *not* joking.' Carl looks angry. 'I haven't felt like this since I was,' he hesitates, 'since I was a teenager. And that was just a crush – a silly childish crush fuelled by raging hormones and peer pressure. This is different, I didn't even feel this with my wife.'

My heart is beating fiercely. Never in a million years did I imagine that Carl Lawson could ever fall like this for me. His voice is hoarse with emotion. His intensity and sincerity are surprising. This man is slowly reeling me in, and I feel no fear or panic. *He* is the reason that I could speak to Gavin without recourse to silly jokes or sarcastic comments. I'm no longer interested in anybody else. I've not even got that 'I know I've made my selection, but I just want to check out what else is on the market' frame of mind. Not that I think there's anything wrong with that attitude. It's common sense. Why settle for second best? But this man, I think, as I luxuriate in his closeness and inhale his Marc Jacobs aftershave, while staring deep into his penetrating eyes: this man is where my search stops.

I take his hand and slowly pull him to the floor.

CHAPTER TWENTY-FIVE

Carl Lawson left this morning at about two. He wanted to stay, but I could tell he was fretting about paperwork he'd left at home and really needed for the office, so I persuaded him that I was okay about him leaving. He didn't want to disturb his chauffeur's sleep, so he rang for a local mini cab, as I drifted into a wonderful sleep, filled with dreams of tropical beaches and four-poster beds, until my hungover best friend called at eight.

'I feel lousy,' she whispers. 'Every movement hurts. How many glasses of sangria did I have?'

'Well, Juan was mixing up his sixth punch bowl when we left,' I say, puffing up my pillow. Carl's side of the bed is all crumpled. I smile at the memories of last night, and imagine him lying there.

'So if I had a glass per bowl, that's five?' I'm silent. 'Don't tell me I had more than five.' I remain silent. 'Holly, tell me. Now.'

'It was definitely less than ten,' I comfort her. 'Don't worry about it. Everyone had too much. You've got far more important things to worry about with this party you've got to organise. People made some great suggestions yesterday. You wrote them down ...'

'I can't read a word. I think the pen must have been leaking.'

'Well, start by ringing the landlord to book the room.'

'I will when *this* room stops spinning.'

'How was Sam?'

'Fine, I think. He left about six, but not before leaving out a specialist dry cleaner's phone number for the housekeeper. Our new cashmere throw looks rather the worse for wear. And we may have to re-varnish just the teeniest bit of the wooden flooring in our bedroom; I misjudged the distance to the en suite. So, how are you? And did I dream it or have you all volunteered as waiters for Trixie's party?'

'You didn't imagine it,' I assure her. 'A few glasses of sangria and we're anyone's. But guess what – Carl came over last night.'

'A surprise visit?'

'Yeah, he'd been away on one of those male bonding things, in the middle of nowhere with no mobile phone range, so we hadn't been able to speak for a few days. I was missing him like crazy.'

'Ooh, poor you. I hate it when I can't get hold of Sam.'

'Yeah, well it seems Carl was feeling exactly the same.'

'That's a good sign.'

'It's more than that. Louise, you wouldn't believe the things Carl was saying last night.'

'What sort of things?' My friend sounds interested.

'Really romantic things. I think,' I can scarcely believe I'm saying the words out loud, 'he's really fallen for me.'

'And how do you feel about that?'

'I'm really happy,' I admit, 'I feel exactly the same. Louise—' I pause, nervous about sharing my innermost dreams – 'I know it's early days and we don't really know each other that well, but I think this could be it. I think Carl is *the* one.'

Silence. My best friend doesn't say anything. Not one word. A few seconds pass. I wait. Perhaps she's throwing up, I think. Perhaps she's fallen back asleep. Perhaps ...

'Holly, isn't this all a bit sudden?'

'If you've got nothing sensible to say then I'd rather you didn't bother,' I snap.

'Look, I'm sorry, Hol. I'm only asking because I care. You've just known this man a few weeks ...'

'I know that. Didn't I qualify what I said with that comment, but I *do* feel like I've known him my whole life.'

'Well, then, that's good,' she says enthusiastically, 'really good. And I *am* thrilled for you. Truly. You deserve someone fantastic; especially after Jake, and the way that bastard treated you.'

'Carl is fantastic.' And he is, I think. I feel such a connection with him. My heart races in the morning when I hear the beep of his text message. I find it incredibly comforting that he is thinking of me the moment he wakes, before he has truly come around to full consciousness, and I panic on the odd occasion I don't hear from him by nine: what if something happens to him, and nobody knows that they need to contact me? I look forward to the day when our relationship is no longer a secret. I yearn to ring his office and be recognised as his girlfriend, not a business associate. Silly, I know, but I want everybody to know how happy I am. How happy *we* are, I correct myself.

'That's brilliant,' Louise is saying. 'Honestly. But I just wonder if you shouldn't be treading a bit carefully. After all, you've only just abandoned your fling lifestyle and admitted that you want a proper relationship. It's early days to be talking about love ...'

'We're not talking about love.' I'm defensive.

'Oh! I thought that's what we *were* talking about.' Louise sounds confused.

'Well, we are, yes,' I agree, 'but you and me. Not Carl. He hasn't mentioned it yet.'

'Oh, right. I must have got hold of the wrong end of the stick. I thought he'd declared his undying and all that.'

'No.' I'm irritated now. 'Look, it doesn't matter. Forget I said anything.'

'Holly, don't be like that. I want you to find somebody wonderful and settle down with him, and if that person's this Carl, and incidentally that's the first time you've told me his name, then I'm really happy for you.'

'His full name's Carl Lawson, but you can't tell Sam or

anyone just yet,' I say hurriedly. 'Technically, he's still my client until tomorrow when we finish this surveillance operations.'

'Not a word. Well once it's over, and after Sam finally completes his deal, which I pray is really soon, we will all meet and I can give him the once-over,' Louise says. 'After all, I can't have my best friend settling down with just anybody.'

'I'd like that.'

'Are we okay, Holly? You're not upset with me?'

'No, you're only looking out for me,' I admit reluctantly. 'I know that, but as soon as you meet Carl you'll see why I've fallen this hard. He's fantastic. He's ...' I search for the words, 'everything I've never had before.'

'I can hardly wait,' she swallows loudly. 'Now if you'd just excuse me, I've got an appointment with a white porcelain appliance.' The line goes dead.

Three hours later and I'm at Investigations-R-Us looking through the weekend reports from the surveillance operations. I was disturbed to see the saucepans still outside Miss Binchy's flat door when I left the house this morning. I really must pop in and see her as soon as possible, to check she is okay. I know she constantly sings the praises of her attentive nephew Seamus but frankly he seems as illusory as Marmalade, the cat I've never seen. This is what happens to old spinsters, I think sadly. They become dependent on the kindness of people they hardly know. Their neighbours become a surrogate family because their blood relatives are too busy with their own lives. And then a selfish thought comes unbidden into my mind: I don't want to end up like that. I don't want to be the batty old lady that a young neighbour takes pity on and keeps an eye out for.

I brush aside these thoughts, and immerse myself in my work. Flamingo seems to have had a busy time. She stayed most of the weekend in Wimbledon with her boyfriend Peter Porter. They spent Saturday night at the cinema; strolled around the shops on Sunday but bought nothing; and enjoyed a pub lunch – roast beef, Yorkshire pudding, mixed vegetables but no potatoes. A quasi-Atkins meal, I think. Interestingly, another bouquet of flowers was delivered, but a neighbour took them in, apparently because she wasn't at home. The florist was called Double Dutch.

Swan spent Saturday morning at a kickboxing class; met a friend for lunch – mixed seafood salad and two (large) glasses of dry white wine; returned home at 4.13 p.m. and had an argument on her doorstep with a florist trying to deliver flowers at 4.27 p.m. The flowers were taken away. 'Swan sure doesn't like whoever it is sending the flowers,' I mutter. Again, the florist was called Double Dutch. In the evening a friend arrived – a tall, slim brunette, dressed in denim jeans, wrap-around top and black leather jacket – with an overnight bag. Neither was seen again until this morning, when Swan waved her off at 7.18 a.m. Swan left for work at 8.30 a.m. Running late again, I think.

I ring Bert, the middle-aged agent who heads up the week-end shifts. He is now enjoying two days' rest. His wife sounds annoyed by the call.

'Hi Bert, sorry to call on your day off,' I apologise when he comes to the phone. 'But did you stake out Poppy's Posies on Saturday?'

'I sent an operative to watch the place, Holly, but there was nothing to report. The guy who sent the flowers to the targets last Saturday didn't show. There was no repeat order. I hear he sent flowers from Double Dutch this time. Tulips from Amsterdam and all that,' he laughs.

'Okay Bert,' I sigh. 'It was worth a shot.' I hang up, disappointed. I had hoped to be able to tell Carl who the mystery sender was. It's a loose end that I don't think we'll ever be able to tie up, although I can't help feeling I'm missing something. A little bell is going off in my head, but I don't know what it's telling me. I try one last shot and dial another number.

'Double Dutch, specialists in spring flowers. Good morning.'

'Oh hi,' I say in my best 'help me please, I am a ditzy female' voice. 'I know this sounds really silly but I had a friend staying this weekend, who, and I can't believe she did this, thought it would be funny to refuse a bouquet of flowers that you delivered to me on Saturday.'

'Some friend,' snorts the florist. 'I'm sorry, but it's not our policy to replace bouquets.'

'I know,' I sigh dramatically, 'and I'm not expecting you to do so. But my friend has left me with a real poser. I just don't know who to thank for the flowers.'

'Where do you live?' I give her Alice Kelly's address. I can hear computer keys being tapped. 'Right, I've got your details here. But I'm afraid that I can't help you.'

'Oh?'

'No, I'm sorry. The sender came into the store and paid for the bouquets with cash. We've no record of the sender's identity.'

'Bouquets?'

'Yes, the customer bought three.' Three? I know the florist really means two, but I can't correct her without raising suspicions. What's the point of questioning somebody who doesn't even remember basic facts, but I push on.

'Was there a card?'

'Hold on, let me see.' A few moments pass. 'Yes, the customer chose a "Thinking of You" card, and wrote a personal message on it. I'm afraid I don't know what that said.'

'Ah well,' I say, 'it was worth a try. Thanks for your help.' I hang up, deep in thought.

'Boyfriend problems?' James asks. He is standing by my desk with a large file of papers.

'No,' I say indignantly. 'What's that?'

'Invoices for the surveillance. Ilyax Insurance is in for a hefty bill. I was going to get accounts to sort it out, and someone should tell Marcus that we are not paying for eight latte coffees per shift, even if it is the graveyard one.'

'I'll do that.' I snatch the papers roughly from him. 'I am the lead manager on this account.'

'Hey, sorry,' he raises his hands in surrender, 'just trying to help. I thought you might be tied up writing the final report on the assignment.'

'I am,' I concede. 'I can't see that anything will happen now to change the conclusion. I'm going to ring the client later to arrange a sign-off meeting tomorrow.'

'This has all been a waste of time,' James says, settling himself on the edge of my desk. 'Those women seem perfectly innocuous. I can't see either of them being a risk to any company. By the way, when is Clive Partridge's appointment as finance director due to be announced? I keep looking out for it on the wires.'

'I don't know,' I reply. 'I'll ask at tomorrow's meeting.'

We chat a bit more about the surveillance before James walks off to make some calls. I dial Carl's mobile.

'What?' he barks down the phone.

'Carl, it's me, Holly.'

'What do you want? I'm really busy here.' I'm taken aback. This is a tone I've never heard Carl use before. He sounds angry and threatening.

'It's about the surveillance,' I reply hesitantly.

What about it?' He sighs deeply and impatiently. 'What is *so* important that you have to ring me right now?'

'I didn't know you were busy.' My stomach is turning anxious cartwheels. This is not the response I had expected. Usually when I call, his voice adopts a tone of real delight and pleasure.

'So you think a big company like this just runs itself?' he blasts. 'That I just sit around all day waiting for you to call?'

'No, I...' I swallow hard to prevent myself crying.

'Look, what is it, Holly? I really don't have time for histrionics. I've got three people hovering outside my door, and a pile of paperwork.'

I adopt a businesslike tone. 'I'm drawing up the bill for the surveillance. I was just reminding you that, as we discussed earlier, the operation ends tomorrow ...'

'Did I say to end it tomorrow?'

'It was a two-week surveillance operation.' I'm flustered.

'But *did I say* that it was to end tomorrow?' Carl enunciates carefully, as if he is talking to a recalcitrant child.

'That was the understanding ...' I say hesitantly.

'Holly,' he sighs again. 'That may have been your under-standing. It was not mine. I asked for a surveillance operation, and, while you recommended a two-week operation, I never actually agreed to it, did I?'

'Well, no, but ...'

'Exactly. Look, I know things have got a bit mixed up between us, but I am still the client here and you are still providing a service. And I want that service to continue.' He goes quiet. 'Is there anything else?'

'Well, I wanted to ...'

'Holly, I haven't time for this right now, I have to go. I'll call you, okay?' He hangs up.

I sink back in my chair in shock. I never imagined Carl Lawson would ever talk to me like that. Just days ago at my flat he appeared besotted. Okay, so I understand he's busy but I wasn't disturbing him with a silly girlie query. This was a business call. Maybe this is what people mean about mixing business and pleasure – even Carl alluded to it – I suppose the line has become blurred.

Perhaps I caught Carl at a bad moment, I console myself. He was busy and thought I was just ringing up for an idle chat. He's probably now feeling just as awful as I am. And yet, there's a small niggling voice at the back of my head that I'm trying desperately to ignore, but which is a bit disturbed by his outburst.

My phone rings. I look at the number, hoping it is Carl ring-ing to apologise and suggest a romantic making-up session. It's my mother. I take a deep breath before answering. I am not in the mood for a 'men are bastards' conversation, and I don't want her to pick up any sense that my relationship is not perfect.

'Hol, I've got such news,' she shrieks down the phone.

'Hi, Mum.'

'Oh yeah, hi. Sorry, I'm just so excited I had to call.'

'What's happened?'

'I've got the gift.'

'What gift? Have I forgotten somebody's birthday?'

'No, silly. *The gift.*'

'Mum, I'm really busy at the moment,' I say, ironically echoing Carl's earlier comment, 'I haven't time for riddles.'

'I went to a psychic fair in Slough with Betty. Did I tell you that Betty's now a whiz on the old Tarot cards? The old dears on her Meals-on-Wheels round love her readings. Of course, everybody laughed when Mildred in the day centre pulled the fertility card. She's 97 after all – but then her granddaughter got pregnant with triplets, and they're not laughing now, especially the granddaughter. I don't envy her one bit.'

'Never mind, Mum. So what's this about you and a gift?'

'Oh yes,' she continues. 'We went to this psychic fair, and well I wasn't there two minutes when Madam Cholet came over and announced I had "the gift". She'd spotted my aura as soon as I walked into the meeting hall. Apparently, I'm surrounded by a haze.'

'No kidding?' I mutter.

'Sorry?'

'Nothing. You were saying about your haze.'

'Yes, it's purple with a flickering lilac centre. It means I'm extremely intuitive and I can pick up on a person's moods without them saying a word. I can sense instinctively if somebody is upset. Obviously I've always been able to gauge your emotional state, but I just put that down to a maternal bond. You couldn't be down without me knowing it. But now it seems it was so much more. Madam Cholet was so excited. She introduced me to all these people. I felt like royalty. Apparently somebody with my aura comes around just once in a generation.'

It seems my mother has discovered her latest passion. I doubt this will be the last discussion of the matter. Her fads generally last six months, enough for Madam Cholet and her friends to have their fun.

'How did Betty take the news of your aura?'

'How would I know? She left soon after we met Madam Cholet. It's funny really. I'd never met Madam Cholet, but as soon as she introduced herself I just sensed that I'd come across her before. There's a little tune that plays automatically in my mind whenever I think of her.'

'So you rang to tell me about your aura?' I really have to get on with my work. Carl's bombshell means I have to sort out another surveillance rota, and some of the agents I've been using over the past fortnight are already booked on other projects. I'll be here until midnight at this rate.

'Well, it's quite a discovery, isn't it? And Madam Cholet says there's every chance it might run in the family. This is my future. Actually I've called because I'm going on a retreat with Madam to explore my hidden potential, and I wonder if we can swap our Sunday lunch. Maybe we could meet this weekend instead of next?'

'I'm not sure what my plans are,' I reply carefully.

'Oh, still seeing that businessman?' Her tone becomes abrupt.

'Yes.'

'So he hasn't gone off with another woman yet?'

'No, Mum.'

'I'm picking up bad vibes about it. Madam Cholet said I should trust these feelings. She says I've got good reason to worry about your new man. Apparently my aura turns red when I think of him.'

And I see red when I hear her comments. 'What a load of bloody rubbish! It's none of her business and, frankly, it's none of yours either. I'll let you know about Sunday, but right now, Mystic Meg, I have work to do. I'm surprised your failsafe intuition didn't tell you. Bye.' I slam the phone down, and it instantly rings. 'What now, Mum?' I shriek into the mouthpiece.

'It's Carl.' He sounds subdued and worried. 'I'm truly sorry for the way I spoke to you earlier.' I say nothing. The old Holly would be full of recriminations, seeking retribution for the outburst. But the new Holly wants to forgive and forget. 'It's no excuse, Holly, but we had a really busy day. We had to fire one of the actuaries for incompetence, so I had meetings with lawyers and it was all so miserable.'

'How was he incompetent?' I ask.

'He was responsible for working out the probabilities for certain events, you know, like how many people would lose their luggage at airports this year, and we think he may have got his calculations wrong. It looks like we may have to make some big payouts as a result. He denies it, of course. But look, that's not important right now. You are. I'm so sorry, babe. Sometimes being a boss stinks.'

'It's alright,' I mutter.

'Are you sure? I couldn't bear for you to be upset with me.' He pauses, then adds in a softer voice, 'My biggest failing, Holly, is that I always shout at the people I love.'

CHAPTER TWENTY-SIX

It is a full day since Carl Lawson made *that* startling statement. I didn't sleep when I finally got to bed last night, many hours after receiving my goodnight text, the sixth text from him yesterday. All apologies. I tossed and turned, analysing his comment over and over again. Questions were buzzing through my mind. Does it mean he loves me? Is that his way of telling me? Did he mean to say exactly that? I can only hope the answer is 'yes'.

I spent yesterday afternoon and most of the evening in a daze, trying to put his comment to the back of my mind as I organised another week of surveillance, and wrote up the weekly report that I'm due to produce at a meeting at Carl's office in three hours' time. It may seem slightly disingenuous, but I do think that I need to retain some boundaries. Handing Carl an official report while we're at a romantic dinner is not really appropriate. But then again, a little gremlin mutters in my head, neither is making out in the client's office.

It was a nightmare organising further surveillance, although this time I'm not assuming that it will end on any particular day. I've got agents booked to cover the next full month, on the understanding that the surveillance could be cancelled at any time. I have promised cancellation fees and double time to get the rota sorted. Seeing my horrendous problem, James helped out and hit the phones. Even Donna managed to track down one or two agents to cover difficult shifts. She has been rather more diligent about work since the fiasco at the pole-dancing evening.

'Bert has just called,' James says, chewing on an energy bar as he approaches my desk. 'He's okay to manage the weekend surveillance again, and he wonders if we want to keep an eye on that Double Dutch florist this Saturday.'

'Great,' I reply. 'That's one less thing to worry about. You look tired. Is everything alright?' James looks like he slept in his shirt. It is crumpled, and I could swear it's what he was wearing yesterday. Maybe he has a new girlfriend. It's funny, but I don't think I've ever thought of James with a woman, or even heard him mention one. Somehow, he has managed to keep his love life off-limits to Donna and Angus.

'Fine,' he yawns before shoving the last piece of bar in his mouth. 'Just some family problems, nothing for you to worry about. Anyway, pot calling and all that. You don't look so hot yourself.'

He's right, I think later when I check my reflection in the mirror. I can't turn up to meet Carl looking like this. I ring Louise for some tips to make me look vivacious and full of life. She advises leaving some cold tea bags on my eyes for ten minutes before I leave.

'They must be cold,' she insists firmly. 'And keep your head back otherwise the tea will drip onto your blouse. I know you. By the way, the party's going really well,' she sounds excited. 'I've booked a swing band, two chocolate fountains, caterers, flowers and an ice sculpture in the shape of Eros. Trixie's step-father, who as I said before is big in frozen desserts, is giving every guest a special ice bag of goodies to take away.'

'Sounds like you've got everything covered.'

'Nearly. I'm still trying to get local authority permission for the firework display and also to release fifty doves to symbolise their love.'

'Good heavens! How amazing.'

I can hear a buzzing noise from her phone.

'Sorry, that's my BlackBerry. Someone has emailed me. I better go. Ciao.'

I have managed a decent rescue operation on my face by the time Carl's secretary shows me into his office (and a silk scarf, twisted into a fancy bow by Donna, really does hide the tea stains). Carl is working on the flatscreen computer in front of him, and takes a few moments to look up. Instantly, his eyes light up with pleasure. It is so blatant that I am sure Jackie must notice. Electricity must be radiating from us. I absolutely glow when I'm in his company.

Once again, he roughly pulls me into his arms as soon as Jackie leaves his office.

'I really didn't know if you'd ever talk to me again after yesterday,' he whispers, his voice hoarse with emotion. 'I was almost beside myself with grief as soon as I put the phone down, babe.'

'It's okay,' I say, ruffling his hair and smiling, 'just don't make a habit of it. Now, while all work and no play makes Carl a dull boy, all play and no work makes Holly redundant. So let's go through these files and then you can take me out for a drink to apologise.'

'Will it be a making-up drink, babe?' he asks, raising one eyebrow.

'It was our first argument,' I joke, 'so it very well might be. You'll just have to wait and see.'

There is little real news in the report. I pass over a sheaf of black and white photographs of the two targets as they set about their daily business. There are snaps of Tracy Bruce wandering around Wimbledon hand in hand with her boyfriend at the weekend and another series of pictures from last night when he arrived late at her Highbury home obviously the worse for wear. There are also snaps of the woman who arrived and stayed at Alice Bruce's house for most of the weekend. Carl appears to pay little attention to them.

'So let me get this straight,' he finally says. 'Two of my staff went to a pole-dancing lesson and you didn't manage to get even one snap of them in skimpy outfits and their legs in the air?'

'It would have raised suspicions if I'd snapped them,' I giggle.

'Call yourself a secret agent?' he laughs. 'I thought you were always ready.'

'I haven't heard you complaining so far,' I reply with a seductive look. 'Maybe I do have the pictures, but maybe I don't want you to see them. I might be jealous.' I watch for his reaction and I see – but this can't be right – a fleeting look of annoyance passing across his face.

'Holly, if you have the pictures then they should be included with this report,' he says firmly. 'Ilyax Insurance has paid for a complete surveillance.'

'There were no pictures,' I admit, mildly irritated by his tone. 'But later I might show you a few of the tips I picked up that night.'

'I'd like that,' Carl murmurs. He smiles, and I immediately forgive him.

It doesn't take long to run through the important points of the report. I mention that both targets again received flowers, but that they came this time from a different florist. Carl nods, not really taking in the information. 'And we'll probably send an agent to watch Double Dutch this Saturday to discover who's sending these lucky girls flowers.'

Carl closes the A4 files. 'Alice Kelly is no longer in the running for the position,' he says.

It's a surprise announcement, and I'm momentarily stunned.

'Does that mean Tracy Bruce has been appointed?' I finally ask. 'Shall I call off the surveillance after all?'

'Discussions are ongoing and no decision has been made, but another internal candidate has put themselves forward only this week so I would like you to transfer the surveillance from Alice Kelly to her.' He hands me another buff coloured folder. 'She's called Carmen Hughes, and she lives in Kensington.' I flick through the folder's contents. Carmen Hughes is another stunning woman. Ilyax Insurance must breed them.

'It'll take me a while to reorganise the surveillance. I'll need to call some agents now to alert them to the new target, and I should call off the team awaiting Alice Kelly tonight.'

'Why don't I get Jackie to show you into another office so you can make calls and sort things out, and then you and I can spend this evening making up?' He places a soft kiss on my forehead.

Chapter Twenty-Seven

Carl is dozing. I rest my head on my forearm and study him. I watch his chest expand and contract with his even breathing. I look at, and envy, the long dark eyelashes that curl out and I count the sprinkling of tiny freckles on his nose. I notice the slight parting between his pale pink lips. This man, I think, could be the last man to occupy that pillow. It just feels so right that I can't imagine waking up with any other man ever again. He is the reason that I won't end up like Miss Binchy. I prod him gently. He stirs slightly, then opens one eye and fixes his gaze on me.

'What time is it?' He sounds groggy.

'About two.'

'Time to sleep then.' His eye starts to close but I give him a prod. 'No babe, not again. I need some shut eye.'

'Can we talk for a little while?'

'What about tomorrow?'

'But I'm awake now,' I giggle, 'and so are you.'

He shakes his head in surrender and opens his eyes. He plumps up the pillows and pulls himself into a semi-sitting position. He leans back against the headboard, and waves one arm at me signalling that I should nestle into his body. I shuffle across, and he wraps the arm around me.

'The things I do for you,' he says, rubbing his eyes with his spare hand. 'So, what do you want to talk about?'

'I'd like you to meet my friends.'

'You woke me to tell me that?'

'You were only dozing,' I tease. 'Besides, it's important. I want them to see us together. I want to feel like part of a couple and not like I'm in some illicit relationship.'

'I thought we agreed, babe, that it'd be better to wait until Ilyax Insurance is no longer your client. It gets complicated otherwise.'

'I know, but I didn't expect you to extend the surveillance indefinitely,' I reply.

'Nor did I, but that's business.' He strokes my nose. 'This is pleasure. Did anybody ever tell you that you've got a gorgeous nose? Very sexy.' He kisses it gently. 'It's almost as sexy as your mouth,' he mutters, softly moving his lips down my face. Carl's lips find their target. 'Perhaps waking me up was a good idea after all,' he mutters. 'Now stop talking.' My treacherous body makes me powerless to refuse.

'So?' I hand Carl a mug of freshly percolated coffee. It's six in the morning and we are both getting ready for work after just a few hours' sleep. He is sitting on the corner of my bed, a towel tied around the waist of his freshly showered body. I perch beside him.

'So?' He looks puzzled.

'So, will you meet my friends?' I repeat the question I posed earlier this morning.

'I just don't think it's very wise.'

'But they're nothing to do with work,' I insist. 'It's only Louise, my best friend, and her husband Sam, who's an investment banker. I've known them for years. Anyway Sam mightn't come. He's busy working on some big merger of some financial companies, and is working all hours. Oh God,' I slap my hand to my mouth in horror at my indiscretion, 'you can't tell anybody that and definitely don't mention it to Sam. He'll be livid that Louise has told me anything.'

'Where does he work?' Carl sips his coffee. I feel gratified that he's finally showing some interest in my friends.

'He used to work at Browns Black, but he was headhunted by that American bank Bush Merriman last year on some mega salary deal. He flew Louise to Paris for dinner on a private jet to celebrate when he got the job.'

'I don't know,' Carl shrugs, but I sense his defences are weakening.

'Go on,' I gently stroke his thigh. 'It would mean a lot to me.'

'What does Louise do?' he asks, reluctantly moving my hand away and adding: 'We've *got* to go to work.'

'She's a party organiser. Actually she's got a big event this Friday. Some trader from Browns Black is having an engagement party in Hoxton.'

'Hoxton?' Carl screws up his nose.

'Should be fun. I'm helping out as a waitress.'

'This Friday?'

'Yes, why?'

'I had plans for us, babe, but if you're busy ...'

'I could cancel,' I offer.

'No,' he shakes his head. 'It's not fair to let your friend down now. There'll be plenty of other evenings for us. *Plenty.* Believe me. All I've got to do now is find somebody to come to dinner at the Ivy with me. It'd be a shame to waste the booking. They're very hard to get.' I playfully thump him. 'Okay,' he says, rubbing his arm. 'I'll order a chicken korma and stay at home in front of the telly.'

'That's right,' I say, 'away from all temptation.'

'You're the only temptation in my life, babe.'

'So if we can't make Friday, what about Saturday?' I ask.

'Oh, sorry, I meant to tell you. I've got the boys this week-end. My soon-to-be-ex is off for a girlie weekend at some luxury spa in Hertfordshire.'

'No!' I can't keep the frustration out of my voice.

'Hey!' He puts his arm around my shoulder, pulls me closer and kisses the top of my head. 'Our time will come, I promise. Let's arrange to see your friends for Sunday lunch soon. Organise it for here, it'd be so much more intimate than going to a big noisy restaurant. And why don't we spend more time together next week?'

'That would be nice,' I smile.

'I'll come over on Sunday evening, and we can plan next week? Maybe I can stay two or three nights?'

'I'd like that,' I kiss him gently.

'So would I,' he replies softly, 'but, for the moment, there's something else I'd like more.' And I watch as, with a gentle flick of his wrist, both our towels fall simultaneously to the floor.

CHAPTER TWENTY-EIGHT

'Donna, this is not fancy dress.' Louise is standing in the penthouse apartment studying my colleague's outfit. Louise is wearing a black Diane von Furstenberg wraparound dress, and has a clipboard tucked under her left arm. In her right hand she is clutching a slimline mobile phone, which she is waving in an accusatory manner at Donna, while its hands-free mouthpiece is wrapped around her ear. 'You wanted to play at waitressing, and that is certainly not an appropriate outfit.' Donna is wearing a white shirt, several buttons left open and tied at the front to reveal (once again) her amazing flat stomach. But her skirt is really stretching the definition of the word. Literally. 'You *cannot* wear that,' reiterates Louise.

'What do you expect me to do, Louise?' Donna asks sulkily. 'I haven't got time to get home and change.'

'Girls, relax,' Angus minces across the room with Pete, the pair of them in clinging white tee-shirts and tight black trousers. 'I have the answer. Donna, if you stand behind the bar all night and serve, nobody will be offended by your fanny frill.' She pulls a face. 'You'll be sent away before the fun begins if you don't behave,' he waves an immaculately manicured finger. Donna spots a hot barman and disappears. 'Darling, you've done wonders with this place. Absolute wonders,' Angus gushes to Louise.

And she has. The ceiling of the vast room, loosely covered in dark indigo sheets, and a wall, painted purple, have been covered by a mesh of fairy lights, giving the illusion of a night sky. Floor cushions, in vibrant purple silks with elaborate beading, are placed along the base of the wall, beside ornate hookah pipes. The room is bathed in soft light – large ornate candelabras create a warm atmosphere. Dramatic floral arrangements of birds of paradise fill empty corners, while old-fashioned wicker birdcages, filled with hanging tropical flowers, swing from the ceiling. Two brushed copper kidney-shaped bars have been installed. We watch a waiter putting the finishing touches to a champagne glass pyramid, made with flat-bowled glasses, set on the top of one bar. The swing band, dressed in 1950s evening glamour, is setting up in one corner. Bamboo screens hide the kitchen from view, but it is still possible to hear the clatter of dishes and pans. Louise has created the impression of a Moroccan palace. I half expect Humphrey Bogart and Ingrid Bergman to walk in. Unfortunately, the illusion is partly spoiled by a large black and white portrait of the happy couple on an easel at the entrance to the room.

'Slightly funereal, don't you think?' Pete mutters.

'The customer is always right,' Louise shrugs.

Outside, the wraparound balcony has been transformed. Garlands of ivy and fern twisted with fairy lights decorate the handrail; aluminium planters are filled with miniature palm trees; and cerise pink floor cushions are scattered at regular intervals. A temporary brick barbeque has been set up in the middle of a newly created rock garden, giving the impression that it is rising from the ground.

'Hi there.' Gavin and James are approaching. I do a double take. I've never seen James look so smart, and Gavin sure cleans up well. They are wearing dark suits, white shirts and black bow ties. Louise hugs them.

'Are you sure you don't mind?' she asks them.

'Mind what?' I ask.

'I've asked them to act as bouncers for the evening,' she replies. 'It shouldn't be a problem. It's only a bunch of City people as far as I can tell. Unfortunately Trixie's fiancé Ciaran is not as organised as she, so I haven't got his list. You'll have to get that off him when he turns up. Oh, talk of the devil.' She nods towards the open door. 'Places, people.' James and Gavin dash to take position by the silken rope at the end of a small red carpet that currently leads to the entrance.

A tall, extremely slim woman in a figure-hugging silver cocktail dress has entered, holding hands with a man in a tuxedo. They are examining their photograph. 'It's pure Versace,' mutters Pete, as he scurries off to the kitchen. 'None of this diffusion range. Check out the Jimmy Choos.' Trixie is walking on improbably high sandals, encrusted with tiny diamanté stones. 'And that's definitely Giorgio Armani,' Angus nods admiringly at Ciaran's suit as he follows Pete.

'Louise, darling,' Trixie air-kisses my friend, 'you've been an absolute marvel. This room looks divine, doesn't it Ciaran? And what a wonderful idea to have the party in Hoxton. *Vogue* said only last month that Hoxton is the new Notting Hill, and one gets so fed up with Chelsea and Kensington.'

'Exactly my thought process,' soothes Louise. 'I've kept the Moroccan theme we discussed, and you were right, I did pick up some great ideas from the *OK!* pictures of Elton's last white tie party. Unfortunately, London Zoo wouldn't hire out the camels we talked about, which is probably just as well. I measured the express lift and I don't think that we'd have fitted them.'

'Oh really? Blast!' Trixie stamps her delicate foot on the floor. 'Melissa Taylor-Green had peacocks wandering around her engagement party.'

'It *was* outdoors at Kew, darling.' Ciaran squeezes her hand. He looks around the room. 'This is amazing, Louise, you have done a fantastic job at such short notice. What time is the fireworks display?'

'Ten,' my friend says. 'Now if you'll excuse us, I've got to check the caterers.' She summons a waiter to fetch two glasses of champagne, as we walk across to the kitchen, where flamboyantly decorated ceramic serving dishes are being loaded with shish kebabs, falafel and couscous, and individual moussakas are being shoehorned into tiny copper bowls. Miniature tagine dishes are being filled and legs of lamb are being butterflied for the barbeque.

'I am really impressed,' I tell Louise. 'It's a little bit of Marrakesh in East London.'

'Thanks,' she smiles distractedly, checking off items on her clipboard. 'Although I drew the line at Moroccan wine; we're having Krug, mint juleps (a homage to mint tea) and beer. Uh oh, I can see the first guests arriving. Take this,' she shoves a silver tray into my hand, 'and stand near the door offering drinks. Quickly.' Louise pushes me out of the kitchen.

I get through three trays of drinks within twenty minutes, as the guests, all dressed in evening wear, swarm through the door. The room echoes with a current of air kissing as the women try desperately not to disturb lipstick while they greet each other. I am just about to circulate with a chilled bottle of Krug when Louise grabs my elbow and marches me into the kitchen.

'What's the matter?' I demand, indignant at the man-handling. 'I haven't spilled anything.'

'Jake is here.' She says it quietly and without emotion, awaiting my reaction.

I stop dead. 'My Jake?'

'Yes. I didn't know he was coming. He must have been on Ciaran's guest list,' she explains.

'He's here ... How does he look?'

'He looks fine,' she replies gently.

'Is he with her? Old Horse Features?' I spit her 'name' out.

She nods, and my stomach lurches.

'Do they look happy?' I ask quietly.

'It's hard to tell,' my loyal friend replies. 'Look, you shouldn't worry about them. You've got Carl now. Forget about Jake and that cow. He was a bastard who treated you badly. Remember that.'

'You're right. I know.' But logic never matters in affairs of the heart. I *am* with Carl now, and I know that I'm head over heels for him, but Jake was my first true love. And no matter how much my heart may mend, there will always be a small part that is forever his. I'm not like my mother. I can't carry hatred around with me. Jake, and his subsequent actions, have had a significant impact on my life. His careless discarding of me made me unable to commit to men. Jake has partly made me what I am today, but Jake is my past, and I've only recently realised he will never play a part in my future. Meeting Carl helped me figure that out – Carl is my future, I tell myself. And I'm ecstatically happy about that.

'Are you okay?' Louise grabs my hand. 'Do you want to go?' I nod. After he dumped me, I had a recurring dream about meeting Jake again, and we'd fall into each other's arms. But never, never in a million years, did I imagine meeting him again while I was wearing a champagne-stained white blouse, black skirt and frilly apron. 'Come on then.' Louise keeps hold of my hand as she guides me out of the kitchen towards the door. Our escape path appears clear but then inevitably, because my life sometimes stinks, I hear Jake call out.

'Holly? Is that you?' I turn slowly to face him. Jake, my Jake, is staring at me. He has filled out slightly, and his hair is now dappled with grey, but otherwise he looks the same. He looks shocked at my appearance. 'My goodness, I never knew.'

'Never knew what?' I ask, slightly confused.

'That you were working as a waitress.'

'I'm not,' I snap. This reunion is not going the way I would have liked.

'Well, I'm sorry, I didn't mean to hit a nerve. When did you give up working at Investigations-R-Us?'

'I haven't.'

'Oh, I see,' he taps his nose with his forefinger, 'mum's the word. An undercover assignment, eh?'

'No,' I reply, and wonder what right-minded young man says 'mum's the word' these days. 'I'm helping out Louise. You remember her?' I nod towards my friend.

'Of course, how are you, my dear?' He leans across me to kiss Louise on both cheeks. What? The bastard kisses my friend and has made no attempt to touch me, his former girlfriend. I seethe with indignation.

'I'm fine,' Louise says coolly.

And then I see *her*. Horse Features, teetering across on tiny sparkly heels, nostrils flaring and tousled mane flowing. God, I think bitterly, even Red Rum would have denied siring you, although he mightn't have been able to dispute the family butt. She stands beside Jake, hooking her arm possessively through his.

'Jake dear, I don't think I've been introduced to the waiting staff,' she simpers. 'What a man of the people you are.'

'Oh, these are old friends,' he replies.

Really?' She arches an over-plucked eyebrow.

'This is Louise,' hands are extended and shaken, 'and this is my old friend Holly. I think I may have mentioned her to you a couple of times.' I'm reeling in shock. Old friend? Okay, so it may be too much to say 'the former love of my life until you came along and stole me away' or even 'the first woman I ever made love to on a beach', but I think we're all grown ups here. 'An old girlfriend' is a pretty innocuous description. Louise clenches her fists in anger.

'Oh yes, I vaguely remember,' says Horse Features dismissively. 'Don't you have mutual friends in common?'

'We have nothing in common now,' I mutter. And in the instant I say it, I acknowledge the truth. I don't recognise this Jake standing in front of me. Where is the man who streaked down Upper Street to persuade me to date him? Or who poured popcorn inside his shirt in the cinema and made me 'come and get it'? 'If you will excuse me,' I say, 'I was just leaving.'

And I turn on my heel and walk out of the room. I don't look back. I don't react. I just make my way outside the building, and dissolve into tears.

'Holly?' James appears at my side. 'Are you okay?'

'I'm fine,' I lie.

'You don't look fine. Come on, I'm taking you home.'

'What about the bouncing?'

'I think Gavin can cope.' We wander in silence along the street looking for a black cab. In my haste to leave I forgot my coat, and I shiver in the night air only to feel James softly drop his jacket on my shoulders. When we reach my flat, James searches the cupboards in the kitchen for a bottle of brandy to warm us. He pours two snifters, hands me one and settles on the sofa beside me.

'Do you want to talk about it?' he finally says. 'We don't have to if you'd rather not.'

'My old boyfriend was there.'

'Which one?'

I'm so upset that I don't flinch at the crass comment.

'He's not someone Donna or any of you have ever heard of,' I reply honestly. 'In fact, he's probably the reason for the guys I dated in recent years.'

'You loved him?' he asks softly.

I nod, and tears fill my eyes. 'Once upon a time. More than he'll ever know.'

'Well, then he didn't deserve you.' James puts his arm gently around my shoulders and pulls me closer. I feel him softly kiss the top of my head. It seems both brotherly and protective. I like it.

'Why do people say that?' I demand. 'It's not true.'

'It is,' he replies. 'The person who deserves you will know everything about you. They'll know your likes, dislikes, endearing habits or strange quirks, and they can't possibly be unaware of the depth of your love, because it will mirror their own.'

'But why wasn't I good enough for him?' I cry. 'Why did he pick her? What was wrong with me?'

'He wasn't good enough for you,' he says quietly.

'No, it was me,' I insist. 'I was the one who let the side down. I was the one who didn't appreciate that he was moving up in the world. I should have been more supportive. I mocked him.'

'How?'

'I made fun of his aspirations. Once we were at supper at some fancy restaurant, and he insisted on the waiter finding grape scissors for the fruit bowl. I couldn't just ignore it, allow him his pretensions, so I handed him a pair of nail clippers out of my handbag.' James bursts out laughing. 'Jake didn't think it was quite so funny. When we got back to my flat, he went ballistic. He kept screaming at me for mocking him. I couldn't stop crying for days. That soon became the pattern of our relationship. He erupted at any potential slight. Sometimes I had to call into work sick because my eyes were too puffy from crying.' I shrug. 'I've never confided that to anybody before.'

'Why would you stay with somebody who screamed at you like that?'

'I loved him,' I reply simply. 'I gave him my heart.'

'He wasn't worth something that valuable,' soothes James.

'How can he still affect me like this? I don't love him any more.'

'He hurt and betrayed you,' says James simply. 'There are no time limits on those emotions.'

James is right, I think.

'What about you?' I ask, pushing my body around so that I'm staring at my colleague's face.

'What about me?' he smiles.

'Ever had your heart broken?'

'Hasn't everyone?' he shrugs. 'But they were only stepping-stones along the path. They broke my heart because they didn't fit it. They weren't my perfect matches.'

'So you believe everybody has a perfect match somewhere?'

'Absolutely,' he says emphatically.

'But what happens if mine is living in a Masai tribe and I never meet him?'

'I've got a feeling yours is closer to home than that,' James replies, nodding at the bouquet of flowers from Carl. And I blush, like a naughty schoolgirl, caught with her secret lover.

CHAPTER TWENTY-NINE

I spent yesterday in bed. Alone. It was a wallowing day. My final day of mourning for what might have been with Jake. And yet, I now know with amazing clarity, that we would never have lasted. His initial attitude towards me last night when he thought I was a waitress, and then his offhand dismissal of me to Horse Features, revealed him in his true light. Obviously I knew he had changed, but last night emphasised how much. It also emphasised how silly I have been. I have spent the past six years foregoing any hope of a proper long-term relationship because I thought no man could ever measure up to Jake. The reality is that Jake probably couldn't measure up to any of them. Those men I dated were better people than Jake because they didn't need to pretend they were anything else to prove themselves. They were comfortable in their own skins and, while they would certainly have loved to drive around in a top of the range Ferrari, that wouldn't have defined them. Sean is just as proud cycling around on his bicycle, with his bright red personalised pennant flapping in the wind. It marks his achievement.

James was brilliant. He stayed for a couple of hours, listened to my tales of woe, and left. I am certain he suspects that I am seeing somebody. He made a couple of pointed comments about the flowers and then my mobile bleeped several times during the evening with texts from Carl. But, like a gentleman, he didn't say anything. I do hope he meets somebody soon. The woman who wins James's heart will be extremely lucky.

He called me yesterday, just to check up on how I was, and to report that Tracy Bruce had again received her weekly bouquet but that, surprisingly, Carmen Hughes, now known as Heron to the surveillance team, had also received one. Poppy's Posies delivered both. It was, as James pointed out, almost like the sender knew we were onto him last week when he swapped to Double Dutch florists. I make a note to pursue this further.

But now, as if the weekend could not get worse, I am about to meet my mother for Sunday lunch. She has specified a darkened restaurant because, apparently, discovering her own aura has opened up her eyes to the auras around her. Crowded places are now out, apparently, the clash of colours gives her a headache. I have decided to take Miss Binchy with me. They haven't met before and it will be nice for my neighbour to have an outing – and I am feeling a little guilty that I haven't seen much of her recently.

'It's so lovely of you to invite me, Holly dear,' says Miss Binchy as we enter the candle-lit restaurant. 'There's only football on the telly this afternoon, even *EastEnders* was cancelled. But we'll be back for Graham Norton, won't we dear? He's such a nice Irish boy.'

My mother is waiting for us at a wooden farmhouse-style table. A gossamer scarf trimmed with fake coins is flung Sophie Loren style across her hair and neck. She is wearing an off-the-shoulder white broderie anglaise gypsy top, with a long floral skirt over an assortment of cotton petticoats. Her wrists are adorned with big bangles and charm bracelets and big gold hoops hang from her ears. Miss Binchy, who is probably no more than ten years older than my mother, is dressed like Emily Bishop from *Coronation Street*.

'It's so lovely to finally meet you, my dear,' Miss Binchy says, settling her ample behind onto a carver chair. 'Please call me Maureen. Are you going to a party later? That's such a lovely costume.'

'It's the costume of my people,' my mother says pompously.

'Really, dear.' Miss Binchy smiles. 'Where are you from?'

'Harrow.'

There's an awkward silence. For somebody who often can't tell me whether it's morning or night or whether the milkman has delivered two red tops, Miss Binchy is today displaying remarkable perceptiveness. I'm beginning to wonder if this was such a good idea.

'So, Holly tells me that you've just discovered your true calling, dear,' she continues. 'Which convent will you be entering?'

'It's not a religious calling,' my mother says indignantly. 'It's a spiritual calling. I see colour wherever I go.'

'Ooh, but so can I dear. I thought that was normal.' Miss Binchy appears confused.

'I see colours where there aren't any,' continues my mother.

'Do you have a black and white telly then? The licence is so much cheaper.'

'No,' snaps my mother. 'I see colours around people. Take yourself, Miss Binchy – Maureen – I see you in a blue haze.'

'Ach, that's probably my rinse, dear. My normal hairdresser wasn't around yesterday. I got a student.'

'I'm not talking about your hair, Maureen. It's your personal aura. I sense great unhappiness in your past.'

'Ah, sure I was unhappy when Ireland lost the Eurovision last year. Lovely song it was. I couldn't believe those cruets won.'

'Croatians,' I correct.

'I sense a great loss in your life, Maureen,' my mother continues, undaunted. 'Perhaps a young man that you never got over?'

'Aye, there was a young man,' Miss Binchy replies.

'I'm right?' My mother sounds surprised. 'And you never got over him?'

'But of course I got over him,' Miss Binchy replies. 'I had no choice.' She pauses. 'The human heart is an amazing thing. Tragedies happen every day. People die in terrible circumstances. Children get taken from their parents. Yet the heart

201

continues to beat, even when you pray for it to stop, and with each beat the pain lessens. Until one day your loss is not the first thing on your mind on wakening. And then the recovery begins.'

'But he was your great love,' I prompt, surprised at her reaction. I cried over the story of a proposal that never came. I now own the coat from a going-away outfit that was never to be worn. He is the reason Miss Binchy is single. He put her life on hold, just like Jake did to mine.

'Aye, he was my great love. I thought I would never get over him,' Miss Binchy nods. 'But I daresay there could have been other loves I would have been happy with. But the Good Lord did not see a reason for us to find each other.'

'It is one man. One love,' says my mother bitterly.

'Really? But that's not fair,' replies Miss Binchy. 'What about the young widows of the great wars? Did they not deserve to meet somebody else?'

'But they couldn't love their second husbands as much. They weren't their first loves, their true loves,' insists my mother.

'Who's to say the second loves weren't their true loves?'

'But the first love is the deepest,' my mum is emphatic.

'No, dear, the first love is the novelty,' replies Miss Binchy softly.

'Don't you ever miss being married?' I ask Miss Binchy.

'You can't miss what you never had,' she says simply. 'But sometimes, dear, on cold, dark winter nights, when it's not possible to go out visiting, I miss having somebody to talk to. I used to have a cat called Marmalade, you know. Beautiful tabby she was, but she died of old age last year.' I look at my neighbour in horror. Today her mind is so clear that she can recall what happened to Marmalade – no wonder I have never seen the cat – but it just emphasises how her grip on reality is fading. This is not just absent-mindedness. This is something far worse. 'And sometimes when I'm ill in bed – which isn't very often, us Binchys have marvellous constitutions – it would be nice to have someone to bring me a cup of tea.'

'You can always call me,' I say.

'Ah bless you, dear,' she pats my hand gently. 'But you have your own life to lead. My nephew Seamus is wonderful too. He's just like a son, and does his best to watch after me. He likes you dear,' she smiles at me. The fog is starting to descend again, I think sadly. I have never met *that* nephew. 'But they're only little niggles. I really am a very lucky woman with many blessings. I have my family, my health and nearly all my own teeth.'

'A relationship is not the be all and end all,' my mother regains her 'all men are bastards' composure.

Miss Binchy nods.

'Indeed it's not, dear,' she says quietly. 'If it isn't right, then a relationship can be the unhappiest place to be in the world.'

CHAPTER THIRTY

I suppose it was inevitable that my mother and Miss Binchy would get on. Despite their opposing views on love and relationships, they have a lot in common. And I'm not just talking about a love of Dot Cotton. It's strange, but today at lunch Miss Binchy appeared the wisest of all of us. She was a woman of the world, even though she'd never travelled further than the Irish Sea. But as lunch went on, I could feel the fog thickening. She started muddling her nephew Seamus with Colm, patting my hand and constantly telling me that she'd a feeling he'd a soft spot for me. And then Miss Binchy became convinced that she'd left an apple pie in the oven. She got so distressed that we cut short our lunch, grabbed a cab and returned home. Even Mum came. Of course, there was nothing in the oven. And then Mum noticed the full dish of cat food.

'Poor thing,' she mouths at me. 'Her mind is going.'

We settle Miss Binchy in her drawing room, on her chintz armchair, and make a recuperative pot of tea. 'I'll have a slice of that hot apple pie,' she shouts after us as we disappear to the kitchen.

'I never want to end up like that,' my mother says.

'Me neither,' I admit.

'I've seen those symptoms before,' she adds sadly.

'Oh?'

'Your father's mother Peg. It was the first stages of Alzheimer's. Poor dear. She was a widow, and I used to visit her every week in the home. Your father couldn't, he found it too distressing. Some days Peggy didn't recognise me, other times she'd be full of questions. Peg could sometimes recall events that happened during the war like they were yesterday, but then she couldn't remember what she had for dinner.'

'Miss Binchy can be like that. What happened to Peg?'

'I don't know. I never saw her again after your father left me.' She shakes her head. 'That man. He did so much damage to so many lives.'

'I'll never let you be alone like that,' I say. 'I'll be here for you.'

'But some day I won't be here for you.'

'Mum. Don't.'

'It's true. And it's selfish of me to impose my beliefs on you. I know I'm just a bitter, twisted woman who blames her ex-husband for all her troubles and has turned into a man-hating shrew.' She pours the boiling water into the pot, puts on the lid and settles it on a tray before facing me. 'But I love you, Holly, and I'd hate to see you end up alone like that poor lady in there, dependent on a cat for company. You need someone. You deserve somebody. After all, didn't I have a relationship, the big day and the meringue dress? Maybe Miss Binchy is right. Maybe there is more than one person out there for us.' My mother hugs me. 'I'd like you to find him.'

I'm overwhelmed but I can't instantly respond because I hear the buzzer to my flat sounding. It's Carl, I think. He's arrived early.

'I think I have found him, Mum,' I say. 'And I'd like you to meet him now.'

I race through to the hallway, pull open the front door and jump into Carl's arms. He looks slightly taken aback by the intensity of the greeting.

'Wow,' he says, when I finally pull my mouth away from his.

'"Hello" would have done just as well, but I'm not complaining, babe. I missed you too.' He nods towards the large tote bag he is carrying. 'I thought I'd move some of my stuff in, so that I'm not scrambling around buying shirts on the way to work.'

I grab his free hand. 'There's somebody here I want you to meet,' I say, pulling him into Miss Binchy's flat. My mother is just passing my neighbour a china cup and saucer. 'Mum, Miss Binchy, this is Carl.' He shakes hands with my mother. Miss Binchy just waves a chocolate biscuit in greeting.

'So you're the new man?' my mother asks. 'The business-man.'

'Guilty as charged,' Carl smiles.

'You've a strange aura,' says Mum.

Carl flushes, and does a rapid series of tiny sniffs.

'I'm sorry. I've come straight from the gym.'

'My mother thinks she's a bit of a psychic,' I explain. 'She reckons she can see coloured auras around people.'

'Oh.' Carl appears to relax.

'Yours is very grey,' Mum continues.

'Is that good?' he asks.

'Does it sound good?' snarls my mother. 'Do you associate grey with happiness?'

'Mum, please,' I warn.

'I can see it too,' Miss Binchy pipes up. 'There's a big black cloud over your head. It sends shivers down my spine.'

'Miss Binchy, you don't have any psychic powers,' I snap, suddenly annoyed with both of them. 'And nor do you, Mum. This farce has gone quite far enough. Come on, Carl, we're going.'

I angrily stomp up the stairs, slam my front door behind me and turn to Carl.

'I am so sorry,' I say. 'My bloody mother is such an idiot. Ignore what she says, and my neighbour is quite barking.'

'It's me who's the idiot.' His tone is quiet but somehow menacing. 'What a set up. I should have realised.'

'Sorry?' I'm bemused.

'What was that downstairs? Were they trying to suss me out? Find out my intentions towards you?'

'No!' I protest. 'I didn't even know my mother would be here.'

'Because I came over here in good faith, hoping to surprise you with plans to move stuff in ...'

'Which I'm thrilled about,' I interrupt. I didn't initially understand the significance of Carl's earlier comments. He is moving his stuff into my flat. That's a sign of commitment.

'And you have your mother waiting to check me out?' He is seething.

'I didn't.'

'Well, I bloody well didn't invite her!'

'What does it matter if my mother meets you?' I suddenly demand.

'Didn't we say this relationship should be kept quiet?' he says slowly.

'But only because of the work conflict,' I reply.

'I am a well-known businessman, Holly, who is getting divorced. That divorce will be very expensive. The last thing I need is for it to appear in the newspapers that I am seeing somebody new.'

'I hardly think my mother will ...'

'That's not the point,' he yells at me. 'It's not what we agreed. I haven't told anybody about us.' Nobody? I'm slightly taken aback. I had felt so happy about our relationship that I wanted to shout it from the rooftops. I had hoped Carl felt the same. 'I'm going for a walk, and I will decide then whether I will move my stuff in as planned or not.'

'How long will you be?' I ask, tears falling down my face.

'I don't know, but I will be back.'

I crumple into a sobbing heap as the door slams. This is our first real argument and it seems so unjust. I never invited my mother to check him out. I can understand part of his reaction, but it does seem rather excessive. I recall one profile I read that said Carl had a tendency to fly off the handle easily, but I dismissed it. I can't help thinking of James's comment about Jake's screaming fit. 'Why would you stay with somebody who screamed at you like that?' Once again, the answer is the same: because I love him.

My buzzer sounds three hours later. It's Carl. He looks sheepish when I open the door.

'I'm sorry,' he says, opening his arms for me to fall into. He kisses the top of my head. 'It's been a lousy weekend. My wife cancelled her plans so I had to play happy families with her and the children. It was so painful. She was constantly baiting me. But that's my problem. I shouldn't have taken it out on you. Can you forgive me?'

'Forgiven and forgotten,' I whisper, although I know even as I say the words that I won't be able to forget his irrational behaviour for quite some time.

'Let's go to bed,' he whispers.

I am just getting under the covers when my mobile buzzes. Carl is in the bathroom. I check the text message.

21.50
From: Carl (moby)
ILY. X

I look up and Carl is standing in the bedroom doorway, neatly folding his shirt like a professional Benetton salesman.

'It's true,' he says tenderly. 'But I don't want to say it out loud until my divorce comes through. I don't want to jinx this relationship. You mean too much. But I think I've found the woman I want to spend the rest of my life with.'

This time I throw open my arms.

CHAPTER THIRTY-ONE

James and I are sitting in the car outside the Kensington flat of Heron, aka Carmen Hughes, and the late entry candidate for Ilyax Insurance's head of human resources. It is the first time we have worked together on this particular surveillance operation, and the first time we have had time to chat since my emotional breakdown over Jake. I feel rather embarrassed about my outburst although James hasn't mentioned it yet. It seems so silly to be getting upset about Jake now that I've got Carl. After his outburst on Sunday, he stayed at my flat two nights running and even promised to meet Louise and Sam for Sunday lunch – which sent me into spasms of terror until Louise agreed to teach me to cook a simple meal.

A toothbrush has been installed in my bathroom wall fitting. A container of Carl's preferred coffee sits in my kitchen cupboard. The video has already taped his favourite American cop series. And, the downside this, his dirty clothes are cluttering up my laundry basket. It's the first time I've felt this comfortable with a man since Jake and yet, I know this sounds silly, Carl and I haven't really talked about where we're heading. There has been no suggestion of my meeting his three children, nor any timescale on his divorce. But it's baby steps, I console myself, and this week I learned that Carl liked *CSI Las Vegas* rather than *CSI New York*. It's something we have in common, but there's so much more I'd like to know. Where does Carl stand on boy bands? *Pop Idol* or *X Factor*? *West Wing* or *Sopranos*? Obviously I also want to discuss some important world issues, like global warming, and whether Sir Bob Geldof should be canonised, but I suppose there's plenty of time to talk about serious matters.

Anyway, I know Carl has been distracted. The announcement about Clive Partridge as finance director is imminent. Apparently, it was delayed while all the details of his salary and benefits package were being worked out. Carl had to call in a remuneration specialist to assess the correct value for somebody of Clive's standing in the international marketplace. He says it takes time to get the balance right, especially as Clive has to be compensated for losing the benefits he had accrued in his years at Egyptia Insurance. In many ways it was an easy assignment for Investigations-R-Us. I just wish others could be like that.

'Heron is up.' James nods at the light that has just come on at an upstairs window of the white stucco-fronted building. Carmen lives in a beautiful residential square with the original Victorian street lights. Most of the parking spaces are taken up with cars that would not be out of place in a Park Lane showroom. I notice that many of the houses have yet to be converted into flats. I can tell because the curtains match in all the windows, and the front door frames are not a mess of bells. There is a gated garden in the centre of the square for the sole use of residents. Each house has its own key, and we watch as the first early birds open the gates to walk their dogs. A milk float chugs down the street, its driver whistling as he makes his deliveries.

To date, like the other candidates, Heron has not displayed any tendencies that might make her unsuitable for the position. She is a fitness fanatic who works out three times a week during her lunch-hour, as Donna found to her cost during her surveillance stint. Other than that Heron has paid one visit to the cinema, made a trip to the supermarket for her weekly shop and spent two evenings at a wine bar with friends.

My mobile buzzes. It's my good morning text from Carl. I

smile as I quickly write my reply: 'And you!' James watches me carefully.

'Is that your secret admirer?' he finally asks.

'What?' I'm taken aback. 'What do you mean?'

'Holly,' he sighs. 'I've sat in this car with you on I don't know how many days over the past month watching women who, frankly, lead quite mundane lives. We are both now Sudoku experts. My new record for finishing the *Telegraph* cryptic crossword is forty-five minutes. Your record for finishing the *Telegraph*'s easy crossword is one hour twenty. We have played countless games of I-Spy, although I still think you cheated over that Z clue ...'

'How dare you?' I retort. 'There really was a stuffed nodding zebra in the back of that car. I couldn't help the fact that it drove off before you saw it.'

'Whatever.' He waves his hand dismissively. 'The point is we have spent lots of time in close proximity with not much to distract us, so it's hardly surprising that I notice your face lights up when you get certain text messages.'

'It doesn't,' I protest, secretly delighted that my pleasure is so obvious.

'It does,' he insists. 'And I've also noticed that somebody texts you at roughly the same time every morning.'

'How do you know that they're from the same person?'

'Your mobile now has two text message alerts,' he points out. 'One type of alert rarely excites you. In fact, you can take ages before you check those texts out. The other type seems to demand an immediate read and response action, and you can't stop beaming for some time afterwards. Plus you also have two types of rings for phone calls too.'

'It could be Louise,' I point out.

'It could be,' he concedes, 'but I don't think so.'

'You seem to have spent an awful long time analysing me,' I retort.

'I can hardly ignore it. You're sitting barely two feet from me, and I am an investigator. Even the most inept detective could work it out. Look, you don't have to say anything and I promise I won't tell Angus or Donna if you confide in me.'

'There is somebody,' I finally concede. 'But I don't want to say more than that.'

'Fair enough,' says James quietly. 'Just answer me this question. Does he make you happy?'

'Yes,' I reply simply.

'Good. I'm really pleased for you. Nobody deserved to take the abuse that you told me Jake directed at you. A temper that fiery can never be controlled.' I shift uncomfortably at this comment. I am still trying to forget Carl's eruption on Sunday and, if I'm honest, his earlier outburst on the phone. 'Anyway, at least I know why you dated the men you did.'

'Don't go all Sigmund Freud on me,' I warn.

'I'm not,' he says quietly. 'I'm just telling you that I understand. Jake destroyed your self-esteem.'

'He didn't.' I don't like this pseudo psycho-analysis. 'I dated those men because I fancied them.'

'Holly,' he says quietly. 'The only thing you had in common with most of them was that you each lived in London. Just fancying them was not enough.'

'Well, I fancy my new man,' I boast. 'And he's definitely not a deadbeat.'

'I'm glad, because you deserve somebody fantastic, Holly.' James's soft tone surprises me, and I'm just about to say something when Heron comes out of the front door. 'Off you go,' James pushes me out of the car. 'Give your skinny jeans an airing. I'll see you at Ilyax headquarters.'

Three hours later James joins me at Starbucks for his mid-morning latte. The back-up team are primed to react if Heron leaves the building in the meantime.

'Do you come here often?' he laughs, placing his mug and blueberry muffin on the table. Before I can respond my mobile rings. 'It's the non-boyfriend ring,' he jokes. I stick out my tongue before answering.

'Holly, it's Donna. Great news. Clive Partridge's appointment as finance director was announced this morning. The stock market loves it. Shares in Ilyax Insurance have raced up. And, get this, you never told me he was so valuable. Clive is on a basic salary of over half a million pounds a year. Is he single?'

'No,' I laugh. 'Get on with it.'

'Worth a try. Right, it's a three-year contract, which I'm sure some shareholders will object to, and there's a special clause if Ilyax Insurance gets bought out or merges with a competitor within his first year.'

'That's unusual,' I muse.

'I suppose, but you don't want to leave a good job and find yourself out of the new one within the year, do you? In that event Clive Partridge will get ... hang on, let me see if I can find it in this announcement.' I hear Donna quietly reading through the announcement. 'Five million pounds.'

'Five million pounds. Shit! That's a shed-load of money.'

'Must be the going rate,' says Donna. 'These insurance companies aren't stupid.' They're not, I think, remembering Carl and his remuneration experts. They can't have got it wrong. It just sounds so much to ordinary people. 'So it's congratulations to you for a job well done. Boris has already put a few bottles of bubbly in the fridge for your return, although he did moan that Investigations-R-Us has not been paid yet. See you back at the ranch. Ciao.'

'Who was that?' James asks.

'Donna,' I reply. 'Clive Partridge's appointment has just been made.'

'Well done you,' he beams, clinking his mug against mine. 'I'm just going to run over to that news-stand and pick up the early edition of the evening paper. Hold tight.'

My mobile rings (special tone) as soon as James runs out of the coffee shop.

'Have you seen the announcement, babe?'

'Just heard about it now. I'm so pleased for you.'

'I couldn't have done it without your help,' he replies.

'What about a celebration later?' I ask hopefully.

'Oh darling, I've just agreed to go out with some of the

guys. It's been a hectic few days and we deserve to let off a bit of steam.'

'No probs,' I say, trying to keep the disappointment out of my voice. 'It was short notice.'

'We're still on for Sunday, right? Meeting your friends?' Sunday, I think, that's four days away. Are we ever going to spend a Saturday night together?

'Yeah, they're really looking forward to it.' Again, I mask my disappointment.

'Me too,' he says. 'That's the other phone. Got to go. Remember. I. L. Y.'

I am still on cloud nine when James comes running up with a copy of the evening paper under his arm. 'Here it is,' he pants, turning to the business section and placing the paper on the table in front of us. We both read the piece in silence. 'That's strange,' he says.

'What is?'

'Final paragraph.'

'Not got there yet.'

'It says the announcement comes on the same day that an actuary at Ilyax Insurance announced his intention to sue for unfair dismissal and sexual discrimination.'

'A man suing for sexual discrimination? That's weird.'

'Sure is. He says he was fired after management learned he was seeing a female colleague. Apparently there's some rule forbidding inter-office relationships.'

'I'm no expert but I'd say that's pretty hard to enforce legally,' I reply.

'It says here: "Peter Porter, 36, alleges he is not the first male employee to fall foul of the rule, introduced shortly after the charismatic Carl Lawson became chief executive at Ilyax Insurance." 'Peter Porter? That name sounds familiar.' He snaps his fingers a couple of times. 'Where have I heard it before?'

My stomach churns. I look at James in shock. My mouth feels dry and my hands clammy.

'Peter Porter,' I finally say. 'Peter Porter is Flamingo's boyfriend.'

James's eyes widen in horror.

'That means our surveillance got him fired.'

'I know.' Guilt is already starting to overwhelm me.

CHAPTER THIRTY-TWO

Carl's mobile was turned off for most of yesterday afternoon. I left six messages but he has not rung back, although he has sent several texts telling me to calm down. Peter Porter, he claims, is a nutcase. His actuarial assumptions were wrong. He was fired for incompetence, and instead of taking it on the chin, he has put together some cock and bull story about sexual discrimination. His departure had nothing to do with any surveillance findings. The texts partly assuage my concerns, but I really wish I could speak to Carl. Investigations-R-Us could be in for a major damages claim if Peter Porter ever discovers its undercover surveillance had revealed his personal relationship to Ilyax. He's an actuary, for God's sake. He'll know to the last penny how much he could expect to earn over his career. Plus I'm more than a little perturbed about the unpaid bills. Boris jokingly brought it up twice last night over our congratulatory drinks, and I hope he was only jesting when he mentioned potential cash flow problems if the invoices continue to pile up.

Not that I've got much time to worry about that this morning. James and I are assigned to Heron, and it seems she's now gone on a shopping trip when she should be working. I dread putting this transgression into her file. It is eleven in the morning, and she is walking in the direction of Leadenhall Market. The City of London is filled with anachronisms such as this – a fourteenth-century arcade, with cobbled walkways and shop fronts painted in green, burgundy and cream, all covered by a massive wrought iron and glass roof, nestling in the shadow of the massive steel tubes of the Lloyd's building, and its neighbouring steel and glass skyscrapers. The market dates back to the Middle Ages when traders came from outside London to sell poultry, cheese and butter. I once heard that a gander was buried here after lying in state. Like Babe in the movies, 'Old Tom' managed to escape a two-day slaughter that finished off 34,000 fellow geese and became a local hero, fed by all the local innkeepers, until he died at the age of 38. I'm not sure that Heron knows any of this. She's heading for a branch of Jigsaw.

I pretend to look at the clothes while keeping a watchful eye on Carmen, but my attention is distracted when my phone rings. Shit! I thought I'd turned it off. The screen says: 'Louise: Home'. I quickly answer, and before my friend can utter a word, tell her that I'm extremely busy and hang up. I switch to vibrate mode and drop it back in my pocket. Within seconds it is shaking away. I answer again and, in slightly more harsh tones this time, hiss that I really am very busy, but a strangulated sound comes through the phone, like an animal in pain.

'Louise? Are you alright?' That sound again: my best friend sounds in trouble. 'Louise! Answer me. Now.' I hear noisy sniffing and snorting, then deep breathing like she is trying to calm herself down. 'It's okay, darling,' I soothe. 'Nice and slowly. Come on now. Breathe in. Breathe out.' From the corner of my eye I see Heron heading towards the changing room, a burgundy linen blouse in her hand. 'Everything will be alright,' I say gently. 'Tell me what's wrong.'

'It's Sam,' she eventually sobs.

'Has there been an accident?' My heart is racing. What on earth is wrong with my best friend?

'No.' She tries to catch her breath. 'I can't find him.'

'You can't find him,' I repeat. 'Where is he meant to be?'

'In the office.' Louise gulps repeatedly, like she's choking.

'And he's not there?'

'No.' A staccato of gulps.

'You think he's with someone?' I quiz gently.

'Yes.' It's my turn to gulp now.

'A woman?' I ask.

'No!' My scandalous accusation appears to stop her gulping. 'Nothing like that.'

'What is it then, Louise?' I ask softly.

'I can't find him,' she repeats.

'Yes, and ...'

'And it's time.'

'Time?' I glance at my watch confused. 'It's just gone eleven.'

'No! It's time,' she shouts down the phone. 'My fertility kit says I'm ovulating. I need Sam here as soon as possible, but I can't find him. Can't you help? What's the point of having a best friend who is an investigator? Can't you find him?'

'Have you tried his mobile?'

'Of course I have. Don't you realise this is a matter of life or death?'

'Woah!' I say, trying to calm her down. 'Is his phone off?'

'No. It's diverted to his answerphone.'

'That's something,' I muse. 'Right, Louise, have you any idea where he might be?'

'His secretary said he's gone to a meeting but she won't tell me where, or which company it is. Apparently there are some stupid bloody insider-dealing rules; she could get sued for telling me, and I could get sued for knowing. Honestly, it's like she signed the Official Secrets Act.'

'Come on now Louise. What about pillow talk? Hasn't Sam spilled the beans when you're getting cosy ...'

'You're joking,' she interrupts. 'He's getting home at three in the morning. All he's fit for is sleeping. Can you help?'

'Well, no, I'm kind of on a job, but ... hold on there ...' I pause for a moment. 'Give me Sam's mobile phone number,' I fish a pen out of my handbag, and jot the number on the back of my hand. 'I'll speak to James. He has a friend who has access to some amazing computer thingummy that's able to trace the location of people through their mobiles. We have to pray that Sam hasn't turned it off since you last called. The tracer only works if a mobile is generating a signal.'

'Is James nearby?'

'Just outside,' I reply. 'I'm not promising anything though. If the computer tells us that he's in a building with hundreds of floors, it could be impossible to find him in time.'

'But he'll have to sign in,' she reasons. 'Can't you just check with the receptionist?'

I suddenly have a brainwave. 'I'll call Gavin. He's brilliant at distracting receptionists. Look, if this has got any chance of working, I'm going now. I'll check in later. Keep calm.'

And then I run out of Jigsaw and back down to Gracechurch Street, where James is sitting in a red Toyota Corolla. I dash to the car, and jump into the passenger seat. He looks at me in surprise.

'What the hell's going on? Where's Heron?'

'In Jigsaw. There's been a change of plan,' I blurt out. 'I need you to ring your buddy who can track people through their mobile phones. I need the location of this number.' I thrust my hand in front of his face. He grips my arm and pushes it away firmly.

'Not until you tell me what's going on.' I briefly explain. Without another word, he pulls out his mobile and starts dialling. I call Donna, who gives me Gavin's number. He answers on the third ring. It sounds like I've woken him.

'Gavin?' I shout. 'I need you immediately.'

'I'm sorry,' he says sleepily. 'I don't do command performances. Please call back later and I'll book you in.'

'It's Holly Parker,' I say.

'Oh!' I can hear the rustle of sheets as he positions himself upright in bed.

'I need you to work your magic on a receptionist.'

'What kind of magic are we talking about?'

'The kind that distracts her long enough for you to scan the visitors' book.'

'Where? When?'

'I don't know where,' I look over at James who shakes his

219

head, 'as yet, but just get ready and I'll call you ASAP. This is an emergency.'

'That's what all the girls say,' he replies. The line goes dead.

'Right,' James says. 'It'll take my friend a few moments. He's going to call back. You do realise though that this could be a case of looking for a needle in a haystack?'

'Yes, but if you could only hear Louise,' I tell him. 'I've got to try.'

I notify the other car that we are pulling out of the surveillance. There is no spare team to replace us, so I tell my undercover agent on the accompanying motorbike to be extra vigilant. The time ticks by. I don't want to ring Louise until we have some definite news. Suddenly James's phone rings. I watch him nod, jot something down and then thank his friend profusely.

'We're all systems go. I have the exact coordinates. It looks like Sam is located in an office building on Bishopsgate, just round the corner from here. My friend can't be one hundred per cent certain from the satellite picture, but it doesn't look like one of the high-rise ones. He estimates there may be about ten floors, possibly a few more.' I ring Gavin to give him the location. We might just be able to pull this one off.

We reach the location in minutes. One building occupies the site. It has blackened glass and a fancy iron sculpture of a rabbit in mid flight just outside its front door. I notice the sign over the entrance and realise it's a small insurance company. A motorcyclist draws up twenty minutes later. A man in leathers and helmet, holding a brown paper package, enters the building. Within minutes he is back outside, and standing by our car.

'Hi there, Holly, but I'm afraid it's a no-go,' he shrugs. 'The receptionist is a man, and immune to my obvious charms.' He winks.

'Shit! Did you manage to get a look at the visitors' book while you were talking? Is Sam in this building?' I feel hassled.

Time is running out. Louise will be desperate by now. 'I need to know that this is definitely the right place.'

James is talking on his mobile. 'It is,' he shouts out. 'My buddy reckons we're within one hundred metres of Sam's phone.' He disconnects. 'It's up to you, Holly, to go in there and woo the security man. Gavin, you stay here. We're going to need you to get the precious cargo to Louise in one piece.'

'But Sam can't wear any biking leathers,' I warn as I advance toward the entrance. 'He needs to keep it all very cool down there. Flowing freely. He's on enforced "boxer shorts cover". I repeat: no leathers!'

The uniformed security guard is sitting behind a large black marble counter, watching a bank of televisions that are screening live feed from all the CCTV cameras in the building. A white plastic sash stretches from the commissionaire's right shoulder to his hip and a medal, attached to a red and green striped ribbon, is pinned to his breast pocket. He smiles as I approach.

'Afternoon, miss. How can I help you?'

'Oh, good afternoon,' I reply. 'I really don't know what to do. You'll think me such an idiot.' My voice is that of 'a desperate little girl lost'. I remember something I saw on telly: when actors want to cry to order they think hard about something profoundly upsetting, like a young puppy dying or starving children in Africa. So I stand in front of the reception desk and concentrate hard on Madonna's acting skills and slowly a tear starts to form. The security man looks slightly concerned. Another tear slides onto my cheek and my body begins to shake. Concern turns to alarm. He pulls a freshly starched white cotton handkerchief out of his breast pocket. 'Thank you,' I smile weakly. He leans across the desk as if to offer a comforting arm, before catching himself. The company has probably issued warnings about inappropriate gestures towards female employees.

'Are you alright there?' he finally asks. 'Nothing can be as bad as this.'

'Oh ...' a sharp gulp of air, 'yes it can.' I sob. 'It's a disaster.'

This is so convincing, I think smugly to myself. Perhaps I should change careers.

'I'm sure that's not true,' he says in a kindly voice. 'What's the matter?'

I wipe my eyes and blow my nose as if in an effort to calm myself down. 'I've forgotten who my boss has come to visit here. His mobile's on divert and I've a really urgent message for him. If I don't get it to him immediately then I'll lose my job, no question about it. He said to interrupt him as soon as the message arrived, but I forgot to write down who he was meeting so he won't get his message. He'll be furious and I'll lose my job.' I let out a deep sigh.

'Right,' the guard says slowly. 'Let me see if I've got this right. Your boss is in this building. You can't remember whom he's meeting, and now you've got an urgent message for him. Is that the problem?' I nod eagerly. 'Well now dear, that doesn't sound too awful. I'm sure we can sort this mess out. What did you say your boss's name was?'

'Sam,' I blurt out, 'Sam Jones-Pickering. He works for Bush Merriman, the investment bank.' The security guard nods knowingly, lifts up a clipboard and runs his finger down the list of visitors who have signed into the building today.

'He's not here,' he finally says, shaking his head sadly as he places the clipboard down on the desk in front of him. 'I'm sorry.'

'But he must be,' I shriek. 'Please check again.' I lean over the desk, and push the clipboard back towards him.

'Okay,' he sighs, shrugging his shoulders. I watch him mouthing the names, as he draws his finger down the list one more time. He stops.

'Sam Jones-Pickering, did you say?'

'Yes!'

'Ah, here we are. There's an S. Jones-Pickering who signed in this morning.'

'Thank goodness. Now please, where is he so I can give him his message?'

'I'm afraid that I can't just let you into the building,' retorts the security guard, indignant I would even suggest he breached company policy. He checks his clipboard. 'There's no record here that you might be visiting. Nobody has warned me about this. All visitors have to be authorised by a member of staff before they can get admitted. We have to be very careful these days.'

'You're a member of staff,' I exclaim. 'Authorise me. Admit me.'

He shakes his head slowly. My hero is turning into a nightmare.

"Fraid I can't do that, miss. Now why don't you tell me the message, and I'll ring the concierge on the floor that Mr Jones-Pickering is on and ask him to pass it on.'

'I can't do that,' I sigh. 'It's rather personal. It'd be embarrassing for him.'

'Believe me, miss, we've heard everything in this line of work. Fred, the concierge on that floor, is the soul of discretion.'

'I can't tell you.'

'Well, you can't come in.' He claps his hands to emphasise the point. 'Are you really willing to lose your job over this?' He smiles kindly. 'I don't think so.' He winks.

'Okay,' I finally say, 'Can Fred tell Mr Jones-Pickering that his wife wants him to return home immediately and make her pregnant?'

Without another word the security guard presses a silver button in a panel on the desk. A glass gate swings wide open, granting me access into the building.

'Third floor, turn left out of the lifts and fourth door along. It's the Ebony Room.'

I dash to the bank of lifts about twenty metres behind the gate, and rush towards Sam and his precious sperm. The Ebony Room has a small metal panel on its door, signalling that a meeting is in process. I rap out a distinct knock and walk straight in. Four men in grey suits and a woman in a bright red jacket are sitting around a wooden table, empty polystyrene coffee cups in front of them, watching another woman scribbling down numbers with a black marker pen on a white board. Sam is not here. They all turn and look at me in surprise. The woman at the board, which I note is headed 'Operation Illinois', tries to shield some of her scribbling.

'Sorry,' I say, blushing. 'I have an urgent message for Sam Jones-Pickering. I must have the wrong room.'

'He's in the men's room,' replies the woman with the marker pen in a haughty tone. 'Now if you'd excuse us.' She shoos me away with her hand. I leave the room, desperately looking up and down the corridor for the sign of a matchstick man with open legs. Never has the sign seemed so appropriate. I start walking and then notice that the loos are right beside the lifts. I run, throw open the door and see Sam standing at the urinal.

'Sam!' I shriek.

He turns in surprise. Momentarily I worry about spillage, and then I shield my eyes from the view.

'Holly, what the hell are you doing here? Get out.' He sounds horrified.

'I'm not looking.'

'That's not the point! What on earth...?'

'Louise sent me. She's in a terrible state. She's been trying to get hold of you all morning. Her temperature is just right and she needs your input immediately.'

'Now?' It's Sam's turn to sound panicked.

'Yes, I've got a motorbike waiting downstairs for you. Hurry,' I urge, before adding, 'But please be careful with you know. Don't panic and, whatever you do ... mind the zip.' I step outside into the corridor. Sam follows moments later.

'What about the meeting?' he says. 'It's important. We're going over the financials of the deal.'

'For goodness sake, Sam, you told Louise that having a baby was more important than work.'

'I know. It is. But this deal is at a critical moment.'

'And so is Louise.' We stare at each other in frustration at the situation. 'Do you want me to tell her that when it came to it, your work was more important than your family?'

'Of course not.'

'Well, sort your priorities out *right* now.' I wave an accusatory finger in his face. He shuffles awkwardly.

'Okay. I'm coming.' He follows me towards the lifts. 'My jacket. It's in the meeting room,' he cries as the doors close.

'Ring from the bike. Tell your colleagues to bring it back to the office. Now run.' We race through the lobby, past the very knowing glances of the security guard, and through the glass doors. Gavin revs up the engine the moment he sees us as James passes Sam a helmet and leather biker's jacket.

As Sam mounts the pillion, he shouts at me: 'I'll get Louise to ring you later.'

'Please, no!' I put up a warning hand. 'My work here is done. From now on, everything else is on a strictly need to know basis.'

And then Gavin accelerates away, taking Sam's precious cargo with him.

CHAPTER THIRTY-THREE

James and I stand on the pavement watching the motorbike zoom off down Bishopsgate, until it turns left at a main traffic junction and disappears from view.

'Well, that's a job well done,' I say.

'Let's hope Sam is just as successful,' my colleague replies. We both dissolve into giggles.When we recover, James adds, 'When I left my flat this morning, I never expected that I'd end up making sure somebody else had sex. It's enough trouble trying to make sure that I do.'

'I know the feeling,' I mutter.

'Mr Wonderful holding out on you?' he enquires. I glare at him. 'Sorry.' James has the decency to colour. 'That's none of my business.' There's an awkward pause. 'Changing the subject then, what did you plan to do today after surveillance?'

'Oh God! Surveillance.'

'Don't worry,' soothes James. 'The back-up team coped. Heron returned to work after spending £248.97 in Jigsaw on a linen blouse and a beaded evening skirt, and has not emerged from the building since. I think we should call it a day, and head off to enjoy the rest of the afternoon. What are your plans for the evening?'

Plans? There is something important I'm meant to be doing. But in all the excitement of the past few hours it's gone from my mind. I search my memory. It's definitely not a date with Carl. How could it be? Mr Elusive is not answering his phone so I can't organise anything, and besides he made it clear yesterday that we wouldn't be meeting up until Sunday. Sunday ... suddenly I remember.

'Oh shit!'

'What?' James looks alarmed. 'What's wrong? Are you meant to be somewhere else right now?'

'You could say that.'

'Can I give you a lift?' He nods towards the car.

I shake my head. 'I don't think I'd be very welcome.'

'Why?'

'I was meant to be meeting Louise at her house, and she was going to teach me how to cook.'

'Cook? I thought Pete had given you some cookery lessons during your ill-fated relationship. He once told me that he'd taught you how to make a perfect risotto. What happened?'

'I discovered Pot Noodles.'

James looks appalled. I shrug.

'I'm a normal woman but I don't like spending time in the kitchen. Pete loved it. I should have realised our relationship was doomed when he spent twenty minutes extolling the virtues of mushrooms. I mean, how excited can you get over fungi? And it turned out that he loved these little dried out old ones that cost a fortune.'

'Porcini?'

'I don't know much about opera, sorry, and please don't change the subject again.' James bursts out laughing. 'Hey, I can't help it. Once Pete told me to separate six eggs for a meringue. I spent ten minutes putting each one into different kitchen cupboards. I thought it was strange at the time, but he was the expert.'

'But this lack of talent wasn't a problem before now?'

'Yeah,' I admit. 'Somehow I've agreed to cook Sunday lunch for Louise, Sam and,' I smile coyly, 'my new boyfriend. And Louise was going to show me how to do it ...'

'Does it have to be a Sunday roast?' James asks.

'Why?'

'Well, I'm not so hot on roast dinners but I'm a dab hand at chilli con carne, even if I do say so myself. I could teach you that.' He looks eagerly at me.

Chilli con carne? I'm about to reject his offer – it's hardly the romantic meal that I had in mind – when suddenly I'm imagining a red gingham checked tablecloth, wicker-covered Chianti bottles, chilli pepper fairy lights around the living room, and perhaps even an inflatable cactus that my mother must have left over from her Frida Kahlo phase. I cringe at the memory. I could buy some chilli pepper plants instead of flowers, and cover my sofa with an ethnic style rug. I could pretend it was a themed lunch ... Listen to me. I'm turning into my mother.

'That would be fantastic,' I gush at James.

'Right,' he smiles. 'Let's hit the supermarket, get the ingredients and then it's back to my place for a quick dab of galloping gourmet.'

'I do hope you're talking about cooking,' I giggle.

'Of course,' he winks seductively. 'What else could I possibly be thinking of?' And strangely I find myself blushing.

An hour later, standing in the compact kitchen of James's flat, teaspoon in mouth while chopping up onions to prevent my eyes watering, I wonder what the Suffragettes actually fought for. On arrival he had handed me a black and white striped apron 'to save those posh clothes you now wear' and donned a navy blue one himself.

'I'm meant to be an emancipated woman,' I splutter, trying not to let the spoon fall out of my mouth.

'You're lucky you're not emaciated with all that junk you eat.'

'There's nothing wrong with ready meals.'

'You won't be saying that after you've tried this. Now shut up and chop.'

So I do. And I learn the painful way not to rub your eyes after chopping chillies, that browning mince does not actually mean turning it into a nice shade of dark chocolate, and a whole host of other cookery trivia that somehow I never learned in my short time with Pete. But the time passes easily, and it seems only minutes before James is talking about putting the mixture into the oven. I move over to the microwave, and throw open the door.

'I'd guess twenty minutes, but you'd better take it out of that cast iron pot. It'll blow your electrics otherwise,' I advise sagely. Not everybody has my talent for mentally weighing microwave ingredients. Nigella would kill for it, I'm sure.

'Holly...' James speaks slowly and clearly. 'We're going to use the grown up one.' He nods towards a hob and oven. 'It's a new fangled invention, I admit, but one I think will catch on. Soon every house will have one, including yours.'

'I'll have you know I'm fully equipped.'

'I'm not denying that,' he retorts. 'But have you ever used it?'

'Of course!'

'Really?'

'I store my paperwork in there. Bills I need to pay, that sort of thing.'

James rolls his eyes heavenwards as he walks over to the freezer and pulls out a perfectly chilled bottle of vodka.

'Right, it's time for the chefs to have a hard-earned rest.' He pours out two large tumblers. I take a huge gulp. The liquid burns as it moves down my throat and into my stomach, reminding me that I haven't eaten since breakfast. Louise owes me big time, I think. I pull out a stool, sit down at a small breakfast bar, and survey my surroundings. James's kitchen is galley-shaped, with a maplewood counter down one wall. A battery of blackened saucepans and utensils hang from a rack attached to the ceiling. Every shelf and cupboard is crammed with kitchen equipment. I spot a marble pestle and mortar sitting atop the fridge.

'You really are the kitchen devil, aren't you?' I say, as he tops up my tumbler. 'I'd never have guessed.'

'There's a lot about me that you don't know,' he smiles enigmatically. 'Call yourself a private detective?'

'Nope. I call myself a corporate investigator,' I correct.

'Same thing. It just sounds posher.'

'So, where did you learn to cook?' I ask.

'My mother. She and my aunt were always baking. I make a mean scone and soda bread. You'll have to try them one day. And then at university, when I had to fend for myself, I experimented a lot. I love dabbling. Take chilli con carne, you don't normally add baked beans but I threw them in one day, and frankly it was my Damascus moment. I became the uni's chilli king. My parties were notorious.'

'So what else is in your repertoire?' I am starting to feel slightly woozy from the vodka.

'Shepherd's pie, fish pie, lasagne, meatballs in tomato sauce, beef Wellington ... pretty much anything apart from straight forward roasts. Anyway, you've got me off the subject. Did you seriously not look into my background? I thought that you'd all have been vying to find out juicy bits of information about me before I joined the company. I'm rather disappointed that you didn't.'

'No.' I'm shocked at the suggestion. 'That would be unethical.' He appears embarrassed at my emphatic tone. 'Did you investigate us? Your future colleagues?' I ask suspiciously. He shrugs. 'You did, didn't you?' I accuse. 'You spied on us.' I'm truly shocked. 'Is nothing sacred? Don't people have the right to their own privacy?' And then I blush at my own double standards and hypocrisy.

'Hey, I'm a professional,' he retorts. 'I needed to find out about the members of my team.'

'And what did you discover?' I challenge, curious despite my indignation.

'Well, I learned that our boss Boris has the most incredible credentials. He really is a bit of a war hero. He has more medals than Steve Redgrave. He served in the first Gulf War and in Northern Ireland. Some of his service files are still sealed so he must have been involved in some very dangerous covert operations.'

'What else?'

'Well, Donna is the classic case of somebody rebelling against her upbringing. She was the youngest child in a family

230

of six boys and her mother died when she was thirteen. It was about that time that her father found solace as a vicar.'

'What?' The vodka nearly comes out through my nose, I'm so shocked.

'Yep, her father started wearing long dresses just about the time she was discovering boys and shortening hers.'

'What about Angus?' I probe.

'God, Holly. I can't believe you haven't done this all yourself long before now,' he sighs, shaking his head in an 'I'm-so-disappointed-in-you' fashion. 'Where's your sense of professionalism?'

'I didn't think it was very professional to use my skills for personal benefit,' I retort.

'Oh right, so you don't want to know about Angus.'

'Of course I do, you idiot, spill the beans.'

'Angus grew up in Glasgow, and in many respects his early life was the mirror image of Donna's. He was the only boy in a family of five girls. His mother is one of six sisters and his father was an only child. Actually, his mother doesn't approve of his homosexuality.'

'She doesn't?'

'No, she has disowned him. She blames university. He was a leading light in his college's theatrical society at Cambridge, and his mother claims the greasepaint corrupted him.'

'Bloody hell,' I say admiringly, gulping down some more vodka. 'I knew you were good, but this is unbelievable inside information. You must have dug really deep to uncover this.'

'Not really,' he laughs. 'I plied them both with drink one night soon after I joined and soon they were singing like canaries. Three light beers and Angus is anyone's. Donna needed a couple of bottles of champagne. To herself.' I playfully punch him. 'So go on. I know you're dying to ask. Did I check you out?'

'Did you?' I ask coyly.

He nods. 'I discovered you were 32, but only after arriving did I discover 36-28-38, because those vital statistics weren't on any official database.' It's getting hot in here, I think, checking the dial on the oven door. 'You graduated with a 2-1, have a good credit record and spend rather more money than your bank manager would prefer in your local wine bars.'

'You're like a Peeping Tom!'

'But you're more of a closed book than the others. It was always a mystery to me why a fantastic girl like you was dating so many losers. But then you told me about Jake and I was able to fill in some of the gaps I'd wondered about,' he says quietly. It's definitely getting hot in here, I think. I can sense tension building up between us, and I feel so disloyal to Carl to even think this, but it's definitely sexual. Calm down Holly, I tell myself.

'Hey, isn't that chilli con carne ready yet?' I gulp down another full glass of vodka. It feels icy cold and soothing. It takes my mind off the moment.

'It's got another three hours or so.'

'You mean I've got to get up at the crack of dawn to cook this?'

'I thought he was worth it.' I blush again. My face feels like a bloody Belisha beacon.

'He is!' I say emphatically, determined to chill the atmosphere.

'I'm glad,' James says softly. 'You deserve that.'

'And he's definitely not a deadbeat.'

'I never said that he was.'

'He's not,' I insist.

'I'm glad.' James walks over to the oven and peeks inside. A jet of heat escapes and steams up his glasses.

'In fact, he's a real high flyer.'

'I'm glad,' he says again, clearing his glasses on his apron.

'A huge high flyer.'

'As I said, I'm glad.' He smiles at me and I suddenly feel all weak at the knees. Why on earth did you drink on an empty stomach, Holly? It's just the alcohol that's making you imagine things that aren't there. Take some of the tension out of the air. Surprise him. Confess.

'Can you guess who it is yet?' I tease in a Rolf Harris voice.

'Tony Blair?' he laughs. James returns to the stool beside me, and his knees gently brush against mine. It feels like an electric shock. This vodka, I think to myself. It's having a strange effect.

'Close, but no cigar.' Keep teasing, Holly. Save yourself.

'Bill Clinton?' James is leaning forward.

I laugh. A panicky laugh. 'You'll never guess,' I babble.

'Tell me,' he urges softly.

'Carl Lawson,' I say. There. It's out there. And my ploy works. The tension dissolves instantaneously. James is no longer laughing. The twinkle in his eyes has disappeared. They are now hard and dark. There is now anger in the atmosphere.

'What did you just say?' His tone is measured.

'Never mind,' I flick my hand at him. 'I was only joking.'

'No, you weren't,' he snaps. 'You said Carl Lawson.' I stay quiet, unable even to look James in the eye. 'As in Carl Lawson, the boss at Ilyax Insurance?' He pauses. Again I fail to react. 'As in Carl Lawson, client of Investigations-R-Us? As in Carl Lawson who used our information to fire somebody? Oh Holly, how could you be so stupid? How could you be so thoroughly unprofessional?'

Chapter Thirty-Four

There is an atmosphere in the office when I arrive the next morning. It might be imperceptible to my colleagues, but to me it is distinctly frosty. James pointedly ignores me, immediately lifting the phone and dialling a number when I arrive, signalling that he does not want to enter into conversation. Momentarily I panic that he has told our boss Boris, but then I remember our drunken argument last night. He promised to keep silent as long as I end the relationship with Carl or withdraw myself from working on the Ilyax Insurance account. Either would be permissible, he said, but I was left in no doubt that there was a deadline. James will tell Boris if I do not act within days. He may give me a week's grace, but that will be it. My head is throbbing with the dual pain of a hangover and a sleepless night. Oh, why did I ever say anything? Why couldn't I have restrained myself from the vodka bottle and kept silent? I only said it to deflect the chemistry that I drunkenly imagined between us. Well, it's certainly not there today.

And yet, grudgingly, I know James is right. I have created the most enormous conflict of interest. I knew all along that dating Carl Lawson and overseeing his corporate investigation was wrong but somehow it seemed so right. For once my personal and business life were working in synchronicity. Positively. But now nothing seems clear. There are some niggling seeds of doubt growing at the back of my mind about the operations for Carl Lawson. They were sown by some of James's comments last night, though I know they were partly fuelled by drink. James couldn't have meant what he said about being manipulated. I haven't been, have I? I'd feel so much better if Carl would answer his mobile and I could speak to him. I want to hear his voice and comfort myself that James's accusations are unfounded.

I have barely sat down, when an email appears on my screen.

To: Holly
From: James
Subject: Ilyax Insurance
Following our discussions last night, I think it inappropriate that I continue on the surveillance of any subjects being considered for the position of human resources director at Ilyax Insurance. Please find a replacement for me on the team as soon as possible.

I look over but James is working on his computer. No quick glance to check I've acknowledged receipt. I feel so sad. It's like I've lost a good friend that I had only just discovered. Before I can respond to the email, Donna comes bounding over to greet me. Today she is wearing opaque black tights which at least give the appearance that she has paid a passing glance to the icy weather outside, even if the bottom-skimming mini skirt and thigh-high patent leather boots suggest the opposite.

'Spill the beans!' she pleads.

'What?' I panic. Surely James won't have told her. He's a gentleman. He'll keep his side of the bargain and give me a few days' grace.

'About Louise?' she says. 'Duh! You go swanning off the job, ask Gavin to deliver a sperm-machine to your best friend and you seem to have forgotten all about it the next day. Good one, Holly.'

'I haven't heard from her yet,' I explain as relief floods through me. 'I must call.'

'I'd have thought she'd have been on that phone thanking you as soon as the dirty deed was done. Maybe he's got more staying power than I gave him credit for.'

'You've never met him,' I retort.

'He's an investment banker. What more do you need to know? They've got to have those mega salaries and top of the range sports cars to compensate for something, if you know what I mean.'

'That's a sweeping generalisation.'

'Nah! It's my experience, so I think we're talking something more than a one-hit wonder. Oh by the way, before I forget, James has asked me to step in for him on the surveillance of Heron. He's got some sort of conflict or other, I don't know. Anyway, I know I blew it the last time, but I promise to blend into the background this time.'

'Okay,' I say wearily.

'Seriously?' She jumps up from the desk. 'You won't regret this. I won't let you down. I'll be so professional.'

The phone rings and Donna leaps into action. She grabs the handset, greets the caller and says: 'Just one second, please.' She presses a button on the keypad to put the call on hold, and informs me Louise is on the line. 'She sounds euphoric. Come on. Talk to her. I want to hear some of the gory details.'

'Holly, I love you. I owe you *big* time.' Louise sounds tired but elated. 'Last night was absolutely fantastic ...'

'Louise,' I interrupt. 'I'm thrilled for you, but I really don't need any details. It's enough to know you're happy.' Donna scowls at me.

'But Holly, Sam was like a man possessed. I think it was all that fresh air he breathed in while on Gavin's motorbike. I'm seriously considering buying him one for his Christmas present. And having Gavin as the driver was inspired on your part. Sam said he gave him some great tips. He's never been like that before.'

'Like what?'

'Well, to coin a motorbike analogy, Sam's pistons were firing on all cylinders.'

'Firing on all cylinders,' I repeat.

Donna looks surprised. I wave at her.

'So are you and Sam having a quiet day together recovering?'

'As if. He leapt out of bed at the crack of dawn. I think he got an email or something on his BlackBerry. I tell you, if I ever meet the guy who invented them – and believe me, it's got to be a guy, no woman would be quite so stupid – I'll give him an earful. Sam can never rest,' she moans.

'I thought that's what you wanted,' I tease.

'He certainly didn't last night,' she admits, and I hear the happiness in her voice. 'But there was some news out this week that could affect the big deal he's working on. God knows what it was. He doesn't tell me anything. Seriously though, Holly, I think last night could be the night that we, and strangely I include you in that, made a baby.'

'I'm sure you're right but try not to get too carried away,' I say kindly. 'It's still early days.'

'I know, but I can feel it. I'm sure. You probably think I'm mad but I'm convinced a little life is starting within me. Call it women's intuition or something. But I'm also ringing to apologise. I know I was meant to be giving you a cookery class last night for the big lunch on Sunday, which I'm really looking forward to. Do you want to reschedule? I could do tonight?'

'Don't worry. I managed to find a stand-in and I think I've found something that even I can cook.'

'A salad?'

'Ho-diddly-ho! Everyone's a comedienne. Let Sunday lunch be a surprise for you.'

'It'll be a surprise if you've cooked it. Did you call Pete for some tips?'

'No, James volunteered. Our unexpected excursion to help you out left us both at a loose end.' I check that nobody is listening in. 'But it was a bit of a disaster. It ended up in a scene about you-know-who.'

'Carl?' She exclaims. 'How did he find out?'

'Too much vodka, no food and my imagination going into overdrive. I told him, and now he's insisted that I either dump Carl or give up his account.'

'Clever move,' mutters my friend. 'He's hoping you're fiercely ambitious and will abandon his love rival. Then he'll sweep in and pick you up.'

'This is serious, Louise. And anyway, he's not a love rival.' I blush at the thought.

'You're right. I'm sorry. But he's got a point.'

'Whose side are you on?' I ask belligerently.

'Yours, obviously, you don't even need to ask that. But you cannot afford to be so conflicted.'

'I know,' I concur, 'but just for once I wanted things going my way in all aspects of my life. It's not too much to ask, is it? This is the first major account that I've ever been in charge of, and I happen to meet the man of my dreams at the same time. Why should I sacrifice one of them? But James has raised some serious doubts in my mind and I really need to talk to Carl.'

'Call him.'

'Gee, why didn't I think of that! His phone has been switched off for a couple of days. I've left several messages.'

'Do you want us to bail out of Sunday? To give you time to talk?'

'No!' My tone is adamant. 'I want you to meet him. I *need* you to meet him to give me an opinion. Anyway, there's no point in talking about this now and you've probably got to go and wave your legs in the air for a while. Speak later?' I have barely hung up when the mobile rings. It's Carl. I note James look over when he hears the ringtone.

'Carl,' I hiss. 'Where are you? I've been trying to get hold of you for days.'

'I'm sorry, doll. I've been travelling. It was a last-minute trip, and the phone connections are not great here.'

'Where are you?'

'I can't say, babe. It's a work trip, that's all you need to know.'

'And you couldn't ring before flying out?'

'Hey, what's this?' He's suddenly annoyed. 'You're sounding like my wife. I didn't have time to call after I spoke to my boys.' I'm hurt, furious and rather irritated by the wife analogy. Wife – he called her wife. Not soon to be ex-wife. Stop it, Holly. You're just overwrought and tired.

'We need to talk, Carl.'

'And we will, on Sunday. I'm really looking forward to meeting your friends.'

'We need to talk now,' I say firmly. 'The newspapers are going crazy about the sacking of Peter Porter.'

'So what? Look, I thought we talked about this. He was incompetent.'

'And are you sure that he didn't lose his job because of our surveillance operation?'

Carl is silent.

'You didn't know he was dating Tracy Bruce until I told you, did you?'

'So?' He sounds defensive.

'But that opens up a huge legal problem for us.'

'How? He can't prove anything.'

'So is it true?' I don't really want to hear the answer.

'Your surveillance did inform us about them, yes. But rules are rules, Holly, and he broke them. Inter-office relationships are out. Look, I've got to go. I'll see you on Sunday at about one. Miss you, babe.' And he hangs up.

CHAPTER THIRTY-FIVE

I have been panicking ever since my conversation with Carl. I can't speak about my concerns to James, who has ignored me ever since our ill-fated cookery lesson. And I really miss him, his corny pretend chat-up lines. And our conversations while on surveillance. Even doing Sudoku is no fun without James to work out the numbers with. He's just another unnecessary distraction, I tell myself. Today I have to tell Carl that I am giving up overseeing the contract. It's better for both of us. He'll see that. We can chat after Louise and Sam leave, but I've got to put my concerns to the back of my mind for now. I've got a lunch to prepare for three guests.

The chilli is in the oven, the rice is waiting in the sauce-pan to be heated and a luscious cream affair from the local patisserie is resting in the fridge. I have destroyed any tell-tale signs that it was shop-bought, but Louise won't be fooled. She knows the only cream I usually use for cooking is Factor Five, slapped all over my shoulders.

I've lit a small collection of Jo Malone scented candles, hung a string of chilli shaped lights that I found in a joke shop along the mantelpiece and placed one of Mum's old inflatable palm trees in the corner of the room. A selection of cacti decorates the windowsills.

I wasn't really sure what to wear. Seduction gear would be inappropriate today and distract us both from the discussion we need to have. In the end I plumped for a pair of black trousers and a pale pink fitted suede shirt that I picked up last week.

Louise and Sam arrive first. My best friend glows with happiness, elegant in a black chiffon skirt and grey cashmere jumper, but Sam looks distracted – as if he'd rather be anywhere else rather than in my flat, particularly after he notices the blow-up palm tree. He shakes his head in obvious disgust as he slowly takes in the other decorations.

'My God, Holly. Have you been watching those awful makeover programmes on television again?' he demands.

'Ignore him, Holly,' Louise says, nudging her errant husband with her elbow. 'He's in a bad mood. There's some major problem with his deal and he'd rather be at his office sorting it out than enjoying a nice meal with us.'

'Nice meal?' He snorts. 'I've tasted Holly's cooking before.'

'Now, now, Sam.' Louise warns.

'Anyway I can't help it if I'm dedicated to my job. Too many blighters in this country think a day's work is collecting their Social Security cheques, and I'm being criticised for wanting to do a proper job. You should talk to that friend of yours, Gavin. He holds down three jobs to fund his PhD. You don't hear him complaining.'

'Sam, Gavin can claim thongs as a tax-deductible expense,' I retort, passing him a bottle of beer and Louise a glass of still water.

'What?'

'Nothing, darling,' soothes Louise. 'I'm not criticising you, but I think you need an afternoon off.' She kisses his cheek softly. 'There may not be too many occasions left after all. Besides, Holly has opted for a themed lunch rather than a traditional roast. It's just something a little bit different, and the decorations are just the final touches to make it special. Personally I think they look lovely,' she turns towards me. 'And so do you. Fantastic shirt. Carl is a very lucky man, isn't he?' She nudges Sam again.

The doorbell rings. My heart jumps a beat, and Louise winks and nods as I mouth a silent 'do I look ok?', dash to the door and press the buzzer for Carl. Oh! Carl Lawson is wearing a football kit. Red shirt, white shorts, striped socks and black boots. It's not quite the look I was hoping for.

'I'm sorry babe,' he says, handing me a bottle of red wine and placing a chaste kiss on my cheek. 'I went to a Sunday morning kickabout with some friends and completely lost track of time. You know how it is.' No, I think, I don't. I have spent the past three days panicking about this lunch. And today I have been so aware of the time dragging.

'Anyway, I suddenly realised I was running late, so I jumped into the car without changing. Can I just use your shower? Promise to be really quick. I'll just say "hello" to your buddies first.'

Louise's face is an open book when Carl walks into the lounge, but like the true friend she is, the stunned expression disappears almost as quickly as it arrived. Sam doesn't react, but shakes hands, as if football players turn up every day for lunch at my flat. This isn't quite the introduction I had hoped for.

'He's very good looking,' whispers Louise.

'Strange dress sense,' mutters Sam. 'Is he another fashion student?'

'He's been playing football,' I explain idiotically.

'Really?' Sam looks surprised. 'He must be good then. I didn't spot any grass stains or mud on his kit.' His comments stir a distant memory that I can't quite grasp. It's like a sense of déjà vu but I push it to one side, and pour myself a much needed glass of red wine. 'Where does he work? Louise didn't say.'

'Ilyax Insurance,' I reply without thinking.

'Ilyax?' Sam looks surprised. 'That's it. No wonder he looked so familiar. He's Carl Lawson, isn't he?'

'Yes,' I say. 'But this relationship is just between us for now.' Sam seems distracted. Louise nudges him.

'We can be confidential, can't we, Sam?'

'Er, yes. Carl Lawson?' he repeats. 'Why didn't you say something before, Louise?'

'I didn't know until today,' Louise says. 'Holly didn't tell me where he worked.'

'He's a client,' I explain. 'I checked out the new finance director at Ilyax Insurance.'

'Clive Partridge?' Sam says. 'That was you? Look, do you mind but I've got to make one quick phone call. It won't take two minutes. I just need to check back on the troops. The team are all working this weekend. I'll just step out onto the landing.' He wanders off to make his call. Louise and I move into the kitchen to put the rice on.

'Something smells fantastic,' she compliments. I beam with pride, before dishing out fresh salsa and guacamole into little bowls. She takes them into the living room while I fiddle with last-minute bits and pieces in the kitchen. I can hear quiet mumbling and then a louder 'I cannot believe you' from Louise. I look up as Sam enters the kitchen.

'Holly, I'm truly sorry to do this. But something's come up back in the office and I've got to go. It's a real pain, I know, and everything smells so delicious. Can you forgive me?'

I look at him in horror. I need him. Carl looked so interested when I mentioned that Sam was an investment banker, and if he leaves now Louise will feel like a spare part.

'Honestly, don't worry,' I say graciously. 'But could you not just stay for a starter? There's no point in rushing to work on an empty stomach.'

'There's really nothing I'd like more, but I've got to dash. Here,' he grabs a handful of tortilla chips and wolfs them down. 'These are great. Did you make them yourself? They're just what the grumbling stomach ordered.' He places a friendly kiss on my forehead. 'You look lovely. I'm sure you'll all have a fun time ... despite the palm tree!' I whip my tea towel against his legs as he dashes through the door. Louise does not say 'good bye' as he leaves.

Carl emerges from the bathroom. His hair, with its dappling of grey, is still damp. He is now wearing a pair of blue jeans and a crisp white shirt with two buttons open to reveal a wisp of chest hair. Three chocolate brown leather knotted bracelets adorn his wrist. I know each child gave him one as a Christmas present.

'Better?' he asks. Louise and I exchange a surreptitious 'he looks gorgeous' look. I explain about Sam. 'Never mind,' he beams. 'All the more for me and I don't just mean the food!' Carl winks at Louise. He looks around the room as I hand him a cold beer.

'I like what you've done here,' says Carl, noticing the decorations. 'So what's on the menu, Holly?'

'We're going Mexican,' I beam.

'Mexican, eh? Nothing with kidney beans, I hope. I can't eat them.' He shakes his head and screws his face up in disgust. 'Did I not mention that?'

I feel sick. I can't believe I was so stupid. I should have asked. I should have checked whether Carl had any foods that he avoided. But then I couldn't get hold of him long enough to ask. Louise is looking at me in horror.

'When you say you don't eat them,' I finally ask, 'do you mean that you just don't like them?'

'No,' he screws up his nose. 'I have a terrible reaction to them. I'll be throwing up for hours if I even go near one.' Shit! I didn't realise people could be allergic to kidney beans.

'Hypothetically speaking, if a dish had initially been prepared with kidney beans but they were all picked out before you ate it, would there be any reaction?' I ask with my fingers crossed.

'Exactly the same. I'd be on my knees throwing up. It's not a pretty picture.' The penny finally drops. 'Oh, my God, please don't say your meal includes kidney beans?' Carl looks horrified. I nod slowly, in abject misery. 'Oh Holly, I'm so sorry. After all the trouble you've been to.' He waves his hand around the room.

'Hey,' says Louise, determined to salvage the situation. 'We've got salsa and guacamole and all types of dips, with pitta bread and tortillas. And I'm sure we can rustle up an omelette for a main course.' I shake my head but Louise gets the wrong end of the stick. She thinks I can't cook an omelette, which would be a correct assumption in normal circumstances. 'I'll do it Holly, you've done enough.' My head is still shaking.

She looks confused, adding slowly: 'You have got some eggs, haven't you?' Bingo! I shake my head in embarrassment.

'I'm sorry,' I lie. 'I forgot to buy some this week.'

'I thought Pete taught you about keeping a basic ingredient cupboard,' she mutters. 'What have you got in, Holl?' My friend Louise is ever the optimist. 'Pasta? Potatoes? Salad?'

'I've got some Pot Noodles,' I finally say. 'And a big pan of boiled rice?'

'Pot Noodles!' Carl exclaims. 'Wow! Fantastic. Haven't had them since student days. We can pretend we're back at university.' He looks at the chilli lights. 'Come to think of it, we used to have some of those in my student digs.'

And that was it. That was how we came to have a Sunday lunch of Mexican dips, Pot Noodles – Louise excused herself on the grounds of her possible pregnancy, and instead had a bowl of plain rice – and a cream dessert, which even she refrained from mentioning was shop bought. I suppose Louise and I could have eaten the chilli but we were so worried that it might infect Carl by osmosis. It wasn't quite the meal I had planned but it worked. We chatted for hours, and every so often Louise would look over at me and, away from Carl's eyes, give me a big thumbs up. And all I could think was how kind he had been not to embarrass me over the chilli con carne and how I must be mistaken about these niggling doubts that keep creeping into my mind. Bloody James, I think bitterly.

And then Louise spoiled it. She didn't mean to, of course, but she did. And it was only because she wanted to go home.

'Holl mate, it's been ...' She hesitates. 'It's been different from expectations, but I've had so much fun. Now I really must be going. I'm meeting a potential client tomorrow. She was at Trixie's party and is thinking of using my services for her fortieth.' She moves across to Carl, and places a friendly kiss on both cheeks. 'It was lovely to meet you. I hope we get the chance again.' Good, subtle. Not too pushy. No clue from Louise that her best friend has already planned her life out with this man.

'It was great to meet you too,' he agrees. 'How are you getting home?'

She looks momentarily confused, forgetting that Sam had taken the car when he abruptly left. 'I'll hail a cab on the street. No problem.'

'I wouldn't dream of it.' Carl is adamant. 'It's getting dark out there. My driver is waiting downstairs. I'll give you a lift home.'

'You're going too?' I ask. 'But I thought we were going to talk.'

'There's nothing I'd rather do, I swear, Holly, but I only got back from my business trip yesterday and I have to prepare for this week. It's been manic since Clive Partridge's appointment was announced.' He stands up. 'Plus I've got all the latest surveillance reports to scan through. But this,' he waves his hands at the dirty plates and empty glasses, 'has been fantastic. I never knew you were such a Pot Noodle expert. It's not everybody who knows to ignore the instructions, and yet still time them to perfection.' He places a soft kiss on my lips. 'You're a very special lady. I'll call you later. '

And then he escorts a very apologetic and confused looking Louise out of my flat towards his car – and I start to cry.

CHAPTER THIRTY-SIX

The illuminated red numbers on my bedside alarm clock seem to mock me as I watch them shuffle through each minute of darkness towards daybreak. There is no way I can sleep. My mind is analysing the events of the previous afternoon. In all my planning, I never once thought of the possibility that Carl Lawson would leave early without us talking things over. If I don't decide today on what path I am going to take, James will tell Boris and I'll be fired. But I can't make that decision without talking to Carl. It concerns him. And it really pissed me off that his mobile was turned off last night. Admittedly he sent the customary good night text but he knows we need to talk, and I'm sure he didn't – and I've replayed the moment of his departure over again several times – mention meeting again. He was friendly but non-committal. I try to tell myself I'm just being paranoid.

Louise obviously rang the moment she got home. She couldn't understand what had happened. Like me, she was certain from all the flirting and chatting that Carl was desperate for quality time alone with me. Carl Lawson is an enigma to me and probably, I reluctantly admit, will always remain so.

I watch the illuminated numbers click over to 6 a.m. It will soon be time to get up. Somehow, despite my distress, I fall into a brief, fitful sleep, and wake at seven to a mad ringing noise. I hit the alarm button in tired frustration, but the ringing continues. I hit the alarm again. It doesn't work. The ringing doesn't stop. I stir myself. This is all I need, I think. A temperamental alarm clock. Then I realise the ringing is coming from my mobile phone. I grab it hoping it's Carl. It's Louise.

'Did I wake you?' She sounds anxious.

'Doesn't matter,' I say, settling myself up against my pillows. 'I need to get up.'

'How are you?'

'Been better,' I admit. 'I hardly slept last night. My mind was going into overdrive. I really needed to talk to Carl, and he knew that, but he left without even taking ten minutes to listen to my worries. Did I do something wrong?'

'No.'

'That's very kind of you to say, but you're my friend.'

'No, you don't understand. You really didn't do anything wrong. Trust me.'

'That's very sweet, but we both know about my luck with men ...'

'No, really Holly, this has nothing to do with your track record.' Listen: Carl Lawson is not who you think he is.'

'Louise, I know you're trying to save my feelings, but really ...'

'Look, stop this,' my friend shrieks down the phone, 'and listen to what I am saying. Carl Lawson is a fraud.'

'What are you talking about?' My head is spinning.

There is a deep intake of breath, and a further hesitation, before Louise continues.

'I shouldn't be telling you this. Sam will go ballistic.'

'Sam? What does he have to do with anything?'

'It's Ilyax Insurance ...'

'Ilyax Insurance? You're really losing me. What's the matter?'

'When Sam came home last night, he confided in me about this big deal he's been working on. He's worried that you may have got into something you don't understand. It's still top secret but his deal is a merger involving Ilyax Insurance. That's why he couldn't stay for lunch.'

'A merger?' I'm confused. 'An insurance company merger? Why hasn't Carl mentioned anything?'

'He doesn't know.'

'But he's the chief executive. He's the boss. He's the top man. Nothing would happen at Ilyax Insurance without him knowing.'

'This is.'

'Why? That's highly irregular.'

'Sam is a bit cagey about the reasons. But do you remember last week I said he'd gone dashing off after hearing about some announcement?'

'Vaguely.'

'He'd just heard about Clive Partridge's appointment. It threw his team into disarray. The company that they're working for is taking over Ilyax Insurance, and its guys will take over the top jobs in the new company. It had all been agreed. The lawyers were just finalising the last few contracts.'

'So Clive Partridge isn't needed?'

'Exactly. His appointment came as a huge surprise to Ilyax's chairman. He only learned about it when the news appeared on the Stock Exchange screen.'

'But the press release had a quote from him saying he was delighted at the appointment.'

'Apparently those quotes are made up by the press officers. It's standard practice. She was only putting out the release that her boss, Carl Lawson, told her to. Why would she question it and ring the chairman?'

'But I don't understand,' I feel like I'm drowning. None of this conversation makes any sense. 'Why don't they just cancel Clive Partridge's contract and announce there has been a major error?'

'It's been signed now.'

And then the penny drops. Suddenly everything falls into place, like the fruits in a one armed bandit, and I understand. 'He's signed a highly lucrative deal. Clive Partridge will get paid five million pounds if Ilyax Insurance is bought out within a year of him signing the contract, so ...'

'You've got it.'

'All the newspaper reports said that it was highly unusual to introduce such a clause ...' I pause, uncertain whether to voice the suspicion that is quickly taking seed. 'But that means Carl Lawson did know about the merger. There must be some connection between him and Clive Partridge, and I missed it because I was so distracted. Oh, my God, Louise. He's been playing me. No wonder he wanted to meet you. He only seemed interested after I boasted that Sam was an investment banker working on a top secret deal.' I can feel the tears starting. 'I am such a fool. How could I ever have imagined that somebody as successful as Carl Lawson would be interested in somebody like me? He must have seen me coming. I'm an idiot.'

'No, you're not,' Louise soothes. 'I was watching him yesterday, and he was definitely not acting. I think he genuinely cares for you. It may have started out as him using you but now there's something there. I can sense it.'

'You're just being kind.' My body is now shaking with the sobs. 'Carl Lawson has used and manipulated me from the very start. I'm ruined. My career is over. I should have spotted the connection with Clive Partridge, but I didn't because I was too interested in getting through the investigation quickly so I could see Carl again. I must have cut corners.' I curl up into a ball. 'I'm ruined. Once this gets out nobody will want to employ me. James was so right to mistrust Carl's motives. Why didn't I listen to him? James was being a friend to me.'

'Holly, come on now. Pull yourself together. This is not helping the situation. How could you know that he was such a total bastard?'

'I should have guessed. My senses should have been tuned in. I am such a fool. He must have been laughing at me behind my back.'

'I'm sure he wasn't,' she says kindly. 'Yesterday he really did look at you with affection. I was watching out for the signs, and I thought he genuinely liked you. It's money and power, unfortunately. They corrupt.'

'What do I do now? I'm finished.'

'Holly.' Louise shouts down the phone. 'Holly! Pull yourself together. This is not the time to get hysterical. We've got to think of a plan.'

'What sort of a plan?'

'I don't know. Something to catch the bastard out.'

'It's too late,' I sob.

'No it's not. We need to work out a solution to this mess.'

'There is no solution,' I sob hysterically. 'I'm ruined. Didn't you hear me? *Why* am I such a fool?'

'You're not. Carl Lawson came into your world at the right time. You were feeling down about your love life, worried about spending the rest of your life on the shelf and probably, and I feel a bit responsible about this, upset by my plans for a baby.'

'I'm happy for you,' I protest.

'Hey, I'd be jealous and upset if I was in your shoes. It's natural. I'm not blaming you. But this sort of whining doesn't help. Now tell me. You've been on a lot of surveillance operations recently. Who were they for?'

'They were women at Ilyax Insurance,' I reply miserably.

'Well, this is all making sense now. Holly, I don't know how to tell you this, but there's another major problem brewing at Ilyax Insurance.'

'What sort of problem?'

'Apparently some female staff allege that they are being stalked by a senior member of staff.'

'Stalked? In what way?' But even as I pose the question, I already know the answer.

'They feel like they're being followed.'

'Which they are,' I say miserably.

'And then this senior member of staff keeps turning up at places they don't expect, like a wine bar they often use, or a sandwich bar. At first the women just thought it was a coincidence but now, after talking to each other, they're not so sure. Some receive regular anonymous bouquets.'

'It's Carl,' I say with conviction. As I utter his name, feelings

251

of utter hatred and anger start to push those of love and desire out of my mind. It is true, I think sadly, love and hate really are different sides of the same coin. He has abused my feelings for him, and my stomach turns at the memory of his touch. I feel violated.

'Sam doesn't know for certain, Holly darling, but he thinks so. Ilyax's chairman is being very cagey about the identity of the guy. But this is a major lawsuit waiting to happen. It will blow Sam's deal out of the water.'

'It *is* Carl. I just know it.' And I am the mug who gave him the information. Even Donna mentioned hearing about a sleazeball working at Ilyax Insurance that night at the pole-dancing. But I was so angry with her for compromising the operation that I didn't pay any attention to the information. I failed to investigate that lead. I start to retch.

'Are you okay, Holly?' Louise sounds tense and nervous. 'I should have called round to tell you this. I can't believe I've been so cruel to use the phone. I'm jumping in a cab. I'll be there in ten minutes. Stay calm.'

CHAPTER THIRTY-SEVEN

I throw myself out of bed and into the shower. My head is spinning. This is a disaster of Pompeian proportions. How could I have been so stupid? Carl Lawson used me. He used Investigations-R-Us to establish the daily routines of women in his company so that he could stalk them. No wonder they were all stunning females. Alarm bells should have started ringing then. Even James mentioned that they could all be top models. And why is it necessary to know the daily routine of a potential human resources director? James was right all along. He expressed concerns about the surveillance operations from the very beginning, said it didn't make sense. And, oh my God, Investigations-R-Us still has to get paid for the work. Even my mother was right about him. Her imaginary sense of auras may just be an affectation she's playing with for now, but she sure picked his true colours. Even my batty old neighbour Miss Binchy didn't like him. No wonder he reacted so badly. He thought old Cagney and Lacey downstairs were onto him.

I've got to confess to Boris this morning, I conclude. I try to imagine the look on his face as I explain how I ...

a) Dated client.
b) Was duped by client
c) Failed to conduct thorough investigation on behalf of client
d) Am unlikely to be paid by client

e) Neglected to find collusion between client and candidate
f) Aided and abetted client's nefarious activities

I've heard of the phrase 'three strikes and you're out'. Huh! That's nothing. I've got more strikes coming off me than a box of matches. I'm doomed. I hear my phone buzzing and feel sick. It's the alert I set up for Carl Lawson. He doesn't know I'm on to him, and that was probably his 'good morning' text, liberally littered with kisses. He played me so well, I think sourly. The flood of text messages was a nice touch that made me feel important. The beauty of text messages to Carl is that he could be sending them from anywhere and I wouldn't know. I just had to rely on his honesty. You stupid cow, Holly. Were you really that desperate for a man that you ignored the warning signs? I feel hollow inside. This man said everything I wanted to hear, and I just lapped it up. Thirty-two-year-old single women, I reflect, are the easiest prey for conmen.

The buzzer rings. It's Louise. I throw on my old comfortable tracksuit. She arrives in my flat with two polystyrene mugs of steaming hot sweet coffee 'for shock,' she explains, and a box of croissants and almond pastries 'for energy' .

'I've rung James,' she says quietly. 'He's on his way.'

'What?' I shriek. 'That's all I need. Somebody walking around saying I told you so.'

'You misunderstand him,' Louise replies. 'He sounded really concerned on the phone. He is coming to help us, not to start blaming anybody. Now, Holly, I need you to be strong. You are going to get through this, and I will be by your side all the way, but right now you have to put Carl Lawson's horrific betrayal to one side. You've got to work out a plan.'

'Plan?'

'Yes, a plan,' she says firmly. 'This man's actions put both of us at risk. Your job looks on the line and Sam's deal might be too. That means my life will not be worth living once he calculates the bonus he missed out on. You have to take a step back from the way you're feeling at this moment and look at this as a professional.'

'What do you mean?' My mind isn't working properly. I feel disconnected, like I'm having an out of body experience.

'Come on Holly,' Louise urges. 'Get some sugar into your system. You need that burst of energy. You need to focus. Imagine a client has come to you with this scenario. He needs proof. What would you do? You're a professional investigator. This should be a walk in the park for you.'

I blink, trying to focus. Investigate, I think. Analyse all the clues. Come on, Holly, don't be a doormat. Don't let this man destroy your life, I admonish myself; even Jake didn't manage that. Concentrate.

'Okay,' I say slowly. Louise has grabbed a big notebook and is sitting back on the sofa, pen poised.

'We suspect that Carl Lawson already knows about the planned merger. And it is a fact that the shares in Ilyax Insurance recently went up,' I say. 'We all naively thought that was because the market liked the appointment of Clive Partridge. But what if it was an insider-trading ring buying shares under the cover of that announcement? They could make a killing once the merger goes through.'

'Good point, Holly,' Louise says encouragingly. 'That's an excellent start.'

'Carl rang me from abroad last week,' I recall. 'I need to find out where he went. He wouldn't tell me. It might be nothing, but it's a mystery and, at this moment, I don't like any loose ends.'

'You're doing really well. I'm so proud of you.'

'We never checked out the florists properly. He used two that we know of. Double Dutch and Poppy's Posies, but we need somebody at either of those stores to ID Carl Lawson as the purchaser of those bouquets. Maybe they've got CCTV; that could help.'

'Florists, right,' she smiles at me. 'I haven't a clue what you're talking about, but it sounds like a great point. Come on. You can do it.'

'I need to look into Carl Lawson's background. There's a connection with Clive Partridge, I just didn't spot it before. And where does the remuneration expert come in?' I'm getting into my stride.

'What do you mean?'

'Well, he said that a five million-pound payoff package was normal for a finance director. He claimed that a remuneration expert has been involved, and conducted research on the subject. I admit that it seemed really high at the time and there were several articles about shareholder outrage, but we never viewed it in this context before. Partridge signed on the dotted line knowing he would shortly be in for a massive payout. There must be a link between the three – Clive, Carl and the remuneration expert. They're in this together.'

'Who's the expert?' Louise is busy jotting down my thoughts.

'I don't know. I'll have to find that out too. And I've got to send Donna pole-dancing again. I want her to chat to Flamingo and Swan ...'

'Eh?'

'Sorry, it's the code names for Alice Kelly and Tracy Bruce. Donna and I were surveying them when they went pole-dancing, and she ended up talking to them. She said they mentioned some creep at work.'

'It sounds to me like we've got a busy few days ahead of us.'

'Yes. Oh God!' I suddenly remember. 'You were meeting somebody about a fortieth party today. You should go to that.'

'You're more important than that,' Louise says quietly. 'Now let's get started.'

Chapter Thirty-Eight

My bell buzzes. It's James. I take a deep breath, calm myself and open my door to greet him. And I wait. I stand there for several minutes. There's only fifteen stairs at most. James is a fit man. He should be here by now.

'James,' I call.

'I'm here, Holly,' he replies. I hear chatting. Oh no, I think, my neighbour Miss Binchy has caught him. She's probably trying to entice him into her flat for a cup of tea and a piece of Victoria sponge. I run down the stairs to see Miss Binchy hugging James. Her small squat body comes up to his chest.

'Holly, dear,' she smiles at me. 'You've met my nephew Seamus?'

I cringe for him in embarrassment at Miss Binchy's obvious mistake. My poor neighbour is particularly muddled today. 'Sorry,' I mouth.

'Isn't he gorgeous?' she continues. 'And he likes you, dear. He told me.'

Poor James. I instantly forget my troubles and worry about him. I need to extricate him from this situation without upsetting Miss Binchy.

'And I like him too, Miss Binchy.'

'Did you hear that, Seamus? She likes you.' James blushes as Miss Binchy nudges him.

'I know, Auntie,' he says quietly, 'but I really have to go to work now.'

Auntie? James is being very gallant, I think. Not many men would play along with an elderly woman losing her mind.

'And will you stop in for a cup of tea later? I'll bake some cakes.'

'I'll try. I might be busy though.' He places an affectionate kiss on the top of her head. Wait, I think. That isn't a play act kiss. James is ...

'You're her nephew!' I accuse. This truly is a day for revelations.

'Guilty,' he says awkwardly.

'You bastard,' I scream.

'Holly, really,' Miss Binchy looks at me in horror. 'If the Good Lord had meant ladies to swear, He'd have made them all fishwives.'

'But he's your nephew!'

'Yes, dear. Didn't I just say?'

'So he's Father Colm's brother?' This is awful. I hit on James's brother, and then I confided in him. He must have been laughing behind my back all this time. I flush with embarrassment and anger. James has the grace to look awkward.

'Yes, dear.' She nods. 'They're my sister's boys.'

'But I thought your nephew was called Seamus?'

'Yes,' Miss Binchy nods again as if indulging a slow-witted fool. How ironic, I think. When she kept telling me that her nephew liked me, I just thought it was another one of her fantasies. But it was reality. Oh my God!

'Seamus is Gaelic for James,' my colleague mutters.

'Why the hell don't you call yourself Seamus then?' I scream. My emotions are in overdrive. I feel angry, hurt, cheated, humiliated and something else. A feeling that I just can't put my finger on. 'You deceived me.'

'This from the woman who's been sleeping with the client,' he retorts angrily. 'That's rich.'

'That's different,' I snap. 'I couldn't tell you.'

'And I couldn't tell you. The time never seemed right,' he snaps back. 'I didn't realise that you were my aunt's new neighbour until it was too late. I only clicked when you mentioned an oil-rig worker ...'

'What oil-rig worker, dear?' Miss Binchy looks confused again.

'And then it would have embarrassed you if I told you, particularly after you confided that you'd hit on my brother.'

'Who hit who, dear?' Miss Binchy's hand flies to her mouth in horror.

'But you told Donna and Angus?' I protest.

'What did you expect? It was funny,' he shouts back, hands on hips. 'Who in their right mind mixes up a Catholic priest with an oil-rig worker?'

'This isn't getting us anywhere,' I finally say. 'I need your help.'

'Which I'm here to give,' he replies in a softer tone. 'Donna, Angus and Gavin are on their way.'

'You told them?'

'They're your friends. I thought you might need reinforcements. They want to help. They're not blaming you.'

'I still don't forgive you for deceiving me,' I say sulkily.

'Ditto. Now go up those stairs and start hitting the phones. We've got a lot of work to do. Auntie Maureen,' he turns to my neighbour. 'Have you got any delicious cakes in the tin? There's going to be a lot of very hungry people working upstairs today.'

'I made a Victorian sponge only yesterday,' she beams. 'I'll just go and get it, and it won't take me two ticks to run up some scones and shortbread.'

Two hours later and we're crammed into my living room and bedroom. 'Never thought I'd get in here,' muttered James as he set up a white board by my wardrobe. Donna was amazing when she arrived. She just ran over to me, hugged me and cried out that all men were bastards, but she had a perfect replacement for me Otto, a Bavarian prince.

Donna and Angus are hitting the phones, calling every airline contact that they have trying to find out where Carl flew to last week. James is trawling through recent Stock Exchange announcements regarding share purchases in Ilyax Insurance. 'Follow the money,' he mutters to himself.

James and I decided that we have to keep the surveillance operations going so as not to alert Carl that we are onto him. He also encouraged me to answer the text messages I received this morning. There was a flurry when I didn't respond immediately to 'good morning'. I check them out.

8.30
From: Carl (moby)
R u ok babe. Worried that hvnt had reply from u. X

8.40
From: Carl (moby)
Please don't sulk about yesterday evening. I would much rather have been with u. Missed u terribly. Sometimes I h8 my job – particularly when I hv 2 make sacrifices. X

8.45
From: Carl (moby)
Ground control to Holly. Come in, Holly. X

9.15
From: Carl (moby)
Was just in meeting with chairman. Couldn't stop thinking of u. XXX

9.18
From: Carl (moby)
Not that u r like chairman. ☺ XX

'My God,' says Louise, reading them. 'He is so manipulative. These texts just reel you in.'

'I know.' I send a reply that I'm fine but busy on surveillance, and finding it difficult to respond. James tells me to add that I want to talk.

9.42
From: Carl (moby)
*Me 2. I really do. But am stuck in meetings most of 2day. Will try
2 call l8r. XXXX*

9.50
From: Carl (moby)
PS ILY

My eyes fill with tears at the last text, and Louise gives
my hand a friendly squeeze. She and Miss Binchy are busy
fussing around the kitchen making tea and refreshments for
anyone who wants them. I notice my neighbour is like a
new woman now she has a purpose in her life. We finish a
round of Victoria sponge, when I tell Gavin that he's coming
with me.

'Where to?' he says.

'I have a plan to find out about the mysterious bouquets.'

When we arrive at Double Dutch, I realise there's no need to
enter. The pavement outside the florist is packed with aluminium buckets filled with parrot tulips. There is every shade
possible of the exotic tulips, including red – the colour that
Carl bought me. Tulips from Amsterdam, I think. I teased Carl
about them, and even Bert made the joke. My antenna should
have been on red alert the moment he did so. Yet another
example of my ineptitude. And frankly I should have personally checked this store out. A lot of things would have fallen
into place.

The outside walls of Poppy's Posies are painted bright red.
Its logo is painted in emerald green writing with the massive
black centres of big crimson red poppies substituted for the
letters 'o'. Buckets of daffodils, tulips, hyacinths and irises
stand outside. Sadly there are no CCTV cameras. We enter.
Two women wearing green tabards over warm jumpers and
jeans are sorting through a pile of burnt orange gerberas,
purple and white irises, and dark red berries on deep green

stems that are lying on an old wooden trestle table. They look up and smile.

'Shout if you need any help,' one says. We pretend to browse at the assortment of containers filled with flowers that stand on little dais around the shop. I wink at Gavin: ACTION!

'I'm sorry,' he walks up to the assistants. 'This is a very embarrassing situation. But my girlfriend here,' he nods in my direction, 'thinks I've been having an affair.'

'Don't lie to me, Clint,' I snarl. 'I know the truth. You've been sleeping with that bitch, and I've got the proof.'

'Babe, I'll prove I haven't.' He turns back to the assistants. 'She says her best friend has been getting anonymous bouquets every Saturday. And she's convinced they're from me.'

'I've seen the way you look at her. Pure lust,' I growl at him.

'I've only got eyes for you, babe,' simpers Gavin. 'You must believe me. I know nothing about the flowers. You've got to help me,' he begs the assistants. 'Tell Kylie you've never seen me before.'

They both readily agree.

'So you ordered them over the phone?' I shriek. 'Big deal. Anyway, maybe these women don't work Saturdays.'

'I do all the deliveries on Saturdays,' one pipes up. Her accent reveals she's from the East End. 'I know all the flowers that go from 'ere.'

'So you're the one who delivered to Tracy?' I stab an accusatory finger at her. 'The slut.'

'I dunno.' The assistant looks confused. 'I'd havta look it up.'

'Go on then,' I challenge.

She looks at her colleague, who nods agreement, wanders over to a battered wooden desk and fishes out a tattered ledger from a shelf underneath. 'When was it made? What's her address?' I give her Tracy Bruce's details.

'And it's every Saturday,' I say, I throwing daggers at Gavin.

'Tracy Bruce, you say?' The assistant runs her finger through addresses scribbled on an old diary page. I nod. ''Ere she is.

You're off the hook, mate.' She turns to me. 'It weren't your boyfriend who sent those flowers.'

'Then who *was* it?' I demand.

'It's old Casanova, mate. That bloke who's always ordering flowers,' she laughs.

'Casanova?' Gavin asks.

'Yeah, tell your friend Trace that she ain't alone. He must send five, ooh, six bouquets every weekend. And how many wouldya say during the week?' Her friend shrugs. 'Two, three, four? He's our best customer.'

'But who is he?' Gavin demands.

'Dunno his name. Sorry.' She shrugs. 'I wanted to send 'im a Christmas card to thank him for 'is business, but he wouldn't give me his address. Funny guy. Only ever pays cash.'

'Nah!' shrieks her friend. 'He paid by card one day. It was strange. A couple of weeks ago he came in with his wife.' I start in shock. Carl Lawson is separated. We must have the wrong man. 'I remember thinking that if she only knew. He was buying her a big bouquet, some sort of special occasion. It was the only bouquet he bought that week. That's why it stuck in my mind.' That must have been the week he switched the other orders to Double Dutch, I think.

'How do you know it was his wife?' My mouth feels dry.

''Cause they had three children with 'em. One wanted a helium and he kept begging his mum for it, and then when she wouldn't let him, he started on his dad.'

'He said "dad"'?

'Oh yeah,' replies the assistant, not realising that we've moved quite far away from our original cover story. 'But his dad didn't have enough money. That surprised his wife, I can tell ya. She was moaning that he'd only just withdrawn three hundred quid that morning and he must 'ave lost it. So he paid by card. I made a special point of reading his name so we did'n havta keep calling him Casanova. Now what was it?' She ponders for a moment. 'Began with a C.' Gavin and I glance at each other anxiously. 'Charlie? Colin? Na.' She scrunches her nose with the effort. 'Got it! It was Carl. I remember 'cause my mum's last boyfriend was called Carl, but he spelt it with a K. There. You can tell your friend her anonymous admirer is Carl.'

Gavin looks at me triumphantly.

'Now do you believe me?'

CHAPTER THIRTY-NINE

It's not definitive and it wouldn't stand up in a court of law, but I now know Carl Lawson sent those flowers to all those women. But I'm puzzled. We only know about two, three women, and yet the florist said he sent six or seven bouquets a week, and Louise said many women had made complaints about 'stalking'. I wonder if he's employed other agencies to conduct surveillance operations? I make a note to ask James to discreetly check with his contacts at our competing agencies. When Gavin and I return to my flat, Donna and Angus are dancing around excitedly. Miss Binchy looks on in amazement.

'What's up?' I ask. Their obvious pleasure distracts me from the painful discovery that Carl Lawson is reconciled with his wife. No wonder he didn't want me to tell anybody about us.

'We found his flight,' they jump around. 'Carl Lawson flew to the Cayman Islands.'

'Cayman Islands? Why there?'

Angus excitedly tells me: 'It's an offshore banking centre. Just the place to deposit large sums of money you don't want traced. Duh!'

'What large sums of money?' James asks.

We all sit in silence thinking.

'Wait,' I say. 'Where's the announcement of Clive Partridge's deal?' Louise passes me a sheaf of papers. 'Here!' I stab my finger on the point. 'Clive Partridge was paid a million-pound signing-on fee. I bet Carl has gone to the Cayman Islands to deposit it before their ruse is discovered. Clive can't go. He's been handling press enquiries and meeting his new team.'

'But we need proof that Carl opened a bank account,' James points out.

I turn to Angus. 'Angus, you must have some ex-lovers who are air stewards.'

'Well there was Justin. He was transatlantic. It's why it couldn't last. The jet lag drove a wedge between us. I was ready to rise when he was ready to fall.'

I hold up my hand to stop any further revelations. 'Right, I want you to get hold of Justin and ask him for a special deal to the Cayman Islands. Here's my credit card,' I fish out my purse, 'and book yourself a flight there today. We need to find out what Carl Lawson did in the Cayman Islands.'

'On the case,' squeals Angus. 'I need a bit of sun. Did I tell you I suffer from SAD?'

'I thought it was GAY,' mutters Donna.

'No joy on the share buying,' James says. 'It's been done through trusts. They're all anonymous.'

'But somebody must know who is the ultimate owner,' I reason.

'Agreed.'

'Follow the money,' I throw his comment back at him.

'On the case,' he echoes Angus.

'What about me?' Donna looks up expectantly.

'You and I are searching through Friends Reunited, Clive Partridge's old phone bills and anything else we can think of to find a connection between the two. And tomorrow night you are going pole-dancing again.'

'And me?' Gavin asks.

'Charm somebody. Find out the name of this so-called remuneration expert. We need to discover another connection.'

'Me?' Louise looks at me proudly. 'What can I do?'

'Isn't it nearly lunchtime?' I joke. 'Miss Binchy, would you be a darling and make some sandwiches?'

'Delighted, my dear,' she smiles. 'But there's no bread in your flat. The only food I found is a big pot of stew.'

'Chilli con carne,' I correct her. James winks at me.

'Holly's cooking,' giggles Louise. 'We've got to try that. There must be something to laugh about today.'

CHAPTER FORTY

It's Friday, almost two months since I first met Carl Lawson, and today I am going to unveil him as the lying, cheating, duplicitous bastard that he is. The past four days have not been easy. There have been moments when I wanted to lie in my bed and sob hysterically about the unjustness of my life. Occasionally I have felt detached from my body, as if I'm floating and looking down on the activity below. I feel shock at his betrayal, and humiliation at how I fell for the way he used me. I thought I had chosen the recipient of my heart wisely – but I acted as foolishly as a teenager desperate for her first real kiss.

My friends have got me through. Miss Binchy and my mother have been marvels. The two have taken over the feeding of the team, although Mum's main contribution has been to ring the pizza deliveryman. They made me eat when I really wasn't hungry, to keep my strength up, they urged, to fight this pain, and my mother even refrained from I told you so – although she couldn't resist bragging about getting Carl's aura right.

Louise has not left my side. She has been there when I've responded to Carl's constant friendly texts, although, surprise, surprise, his week has been so tied up with meetings that we never did get the chance for that chat. We will today, I think grimly. And James has been spectacular. I have partly forgiven him for misleading me about his auntie. Pot calling, and all that. He confided that he empties the cat bowls so Miss Binchy thinks Marmalade is eating his meals. And when this is over, I have promised to accompany him and his aunt to see a specialist. We are certain she is in the early stages of Alzheimer's, but we want to know if there is anything that can be done.

Louise is particularly impressed by him. 'How come you never really mentioned James before?' she asked after he left one night.

'I have,' I protested. 'Anyway, you've met him before.'

'I know, but I didn't really know him. He is such a genuine nice guy – a complete rarity in this world. I'd say you've been looking in the wrong place, my dear.' I must have looked confused. 'I think your Mr Right actually sits in the office barely three desks away from you, and you never really noticed.' I laughed at her, but deep down inside something stirred and I had an uncomfortable feeling that not only was she right, but that I had now blown everything.

Gavin accompanies me to Ilyax Insurance. The others will meet me at the Corney & Barrow wine bar in The Royal Exchange, for a much needed drink, in one hour's time. As Gavin and I enter the company's reception area, he springs into action. I do not want Carl Lawson to have advance warning of my visit, and Gavin sweet-talks the receptionist into letting us come in without passes. I am a stripper, apparently, and it would spoil somebody's fortieth birthday if he got wind of my arrival. A quick (and giggly) exchange of phone numbers and we're in.

We make our way to Carl's office. I hide in the women's toilets, while Gavin distracts Jackie, Carl's secretary, with some cock and bull story about being lost. I sneak past and enter the room without knocking.

'Jackie, babe, what is it?' Carl doesn't look up. 'I'm busy at the moment. On the other hand, if you're wearing suspenders ...'

'I'm not,' I say sharply.

'Holly! What the hell are you doing here?' Carl stares at me, shocked.

'I wanted to see you.'

'And me you, babe.' He starts to get up, his arms outstretched to hug me. 'I hope you weren't upset by my joking with Jackie. We always muck around like that.'

'Not at all,' I insist, sidestepping his hug. He looks confused. 'Although I think it is a highly inappropriate conversation for a company boss to be having with his PA. Some might class it as sexual harassment.'

'You're angry, babe,' he soothes. 'Don't be. It doesn't suit you.'

'I'm not angry.' I shake my head and the relief on his face is visible. Carl holds his arms out to me again but I stand immobile. Irritation and confusion flash across his face. 'I'm not angry,' I repeat. 'I'm livid.'

'It's only banter, babe. Come on,' he entreats. He beckons me closer.

'No, that's not why I'm livid,' I respond. 'I'm livid because you're a lying, cheating, duplicitous bastard.'

'What?' Carl recoils in shock. 'What's this about? Babe, I'm sorry I haven't called but I've been busy. But, honestly, don't come all heavy on me now. You're not my wife.'

'No,' I shake my head, 'and I count my blessings on that one. I hear congratulations are in order.'

'Eh?'

'You're reconciled.'

'No we're not,' he bluffs. 'Who told you that?'

'Your wife's sister,' I retort. 'Of course, she didn't know who I was, but I've always been very good at undercover work.'

'She's lying!' he protests.

'Why would she?'

'Because she's jealous. She fancies me.'

'I don't think so,' I sneer. 'She seems like she's got her head screwed on.'

'Is this what this is all about?' His tone becomes defiant. 'You're angry because you found out that I'm back with my wife. You're going to do the little wronged girlfriend act? For Christ's sake, all I did was lie down on top of you.'

I recoil as if I've been slapped. I'm shocked at his coarseness, and that the man I loved could so devalue the intimate times we spent together.

'You told me that you loved me,' I say quietly.

'No, I didn't,' he retorts. 'You assumed it.'

'ILY,' I say.

'That could mean anything,' he snarls. 'You're playing in the big people world, so grow up.'

'You used me.'

'What?' His lip curls in amusement. 'You came into my office the first time as a mousy, frankly unremarkable woman. But I could tell that you were interested. You got that gooey-eyed look. And then the next time you arrived. Wow! You stuck your cleavage in my face so often that I thought I was a pig snuffling for truffles.'

'I didn't.' I redden with shame.

'Face it. You got what you wanted. I'm sorry you didn't understand the rules. Now I'd like you to leave my office.' He takes a step towards me, as if ready to push me to the door.

'What does Banco Cayman account number 78642-41681-52342 mean to you?'

I swear panic flickers across Carl's face.

'Nothing,' he bluffs. 'Should it?'

'I would have thought so. You opened it just over a week ago and deposited more than one million pounds.'

'Why would I do that?'

'It's the ill-gotten gains from your plan with Clive Partridge. And you nearly got away with it, too. I found the connection. Finally. You and Clive went to school together.'

'No law against that,' he shrugs, a cocky air returning to his demeanour. He doesn't get it, I think; I've rumbled him. 'Anyway,' he goes on, 'You said he was the right man for the job. That would be an interesting story, wouldn't it? Corporate investigator fails to find link because she's sleeping with the client.'

'I didn't say he was the right man. I told you that there were no skeletons in his closet, but that the final decision was yours. And there is a law against fraud and obtaining money by deception. That remuneration expert you spoke so highly about ... I'm not surprised. He's your wife's cousin. Admittedly only a second cousin, so that was quite a link to find. But I did.'

'Bully for you, top of the class, kiss the teacher. What does that prove?'

'The three of you will share a big payout if Ilyax Insurance is taken out within the year.'

'But there's no chance of that.' Still bluffing.

'Really? You know nothing about any merger discussions?'

'No!' he retorts.

'Do you want to tell me why you've been buying shares through Carroll Stockbrokers via anonymous trusts?'

'I haven't.' Carl slumps in his chair.

'Your private stockbroker likes a drink, Carl, at the American Bar in The Savoy. So does my friend James. They had a great chat. He was very informative.'

'It's all supposition, Holly. You can't prove this. So what? I heard about the secret merger talks, but I should have been informed. I'm the boss. Those old tossers on the board are planning to get rid of me.' He stabs a finger at his chest, anger welling up inside him. 'Who the hell do they think they are? I like to think of my share purchases as an unexpected redundancy package. I'm entitled. I've made this company what it is.'

'You used Investigations-R-Us, and six other firms, to follow female employees, to discover their patterns so that you could stalk them,' I continue, ignoring his outburst. 'I hear you fired Alice Kelly last week. Was that because she was gay? Did she reject your advances?' I taunt. 'Was your male pride hurt? Oh, by the way, we're going to help her with her sexual discrimination claim against Ilyax. I'd like to see you defend that in a tribunal.'

'You bitch,' he moves as if to hit me.

'I wouldn't,' I warn, as the door opens and Gavin appears. Carl steps back.

'You can't prove any of this,' snarls Carl.

'Really?' I look around at my surroundings. 'What a tidy

office. It's sparkling. Those cleaners you employ do a really thorough job.'

'So what? It's what they're paid to do.'

'Indeed, but last night I paid them not to turn up. And I sent in my own team of cleaners.' James, Gavin and Angus donned overalls (much to my gay colleague's distress), grabbed some buckets and brooms and, wearing official looking swing badges (put together on the computer), swept the offices. Well, kind of. Today Carl Lawson's office has more bugs than a Bushtucker Trial. Unfortunately the recordings will be inadmissible in a court of law, but that's not the point. We don't want to go that far. 'Our conversation has been recorded. Indeed, a team of my associates is sitting in a van outside listening to us as we speak.'

'What do you want?' He finally says, his tone desperate and pleading. 'Do you want us to be together? Because if that's what you want then, babe, I'm willing. I love you.' He falls to his knees.

'No,' I reply quietly, looking down at him. 'No, you don't. God, you're pathetic! I couldn't want anything less. But I do have some requests.' I lay out my demands.

Carl's first act, on recovering his composure, was to sign the invoices from Investigations-R-Us, and authorise immediate payment. Gavin hovered menacingly as he made the call to the accounts department. Clive Partridge is to resign today for personal reasons, forgoing all his contractual rights, and repaying one million pounds back to Ilyax. The account in the Cayman Islands is to be closed. Carl's stockbroker is to sell his recently acquired shares in Ilyax. All profits will go to a charity for research into fertility – I thought Louise deserved something. Alice Kelly and Peter Porter are to be reinstated immediately. And Carl Lawson is to resign. He has no choice on any matter. The police don't take too kindly to insider dealing, sexual harassment and stalking. And I have the evidence.

Angus, Louise, Donna and James burst into spontaneous applause when Gavin and I walk into Corney & Barrow. They rush to hug me and pour champagne down my throat.

'She was magnificent,' gushes Gavin. 'I was so proud.'

Strangely I feel no satisfaction.

'It just feels all wrong somehow,' I say. 'Carl Lawson may have lost his job, but there's no mark on his personnel file, so he'll get another. And Clive Partridge won't suffer either. They are getting off scot-free. I don't care if I lose my job over this, I just want them to feel real pain.'

'But you know we couldn't really go to the police,' says James. 'It would have put Louise and Sam in a terribly awkward situation. He told her about a secret merger, and she told us. The law is really strict about that and we didn't sign any confidentiality agreements. And then the scandal about Clive and Carl could destroy Ilyax Insurance. Think of the thousands of staff who work there whose jobs could be put at risk. Or the women he stalked who would then be stalked all over again by the tabloid press. They've suffered enough. No.' He puts his hand gently over mine, and I feel all tingly. 'This is the best way. Honestly.'

'But that bastard walks free.'

'And so do you ...' There's an awkward pause.

'I'm truly sorry about getting Investigations-R-Us into this mess,' I say quietly.

'Well, you got us out of it. It's time to put it all behind you.'

'It'll be hard,' I say. 'I thought I loved him. I thought we had a future.'

'I know.' James places a comforting arm around my shoulder as I start to sob for what could have been. As I finish sniffing, I notice the others have moved away.

'I'm embarrassing everyone,' I sniff. 'I'm sorry.'

'You're not embarrassing me,' he smiles.

'I'm sorry about everything,' I say. 'About lying.'

'Me too. I should have told you as soon as I realised my aunt was your neighbour, but the lie just became too big and I couldn't expose myself. I thought you'd never speak to me again.'

'You should be so lucky,' I poke him playfully. But he grabs my fingers and slowly strokes them.

'Holly, this is not about you now,' he says quietly. 'It's me. Not you. And if I don't say this now I'll never know and I'll probably never pluck up the courage again. I'm falling for you, Holly, have been for ages. And I don't care if you want to keep up this sleek, confident career woman façade or fall back into the scruffy disorganised girl I first fell for. I like you whatever way you come.'

I can't speak. I feel all jittery and nervous. James is holding my hand and whispering sweet nothings at me. And I feel really happy. Ecstatic, in fact. This is real, I think. This man will never lie to me. He's true and honest and decent. And – oh God, Holly, why didn't you notice this before? – incredibly sexy.

'It's you, Holly. You're what I want. What do you say?'

I lean closer to him and whisper in his ear.

'I say shut up and kiss me.'

And he does.